D1733315

Selected Works of
BA JIN

GARDEN OF REPOSE
BITTER COLD NIGHTS

FOREIGN LANGUAGES PRESS BEIJING

First Edition   1988

Translated by
Jock Hoe

Illustrations by
Huang Yinghao

ISBN 7-119-00575-8
ISBN 0-8351-1055-9

Published by the Foreign Languages Press
24 Baiwanzhuang Road, Beijing, China

Printed by the Foreign Languages Printing House
9 West Chegongzhuang Road, Beijing, China

Distributed by China International Book Trading Corporation
(Guoji Shudian), P.O. Box 399, Beijing, China

Printed in the People's Republic of China

CONTENTS

In Chongqing (1941)

In Beijing　(September 1949)

FOREWORD

I began writing novels in spring 1927, when a friend of mine and I were living in lodgings in the Latin quarter in Paris. In an essay entitled "Reminiscences", written later, I described the room:

It was a small room. The window was open all day. Below it was a quiet street with only a few people. At the corner of the street was a small café and from my window I could see people walking in through its wide-open glass door. But I never heard any noise of drunkenness or gambling. Directly opposite me was an old, high building, which obstructed not only my view but also the rays of the sun, thus making my small room, already filled with the smell of gas and onion, look even more gloomy and depressing.

In the same essay I wrote about life at the time:

My life was very simple and monotonous. Every morning, I went for a walk in the Luxembourg Park. In the evening, I went to a night school for my French lessons. During the day, I stayed at home and let the old and shabby books eat away my youth, books which nobody would bother to read. Very often, after some unbearably quiet moments, the air suddenly began trembling. So, too, the street and even my room. The rumbling sound reverberated in my ears and I completely forgot where I was. Everything around me seemed to be undergoing great changes. Gradually, however, the sound died away. Experience told me that a heavily loaded lorry had gone past on the cobbled street below. Soon, silence resumed its reign. Slowly I stood up, walked to the window and leaned out to look at the seemingly wounded street. I looked at the small café, which was also very quiet, and I could see a few people drinking and humming a tune or two. An unbearable feeling of loneliness once again overwhelmed me.

After eleven o'clock, my friend Wei and I came out of the night school and we walked on the quiet street, which was drenched with rain. With my eyes set on the almond-coloured sky and the two tombstone-like towers of Notre Dame, I could feel the inextinguishable flames again burning in my heart. One evening, I was walking by myself on the path beside the Panthéon and came to the bronze statue of Rousseau. Unintentionally, I stretched out my arm and

i

stroked the icy stone base as if I were stroking someone very dear to me.   I looked up at the giant, who was holding a straw hat and a book in his hand, the thinker whom Tolstoy called "the conscience of the whole eighteenth-century world".   For a good while, I stood there, all my miseries forgotten, until the heavy footsteps of the policeman made me realize all of a sudden what kind of world I was living in.

Every night, I got back to the lodging-house, tired.   After a short rest, I lighted the gas stove and made tea.   Then the bells of Notre Dame began ringing out their mournful notes, which knocked heavily at my heart.

In circumstances like these, memories of my past again came back to torture me.   I thought of my life in Shanghai, my friends in their battles.   I thought of my past loves and hates, joys and sorrows, hopes and struggles, pains suffered and sympathies received. As I thought of all my past, I felt a severe pain in my heart as if it had been cut through by a sharp knife. The inextinguishable flames began to burn fiercely again.

Then it happened.

In order to alleviate the pain in my young and lonely heart, I began writing about the few things I had gleaned from life.   Every night, listening to the chimes of Notre Dame, I wrote in my exercise book something which read like parts of a novel.   Within three months, I completed the first four chapters of *Destruction*.*

So, even I myself had never expected that I would turn out to be a writer.   I went on writing for the next thirty years and whiled away, at my desk, the best time of my life.   Many a time, I have said that I would "give up art" and "put an end to my writing career".   But I have not been able to do so.

My major works were all written in the twenty years from 1927 to 1946.   In the long period before Liberation (1949), my life as a writer was painful.   I have confessed before: "When I am burning with passion, my heart is about to explode and I don't know where to place it;   I feel that I must write.   I am not an artist, and writing is only part of my life, which, like my works, is full of contradictions.   The conflicts between love and hate, thought and action, reason and emotion — these combine to weave a net enwrapping my whole life and all my works.   My life, as well as my works, is a painful struggle.   Every novel of mine carries my cry in my pursuit of light. . . .   At the same

---

* Ba Jin's first novel. — *Trans.*

time, the picture of extreme pain and suffering is like a whip lashing me from behind." Inevitably, I could only pick up my pen and write. I wrote to my heart's content, throwing all caution to the winds.

Time marches on. Read in the present new age, my works appear to have so little force; they are so colourless.

Even so, I have made selections from my past writings to represent the fruits of several decades of my literary endeavour. What gives me courage in reprinting these old pieces is my firm belief in writing, which is still very much with me. In 1955, I wrote:

> I will never lose hope. There may be different styles and emphases in my works, but the basic thinking which prompts their creation is the same. Ever since I started writing, I have never stopped attacking my enemies. And who are they? All the outmoded, old ideas, all the absurd systems which have been obstructing the path of social progress and man's development, all the forces which seek to destroy love — these are my enemies. . . .

My works, I hope, will bear witness to my words above. I have been writing for over fifty years. I have been searching, all my long life. I am nearing eighty now, but I am still searching. During the ten calamitous years of the "cultural revolution" (1966-76), I was forced to give up writing for a long time. But now my pen is finally back in my hand. In my heart, the fire is still burning. In my mind, is still the same old voice which continually urges me, "Keep writing, keep writing." I feel inside me emotions rising and falling like mighty waves, waiting for a free outlet. So deep is my love for my country and my people!

I want to write. I will continue to write. Let that fire burn me out, fiercely. When only the ashes of my body are left behind, even then, I know my love and my hate will never disappear.

Ba Jin
Shanghai, February 1981

GARDEN OF REPOSE

REPOSE

1944

I

After drifting about away from home for sixteen years, I went back only recently to my hometown, which has since become part of the "rear area" in the present War of Resistance. Although I was born and bred there, nothing seemed in the least welcoming. I did not see a single familiar face in the streets. In fact, even the narrow lanes with their smooth paving-stones had vanished, completely replaced by wide roads smothered in clouds of dust. The streets and lanes, once so secluded and quiet, were now bustling with activity. The thresholds sheathed in iron and lacquered in black, that used to stretch across the gateways of the rich mansions, had all been sawn away, to allow the brand-new private rickshaws to pass proudly in and out. And as for the imposing shopfronts, I was almost dazzled by them. Once, I had the temerity to step into a high doorway of the department store. No sooner had I pointed to some item lying in the shop-window and asked its price, than the shop-assistant shouted at me so rudely that I was terrified into beating a hasty retreat.

I was staying at a small hotel like any visitor a long way from home. The room was not exactly cheap. It was tiny. If I opened the window, the room would reek of coal dust, but if I closed it, not a ray of sunlight could get in. I was hardly ever in the room at all, except when I went to bed. I liked to wander about the streets, strolling along, silent and alone, indifferent to either the noise or the quiet. Sometimes, I would walk along, head down, absorbed in my own thoughts. Sometimes, I would stand at a street corner for an hour or so, listening to some blind story-teller, or perhaps, I would seek out a physiognomist to chat with.

3

One day, I was wandering along deep in thought, when, suddenly, someone caught me by the arm. I looked up, startled, thinking that I had accidentally trodden on someone's foot.

"Good heavens! Are you here? Where are you staying? You're back, and you haven't even been to see me! You ought to be shot!"

In front of me stood Yao Guodong. We'd been at primary school, secondary school and university together. Although we had been in the same classes at all three, he had graduated from the university and gone on to study overseas, but I had stayed at the university for only six months, because my uncle, who had been paying for me, died. Afterwards, I became a writer, producing some six novels, which no one paid much attention to. He had taught at a university for three years and been a government official for two. Then he had gone back to while away his days on the hundred or so acres his father had left him. Five years ago, he had bought the residence of the Yang family, an old family in the same town that had fallen on bad times. I knew all about that. He had married and had children. His wife had died, and he had remarried. I knew all that too. He had never written to me, and I had never tried to find out his address. When he passed through Shanghai after giving up his government post, he had found out where I lived and dragged me out for a meal at a restaurant serving Shanghai food. The wine encouraged him to pour out to me his aspirations, his achievements and his disappointments. I interrupted very infrequently. Only when he got to asking me about my life as a writer, the sales of my books and how much I got for my manuscripts, did I manage to put in a few brief phrases. At the time, I had published only a couple of short story collections and occasionally one or two short magazine articles. For some reason, he'd not only read them all, but had read them with care. "Not badly written at all! You really know how to write! You just need a greater boldness of vision," he said, nodding his head and reddening a little. I blushed too, not knowing what to answer. "Why do you write about such insignificant people and about such trivial events? I'm going to write a novel too, but I shall write about some earth-shaking events, about the great achievements of heroes and martyrs!" He threw back his head spiritedly, fixing his large sparkling eyes on me.

"Fine, fine," I muttered, feeling rather abashed in his presence. He was silent for a moment, then suddenly let out a loud guffaw. The next day, he took the boat. But his novel was never published. It seemed as if he never even picked up his brush.

This was the friend who was standing before me now. Tall, broad-shouldered, with a wide long face, a broad forehead, thick eyebrows, a beaked nose and a thin upper lip over a fleshy lower lip, he had not changed much at all. He had grown just a little fatter, a little paler. He grasped my small skinny hand in his moist chubby palm.

"I knew you'd bought the Yang residence, but I didn't know whether you were in town or not. I thought you'd have gone to the country because of the air-raids, and was afraid your gate-keeper wouldn't let me in. Just look at my clothes!" I said, a little disconcerted.

"All right, all right! Don't start making fun of me! After the terrible bombing last year, I went to the country for two or three months, but then we moved back again. Where are you staying? Let's go and see. Then I'll know where to find you later," he said with a frank and open smile.

"At the International Hotel."

"When did you get here?"

"About ten days ago."

"And you've been living at the International Hotel ever since? You've been back in your hometown for over ten days and you're still staying in a hotel? You're mad! You've got well-off relatives, haven't you? That rich uncle of yours has been doing even better in business these few years, buying up land every year. Why don't you go and see him?" he thundered, letting go my hand. He was talking so loudly, as if he wanted everyone in the street to hear.

"Not so loud, not so loud," I warned him anxiously. "You know they haven't had anything to do with me for a long time. . . ."

"But it's different now. You're famous! You've written lots of books," he interrupted, without letting me finish. "I admire you greatly too."

"Don't you start taking the mickey now! I don't even earn enough in a year to buy a decent Western suit. How can they think anything of me? Even if they were not afraid of my borrowing money from them, they'd be sure to think that a poor relation like me would make them lose face. By the way, have you finished that great novel of yours?"

He was surprised for a moment, and then burst out laughing. "What a marvellous memory you've got! I wrote for a couple of years after I came back home, and messed up thousands of sheets of paper. But I didn't manage to finish even twenty thousand characters. I don't have the talent. Later, I thought of doing some translations from the French, but it didn't work. I tried a novel by Hugo. People write such beautiful language, but by the time I've finished with it, it seems like nothing at all. When I put the original aside, I couldn't even make head or tail of what I'd written. After translating a couple of chapters of Quatre-vingt-treize, I threw it away. Studying literature at 'varsity was a complete waste of time. Since then, I've given up. I'm ready to acknowledge defeat to you, old chap! I'm not going to blow my own trumpet anymore. Well, let's not talk about all this now. Take me to your hotel. The International Hotel, did you say? How is it I don't know what street such a grand hotel is in?"

I couldn't help laughing. "Things with big names usually turn out to be tiny. It's near here. Let's go."

"Hello, what kind of philosophy is that? Oh, well, I'll find out when we get there." As he spoke, a happy smile spread over his face.

2

"What! You live in a room like this!" he exclaimed in astonishment as he came into the room. "Impossible! Impossible! I can't let you stay here! It's so dark, and you haven't even got the windows open!" He threw open the casements, broke immediately into coughing and moved hurriedly away, fumbling for a handkerchief with which to wipe his nose. "The stench of the coal is terrible! How can you stand living here? You're simply killing yourself!"

I gave a wry smile, and answered casually: "I'm not like you. My life's not worth anything."

"All right. Don't you start on me again," he said seriously. "You're moving to my place. I don't care whether you want to or not. I insist on your coming."

"There's no need," I said evasively. "I'm leaving in a couple of days."

"Is that all the luggage you've got?" he exclaimed, pointing suddenly to a small leather suitcase in the corner of the room. "What else have you got?"

"Nothing. I didn't even bring any bedding with me."

He went up to the bed and inspected it for a moment. "You're a fine one! Such filthy blankets, and you can actually sleep there!"

I did not say anything. I just smiled.

"Oh, well, the less luggage, the better. I'll move it for you straightaway. I know what you're like, so when you're at my place, I won't disturb you at all. If you feel like it, I'll come, and we can chat together morning and night. If you're not in the mood, I'll leave you alone for days on end. If you want to write, the guesthouse in my garden has very nice surroundings and is very quiet. No one will bother you. Is that all right?"

I could not find any reason for refusing such a genuinely sincere invitation. Besides, as I listened to him speaking, I was tempted. But he did not wait for me to answer. He just called the hotel boy to make up my bill, settled it before I could, and then told him to take my suitcase downstairs.

We got into rickshaws, and twenty minutes later, we were at his place.

3

Huge lustrous gates in black lacquer set in a high wall of grey brick. The words "Garden of Repose", written in seal script in large red characters the size of hand-basins, looked proudly down from the lintel. The inner gate, normally closed, now opened for our rickshaws. A white wall-screen welcomed me. On it were inlaid within a blue circular frame, four decorative characters in seal script, the colour of red ochre: "To be long enjoyed by future generations!" My eyes had scarcely taken in the words, when my rickshaw turned behind the screen. The wheels rolled for a moment in a courtyard covered in square paving-stones, and came to a halt before a second gate. Taking my suitcase, my friend strode across the threshold, while I followed close behind with my duffel bag in one hand. We entered a paved courtyard, square in shape. Opposite us was a large hall. The inner courtyards were completely hidden by a row of doors painted in gold. In a corner of the hall stood three almost new rickshaws.

From somewhere came the sound of several people talking at once, but there was not a soul to be seen.

"Zhao Qingyun! Zhao Qingyun!" my friend called. We walked across the courtyard. My friend glanced over to the left to where the porter's lodge was, but the doors were wide open, the tables and chairs all unoccupied. I looked over to the right, but the row of doors there were tightly shut. At the top of the steps beside the hall was a small double door, above which was pasted a strip of paper on which were written, once more in seal script, in deep black characters, the words "Garden of Repose".

"Why is 'Garden of Repose' written up everywhere?" I wondered with curiosity.

"There! This is where I've invited you to stay. And I guarantee you satisfaction!" cried my friend, pointing to the small doorway. Without waiting for an answer, he began to shout: "Lao Wen! Lao Wen!"

I heard no reply from his servants, and feeling that it was not altogether appropriate for me to let him continue to carry my luggage, I put out my free hand and said: "Give me the suitcase."

"It's all right," he said. And as if afraid that I might snatch the suitcase from him, he quickened his pace, hurried up the stone steps and went through the small doorway. I had no choice but to follow him.

When I stepped across the threshold, I saw at the far end of the corridor a gallery enclosed by a stone balustrade, beyond which were rockeries, trees, flowers and other plants. At the same time, I heard the sounds of an altercation.

"Who's quarrelling in the garden?" my friend muttered in surprise. No sooner had he spoken than a group of people turned into the gallery following the balustrade from the left. When they saw my friend, they stood stock still, and greeted him respectfully: "Sir!"

There were in fact only four people: two servants in long gowns, a young man who looked like a rickshaw puller, in a short jacket and barefoot, and a young boy neatly dressed in school uniform. The boy was being dragged along by the right arm by the younger of the two servants, but was resisting vigorously. He kept shouting: "I'll be back! You can drive me out, but I'll be back!" When he saw my friend, he glared at him angrily, pulled a face, and said nothing.

My friend, however, smiled. "What are you doing back here again?" he asked.

"This is my house, why shouldn't I come in?" the boy said

obstinately. I looked at him: at his long narrow face with its
fine delicate features. His nose however curved a little to the
left, and his upper teeth showed ever so slightly. He couldn't
have been more than twelve or thirteen.

My friend put down the suitcase and told the young servant:
"Zhao Qingyun, take Mr. Li's suitcase into the lower guest
room. And you'd better give it a sweep while you're about it.
Mr. Li is going to stay there." The young servant acknowledged
the order, throwing another glance at the young boy before letting go his arm. Then he took my suitcase, and went off following the stone balustrade to the right. My friend then continued:
"Lao Wen, go and tell your mistress that I've invited a close
friend to stay. Ask her to get out a couple of sets of clean bedding and have a bed made up in the lower guest room. And
get the wash-basin, teapots and other things ready." The old
white-haired servant, some of whose front teeth were missing,
replied: "Yes, sir!" and went off along the gallery to the left.

Only the rickshaw puller was left, standing in stupefaction
behind the boy. My friend waved at him and said briefly:
"You can go now!" and so, even he left.

The child said nothing. Neither did he leave. He just glared
sulkily at my friend.

"He's a good subject for you. You can write all about him.
I'll introduce the two of you," my friend said with a smile, looking very pleased with himself. Then he said more loudly: "This
is Master Yang, former owner of this mansion, and this is Mr.
Li, novelist."

I nodded to the boy, but he ignored me. He stared at me
with suspicion and hostility. Then he put his hands in his
trouser pockets, and began questioning my friend, just like an
adult.

"Why aren't you chasing me away today? What are you
playing at?"

My friend didn't get angry however. He continued to laugh
quietly as he looked at the boy, and said unhurriedly: "It's
lucky Mr. Li was here today, so that I could introduce him to

you. In fact, you're not being very polite. Since the house has been sold, it belongs to the person who bought it. Why do you have to keep coming back to make trouble?"

"It was the others who sold it. I never sold it. When I come, I don't do any damage. I just pick a few flowers. In any case, you people hardly ever come to admire them. What if I do pick one or two. How can you be so stingy!" The boy threw back his head, full of assurance.

"Then why are you always quarrelling with my servants?" my friend asked with a smile.

"They're so unreasonable. If they see me come in, they drag me out. They claim I'm here to steal. The bastards! Now that the house has been sold, what do I care about any of your things? It's not as if I were starving. We don't have as much money as you, that's all. In any case, what's the good of having a bit more filthy lucre?" The boy had a tongue and was clearly a clever talker. His eyes flashed, and as he spoke, his face reddened.

"So you let them sell the house? You're a fine one to talk! Even if you hadn't let them, they'd have sold it anyway." My friend burst out laughing. "It's marvellous! How old are you now?"

"What's that got to do with you?" The child turned angrily away.

The young servant appeared. He stood before my friend and said respectfully: "The guest room is ready, sir. Will you go and have a look?"

"You can leave now," my friend instructed.

The young servant looked towards the boy and said: "What about this. . . ."

My friend cut him short, without waiting for him to finish: "You may as well let him stay to talk to Mr. Li." And to me, he said, pointing to the boy: "Lao Li, you should talk to him. You mustn't let such a good subject slip away."

My friend left, followed by the young servant. There was just myself and the boy left standing by the balustrade. I looked at him, and he looked at me. The angry expression on his face gradually disappeared. He was measuring me with a suspicious eye. He didn't move away, nor did he say a word. Finally, it was I who spoke: "Why don't you sit down?" I patted the stone balustrade with my hand.

He did not answer. He did not move.

"How old are you?" I asked.

He answered softly, as if speaking to himself: "Fourteen." Suddenly, he came up to me, his eyes shining, caught me by the arm and implored: "Please, pick a camellia branch for me, won't you?"

I followed the direction of his gaze. Beyond the stone balustrade, on the side where the rockeries were, beside the cassia tree, stood a camellia bush, more than ten feet high, its thick green leaves set off by the mass of red blossoms.

"Those over there?" I asked, without thinking.

"Please pick one for me. Quickly! They'll be back in a moment," the boy begged earnestly. His eyes were so beseeching that I couldn't say "no". I knew that my friend would not reproach me for picking the flowers in his garden indiscriminately. And so I climbed over the balustrade, went over to the camellia tree, and broke off a branch, one with four flowers.

He stood on the other side of the balustrade, waiting for me with his hand outstretched. I presented the flowers to him from beneath the balustrade. He took them, smiled happily, and with a brief "thank you", turned and ran off.

"Wait a moment! Wait a moment!" I called to him from behind. But he had already run out of the garden without hearing me.

"What a strange child," I thought.

4

The garden was very quiet. Now I was the only one there. My friend, having left me, paid me no further attention. I

stood outside the balustrade for a few minutes, but not a single
servant came into the garden to pour me a cup of tea.   And so,
I began to stroll around the rockeries, following the little crooked path.   There were a number of rockeries, none taller than
I, but each of a different shape, covered with creepers
and moss, with little hollows in which bloomed wild flowers
of all descriptions, white, yellow and red.   The tropical orchids bordering the path were not yet in flower.   The path led
eventually to the steps of a guest house.   The sills were
rather high, while the former paper windows, now set with
glass, were completely screened by silk curtains, embroidered
with birds and flowers, so that I couldn't see the furnishings
inside.   This must be the upper guest room, I thought.
Below the windows, in the corner of the wall, grew a tall magnolia tree.   The ends of some of its branches, which were still
covered with dying flowers, stretched out over the wall patterned in plum blossoms in the upper part.   The spoon-shaped
white petals lay heaped up in the corner of the wall.   Some
were already turning brown, but I could still smell the lingering
perfume that wafted over to me.

I stood for a moment beneath the tree, and then bent down
and picked up some petals, caressing them gently between my
fingers.   Magnolias were old friends of mine.   I too had had a
garden when I was young, and, as a child, magnolia flowers
had been the ones I loved most.   Without thinking, I raised
the petals to my nostrils.   All at once, I came to my senses with
a start, and looked all around me.   I could not help smiling
at my odd behaviour.   I threw the petals to the ground.   But
then, I thought: That young boy had probably had such a feeling
as I had just had.   What a pity, I thought, that I had not run
after him, and dragged him back to question him.

I did not go up the steps to look inside the hall.   (At the
top of the steps on the left, in front of the door, I could see a
long mahogany table, together with a round porcelain stool.)
Instead, I followed the wall along to the right.   I passed a
tub of goldfish, passed the drooping branches of two crab-

apple trees, and a tree of plum blossoms, and came directly
to a rectangular flower terrace. On one side was a wall, while
directly facing the other side was a reception hall, whose windows were all inlaid with glass. I guessed that this was the
so-called lower guest room which my friend had prepared
for my temporary stay. On the terrace grew three peony bushes.
Below it was an area paved in stone, while in the courtyard, two
cassia trees stood like sentinels on each side of the room.
To the left and right, beyond the balustrade, were placed three
large pots of orchids on round green porcelain stands.

I went up the steps, and was about to enter the room, when
my friend's voice stopped me. He called from afar: "Lao Li!
Why are you all by yourself? When did the Yang boy leave?
What did you talk to him about?"

As I turned to look at him, I replied: "You all went off, so,
of course, I'm all by myself. . . ." But I didn't finish what I
was saying, for I saw behind him, a woman with curled hair,
wearing a grey knitted cardigan over a light green cheongsam.
She was accompanied by an elderly woman servant carrying a
pile of sheets and blankets in her arms. I realized it was his
wife and a servant, coming to make up my bed. So I went over
to greet them.

My friend, immensely pleased, presented us: "Let me introduce you. This is my wife, Wan Zhaohua. You can just call
her Zhaohua from now on. This is Lao Li — the one I'm always
telling you about." His wife gave a light smile, and nodded
almost imperceptibly, while my head bent so low that it was
almost a ceremonial bow. I looked up to hear her say: "I've
often heard him speak of you, Mr. Li. We can't possibly look
after you properly. I'm afraid we're sure to forget something. . . ."

My friend interrupted, without giving me time to answer.
"The thing he hates most is to be treated like someone special.
It's best to leave him free to do exactly as he likes. Just settle
him down in the room and leave him to it. That'll do."

His wife glanced at him. Her lips parted slightly, but she

said nothing. She just smiled at him, and he smiled back. I could see that they got on very well together as a couple.

"Even if Mr. Li is an old school friend of yours, he's still a guest. How can we not do our best to look after him!" his wife said, smiling. She was speaking to her husband, but her eyes were fixed on me, without the slightest shyness.

Her face was the shape of a melon seed, and not very long. In it were set a pair of large black eyes, a straight nose and rather thin lips. She was slight-shouldered, slim-waisted, and rather tall. Standing beside her husband, she reached as high as his eyebrows. She could only have been twenty-two or twenty-three. A smile always hovered on her face. She was a very approachable and a very beautiful woman.

"Well, you'd better see to getting the room tidied up. You do the cooking yourself tonight, so that I can spend a pleasant evening drinking with him," my friend urged his wife, with a smile.

"It's really too great an honour to have your wife do the cooking herself," I interrupted at once, out of politeness.

"Well, you go and keep Mr. Li company in the upper guest room. He's been here for hours, and we haven't even offered him a cup of tea," she said apologetically, turning to her husband. Then she gave me a slight nod, and went towards the lower guest room. The elderly woman servant had already gone in long ago. Even the old servant, Lao Wen, carrying more things in his arms, had gone in.

5

"Well, what about it? Do you want to go and sit in the upper guest room as my wife suggests, or would you rather sit on the balustrade? Or perhaps we could go for a walk in the garden," my friend asked with a smile.

We were standing in the gallery at the left-hand end of the balustrade with my back to the rockeries beyond. My eyes fell onto a glass window which was not completely screened by its curtains. Through the window I could see bookshelves stacked with books sewn with thread in the traditional Chinese way. I guessed it was my friend's library, but I was surprised that he should like reading such books. I could not help asking him: "Hey! Have you taken to reading ancient books now?"

He gave a laugh. "Sometimes when I'm bored, I read a few. Actually, it's the library of the Yang family. It came with the house. Even if I don't read them, they make a nice decoration."

At the mention of the Yang family, the young boy came at once to my mind. So, sitting down on the stone balustrade, I asked him: "Tell me all about this Yang boy. Tell me as much as you know."

"Did you get any material to write on? What did he talk to you about?" Without giving me an answer, he questioned me instead.

"He didn't say a thing. He wanted me to pick him a branch of camellias, and ran off as soon as I'd done so. I couldn't hold him back," I replied.

He scratched his head once or twice, and then sat down with me on the balustrade.

"To tell you the truth, I don't know much either. He's the son of the third son of the family. There were four brothers in all. The eldest has been dead for some years. The other three seem to be in town somewhere. The second and fourth are making a lot of money in business. The third one's never had a proper job. He's a notorious wastrel. He dissipated his family's fortune completely. I gather he died later. Now the family depends entirely on his elder son, the young lad's brother. He keeps them all on his job with the post office. But the young lad's also been a disappointment. He doesn't study properly, but keeps coming into our garden to pick flowers. One day, I even saw him talking to a beggar at the gate of the Temple of the Grand

Immortal next door to us. If he gets in here, he refuses to go
when we try to chase him out. Even if we do manage to get
him out, he slips back in again. It's not that he's so clever,
it's our gate-keeper, Old Man Li, who let's him back in. Li
was originally the head porter for the Yang family. It appears
he was the gate-keeper for them for over twenty years. The
second son recommended him to me. I can see what a devoted
worker he is, so I haven't the heart to reprimand him. Once
when I just started to say something to him, and tears came
to, his eyes. What can you do? He loved his old master.
That's perfectly human. Besides, the boy keeps his hands clean,
he doesn't steal anything. As long as I don't see him, he might
as well be allowed in. It's just that my servants can't stand
him and keep chasing him away."

Seeing my friend had stopped short, with my curiosity still
unsatisfied, I pressed on with my questions: "Is that all you
know? I don't understand why he keeps coming in for flowers?
What does he want them for?"

"I don't know either," my friend answered indifferently,
shaking his head. He had not thought that the boy would
arouse such an interest in me. "Perhaps Old Man Li knows
a bit more. You can have a chat with him later. And I'm
sure the boy will come back, so you can ask him as well."

"But you must promise me one thing. When he does come
again, you must let me deal with him. You'd better tell your
servants not to interfere."

My friend smiled contentedly, and nodded. "I'll do as you
say. Do whatever you like. Only, when you've found enough
material for a book, you must let me have the honour of reading
it first."

"It's not because I want something to write about. I'm
genuinely interested in what the boy's up to. I think I
understand a little of what he feels. You know, we had a big
garden at home once too. Eventually, it was sold together with

the house. I'd like to go and have a look at it too," I said
seriously.

"Then why don't you go and have a look? I can still remember. It was in Shuwa Street. Who's living in your old
house now? Have you made any enquiries? Once we know
who's living there, I'll find a way of getting you in. I guarantee it," my friend said with warmth and sympathy.

"I've asked," I replied, shaking my head despondently. "It
was sold sixteen or seventeen years ago, and has changed owners
several times. It was rebuilt a number of times, and now it's
a department store. Just like that young lad, I never had a
say in selling the house either, and I've never spent a penny of
the money got from selling it. The others sold it. They destroyed
the only thing that can remind me of my childhood."

"What's there to be so sad about? You can buy another
house, and set up a garden just like the old one. It'll be the
same, won't it?" my friend said kindly to cheer me up. But
I found his words quite unacceptable.

I shook my head and gave a wry smile. "There's no chance
of my becoming a millionaire, and, in any case, I wouldn't want
to do anything so evil."

"How can you talk like that! Are you rebuking me?" my
friend said reprovingly as he stood up. But his face was smiling
once more, so that I knew he wasn't angry with me.

"Why should you think I mean you? I meant the fools who
buy houses and bequeath them to their sons and grandsons to
sell," I said, beginning to get irritated nevertheless.

"Well, you can set your mind at rest," my friend said. "I
won't be leaving this garden to my son to no purpose." He
looked up, his eyes smiling, gesturing with his right hand, as
if to give expression to the great aspirations he had. I said
nothing. After a moment, he continued: "Let's finish with all
this gossip. It's uncomfortable sitting so long on all this stone-
work. Let's go down to the lower guest room. Zhaohua
will have tidied up your room by now."

6

I followed my friend into the lower guest rooh. On hearing our footsteps, his wife, who was standing by the square marble table by the window arranging flowers in a vase, turned towards her husband and smiled at him affectionately before giving me a smile. "The room's all ready. I don't know whether you'll like it or not, Mr Li. I'm no good at interior decoration."

"It's perfect, perfect!" I said with satisfaction, casting a glance round the left-hand section of the room. The sincerity of my words and my expression must have been obvious to her, for her smile spread all over her face.

I had the feeling that each time she smiled, the room became much brighter, and at the same time, the "nameless burden" on my heart also seemed to grow a little lighter, (whether it was loneliness, anxiety, regret, yearning or compassion, I could not say, but I felt something for ever weighing on my mind, a heavy burden which I could not throw off, a burden which forced me to write). Now she was standing at the window, holding the large crackle-glaze porcelain vase in one hand, while, with the other, she was arranging the red flowers of the camellia branches around the rim. The windows were hung with pale blue curtains, softening considerably the sunlight that illumined her face. It would certainly have made an attractive painting. I guessed that the square table was to be my writing-desk. The bed had been set up in the corner. It was really a divan. There was even a small footstool by the bedside as was the custom. A gauze mosquito net hung from a ring above the bed. On a small square stool at the head of the bed, which faced the window, rested my suitcase, and not far from the foot of the bed were two armchairs separated by a tea-table.

She put down the vase and moved away from the table, and, going towards her husband, said to me: "Please sit down, Mr. Li," and gave instructions to Lao Wen who had just finished

arranging the armchairs: "Lao Wen, go and make Mr. Li a cup
of tea." And then to the elderly woman servant who, having
arranged the blankets, was standing at the head of the bed,
she said: "Mrs. Zhou, remember to send over the thermos of
hot water shortly." Then she turned to me: "Mr. Li, if you need
anything, please don't hesitate to ask them to bring it to you.
You must make yourself at home."

"I never stand on ceremony.   Thank you, Mrs. Yao. I've
put you to so much trouble today," I said gratefully.

"Mr. Li, you just said you don't stand on ceremony! What's
this 'thank you', 'putting you to so much trouble'! If that's not
standing on ceremony, what is?" Mrs. Yao said with a laugh.

My friend interrupted: "Lao Li, I notice that's the first time
you've used my name 'Yao'. You haven't addressed me by either
my surname or my first name.   I was afraid you'd even forgotten what I was called!" he cried, bursting into a laugh.

In reply, I laughed too: "With a name as imposing as Yao
Guodong, how could I forget! Just like your name, you're a
pillar of the state!"

"My father gave me the name.   I can't be held responsible,
so there's no need for you to make fun of me.   In any case,
it's not certain that my father meant anything by it," my friend
argued, laughing.   "For instance, if a Japanese calls his son
Kametaro,* it surely doesn't mean that he wants his son to be
a turtle."

"Of course not.   He wants his son to live as long as a
turtle." I also laughed.   "And then there's your other name,
Songshi. Does that mean you're going to have to recite poetry
all your life?"

Mrs. Yao, repressing a smile, said to her husband softly: "Let's
go back and let Mr. Li get a little rest. He must be tired. And
I have to get tonight's dinner ready.   You can chat at your
leisure tonight while you're drinking."

"All right, all right," her husband nodded several times,

_____
* Kametaro means turtle in Chinese.

glancing at her with a smile. "It's very quiet here. It's not at all bad as a place in which to write. But it's too quiet. Will it worry you at night?" He went on at once, without waiting for me to reply. "If you're nervous, you can get one of the servants to call me, and we can have a chat together."

I smiled in answer. "If you feel in the mood, please do come and chat. I'd like that. But don't worry, I won't have any fears."

Accompanying his wife, my friend left. I could still hear his laughter through the window. He had really enjoyed himself today.

I sat down in the cane chair before my table. I felt a little tired, but was much more at ease in my mind nevertheless. I looked up and listened quietly to the song of unknown birds chirping in the trees outside my window.

7

In the evening. Lao Yao (as I now began to call him) and I sat at a small ebony table opposite each other, eating the food prepared by his wife and drinking long-preserved Shaoxing wine. The food was good, the wine was good, and his happy mood was even better. His speech flowed like water. He did not give me a chance to get even one word in. He criticized people of every kind, gave his views on every subject. He was not satisfied with anything. He complained continually. But from his never-ending grievances, I learnt one thing: There was nothing in his own life that he was not satisfied with. He looked on his second marriage as the greatest possible happiness. He was pleased with this new wife of his. He loved his new wife.

Putting down his wine cup suddenly, he turned to me with a smile: "Lao Li, what do you think of Zhaohua?"

"Not bad at all! You must be very happy," I answered in approval.

He closed his eyes gladly for a moment, tapping the table with three fingers of his right hand. Then he nodded several times, picked up his cup again, and drank a large mouthful. Then suddenly he began to smile to himself.

"Lao Li, you should get married soon. With a family, you'll feel more settled." He paused for a moment before continuing: "Don't keep dreaming of love. That's all fantasy from novels. Look at Zhaohua and me. We've never spoken of love. We got to know each other only through being introduced. But now we're married, we get on very well together. We're very happy."

"I heard that you were related," I interrupted.

"We are, but very distantly. We hardly ever saw each other. To tell you the truth, I like her much better than my first wife." He began to blush, for his happiness made him more flushed than before.

"If someone as satisfied with married life as you are is still so full of complaints and grievances, then wouldn't I be better off as I am, free to come and go as I please?" I interrupted once more.

"You don't understand. You won't understand even if I try to explain. Love for us Chinese is something quite different from that for Westerners. They marry only after they have found love, whereas we Chinese begin to love only after marriage. I think our way is more fascinating." He spoke slowly and deliberately, pleased with himself, as if expounding some great theory, emphasizing his words at the same time by gestures with his right hand.

I couldn't keep my patience, and so broke in: "All right, all right. You'd better take your grand theory and talk it over with Dr. Lin Yutang. He might ask you to write a new *Six Chapters of a Floating Life* with which to fool the foreigners. I don't understand you at all."

"You don't understand? Look, isn't this the best proof?" His laugh was tinged with pride, as he turned to look towards the entrance of the room. I turned too. His wife came in, followed by Mrs. Zhou, a lantern in her hand.

I stood up at once.

"Please sit down, sit down. I'm afraid the meal wasn't very good. I don't suppose it was to your taste, Mr. Li," she said with a smile, revealing for a brief moment the whiteness and the evenness of her teeth.

"It was excellent. I've eaten so much. But I've put you to so much trouble today. Have you yourself eaten, Mrs. Yao?" I replied with a smile, still standing.

"Yes, I have, thank you. Please sit down. There's no need to be polite," she said. I sat down. She came over and stood beside her husband. He looked up at her. "Have a bit more," he said, handing her the chopsticks. She refused them, shaking her head: "I've just had my supper. I think you've had enough to drink, don't you? Don't get drunk. You told me that Mr. Li doesn't drink much. You'd better start eating rice or the dishes will get cold." Lao Yao nodded, and called for the rice.

"All right, let's not drink any more. Lao Wen, Mrs. Zhou, would you bring some rice?"

"Has Xiao Hu still not come back?" he asked his wife anxiously.

"I sent Old Man Li to fetch him. He's already been gone for some time. He should be back by now," she replied.

"Did you save him some chilli sauce?" he then asked.

"Yes. I've kept him some of everything he likes."

Bowls of rice were brought to the table. I picked up my bowl to eat, not wanting to disturb a conversation between man and wife. Suddenly, I heard a child's voice cry: "Dad! Dad!" I looked up, and saw a ten-or eleven-year-old child, dressed in Western clothes, run over to my friend.

"You're back! Did you have a good time at Granny's?" my friend asked affectionately, stroking the child's smoothly combed hair.

"Marvellous! I played chess and poker with my cousins.

Tomorrow's Sunday. If Old Man Li hadn't been so insistent, I wouldn't have come back. Granny wants me to go back tomorrow to play. She said next time there's no need to send anyone to fetch me. They can send me back in their rickshaw."

"All right. Next time, we won't send a rickshaw for you. You can play to your heart's content," my friend said, laughing. "You're back, and you haven't said hello to your mother. She was very worried about you."

The child was standing on my friend's left, and his wife on his right. He looked up, glanced at his stepmother, greeted her briefly and turned away. His stepmother smiled at him tenderly, and then said softly: "Xiao Hu, you haven't said hello to our guest. This is your uncle."

"Say hello to your uncle," my friend said, pushing the child forward by the shoulder.

He moved a few steps forward and bowed to me, mumbling indistinctly: "Uncle."

You could say that the child was a smaller edition of my friend. The face, eyebrows, nose and lips were an exact replica of his. Only the clothes were different. Lao Yao was wearing a long blue silk gown, while the boy was dressed in a coffee-coloured Western jacket, short khaki pants, a white shirt and a maroon tie. In build and stature, he was like the Yang boy, but in dress and manner there was little resemblance.

"Look, Lao Li. Isn't he like me? This is the second of my treasures!" Lao Yao said proudly, bursting into a laugh. I glanced directly at his wife. She was blushing, and kept her eyes on the ground. I knew from this that she was the first of his treasures.

Seeing that I remained silent, Lao Yao leaned forward and gave the boy a slight push with his left hand, saying: "Go up closer and let Uncle have a better look at you!"

The child moved forward another couple of steps. Turning his head with an air of indifference, he said ironically: "Have a look then." He stood in front of me, his arms crossed, sizing me up with an expression full of arrogance and disdain.

"Is there a likeness?" my friend asked insistently.

"Yes, indeed! . . . Only, I think. . . ."

He was so pleased at hearing my "yes, indeed", that the "only" which followed was as if lost. He at once held his left hand out to his son and said: "Xiao Hu, come over here. Your mother's kept some chilli sauce for you. Would you like to eat something?"

"I'm full now. I'll have a snack before I go to bed tonight." The child ran over to his father, seized him by the hand, and like a spoilt child began to beg: "Dad, when I was playing poker with my cousins today, I lost 450 dollars. Please pay me back."

"All right. Your mother will give you 500 dollars later," his father answered readily. "Tell me, what did you get to eat at Granny's?"

"Mum, you'll give it to me later, won't you?" Instead of answering his father, the child turned with a smile to his step-mother. This time he pronounced the word "Mum" much more affectionately.

"I'll give it to you as soon as we go in. Your father's talking to you. You can come in with me in a moment. I want to see you change your clothes and go over your lessons," his stepmother said tenderly, with a smile.

"All right," he answered discontentedly, screwing up his eyes and twisting his lips to one side in a pout. I had noticed this expression already, when comparing his face with his father's. Because of it, taking his face as a whole, the child really didn't resemble his father at all.

Perceiving this expression of Xiao Hu's, my friend's wife glanced at me without a word. The smile remained on her face, but her eyes hid an indescribable sadness. By the time I looked at her more attentively, she was talking happily to her husband, and the sadness in her face was no longer to be seen.

Mrs. Yao left first with Xiao Hu. Lao Yao and I finished our meal and went on talking for some time. He was no longer in a complaining mood, but talked instead only of the merits of his wife and his son. I learnt that after three years of marriage, his wife had not borne him a child. His first wife had left him a son and a daughter, but the daughter had died two months after her mother.

That night, I slept in that vast empty guest room. The doors creaked in the wind, the leaves fell from the trees, the birds amongst the branches flapped their wings in agitation, sand and stones whirled in the air. I was not afraid. But I wasn't used to the surroundings, and I could not get to sleep peacefully.

I thought about my friend, about his wife and his son. And I thought about the Yang boy. I thought for a long time. I compared the two boys. And I wondered whether Mrs. Yao's family life was as happy as her husband claimed. The more I thought, the less I could sleep. Then I became annoyed with myself, and rebuked myself, saying: "Why do you worry about other people's affairs? Everyone has his own way of life. It's no use your bothering about it. You'd better get some sleep instead."

But outside the window, the night was already beginning to fade. The little birds in the trees and on the eaves were already chirruping querulously to one another.

8

I did not get up until ten o'clock; by then the golden rays of the sun were already flooding the room with their light. Lao Wen came in to bring me water and to make tea for me, while Mrs. Zhou brought me my breakfast. At midday, Mr. and Mrs. Yao came and lunched with me in my room.

"It's only for this once, for the sake of politeness. In future, we'll leave you on your own and forget all about you," Lao Yao said with a smile.

"That's fine, fine. I'm used to living without a fuss," I replied contentedly.

"But if you need anything, Mr. Li, please just call the servants. You must make yourself at home," Mrs. Yao said. She was wearing a light green cheongsam, with a short white jacket on top. When she heard me tell my friend that I had not slept well, she remarked: "No wonder! The room's too big. I forgot to tell Lao Wen yesterday to put up a screen. It'll be a bit better with a screen to partition it."

Not long after the bowls, chopsticks, glasses and dishes had been cleared away, the screen was brought in. It was of purple silk stretched over a black lacquered frame. It separated the sleeping area from the rest of the room, turning it into a bedroom.

We three remained in this "bedroom" for a moment to chat. They sat in the two armchairs. Lao Yao sat smoking, lazily blowing smoke-rings from time to time, while Mrs. Yao sat upright, sipping tea slowly from the cup in her hand, as if plunged in thought. I sat in the cane chair by the window, my legs crossed, completely relaxed. We talked about what was happening in the city. I kept plying them with questions.

Eventually, Mrs. Yao whispered something to her husband. Standing up, he threw away his cigarette butt, took a few steps about the room, and then said: "Neither of us will be home this afternoon. Her mother," (he turned to look at his wife) "has asked us over for a visit, and we have to go with her to the opera as well. Do you like Peking Opera? I could go with you. But there aren't all that many good actors here."

"You know I've never liked watching old opera," I answered.

As his wife stood up, he continued: "I thought perhaps you might have changed. Many people gradually become more flexible as they get older."

"But there are also those who become more stubborn with age," I answered with a laugh.

My friend laughed, and so did his wife. "He's really talking

about himself," she said.   "He's always convinced that he's
getting more tolerant."

   "Talk about me! You're just the same.   For instance, you
don't like listening to Peking Opera, but the moment your
mother talks of going, you go with her.   I've never heard you
say you didn't want to go.   You like foreign films, but if
there's no one to go with you, you don't go.   And so people
who don't know would think you're an opera fan!" my friend
teased his wife.   But she didn't respond.   She just smiled, and
purposely directed her gaze outside the window. But a faint
blush was just visible beneath the light powder on her face.
Then she glanced back at her husband, her lips trembling slightly, as if begging him not to go on.   But once he began talking,
it was difficult to stop him.   "Lao Li's not a stranger.   It
doesn't matter if he knows.   He won't put you into his novels."
She flushed, and at once turned away, pretending to look at
something else.   "In fact, he'll make a good companion for
you! He likes foreign films too.   If there's a good one on, you
must make him go with you.   By the way, Lao Li, if you should
feel a bit depressed while you're here, and would like to read
any ancient books, there are plenty in my library. I can give
you the key." He was the first to laugh at this suggestion.   "I
know you won't want to read all that old stuff.   My wife has
a lot of novels — new ones and old ones.   She's got the whole
series of novels published by the Commercial Press.   Of course
they're not the sort of thing novelists like you write, but they're
novels just the same.   I've read a few.   Even though they're
classical Chinese, they're very vivid nevertheless.   We've also
got the latest novels in modern Chinese."

   His wife seemed to be afraid of his saying too much.   Her
blush had already disappeared.   Now she turned towards him
and said urgently: "Once you start talking, you can't stop.   You
should let Mr. Li have a rest. I have to go and tidy up. . . ."
Her face was, as ever, covered with a smile, a smile more
luminous than the sun.

   "All right, I'll stop then.   You're so impatient!" My friend

smiled contentedly at his wife. "We've disturbed Mr. Li long
enough for today. Let's go. We'd better let him get on with
his writing in peace." I smiled at them both. I stood up and
saw them out. Now I was master of this half of the lower
guest room. I stood beneath the window, near the stone
balustrade, and watched them disappear. They were conversing intimately, passing along the balustrade, past the upper
guest room, to their own quarters farther in.

9

They didn't come in the afternoon. Nor did anyone else come
to disturb me, apart from Mrs. Zhou, who came to fill my
thermos, and Lao Wen, who brought me dinner.

After dinner, Lao Wen brought me water for washing my
face. Without thinking, I said to him: "I'm giving you too much
trouble. In future, there's no need. . . ."

Lao Wen stood with his arms by his side, screwing up his
aged eyes for a moment. "Li *laoye*,* how can you say such
a thing? You're an old friend of our master's. It's our job as
servants to make sure that you're waited on properly. If
anything should be lacking in our service, you must be frank
in pointing it out."

His words made me uneasy. It was the first time that anyone
had ever called me *laoye*. The word was extremely disagreeable to me. I knew that he would keep on addressing me in
this way in the future, and would go on doing so till I left the
Yao family. I couldn't bear it. I thought it over. The only
thing to do was to speak out. "You're an old man. You're
different from the others." (Sure enough, my words had an
effect. His face broke into a smile.) "Please don't call me
'Li *laoye*'. Down where I come from, we use 'Mr.' Why don't

* *Laoye*: a respectful term used in addressing members of the
gentry.

you follow our custom and just call me 'Mr. Li'?"

"Very well, I'll do as you say, Li *laoye* — oh, I mean Mr. Li. As for being an old servant, I've been in the Yao family for over thirty years. I've watched the master grow up. He's so kind-hearted, generous and understanding towards other people, just like his father, our previous master."

"What about your mistress?" I asked.

"Do you mean the present mistress?" he asked. I nodded. Lao Wen then continued: "Since she came into the household three years ago, the mistress has never scolded me even once. Before she came, everyone said she was a very modern young lady, and we were afraid she'd be full of new-fangled ideas. But since she's arrived, everyone's been full of praise for her. She's as kind-hearted as she's beautiful. She's always smiling. She's especially considerate towards me, saying that I'm an old family servant. She even consults me on some matters. We're lucky to be able to serve such a master and mistress." His lined face became even more wrinkled with his smiles, but his tiny eyes were filled with tears, as if he were about to cry.

After I had washed my face, he came over to the tea-table to take away the wash-basin. My curiosity had been aroused by what he'd told me, and so I immediately began to question him further. I wanted to hear more from him.

"What about your first mistress?"

Lao Wen put down the wash-basin, glanced at me, and stood by the tea-table, his hands by his sides, shaking his head. He replied: "It's not just servants' gossip, but the previous mistress was a lot inferior to our present mistress. She really can't be compared to her. The first mistress left a son, and also a daughter. Then the daughter died too. . . ." He suddenly broke off what he was saying, and turned to look towards the door.

"I've met the boy. He looks exactly like his father," I said, hoping in this way to get him to say more.

"But his temper is altogether different from his father's." He looked at me, and then glanced at the door again. He seemed to want to take back his words, but it was already too late. He knew that I'd clearly heard what he'd said.

"Don't worry. Just say what you want. I won't tell anyone else. You're quite right. I noticed it too. Young Master Hu's attitude to Mrs. Yao is not very good."

"Mr. Li, you don't know the worst of it. Master Hu has always had a terrible temper, not only towards his stepmother, but towards his own mother as well. He was nearly seven when the first Mrs. Yao died. He didn't even shed a single tear. His grandmother over-spoils him, and his father spoils him too. The mistress simply can't do anything with him." He came up to me and, lowering his voice, continued: "I've heard Mrs. Zhou say that the mistress has been in tears many times because of him, but even the master doesn't know about it." He stopped for a moment, and then went on in a low voice as before: "When Mrs. Yao went back to visit her parents, she wanted to take the boy with her, but he absolutely refused to go. His grandmother said that our mistress was incapable of looking after her daughter's son properly. For two years, Mrs. Zhao, his grandmother, hasn't visited us, but frequently sends someone to fetch Master Hu to her place to play. Mrs. Yao still goes to see the Zhao family at New Year's and at festivals. Last year, the Zhaos were afraid of the air-raids, and so went back to the village for over six months, taking Master Hu with them for three or four months. He didn't want to come back under any circumstances. The master and mistress had to send me many times to fetch him before he would come back. When he was back, he threw such a tantrum, demanding who would take the responsibility if he were killed in a bombing raid. Since the master didn't scold him, the mistress couldn't say a thing. Actually, while staying with the Zhaos, he never opened a book, but spent all day gambling with his cousins. . . ."

"Why is Mr. Yao so blind to all this? It's a father's duty to educate and train a child such as your young master," I interrupted.

"Yes." Lao Wen gave a worried sigh. "The master spoils him. He lets him do anything he likes. It's been this way since he was small. It makes us servants, watching from the sidelines, so anxious." Suddenly, forgetting himself, he raised his voice: "He's not young. He's twelve already, and he's still in his fourth semester at senior primary school." Then, lifting his head in exasperation, he said, as if to himself: "What's said is said. What's it matter if others hear me? The worst that can happen is that I'll be packed off home."

"He's twelve! I thought he was ten at the most."

"People who are up to all kinds of tricks don't have enough energy left for growing. What's to be done?" Lao Wen's voice was still tinged with anger.

"That Yang boy yesterday was about the same age. . . ."

"Master Yang?" Lao Wen asked in surprise. But without waiting for me to explain, he went on at once: "I know, the one who's constantly running in for flowers. His family used to be very wealthy. I gather they were even richer than our present master. But they're bankrupt now. However, they can still manage. I've heard the gate-keeper, Old Man Li, say that Master Yang's not fourteen yet, but has been three years at secondary school already, and doing very well."

"But didn't Mr. Yao say that he doesn't study diligently?" I asked.

"That's what he says! I'm talking about what Old Man Li says. In fact, I don't know whether it's true or not. I've always thought, if he's so good at schoolwork, how is it he's always coming into the garden to pick our flowers? I don't understand what's behind it at all. I've asked Old Man Li, but he won't say. If I insist on asking, he starts to shed tears. Yesterday, he spoke to me again about the matter, saying that as long as the master doesn't know, and Zhao Qingyun doesn't see, just let Master Yang in to pick a few branches. Actually, I don't want to make trouble for him. He's a nice child. The house was theirs originally before it was sold. Besides, a couple of branches of camellias aren't worth all that much. In any case, neither Mr. Yao nor his son appreciates flowers. Mrs Yao is the only one who gets any pleasure from them. In fact, the mistress has said, 'What's so important about a couple of branches of blossoms? If he likes flowers, then give him one or two branches.' It's only Zhao Qingyun who's so upset. Lao Liu, the gardener, asked for three months' sick leave, and now Zhao Qingyun is in charge of the garden. And the thing he hates most is other people running into his garden. Mr. Yao has also ordered that Master Yang not be allowed in, saying that he's afraid Master Yang will set a bad example for Master Hu. And so, whenever Zhao Qingyun runs into Master Yang, they quarrel. He tries to chase him out, and the other refuses to go. Master Yang may seem to be small, but he's pretty strong. And he knows how to answer back. Sometimes, Zhao Qingyun can't manage on his own, and so if I happen to be about, I have to give a hand."

"Since Mr. Yao's afraid his son will be badly influenced by Master Yang, does that mean that your young master likes playing with Master Yang?"

"Good heavens, no. Why would our young master want to keep Master Yang's company? He's very snobbish. He never looks at me directly, and can't even bring himself to speak to me properly. The master's really being much too cautious."

"Mrs. Yao's a very understanding person. She could persuade your master not to be so neglectful of Master Hu's education," I said.

Lao Wen shook his head in discouragement. "It's no use. Mr. Yao can understand everything, but in this one matter, he seems to be a bit blind. If you talk to him about it, he won't listen." He bent over slightly, and with a serious expression, whispered to me: "I've heard that the mistress has told our master several times how Master Hu refuses to study at home; how he's always going to his grandmother's to gamble and picking up bad habits; how difficult it is for her as a stepmother to keep an eye on his upbringing; and how, in order to stop gossip from the Zhao family, the master should take his upbringing in hand. But Mr. Yao says that all young people are like this, that he'll change when he grows older, that Master Hu is very clever, and that there's no need to worry about his upbringing. After running up against a wall so often, the mistress doesn't dare keep bringing it up. The Zhao family don't like her at all, especially old Mrs. Zhao, the grandmother, and her two daughters-in-law. They not only spread gossip about her outside the family, but often encourage Master Hu to make life difficult for her as well. The master doesn't take the slightest notice. The mistress has told Mrs. Zhou that it's lucky she herself hasn't borne a son; otherwise, she'd have an even worse time as a stepmother."

"Mrs. Yao really does have a bad time," I said in sympathy, and with indignation.

"Ah, yes. If Mrs. Zhou hadn't told me, how would I have known? The mistress is always so full of smiles. Whenever she meets people, she chats with them and laughs with them. I only hope the spirit of the old master will bless her and give her a couple of sons, so that, when they grow up, they'll accomplish great things and bring credit to her." The old man's sincere wish for her happiness echoed faintly in the vastness of the guest room. I saw him wipe away a tear with his hand. Feeling sad, I got up and walked about the room for a moment in silence.

I felt Lao Wen's eyes fixed on me as I moved, and so I stood still, gazing at his slightly bent head, while waiting for him to speak.

"Mr. Li, you mustn't tell anyone else what I've just told you," he begged me cautiously. The angry expression on his face had disappeared completely. Instead, I saw a beseeching look of helplessness, his toothless mouth a dark cavity.

"Don't worry. I certainly won't tell anyone," I said with emotion.

"Thank you. I've poured out to you today everything I've had bottled up inside me. Mr. Li, even though we're servants without any education, we can still tell the difference between good

and bad, between right and wrong.   And it hurts us too." Lao
Wen looked down and, picking up the wash-basin in both
hands, went out heart-sick, weeping as he went.

I stood alone at the door of the lower guest room.   I had
drawn so much out of him and had learnt so much from him.
But was my curiosity satisfied?

No. I only felt the sharp claws of some savage beast tearing
at my breast.

10

The next day, when Lao Wen brought in my lunch, he told me
that the previous night, Xiao Hu had once again not returned
home. He also told me a few things about him, and got onto
how he was even spreading gossip about his stepmother outside.
I was not at all pleased when I heard this.   After lunch, I
couldn't work inside, and I didn't want to wander round town
either.   I walked about in the room and around the garden
for I don't know how long, and then, tired out, sat down in
the armchair to rest.   But I got bored with just sitting, and
so got up again.   Finally, I was so fed up I did not know what
to do.   Then I suddenly thought that I might as well go to the
cinema to pass the time.   Just as I turned from the balustrade
into the corridor, I saw Mrs. Zhou bringing me my dinner, explaining that she was serving because Lao Wen had asked for
leave to go into town.

So I had to go back to my room to eat.   Mrs. Zhou made the
tea and filled the wash-basin.   She did her work with great
dexterity.   She was a sturdily-built woman of about forty, her
hair done in a big bun at the back, with a rather long face,
yellow skin, high cheek-bones, thick lips and bushy eyebrows.
She did not like speaking in my presence.   I deliberately asked
her whether Master Hu was home or not.

"Him! Needless to say, he's at the Zhaos' again. When Mrs.
Yao goes to visit her family, she begs him to go with her, but

he won't. All he's interested in is going to the Zhaos' to gamble," Mrs. Zhou said disdainfully, pursing her lips.

"Does he not even obey if Mr. Yao tells him to go with her?" I went on to ask.

"Even the master lets him do anything. He's the little tiger, the little emperor of the Yao family." She turned away, unwilling to say more.

After dinner, I went out the main gate, intending to go to a cinema in the town centre. The gate-keeper, Old Man Li, was sitting just inside the gate on an old-fashioned wooden armchair, smoking strong tobacco. On seeing me, he stood up, put down his pipe and addressed me respectfully: "Li *laoye*," smiling at me amiably.

As I went out the gate, this "Li *laoye*" sounded so disagreeable to my ears that I turned back. He'd just sat down again, but stood up at once.

"Old Man Li, sit down. There's no need to be polite." I motioned to him to sit down again, saying to him quietly: "Please don't call me *laoye*. Everyone calls me 'Mr'. You know what I mean."

"Yes, Mr. Li, I understand," he said respectfully.

"Sit down, sit down." Seeing there was no one else about, I decided to take this opportunity to find out about the Yang boy. I sat down on a wooden stool opposite him, so he was forced to sit down too.

"I hear you worked for a long time in the Yang family. Is that so?" I asked, looking at his bald head.

"Yes. I entered the household just after Mr. Yang, the grandfather, had finished building the house. That was the 32nd year of the Guangxu Emperor (1902) over thirty years ago. At first, I was a sedan-chair bearer. In the 6th year of the Republic (1917), I got into a fight, fell and broke my leg. The old master paid for my medical treatment, and asked me to be the gate-keeper." He bent down and knocked his pipe against the sole of his shoe. The ash fell to the ground, and he at once rubbed out the sparks with his foot. He put the pipe down on the chair behind him.

"Is everyone in the Yang family well?" I asked, putting on an air of concern.

"The old master died in the 20th year of the Republic (1921). And the eldest son's been dead over five years now. He had only one son, who went off after the house was sold, and there hasn't been any news of him since. The second son's in business in Hengyang and doing well. The fourth son is the deputy-manager of some big company here in Chengdu, and is also very well-off. The third son's the only one that's dissipated all his inheritance. He finds it hard even to get anything to eat. . . ." He gave a succession of sighs, shook his head several times, and stroked his beard once or twice, a white beard only an inch long.

"The young boy who came yesterday was one of the Yang family, wasn't he?"

"Yes. He's the son of the third master. He's just like his father, with delicate features, and very intelligent, but also very self-assured. When the third master was young, his father was extremely fond of him, and used to give in to him on everything. Later when he grew up and married, he was led astray by his friends, and frittered away all his fortune. He even spent all his wife's dowry. Later, his wife and elder son fell out with him, and only this younger son is on good terms with him."

"Is he still alive then?" I interrupted suddenly.

"Er . . . I don't know." He shook his head several times. I noticed his eyes. Although he had turned his face to hide them from me, I saw nevertheless that they were filled with tears. I realized he wasn't telling me the truth. He was hiding something. But I still hoped to fish the truth out of him.

"Isn't the elder son working in the post office? In that case, the family must be able to manage. The younger son's still at school, and it costs a packet nowadays to keep young people in school."

"Yes. The brothers get on very well. The younger son studies very hard. The elder boy is very fond of his brother. It's just that he hates his father. The younger brother always comes second or third in the exams at school." As he spoke, he smiled, stroking his beard between his fingers, but the tears in his eyes had still not dried.

"That's right. I could see that. He really is a fine lad." I praised him deliberately. "But there's one thing I don't understand. Why's he always running in for flowers, causing trouble for the Yao family servants? If he likes flowers, he can buy them. They're not expensive. Why does he have to pick other people's flowers?"

"Mr. Li, you don't understand. The boy is kind-hearted. The flowers aren't for himself."

"Even if they're for someone else, he can still buy them. You can buy camellias outside," I continued. I was beginning to see the light.

"There aren't many camellias available outside. And even if there were, they can't compare with those here in this mansion. They were planted over thirty years ago. There were already camellias in the garden when Third Master was young. Altogether two trees, one red, one white. The white one was badly chopped by Master Hu the year before last. Now only the red one's left. Third Master loved that tree. He didn't have a proper job, but that time they talked of selling the house, it wasn't his idea at all. Second Master and Fourth Master wanted the money to start a business, and so they kicked up a fuss, insisting on selling. Eldest Master's eldest son was only twenty-six or -seven, and hadn't yet married. He was very quick-tempered, and ordinarily looked down on his uncles. He also demanded that the house be sold, saying that the family property should be divided up completely, so that he could go abroad and study, and never come back to Sichuan again. Third Master had already spent all his wife's money, and so she was anxious to have the place sold in order to have something to live on. Everyone wanted to sell. Even if Third Master had said he didn't, it would have been no use. At the time, everyone was in a hurry. They were afraid that one or other of them would change his mind if they waited too long, so they got only a very low price for it. Once they got the cash, it was divided among everyone. Third Master didn't get a penny." Once more, he stopped speaking, his lips completely hidden by his short, thick, white moustache.

"How can he have got nothing? Surely his wife and the others must have given him something after getting their share. He needed money for food and lodging," I pursued in surprise. I was sure he was hiding something important from me.

"Yes. What you say is right, Mr. Li," he replied respectfully.

I knew he would not tell me any more. He probably guessed I was trying to dig information out of him, trying to find a way to get his inner secrets out of him, so he said this "yes" to keep me quiet. If I continued to interrogate him, not only would I probably have no luck, but I would increase his suspicion of me. It was better to stop here, and wait for another opportunity.

Just as I was thinking this, a human figure suddenly flashed past. Old Man Li stood up at once. His round face had completely changed colour. It was moved by fear, as if he'd seen something that he was afraid to see.

I was startled too. I got up and stepped out the main gate. I looked up the street, but saw only someone's back. He was tall and thin, with long hair thick with dust, and was wearing a lined grey cotton gown, so dirty and greasy as to be almost black. He was hurrying away as if afraid of being pursued.

I I

I followed the direction he'd taken. As I passed a building that looked like a temple, I caught sight of three large characters for "Temple of the Grand Immortal". I suddenly remembered Lao Yao's words. He said he'd seen the Yang boy with a beggar at the doors of this temple. He'd also said that the Temple of the Grand Immortal was next to his residence. In fact, it was more than half-way down the street from his house. My curiosity drew me into the temple.

It was very small. The air may once have been thick with the smoke of incense, but now the place was desolate and deserted. The tablet of the Grand Immortal stood all alone in the god's niche. Only a corner of the curtain remained. On the wall still hung a few dilapidated boards with inscriptions like "Your prayer will be answered". The altar had lost a leg, and in the censer a single stick of incense was burning. There were no holders for candles. Instead, there were two large turnips in which were stuck two burnt-out candles. In a short fat glass bottle in the middle of the altar was a branch of red camellias. They were clearly the flowers I had picked for the Yang boy the day before.

Strange! How had those camellia blossoms got there? I pondered over it. I felt sure I was on the verge of solving a mystery.

Beside the niche was a small door leading to the back. I went in through it. Behind, I found some stone steps, a small court-yard and a brick wall. At the top of the steps, against the wooden wall of the niche, on a heap of straw, was spread a mat, over which lay an old blanket. Beside the pillow stood a wash-basin containing a few odds and ends. In one corner of the courtyard, against the brick wall, a small stove had been constructed out of a few bricks. On it was a small earthenware pot which was now boiling, giving off steam.

Who was here? Could it be that the Yang boy had some connection with this person? Or was he perhaps a disciple of the Grand Immortal? I was puzzled. I stood on the steps lost in thought, staring at the earthenware pot on the broken-down stove.

I heard the sound of a weak cough behind me. I turned

round. A man was standing there, tall and thin, with long dishevelled hair, his long grey gown filthy with grease and dirt. It was the man who had just fled from the Yao family gate. He was sizing me up, his eyes filled with fear and suspicion. I looked at him closely too. His long dirty face looked as if it hadn't been washed for many days. He looked old, but he had delicate features. His eyes were very bright, his nose curved slightly to the left, and his upper lip was thin. And though his lips were closed, his upper teeth were partly visible. How strange! I seemed to have seen him somewhere before.

He remained standing there, measuring me up. He did not say a word, and did not move away. As he looked at me, I began to squirm uneasily, as if all the grease and dirt on his body had stuck to mine. I couldn't bear this silent appraisal any longer, and so I broke the silence by asking:

"Do you live here?"

He nodded expressionlessly.

After another moment, I spoke again:

"What you've got in the pot is boiling." I pointed to the earthenware pot on the stove.

He nodded again.

"Are you the only one here?" I asked, after another few minutes.

He nodded again.

Was he a mute then? I stood there for another moment. We looked at each other for three or four minutes. It suddenly came to me: His nose and lips were an exact replica of the Yang boy's. The eyes were also alike.

It was an unexpected discovery. Surely he could not be the third son of the Yang family? He couldn't be the Yang boy's father?

I should have asked him. I should have made him tell me who he was. It was no use. He would not speak. He would only nod. How would I be able to understand him? Even if he wasn't a mute, even if he really was the boy's father, he would never reveal his secret to a stranger like me. So what was the use of my continuing to stand there so idiotically?

I went out the small door in disappointment. He followed me out. When I came to the altar and saw the camellia flowers in the bottle, I could not help asking another question:

"Are those flowers yours?"

He nodded again. This time, I saw the trace of a smile on his lips.

"I picked these myself the day before yesterday from the Yaos' garden," I said, pointing to the camellia branch.

He glanced at me as if uncertain whether to believe me or not, smiled slightly (at least so it seemed to me, though he may not have smiled at all) and, after a while, nodded again.

I could not help myself, and found myself asking again:

"Did Master Yang give them to you?"

He nodded again, and then simply left me standing there, going across the paved courtyard to stand at the doors of the main entrance. I did not see the expression on his face clearly. The light in the temple was very dim, for night was approaching.

My spirits dampened, I went out of the temple. Behind me I heard the sound of the doors closing. I turned round. The doors, lacquered in black, had lost their shine. Locked inside the temple behind them was the mute who could only nod.

Standing there before the entrance, I took out my watch. It was only ten minutes past six. I at once hailed a passing rickshaw, asking the young puller to drop me at the Rongguang Cinema.

My mind was filled with the secrets of many people. Now I needed to rest. I needed to forget.

12

When I got back to the Yao mansion, it was not yet half past nine. Xiao Hu was standing in the main hall shouting at Zhao

He followed me out.

Qingyun. He was using the most vulgar language. Zhao Qingyun was sitting on the doorstep of the porter's lodge. He was wearing a short jacket, his sleeves rolled up almost to his shoulders, showing two firm muscular arms. He was answering back in language that was alternately cold and then heated. Lao Wen was sitting on a black lacquered bench inside the second gate, on the right, smoking his pipe.

Lao Wen stood up and greeted me: "Mr. Li. You're back."

"What's the matter with him?" I asked, pointing at Xiao Hu.

"He came back in a temper because he lost at gambling. He blames Zhao Qingyun for going early to fetch him. It was Mrs. Yao who ordered him to go and get him. She said he had to revise his lessons in the evening; besides, to get to class at seven in the morning, he has to get up at six. In fact, what kind of study does he do? He's just muddling along wasting his time." Lao Wen shook his head and sighed. "In a month, he takes at least ten days off, and is late for another fifteen. After seven years in school, the characters he can recognize wouldn't even fill a basket. He's simply storing up evildoing for himself."

"Hasn't Mr. Yao come back?" I asked.

"It's still early. Mr. and Mrs. Yao have gone to the opera today with Mrs. Yao's mother. They won't be back till twelve. When Mr. Yao's not home and he throws a tantrum, no one pays any attention to him. But Zhao Qingyun is stubborn, and won't let him get away with it. So Xiao Hu just brings trouble on himself."

In the hall Xiao Hu was jumping and shouting to all and sundry, his language becoming increasingly coarse. Once he leapt into the courtyard threatening to hit Zhao Qingyun. Zhao stood up, squaring his shoulders, and shouted back:

"Fuck you, mate! You make one move, and I'll make mince-meat of you, or my name's not Zhao!"

Xiao Hu retreated in fright. At that moment, the sound of a rickshaw bell and the cries of pullers were heard from outside the second gate. Xiao Hu at once ran forward a couple of steps, pushed his hands into the pockets of his Western jacket, and, with a cry of satisfaction, laughed: "All right, hit me then. Dad's back. Just see if you dare."

A house rickshaw and two other rickshaws stopped at the second gate. From them descended a plainly-dressed middle-aged woman, a young girl, her hair in plaits, wearing a floral cheongsam, and a sixteen- or seventeen-year-old youth in a blue school uniform. They crossed the threshold one after another. Lao Wen dropped his arms to his sides and greeted them. They answered him with a nod.

When Xiao Hu saw that it wasn't his father return-ed, he turned and ran off. He ran up the steps of the main hall, stood there, and began swearing at the top of his voice again. When the woman and young girl passed him, he paid no attention to them. Nor did they look at him. Only the youth stopped and asked him with a smile: "Cousin Hu, who are you quarrelling with?"

"Mind your own business!" answered Xiao Hu, turning angrily away.

The young man smiled as if nothing had happened, and went in through the side door into the inner courtyard.

"Was he Xiao Hu's cousin?" I asked Lao Wen.

"Yes. They are his widowed aunt, her daughter and her son. They know what Master Hu's temper's like, and keep away from him whenever possible. When Mr Yao's not there, Master Hu doesn't give them any consideration. His aunt be-longs to his parents' generation, but you see he doesn't even greet her. She's Mr. Yao's elder sister, not quite two years older than he. Her husband died young, but left her with some land, so the family manages to survive. Mr. Yao's been good enough to let them live here. Perhaps also because the mansion has too many rooms. It's too big for just a family of three to live in. Mr. and Mrs. Yao treat this aunt very well. It's just Master Hu who despises them. He's always telling people that his aunt and her family haven't any money to speak of, whereas the Yaos have nearly a hundred acres of land. If somebody has lots of land, it's because his ancestors left it to him! Her son and daughter are both studying at the university. They've never been rash with their money. Everyone's full of praise for them. They are really capable." As Lao Wen talked about Xiao Hu, he began to get angry. As soon as he began to speak, he let out all these grievances. I understood how he felt. I knew whence his anger sprang.

"I think I'll just have to tell your master that if things keep going the way they are, not only will it harm Xiao Hu for the rest of his life, but your mistress will be hurt by it as well," I said.

"It's no use, Mr. Li. No use. This is the only matter on which the master doesn't see clearly. Besides, there's also what the Zhao family puts him up to. The trouble is that they have even more money than Mr. Yao, and all Master Hu thinks of is money. Mrs. Yao's family doesn't have much money at all. They're even worse off than Mr. Yao's sister, so, of course, Master Hu has no respect for them at all. The year Mrs. Yao came into the family, he went to visit the Wan family twice, but since then, he'd rather die than go there again."

"How many are there in Mrs. Yao's family?"

"Apart from her mother, there's her elder brother and his wife, and their two sons. The brother is ten years older than Mrs. Yao, and is teaching at a university. It seems he's got a very good name. The two sons are studying away from Sichuan. Even if they haven't much money, the Wan family live together very harmoniously. That's what you call a family! Not at all like the Zhaos. Not a single one of them has a decent job. All they can do is to show off their wealth, and gamble. Even we servants find it shocking. Mr. Li, just think. If Master Hu goes to the Zhao family day after day, how can he become a decent person!"

"I didn't realize you understood so much," I said, praising him.

"Mr. Li, you're too complimentary. What's the use of servants like us understanding things? We'll be servants all our lives. In the master's presence, we don't even dare let out a fart. He's so well-read, so widely-travelled, how dare we contradict him? Even if we wanted to take up cudgels on behalf of Mrs. Yao, we wouldn't dare say a word to him. Besides, they're a very loving couple. Outside the family, there's no one who doesn't comment on how much Mr. Yao loves his wife! . . . Master Hu's gone in. Mr. Li, you should go in and rest too. I've kept you long enough. I'll go and fetch you some water to wash with." He pushed the tobacco pipe which he'd been squeezing between his fingers into the back of his trouser belt, and went off into the courtyard, sighing and shaking his head. I could only follow him into the Garden of Repose.

13

And so I continued to live at the Yaos'. My friends gave me complete freedom, and provided me with every convenience. The garden was quiet, and few people ever entered it. Whenever guests came, he would receive them in the upper guest room. In fact, apart from early morning and evening, he was not much at home. I knew that he was not in any kind of business, and I'd heard that he was not much interested in the social round. I asked Lao Wen what Mr. Yao went out to do during the day. Lao Wen said that he often went to the Zhengyu Gardens to take tea and listen to traditional Chinese music, and that sometimes he dragged Mrs. Yao along with him.

I began my work on the sixth day after moving into the Yao household. It was my seventh book and my fourth novel. It was the story of an old rickshaw puller and a blind woman story-teller. Before making my way back to my hometown, I had discussed the story line with an elderly man in the world of letters. He was editing a literary collection for a big publishing house at the time, and wanted me to give the completed novel to them to publish. I had agreed. I had to keep my word. My work was going very well. I stayed in the lower guest room writing, and by the end of the week, I had already written over 30,000 characters. I estimated that I could finish the novel in about three weeks.

Every day after dinner, I went for a walk along the streets. Sometimes I went rather a long way, but other times I would come back after going two or three blocks, and sit down on a stool inside the main gate to chat with Old Man Li. We talked about everything. But as soon as I touched on the Yang family, he would either shut up or change the subject. I felt that he was on his guard against me.

I passed the Temple of the Grand Immortal every day, but the doors were always shut tight. I would push them gently, but they wouldn't open. Once I was just a few steps from the entrance when I saw a young boy come out. I recognized him. It was clearly the Yang boy. He flew off as fast as he could, and in a flash had disappeared into the crowd. I went up to the temple. One side of the door was open, and the mute was standing in the doorway. I looked at him and he looked at me. His face hadn't changed, only his eyes were filled with tears, while in his left hand, he was holding a book, thread-bound in the traditional way.

He stepped back, intending to lock me outside, but I immediately blocked the door with my right hand. Looking down at the book in his hand, I asked: "What book's that?"

He nodded stupidly, lifting his hand slightly. The book was open. It was printed from engravings on stone, and the text was in large characters, some of which had little red circles beside them. I caught sight of the lines by Bai Juyi:

"Gazing at the moon, we shed sad tears;
Separated in five different places, we know one feeling of homesickness."

I recognized it as an old edition of the *300 Poems of the Tang Dynasty*, published over twenty years ago.

"Are you reading Tang poems?" I asked gently.

He nodded again, retreating a couple of steps.

I moved forward, and asked again amiably: "What's your name?"

He nodded as before. Tears trickled from the corners of his eyes, but he did not wipe them away. He seemed quite unaware of them.

I looked up at the altar. A stick of incense was burning in the censer. The camellias were still in the bottle, though they had already faded. I spoke to him again: "You really ought to change the flowers."

This time he forgot even to nod. He stared at the flowers stupidly, his tears staining his cheeks like two threads.

I suddenly remembered that it was Saturday. I had been with the Yao family for just a fortnight. The day the Yang boy came for the flowers had been a Saturday. He probably came here every Saturday to see his father. There was no doubt, the mute was the third son of the Yang family. According to Old Man Li, when they had sold the house and divided up the proceeds, the third Mr. Yang had not received a penny. It was probably at that time that he'd been driven out by his family. As to how he came to be living in the temple, and how he'd become a mute, there must surely be a long story behind it. But how could I find out? He would not tell me himself. Nor would the Yang boy. What about Old Man Li? At present, he would not talk to me about the Yang family.

The mute coughed beside me, not just once, but five or six times in succession. I looked at him with sympathy, trying to think how I could help him. He forced himself to stop coughing and, pointing to the door, gestured for me to leave. For a moment, I hesitated, and then went out without a word.

The door closed behind me. I didn't turn to look. The moon, in its first quarter, hung suspended in the pale blue sky. Night had not yet come, and the evening air was cool and fresh.

I walked slowly down the street, trying to forget these seemingly mysterious events.

14

"Lao Li! Lao Li!" a familiar voice called from behind me. A huge figure jumped down from the rickshaw heading directly towards me.

I came to a halt and looked up. Lao Yao was standing before me, his face wreathed in smiles.

"I was just getting worried that I mightn't be able to find you. I never thought I'd catch you on the way home. What luck!" He laughed with satisfaction, and turned to the rickshaw puller at once. "You can take the rickshaw home," he instructed.

The man acknowledged the command, lifted the shafts and trotted off.

"What's the news? You look so happy!" I asked.

"Now that I've run into you, my troubles are at an end," Lao Yao laughed. "I'd arranged to go with Zhaohua to the pictures at seven. I'd already bought two tickets, but never thought that once I got to the Zhaos' they'd want me to stay for dinner and take the old lady to the Sichuan opera. There was no way I could refuse. But what was I to do about my wife's going to the pictures? I thought, I'd better get you to go with her. Only I was afraid you wouldn't be home. But now there's no problem."

"You can go to the opera after you've seen the film," I said.

"But I still have to rush back to the Zhaos' for dinner. Now I'll go home first to tell Zhaohua."

"If you don't go with her, your wife may not be pleased about it."

"No, no!" he said, full of confidence, shaking his head. "No one has a better disposition than she has. And she knows that I normally don't like films very much anyway. I just go to keep her company."

"Didn't the Zhaos invite your wife to dinner?"

"Why do you keep on about it? You're fast becoming an old woman," Lao Yao exclaimed with an accusing laugh.

"Let's go. Zhaohua will be waiting for us at home. And I have
to hurry back to the Zhaos'. They're at the South Gate, and
we're at the North Gate."

I gave a laugh and followed him. However, he answered my
question on the way, and also explained to me: "Old Mrs. Zhao
doesn't like seeing Zhaohua. She says that it makes her think of
her own daughter, and she can't bear it. Since my first wife
died, the old lady hasn't been to our place once. Actually,
Zhaohua was very friendly with the Zhaos' at first, but later,
they kept saying that they were afraid it would cause old Mrs.
Zhao too much pain, and so they didn't dare invite her over.
She's never been to the Zhaos' since then. Actually, you
can't blame them. The old lady loved her daughter too much.
That's only natural. Besides, my first wife was her only
daughter."

"In that case, doesn't it make her think of her only daughter
when she sees you or Xiao Hu?" I queried, not satisfied
with his explanation.

"She loves Xiao Hu very, very much. Going to the opera this
evening was his idea." He seemed not to understand what I was
driving at, answering me only with words that I found dis-
pleasing.

We reached home. Lao Yao asked me to wait in my room.
I stepped over the threshold into the Garden of Repose, and
heard him tell Lao Wen: "Go outside and call a rickshaw for
Mr. Li."

15

I wandered in the garden for ten minutes or more, watching the
night slowly cast her net over the ground from the walls and the
trees. Two or three ravens sighed with fatigue as they flew
through the tree-tops. A tiny bird flew down suddenly from
the cassia tree, through the green foliage of the camellia bush,
which was no longer in flower, and came to rest on the rockery.

Lao Yao and his wife came. His wife was smiling as usual. She was wearing a short narrow-waisted black velvet jacket over a light grey woollen cheongsam. Lao Yao had changed from his long gown into a Western suit, and over his arm was carrying a light overcoat with a double lining.

"Lao Li, let's go. You're not taking anything?" Lao Yao called happily, standing by the stone balustrade.

"I'm coming. I'm not taking anything," I said, as I went up the steps and, following the balustrade, went over to meet them.

"Mr. Li, I'm so sorry. We're interrupting your work again," Mrs. Yao apologized with a smile.

"Mrs. Yao, you're much too polite. He knows," I said, pointing to her husband, "that I'm a film fan. You apologize even when you invite me to a film. What can I possibly say in reply?" I laughed.

"All right. Let's stop all these formalities and go, or we'll be late," urged Lao Yao from beside us.

We went out the gate of the garden. Three rickshaws were waiting for us at the second gate. The two of them got into the house rickshaws, while I took the hired one, and we went out the main gate one behind the other.

After two blocks, my friend said good-bye to his wife at the intersection. After another six or seven blocks, our two rickshaws stopped at the entrance of the cinema.

I looked up at the clock, and saw that there were still eight or nine minutes before the film would begin. There were very few people in the foyer — a dozen or so. The film was *Tears of Love Amidst Clouds of War*. There wasn't a single well-known star in it. Moreover, it was a story of the American Civil War, and I doubted that it would suit the taste of the local audience.

The cinema was very large, and it was only just over half-full. There were five empty seats in the row in front of us. Mrs. Yao began reading the programme, but the lights went out before she finished.

On the screen appeared the life of a harmonious family in a

beautiful and peaceful country setting. Then followed a succession of simple tragedies. My heart went out to those fine people in their miserable destiny. I saw Mrs. Yao wipe her eyes
frequently with her handkerchief, and from time to time I heard
her sigh softly.

When it came to where the father had returned from the war,
and was lying on the sofa dying, the film broke. The lights
went on again. Mrs. Yao let out a sigh but said nothing, keeping
her eyes to the ground. I, however, looked round at the other
seats, without any real purpose.

For a moment, I was taken aback. Three rows in front of
me, on my right, was the Yang boy, dressed just as I had seen
him earlier at the door of the Temple of the Grand Immortal.
He was talking to a middle-aged woman seated beside him. Her
face was lightly powdered, her hair brushed back into a small
chignon, and over her blue-flowered cheongsam, she was wearing a grey woollen jacket. On her right sat another young man
in a grey Western suit. She turned slightly to say a few words
to him, and when she smiled, he smiled in reply. After a while,
the young man suddenly turned to look behind him. I saw his
face clearly. Apart from his hair, which was smoothly combed
and oiled, and the pallor of his face, he was the spitting image
of the Yang boy.

What a coincidence! So many things suddenly came together.
Who would have thought that I would run into the Yang boy's
mother and brother in this cinema.

The lights went out again. The film continued. Finally the
war ended, and the soldiers returned to their homes. The honest
young woman, after waiting for a long period in despair, finally
saw her lover return to her on the family farm re-established
with her mother.

Everyone got up to leave. The lights went on again. Mrs. Yao
glanced at me, and then got up. I said to her briefly: "Not a
bad film." She nodded and replied: "I never expected it."

Mrs. Yao was afraid of the crush and suggested we let the
others leave first. By the time we reached the entrance, all the

rickshaws had been taken. I saw Mrs. Yang and her sons take the last three.

Their rickshaw man was waiting for us at the bottom of the steps. When he saw her, he called: "Mrs. Yao! The rickshaw's over here!"

"Where's Mr. Li's rickshaw?" she asked.

"I hired one," he replied, "but someone grabbed it. There aren't many today. We'll probably be able to get one farther on. Will you get in first?"

I said at once: "Mrs. Yao, please go home first. I'll just call one for myself farther on. If there aren't any, then it's just as easy to walk."

"You go ahead. I'll walk with Mr. Li part of the way. I'll get in when we manage to hire him one. In any case, it's a nice evening. The moon's out." Mrs. Yao gave her instructions to the rickshaw man softly, without asking my opinion.

"Yes, Mrs. Yao," he replied respectfully.

And so I went down the steps with her, while the rickshaw man went slowly ahead pulling the rickshaw. The two of us followed behind.

16

We followed the rickshaw round the corner and left the noise of the people, left the brightness of the lights, and entered a small quiet lane paved in stone. I did not speak. My ears were filled only with the regular tap of her low-heeled shoes.

The moon shone weakly down.

"I haven't been out walking for two years. I go by rickshaw everywhere," she began, for she seemed to notice that her silence made me uncomfortable.

I took the opportunity to repeat: "Mrs. Yao, I think it would be best if you went back by rickshaw first. There are still quite a few blocks to go. I'm used to walking, so it doesn't matter."

I did not say this entirely from politeness, for I was afraid the walk would tire her. Moreover, I felt rather awkward accompanying her in this way.

"It doesn't matter, Mr. Li. There's no need to worry about me. If I don't practise walking, I might forget how to in future." She glanced at me with a sly smile. "Last year, during the alerts, we fled from the air-raids in our own rickshaws, but when we got to the countryside, we had to do quite a bit of walking from time to time. There haven't been so many air-raid warnings these past couple of years. My husband not only doesn't like walking himself, but won't let me walk either, nor will he let Xiao Hu walk."

"Are you very busy in the house, Mrs. Yao?"

"No. I've lots of time. There are only three of us in the family. The servants are not bad. When anything needs doing, they do it very well without being told. I've nothing to do, so I read to pass the time. I've read several of your works, Mr. Li."

The thing I hate most is to hear people say to my face that they have read my books. When I heard these words from her lips, I felt even more embarrassed. I said apologetically: "They're very badly written. They're not worth reading."

"Mr. Li, you're too modest! You're an old friend of us. You mustn't be polite with me. My husband often mentioned you to me. I'm in no position to criticize your books, but I've read them, and I'm sure that you're an honest and kind-hearted person. It seems to me that he is very lucky to have a friend like you. He has lots of acquaintances, but there aren't many who are real friends," she said with sincerity, softly but clearly, and in such a sweet voice. Nevertheless, I detected in her tone just the touch of a hidden sorrow. I sympathized with her, thinking: And what about you? What real friends do you have? Why don't you think about yourself? But I couldn't say such a thing to her directly. All I could do was to signal my agreement.

We went on for three blocks. I said nothing, for my heart was too full of unspoken emotion.

"It always seems to me that novelists must have the heart of a Buddha in the face of human misery in the world today. Otherwise, how can one man endure the sufferings of so many people? How can the pen of one man pour out the griefs of so many others? That's why, Mr. Li, I'm sure that one day you'll be a great help to my husband. . . ."

"Mrs. Yao, you're being polite again. What help can I possibly be to him? He has a very comfortable life. He's far better off than I am!" I said with feeling. I thought I understood what she meant, and yet at the same time feared I might have misunderstood what she was really saying, and so I uttered these meaningless words both to reassure her, and to express my helplessness in the situation.

"Mr. Li, I'm sure you understand what I mean, or at least one day you will understand. I believe that you novelists see into things much more deeply than other people. Ordinary people see only the surface, but you explore into the depths of men's hearts. I think too that your life is very hard, because by seeing so deeply, I'm afraid you also see a great deal of suffering, and very little happiness. . . ."

Her voice trembled slightly and trailed off into the distance like a sigh, a sob. It stabbed my heart, penetrating to its very depths.

I lost the power to resist. I forgot myself. I wanted desperately to reveal my feelings. I said to her earnestly: "Mrs. Yao, I still can't say whether I understand you or not. But you have no need to worry. Please remember that, with a wife like you, Lao Yao must be the happiest man in the world. . . ." I was so moved that I could not finish what I wanted to say. And then, I was suddenly afraid that she might misunderstand me, that she might turn my words into a joke, into an offence even.

She was silent, so much so that she didn't make the least sound. She kept her head down slightly. After a while, she looked up again. But she didn't answer me at all. I did not dare say anything to her either. Her eyes looked straight ahead into space, so that I couldn't see the expression on her face.

I could not bear this heavy silence, nor did I wish to escape from it. She said nothing about getting into the rickshaw, and so I had to accompany her all the way home. Whatever impression my words, had left on her, since I had spoken my true feelings, I had now no choice but to be ready to take the consequences. And I had no regrets.

Her steps were no longer as regular as before. She had no doubt lost the tranquillity of her mood. I wished I could discover what she was thinking at that moment. But how could I find out?

We were still two blocks from home. At the intersection, she suddenly turned towards me and her sweet, gentle voice broke the silence. "Mr. Li, I hear you're writing another novel. Is that so?"

"Yes. I've nothing to do, so it passes the time."

"But it's not good for your health to write so much every day. Mrs. Zhou says that you're bent over your desk writing away all day. And besides, the desk is too low. I'll change one for you tomorrow. But you should write less, Mr. Li. You don't look too well," she said with concern.

"Actually, I don't write very much," I said gratefully. Then I added: "If I don't write, there's nothing to do. Apart from going to the cinema, I don't have any other liking, and there are not many good films recently.

"I, on the other hand, like reading novels. Reading novels is almost the same as seeing films. I often wonder how one man's brain can think about so many complex situations at the same time. Mr. Li, have you already worked out the plot of your novel? What kind of characters are you writing about this time?"

I related to her the plot of the novel. She seemed to listen attentively. By the time I came to the end, we were already home.

The man pulled the rickshaw in first, while Mrs. Yao and I followed behind. Old Man Li was standing respectfully in front of his wooden armchair. Behind him, a dark shape stood leaning against the wooden partition. Even with the light from the red lantern hanging from the eaves above the door, I could not see his face clearly. Besides, I gave only a quick glance, but I could tell at once that it was the mute from the Temple of the Grand Immortal. However, by the time I'd finished saying a few words to Mrs. Yao and turned back from the inner gate to look out, I saw only a long shadow slip away and disappear in flight down the street.

I had no time to pursue the matter. I accompanied Mrs. Yao across the courtyard and went in through the second gate.

"This is the first time I've walked so far since my marriage into the Yao family," she said with a smile that seemed evocative of her happiness. After a while, she added: "I'm not in the least tired." After another couple of steps, she continued: "I must thank you."

I thought she would leave me to go into the inner courtyard, so I answered with a smile: "Not at all. See you tomorrow."

But she remained there looking at me, hesitated a moment, and then finally spoke out: "Mr. Li, why don't you let the old rickshaw puller find happiness with the blind girl? There's so much pain and so little happiness in the world, and it's so rare for things to come out as we want them. But you novelists could provide the world with more warmth, wipe the tears from every eye, and bring happiness to everyone. If I could write, I definitely wouldn't let the blind girl drown herself. I wouldn't let the old rickshaw puller go mad." She spoke earnestly, her voice filled with sympathy and pity.

"All right," I said, laughing. "All right, Mrs. Yao. For the reasons you give, I'll let them live happily ever after."

"Then thank you. See you tomorrow." She smiled gratefully, then turned and left.

At the time, I had spoken for the sake of speaking, but I had no intention of changing the ending of my story to suit her ideas. But after returning to my room, I felt completely alone as I sat facing the mute electric lamp. I spread out my draft, but I could not write a word. When I pushed it aside, I felt the need to pour out the emotions that filled my heart. I heard her voice as I sat in the cane chair before the table. I heard her voice as I walked back and forth about the room. I heard her voice as I went to sit in the armchair again. "Provide the world with more warmth, wipe the tears from every eye, and bring happiness to everyone." These words echoed in my ears repeatedly and unceasingly. Finally, they seized possession of my soul. Suddenly, a new vision of the world appeared before me. For the first time, I saw my own weakness and failings. My life till now, my works, my projects, all had been a waste. I had increased the suffering of mankind. I had filled the eyes of the pure and the honest with tears. In this world full of suffering, I had not brought a single sound of joy or laughter. I had locked myself into a little world of my own making. I had lived selfishly, dissipating my youth onto pages of white paper. I had spent my days garrulously pouring forth those tragic stories. I had made the kind-hearted suffer, killed the warm-hearted and the sincere, added to the misfortunes of the unfortunate. I had allowed a good-hearted blind woman to leap into the river, an upright old rickshaw puller to go mad, and a pure and honest young maiden to end her own life. Why could I not stretch out my hand to wipe away the tears of others? Why could I not dispense a little warmth to decrease the hunger and cold in this world? Her words illuminated the innermost recesses of my heart, enabling me to see for the first time its utter emptiness. How empty they were — my work, my life, my writings.

Despair and regret would soon make me mad. I had already fallen from the throne in the kingdom I had created. I could not bear the light of the electric lamp. I couldn't bear the furniture in the room. I ran into the garden. I walked back and forth between the two old cassia trees for a long, long time.

That night, I went to bed very late, but I slept badly. One nightmare came after another. Even in my dreams, I couldn't accept myself.

17

The next day I got up quite early, but I had a headache, and my eyes were sore. However, I did not lie down. I felt angry with myself. I opened my draft to write, but I could not. I had no wish to write, but I forced myself to do so. From half past seven in the morning right up to half past ten, I wrote altogether over five hundred words. In those three hours, I kept hearing her voice: "Why don't you let them live happily ever after?" I still wanted to stifle it with all my force. But little by little, my brush refused to obey my command.

I re-read several times the five hundred or so words that I had written. I saw Mrs. Yao's influence on that short section for the first time. I threw aside my brush angrily, and yet I could not explain the reason for my irritation. Just at that moment, Lao Yao came in.

I looked up from my desk in answer to his greeting, and forced myself to smile at him, but I remained seated in the cane chair without bothering to stand up.

"What's wrong? You don't look at all well!" he cried in alarm.

"I didn't sleep well after I finished writing last night," I answered quietly. I was lying.

"Ah, yes. I heard you coughing in the room when I came back at midnight last night." And then he continued: "Actually, you're not in very good health. You shouldn't stay up too late. In any case, the garden's very quiet, and you've got plenty of time. Why do you insist on writing in the evening?" From his voice and his expression, I knew that his concern was sincere. I was grateful to him, and so I thought of taking this opportunity to talk to him about Xiao Hu, to give him some frank and friendly advice.

"Did you come back with Xiao Hu?" I asked.

"Yes, I did. Xiao Hu knows a lot about Peking Opera. He takes a great interest in it," Lao Yao replied, laughing proudly.

"But it's too late. It's not very good for him. Boys should normally go to bed early, and besides, in the evenings, he still has his lessons to go over. His grandmother spoils him too much. I'm afraid it'll hold him back. As his father, you ought to realize that," I said earnestly, speaking slowly on purpose, so that he would hear each word clearly.

He began to laugh. He slapped me on the shoulder. "My dear chap, you talk just like an old bookworm. I've got Xiao Hu's education well in hand. At first, Zhaohua didn't approve of my method either, and used to talk just like you. But I've convinced her now. With children, the thing to be afraid of is if they don't like playing. Besides, it's not as if we hadn't any money. Children who like to play are very lively, whereas those who don't are pallid, skinny and slow-witted. Even if they do read a few more books, they don't necessarily learn anything from them. I'm not just boasting because I'm his father, but whenever Xiao Hu goes visiting, everyone praises him!"

"I'm afraid Xiao Hu doesn't visit many families apart from the Zhaos," I said coldly and ironically.

It was as if he hadn't understood me. He continued to laugh, looking very pleased with himself: "But there are quite a few people in the Zhao family alone!"

"It's his grandmother's house. That a grandmother should dote on her grandson is the commonest thing in the world," I said seriously. "But what about other people? Do they all love him?" I had meant to avoid saying things like that, but I finally spoke out.

He hesitated a moment, but nevertheless he answered, lifting his head proudly: "Whom do you mean? In our own family, for instance, Zhaohua has never said anything bad about him. My sister doesn't like children very much, but she doesn't get on badly with Xiao Hu. The boy's just too intelligent, too conceited. But it's natural. A clever child can't help being conceited. I will have to correct him later."

"Indeed, that's very important. Otherwise, I'm afraid your

wife's going to have a tough time in future. It seems to me that you can't help doting on him, but you must be careful not to spoil him." I gave this advice sincerely, and was not in any way sneering.

"What's all this nonsense?" he exclaimed, bursting into laughter. "You've never married. You can't know about being a father. There's no need for you to worry on my behalf. In any case, I'm not a fool."

"Nevertheless, I think an onlooker often sees best. You should think about it," I said obstinately.

"My dear chap, an onlooker doesn't see best in this game. I have great hopes for Xiao Hu, so, of course, I won't neglect his upbringing." He patted me on the shoulder. "Let's not talk about this anymore. It can't lead anywhere, because you're a complete amateur." He began to laugh with a satisfied air.

I did not laugh. I turned away, biting my lower lip. I was secretly mad at myself for not being able to express myself better. I couldn't open his eyes and make him see clearly what was really going on. I could not make him understand what was hidden in the soul of the woman he loved.

Just at this moment, his wife entered. She was dressed as she had been the day before, her smile lighting up her whole face like the sun. She greeted me before saying to her husband: "The Zhaos have sent someone to fetch Xiao Hu again."

"Then let him go," her husband answered without giving it a moment's thought.

"I don't think it's very good for Xiao Hu to play so much. He's had very little time recently for going over his lessons. I'm worried that this year again, he might. . . ." She expressed her view in a very soft voice, but when she got as far as "might", she stopped herself and looked at her husband hopefully, waiting for him to answer.

"It doesn't matter, really it doesn't," he said, shaking his head. "Last time, the school wasn't fair. It wasn't his fault. Besides, today's Sunday. The Zhaos have come for him. If we don't let him go, they'll say all kinds of things. Actually, everyone in the Zhao family loves him, so when he goes there, we don't need to worry."

She hesitated for a moment, glanced up at him, and, lowering her eyes, said slowly: "But to go there every day and never study, to learn the manners of a rich young gentleman, that's not good either."

"Dad! Dad!" Xiao Hu called happily from the window. He ran into the room, his head gleaming with sweat. He was wearing a white open-necked shirt and white duck shorts. Seeing his stepmother, he greeted her hurriedly and briefly: "Mother," and then mumbled an indistinct greeting to me. He bowed to me slightly, but so quickly that I just saw his head flash up and down.

"What is it? Why are you so happy?" my friend cried, his smile full of affection.

"Grandma has sent a rickshaw for me to go and play," Xiao Hu answered as he ran up to his father and began shaking his hand.

"Good, but you must come back early today," Lao Yao said, stroking the boy's head.

"I know," the child answered happily. He let go his father's hand and continued: "I'll go and get my clothes." Without another glance at his father or mother, he ran out.

Mrs. Yao gazed out the window, as if in thought.

"For a father, you're certainly easy to get around," I said to Lao Yao jokingly. I didn't like this "upbringing" of his.

Mrs. Yao looked over towards me.

"It's a father's affection for his son. There's nothing I can do," Lao Yao said, shaking his head. From the expression on his face, I knew that he was not altogether satisfied with this kind of "upbringing" either.

"I'm worried that if Xiao Hu plays too long, he won't feel like studying," Mrs. Yao put in, smiling at her husband.

"No, no, that's not possible," Lao Yao said at once, shaking his head. "You worry too much. I know a sure way in which to stop him from getting into bad habits."

"Mr. Li, do you believe in his way?" She smiled at me, her lips pursed.

"No, I don't," I answered, shaking my head. "According to him, he has a sure way for everything."

His wife nodded and said: "That's a fair statement. He's so conceited about everything. He doesn't like listening to advice." She glanced at him again.

He was still smiling happily. His lips moved. He was about to say something, when Mrs. Zhou's face appeared.

"Sir, your sister would like you to go and see her. She says she has something to talk over with you," Mrs. Zhou said.

Lao Yao said to me: "In that case, we'll go on with our chat this afternoon. But Zhaohua can stay for a while." He followed Mrs. Zhou out at once.

Mrs. Yao was standing at the window gazing at her husband's back, when she suddenly turned towards me and said: "Mr. Li, I've already spoken to my husband about the writing desk which will be brought over shortly."

"Thank you. Actually, it doesn't matter if it's not changed. This table's not bad," I answered politely.

"The table's a bit low. You do so much writing each day, it's not comfortable bending so low," she said.

"I'm used to writing like that. It's not a problem. I don't feel happy about giving you so much trouble."

"Mr. Li, you mustn't be so polite in future, all right? You're an old school friend of his, so you mustn't be polite with me." She smiled amiably.

"I'm not being in the least polite. . . ." My words were interrupted by a noise.

"What's going on?" she exclaimed to herself in alarm, heading towards the door. I followed her.

The Yang boy was standing by the stone balustrade, quarrelling with Zhao Qingyun. He was shouting: "I've come to talk to Mr. Li. You've no right to stop me."

"Mr. Li doesn't know you. You've obviously sneaked in to

steal.   You think I don't know all about you!" Zhao Qingyun shouted, his face reddening.

"Zhao Qingyun, let him come in," Mrs. Yao ordered from inside the door.

"Yes, ma'am," Zhao Qingyun answered, and said no more.

The Yang boy came through the door and bowed to her: "Mrs. Yao." She nodded and smiled, returning his greeting softly: "Master Yang."

He then turned to greet me: "Mr. Li."

"Come in and sit down. What do you want Mr. Li for?" she asked gently, and without waiting for him to reply, she said to me: "I must go now.   If Master Yang wants any flowers, Mr. Li, please pick a couple of branches for him."

"Thank you, Mrs. Yao," the Yang boy replied gratefully.

As she left, I saw the boy's eyes follow her departing figure.

18

"Sit down." I was the first to speak.

He looked at me. His lips moved, as if he were about to say something, but he said nothing.

"Have you come for some flowers?" I asked him, smiling.

"No." He shook his head.

"Then, what did you want to talk to me about?" I stood by the side of the table, my back to the window.   His hand was resting on the arm of the cane chair, while his eyes were directed towards the window screened by the curtains.

"Mr. Li, I want to ask you something . . ." He choked back the rest of what he was going to say and turned to me with beseeching eyes.

"What about? Just tell me everything," I said to encourage him.

"Mr. Li, please don't go to the Temple of the Grand Immortal again.   Please!" He kept blinking, as if he were going to cry.

"Why? How do you know that I've been to the temple?" I asked, stunned.

"I, I. . . ." His face reddened. He stuttered, unable to answer.

"What relation are you to the mute?" I asked.

"The mute? What mute?" he answered in surprise.

"The mute in the temple."

"I don't understand." He avoided my gaze.

"I saw the camellia flowers you took there."

He said nothing.

"Yesterday, I saw you with your mother and brother at the cinema."

His lips moved slightly. A sound escaped him, and he at once looked down at the ground.

"Why don't you want me to go to the Temple of the Grand Immortal? Just tell me the reason, and I'll do as you say."

He looked up at me, the tears streaming down his cheeks.

"Mr. Li, please don't interfere in things that don't concern you," he sobbed.

"Don't cry. Tell me what the Temple of the Grand Immortal has to do with you. Why don't you tell me the truth? I may be able to help you," I said earnestly.

"I can't tell you! I can't!" He wiped his eyes with his hand as he spoke.

"All right, don't tell me. I know everything. The man in the temple is your father. . . ." Before I had finished speaking, he dropped his hand, and shaking his head vigorously, he shouted in denial:

"He's not! He's not!"

I went over to him and took both his hands in mine to calm him. "Don't be upset. . . . I won't tell anyone. It's not your fault. Tell me, how did your father get into this situation?"

"I can't tell you! I can't!" He snatched his hands away, and ran towards the door.

"Don't go. I've something more to say to you." I tried to call him back. But the sound of his footsteps gradually disap-

peared into the distance. But the sound of his sobbing as he
ran off continued to echo in my ears long after he had gone.

I did not move from where I was, for I knew that I couldn't
catch up with him.

19

Before lunch that day, the writing-desk was indeed brought to
my room. The surface of the desk was smooth and shiny. I
thought I could see reflected in it Mrs. Yao's smiling face.

Although I sat at the writing-desk the whole afternoon, I
did not write a single word. I kept thinking of the young
boy.

Finally, I could not sit there any longer. My mind was in too
great a turmoil. The garden was too quiet. Without waiting
for Lao Wen to bring me my evening meal, I bolted the door
of the room and hurried out.

As I was passing the Temple of the Grand Immortal, I saw
that the door was slightly ajar, and so I paused before it and
pushed it a little. It opened slightly, but there was no one
inside. I turned and left.

I turned right at the intersection and went down a block.
I saw a snack shop selling soya-bean junket and decided to stop
there, choosing a table near the street to sit at.

While I was eating, noise arose suddenly from next
door. I put down my bowl and went outside to have a look.

Next door was a shop selling fried rice-cakes. A crowd was
gathered round the stall in which the cakes were displayed. I
heard the most vulgar abuse being shouted.

"What's going on?" I asked a bystander dressed in a short
jacket.

"He stole a cake. They're beating him up," the man replied.

I forced my way through the crowd into the rice-cake shop.
A strong, rough fellow had seized someone by the right

shoulder, and with the stick used for mixing the dough, was beating him repeatedly on the head and on the back. The man had his head down, trying to protect himself with his left arm and groaning, but not otherwise uttering a word.

The fellow beating him was shouting menacingly: "Go on, tell us! Where do you live? What's your name? Tell us the truth, and we'll stop beating you, then you can get the hell out of here!"

The victim said nothing. His clothing had been ripped from his shoulder down his back, revealing a big patch of dark flesh. It was none other than the mute from the Temple of the Grand Immortal.

"Speak up now! Tell us and we'll let you go. You're not dumb, so why don't you say something?" a bystander interjected.

The man being beaten still said nothing. His face was already swollen, his back covered with bruises. The blood poured from his nose. His lips were red with it, and there was even blood on his left hand.

"Let him go. You'll beat him to death! He's a mute. . . ." I was saying this to the fellow beating him, when suddenly I heard a terrified cry of pain. I turned round.

The Yang boy, red in the face, his tears flowing, ran to the mute, pushed away the fellow's hand and shouted:

"He hasn't committed a capital crime. What are you hitting him for? Look at what you've done to him! You only know how to bully innocent people."

The crowd stared at the boy in surprise. Even the man doing the beating let go without a word. He looked at the boy as if at a loss. The victim kept his head down, looking at no one, and continued to keep quiet.

"Let's go," the boy said to him affectionately, and, pulling a handkerchief from his trouser pocket, gave it to him. "Wipe the blood off your nose." The child took him by the right hand, squeezed it firmly, and said once more: "Let's go."

No one interfered. No one tried to stop him. The child

helped him slowly down the middle of the road. The eyes of
the crowd followed them as if watching the strange plot of some
play.

The two figures disappeared. The crowd broke into animat-
ed discussion. Everyone wondered what relationship there was
between this "kid" and the "beggar". From what they were
saying, I learnt that the mute had been caught taking a rice-
cake without paying for it. That was what had led to the
dispute.

"Your rice is cold, sir. Please come back and eat," the waiter
of the restaurant next door came over to say. "I'll get you a
hot bowl instead."

"Thank you," I answered. I decided to go to the Temple of
the Grand Immortal when I'd finished my meal.

20

I went to the Temple of the Grand Immortal. The door was
still ajar, so I pushed it open and went in. Then I closed it
again.

There was no one in the front room and no sound from the
back either. I turned to go to the back room.

The mute was lying on the bed. His face, dark red, was
swollen in several places, and his nostrils were stuffed with
two balls of paper. He looked at me absent-mindedly. He
seemed to think of something, but when he tried to move, he
fell back again, groaning with pain.

"Don't be afraid. I haven't come to harm you," I gestured
gently, trying to calm him.

He looked at me doubtfully.

From outside came the sound of footsteps, of leather shoes.
I knew that it must be the Yang boy coming.

And indeed it was. He was holding several things in his
hands, including a medicine glass and a thermos flask.

As soon as he saw me, his face changed colour. "You here again! Are you spying on us?" he asked rudely.

I felt acutely embarrassed. I had never thought he would speak to me like that. I blushed, and stammered in reply:

"You mustn't misunderstand me. I sympathize with you. I came to see if I could be of any help. I had no intention of doing you any harm."

He glanced at me and his eyes immediately softened. But he said nothing. He went up to the bed and put down the medicine glass and the other things. I went over to help him, first taking the thermos from his hand. He arranged the things beside the pillow, and then took the thermos back from me. He smiled at me slightly and said: "Thank you. I'll go and fetch some boiled water." He bent down and picked up the hand-basin.

"I'll go with you. You can't carry it all by yourself. Give me the thermos flask," I said, touched.

"No, I can do it." He would not let me take the things he was holding. He looked over at the sick man on the bed: "Please keep him company." He went out, taking the wash-basin in one hand and the thermos in the other.

I went up to the sick man's pillow. He opened his eyes to look at me. But his eyes, dull and weak, filled with deep suffering, seemed to me like an oil-lamp that had run dry, its feeble light gradually weakening as if about to go out.

"Don't worry. Have a good rest and get well," I said, bending over to comfort him.

He opened his eyes wide again to look at me, as if he hadn't understood what I had said. His face trembled and his whole body shook. Not knowing what to do to look after him, I asked in some confusion: "Are you in pain?"

"Thank you," he said with an effort. His voice was low, but I heard it clearly. I was startled. Then he wasn't a mute! Why then had he said nothing up to now?

Outside, I heard the sound of approaching footsteps.

"He's a good child," he continued. "Please look after him well. . . ." He had no strength to say more.

The boy came back in, carrying the thermos and the washbasin.

I took the basin from him, knelt down and placed it on the ground beside the sick man's pillow. Then I soaked the face towel in the water which half-filled the basin, and wrung it out.

I stood up without a word and moved aside, watching him wash the invalid's face, wipe down his body, change his clothes, and clean his nostrils, changing the paper for two clean wads of cotton wool. Then he gave the sick man some more medicine. I watched the movements of his two hands attentively. What infinite patience and concern they showed. It was not a job for a twelve- or thirteen-year-old boy, and yet he was so careful, so thorough, as if he'd been trained for this kind of work.

The invalid said nothing. He never even let out a groan. He stared at the boy with wide-open, lifeless eyes, obediently doing everything the boy asked him to do. On his swollen face slowly appeared a kind of tearful smile. His eyes were full of a father's affection. When the boy had finished everything, he suddenly stretched out his skinny hand and clasped the child's left hand firmly. "Forgive me," he said in a low voice. "You are too good to me . . ." and the tears streamed from his eyes.

"None of us is any good to let you suffer on your own," the boy managed to say in a choking voice, and then for a long time he couldn't say another word. He sat by the side of the bed.

"I brought it on myself," the invalid said painfully, one word at a time, his voice shaking terribly.

"There's no need to talk. Look what's happened to you! As for us, we're OK," the boy said in tears.

"That at least makes me happy," the invalid sighed.

"But you, . . . why do you have to hide? Why do you have

to punish yourself? . . ." The child wept broken-heartedly. He bent down and laid his head on the sick man's shoulder.

The invalid stroked the child's head lovingly. "Don't be upset. This suffering of mine isn't anything to worry about."

"No, no. We must get you into hospital!" the child cried, shaking his head in grief.

"Going to hospital's no use. The hospital can't cure my illness," replied the sick man firmly, weakly shaking his head. The boy said nothing. "I'm much better now. You can go home. Don't let the others worry." In speaking, the invalid had to pause to take breath several times. His voice became weaker, and in the greyish-brown light of the approaching evening, his face became even worse to look at. Only his eyes retained a little life as they gazed with love at the child's slightly trembling body.

"Then come home with me. It must be better there than here," the child cried beseechingly, raising his head.

"Where do I have a home? What right do I have to disturb you? It's your home," the sick man said bitterly, shaking his head.

"Dad!" The child couldn't hold back his own feelings and began to weep. "Why mustn't you come home? Surely our home is also your home? Am I not your son? It's nothing to be ashamed of! Why daren't I recognize my own father?. . ." The child bent his head once more, burying it this time in his father's chest and weeping with loud sobs.

"Han'er, I know you have a kind heart. But your mother and brother won't forgive me. Besides, I can't change my temperament. I've done you all enough harm. I can't bear to once more. . . ." He put his arms round his son's head and sobbed for a long time. I stood at the side, scarcely daring even to breathe. I felt I had no right to know this family's secret. I had even less right to watch this father and son's pain. But it was too late to steal out of the temple now.

The father sighed suddenly and, raising his voice, said: "Go home now. I would rather die than go back to your family."

The father began to weep soundlessly. The child did not lift his head, but wept even more broken-heartedly. I could not see the expression on the father's face clearly. I could only see his two hands pressed against the back of the boy's head. And soon, I couldn't even see his hands.

I went over, bent down, and tapped the boy lightly on the shoulder. I had to do this three times before the child looked up and turned his face towards me. I said to him sympathetically: "Let him rest for a while."

The child stood up slowly. His father breathed out softly. There was no other sound.

"He's tired. His spirit's not up to it. Don't talk to him too much. Don't break his heart. Don't upset him," I continued.

"Mr. Li, what do you think we should do? He definitely won't come home, and he won't go into hospital. But how can he stay here!" the child said.

"I think that if your mother and brother would only come and fetch him, he would certainly go home," I said.

There was a long moment of silence before the child answered in a voice full of pain: "They definitely won't come. You don't know what they're like. If he were willing to go into hospital, then it would be all right. Only I don't know how much it costs to stay in hospital." His voice was so low that I was the only one that could hear him.

"Then send him to hospital tomorrow. Even a third-class ward would be better than here. If you haven't any money available, I'll think of something," I said earnestly. I had raised my voice slightly, for I thought that the sick man was already asleep, as I hadn't heard a sound from him all this time.

"No, we can't let you pay." The child shook his head in refusal.

"Don't be so obstinate. What's important is your father's health. We'll talk about the other things later. When he's better, we can find him some work to do," I said in explanation. "Do you think he's willing to go to work?"

"Then we'll do as you say," the child said gratefully.

"We'll meet here tomorrow before nine, and take him to the hospital together. That's decided then. Are you going to school tomorrow?"

"It doesn't matter if I miss a couple of classes in the morning. I'll meet you here tomorrow definitely, Mr. Li. You go back first. I'll light a candle and keep my father company for a while."

The sick man coughed weakly, and then it was quiet again. The child struck five matches before he could get the candle to light.

"All right, I'm going. If anything happens, you can find me at the Yaos'."

I waited for his answer before I stepped out through the small door into the darkness of the courtyard.

2 1

I went back to the Yaos'. As I went through the main gate Old Man Li stood up to greet me.

"Your third master's ill in the Temple of the Grand Immortal. I've just settled with his son that we'll take him to hospital tomorrow," I said to him. I told him this news, because I knew that, apart from the young boy, he was the only one who cared at all for the third Mr. Yang.

Li's eyes widened, and he stood with his mouth gaping, unable to say a word.

"There's no need to pretend to me. Your third master's been to see you. I saw him. Don't worry. I won't tell anyone," I said, reassuring him. "I'm telling you because I'm sure you'll find time to see him," I added.

"Thank you, Mr. Li," Old Man Li, said gratefully. Then he asked anxiously: "Mr Yang's illness is not serious, I hope?"

"No. He'll get better with treatment. But he can't keep

on staying in the temple. You're a sensible man; why don't you urge him to go home and live? From the look of things, they manage well enough."

Old Man Li sighed bitterly, and then said: "Mr. Li, I know you're honest and kind. I don't dare deceive you, but it's too long to explain it all to you, and it's too painful for me. I'll tell you about it another day." He turned his face towards the gate, looking out into the street.

"All right. I'll go in and get Lao Wen to come and look after the gate for you. You go to the temple and have a look."

"Yes, I will," he said at once. I'd already stepped across the main gate and gone down the steps when he suddenly called to me from behind. I turned round. He implored me rather awkwardly: "Mr. Li, please don't say anything to Lao Wen about Third Master."

"I know. Don't worry." I nodded to him gently.

I went through the second gate into the courtyard. The front doors of the porter's lodge were wide open. On the square table an oil lamp was burning. Lao Wen was sitting on the doorstep, smoking his strong tobacco in solitude, puffing away on a pipe pressed between the fingers of his left hand. The pipe glowed on and off. His old, kind face would appear indistinctly before my eyes for a moment, and then vanish as the light of the pipe went out.

I went towards him. He stood up and came down the stone steps to meet me.

He greeted me with a smile: "You're back, Mr. Li."

We stood in the courtyard chatting. I simply told him that Old Man Li was going out to do something for me, and asked him if he could look after the gate for him.

"Of course, of course," he said readily.

"Are Mr. and Mrs. Yao home?" I took the opportunity to ask.

"They've both gone to the pictures."

"Is Xiao Hu back?"

"Once he goes to his grandmother's, he refuses to come back

before eleven or twelve o'clock. Before, Mrs. Yao used to send someone to fetch him, but Mr. Yao let him have his own way, and won't let Mrs. Yao send anyone," he said indignantly. I could feel him scanning my face in the darkness as if to say: "Why don't you think of something? Why don't you say something?"

"It's no use my saying anything. I tried to persuade him this morning, but he thinks Xiao Hu's perfect," I said, as if defending myself.

"Yes, that's it. Mr. Yao's like that. I think that if only Master Hu reforms when he gets older, then it'll be all right," Lao Wen added.

I did not say any more. Lao Wen, biting on his pipe, went slowly out the second gate.

The moon pushed its way through the clouds, slowly lighting up the courtyard. The whole mansion was extraordinarily silent. The sound of a bamboo flute came from a direction I couldn't make out. The moon was hidden once more by a large grey cloud. I felt the darkness envelop my body, and my heart was seized with a nameless anxiety. I walked about the courtyard for a while. The sound of the flute ceased, but the moon continued its way in and out of the clouds. Zhao Qingyun came out from the inner courtyard. He didn't come into the porter's lodge, but went straight out through the second gate instead.

I went into the Garden of Repose and entered my room. The sound of the flute began again. It was from next door. After the flute ceased, from the direction of the surrounding wall came the sound of a young woman's laughter.

I could not sit in my room, so I walked through the Garden of Repose, and finally out of the house. Lao Wen was sitting in the wooden armchair, but I was not in the mood to talk to him.

In front of the gate of the house almost opposite ours, a crowd had gathered. Two men and a woman, all three of them blind, were sitting on a wooden bench singing an aria

while accompanying themselves on the *huqin*, a two-stringed
Chinese violin. It was from an opera I knew well: *The Tang
Emperor Minghuang Awakens from His Dream.*

After some ten minutes, Tang Minghuang's "sweet dream"
is shattered by a courtier. The blind people stopped singing
and the *huqin* became silent. A woman, probably an old nursemaid, came out from the inner gate to give them some money.
The blind people got up, thanked her, and then, tapping out
their way with bamboo sticks, went off down the street. In
front was the young man who had sung the part of Yang Guifei.
He seemed to still have an eye which could see the light, for
he could find his way along the road under the moonlight
without using his bamboo stick. He led the way, playing the
huqin at the same time, a melody full of heart-breaking grief.
Behind him was the old blind man who had sung the part of
An Lushan. One hand rested on the shoulder of his young
companion, while he held his stick in the other, his *huqin*
pressed under his arm. I recognized his face, and I remembered his name. Fifteen years ago, I had often had the opportunity to hear him sing. Now he sang only supporting
roles. At the back was the blind woman who'd sung the part
of Tang Minghuang. Her voice was still just as good. Fifteen
years ago, I had heard her sing *The Nanyang Pass* and *The
Recommendation of Zhuge Liang*. Now she was a middle-
aged woman of about forty. Her left hand rested on the
shoulder of her old companion while her right hand held the
stick. I remembered that fifteen years ago, someone had told
me that she was the old man's wife. Her short, plump body and
flat, round face hadn't changed greatly. She was just a good
deal older.

The grief-stricken strains of the *huqin* faded farther and
farther into the distance. The three tottering figures that
seemed about to fall at any moment finally became fainter.
I suddenly thought of the old rickshaw puller and the blind
girl in my novel. This poverty-stricken couple before my eyes,
were they not the incarnation of these two characters? What

kind of ending could I arrange for them? Was there no way
in which I could offer them some happiness?

I was worried by all these thoughts. I did not want to
return to the tranquil garden. I remained standing in the
middle of the street. Their shadowy figures came and went
before my eyes, sometimes clear, sometimes indistinct. Suddenly I thought of chasing them, and strode quickly after them.

I passed the doors of the Temple of the Grand Immortal once
more. I heard the blind man singing nearby, but my
feet were as if drawn by a magnetic force, and I stopped
before the two doors from which the lacquer was peeling. I
hesitated for a moment, and was about to stretch out my hand
to push open the door when it suddenly opened. The Yang boy
came out. He was a little surprised to see me. Then he greeted
me amiably: "Mr. Li."

"Are you just back?" I asked gently.

"Yes," he replied.

"Is he a bit better?" I asked again. "Is he asleep?"

"He's a little better, thank you. Old Man Li's there."

"Then you should go home and rest. You've had a tiring day
today."

"Yes. I'll wait for you tomorrow before nine. Mr. Li, if
you're busy, it won't matter if you're a bit late."

"No, I've nothing on. I won't be late."

And so we parted at the door. I waited till his figure had
disappeared, and then went to push open the door of the temple.
I pushed it gently. The door opened slowly, without emitting
any sound.

I went into the courtyard. It was lit at the back by a candle.
I heard Old Man Li's voice filled with sobs: "Third Master,
you can't act like this. . . ."

I had no right to listen in on their conversation. I had even
less right to interrupt them. I hesitated for two or three minutes
before quietly withdrawing. I heard "Third Master's" reply:
"I haven't the face to harm my child anymore."

I went back to the house. Inside the second gate, it was still very quiet. In the porter's lodge, the big wick of the oil lamp had been snuffed out. There was not a soul to be seen. The moon had already scattered the clouds, and hung suspended in the sky like a huge electric light bulb.

Head down, I wandered about the courtyard for a while. Suddenly, I heard a familiar voice calling: "Mr. Li." I recognized Mrs. Yao's voice, looked up and answered.

She was wearing a short white jacket over a slate-blue cheong-sam of light wool. On her face was her usual kind-hearted smile. The rickshaw man pulling the empty rickshaw, went on up to the main hall.

"Are you back from the cinema, Mrs. Yao? Where's Lao Yao?"

"He met a friend on the way back and wanted to discuss something with him. He'll be back in a moment. Have you been back long, Mr. Li? We wanted to ask you to the pictures, but when we went to look for you in your room, we found you'd gone out without having dinner. Did you have something outside, Mr. Li?"

"Yes, I had something to attend to, and so I had dinner out. Was the film today all right?"

"It was *Innocence in a Sea of Bitterness*. It was good, but a bit too tragic. It's upsetting to see a film like that." She frowned slightly, and her smile disappeared.

"Ah, I've seen it. It's the story of a doctor and a young girl. In the end the two of them are hanged because of a false accusation. The two main actors were very good."

She stopped for a moment, and then said reflectively: "I'm amazed that people can behave so viciously towards each other. A kind-hearted doctor and an out-of-work actress. They never did anyone any harm. Why did they have to be hanged? Why can't people behave better towards one another? Why do they have to take revenge on one another?"

She looked up at the sky with an expression like grief on her face. The silvery white moonlight made her face appear even purer. For the first time, she had unveiled to me the secret of her heart. Another side of her life was finally revealed to me. The hostility of the Zhao family, the contempt of Xiao Hu, the lack of understanding of her husband. . . . How deep must have been the desolation in her heart. . . .

Sympathy hurts me. Actually, the feeling I had for her was more than sympathy, but there was no way in which I could express it. All I can say is that, even though in present-day society I am a lowly person of no consequence, my life not worth a penny, if at that time, I could only have made her happy, I would have nothing to spare in this world.

But how could I make her understand this feeling of mine? I couldn't tell her I loved her, because perhaps it was not love. Besides, I had no other thought but to bring her happiness, to make that smile light up her face forever.

"It's a case of people being hurt by traditional morality. But the plot of the film is completely imaginary. I know that there's still a great deal of warmth in the world." I said this to reassure her. Although my words were simple, I poured all my heart into them. I stressed every word, so that she would believe me, so that her sorrow would be driven away.

Lowering her gaze as she glanced at me and, nodding slightly, she said to me in a low voice: "I understand. Only I feel that my own life is too comfortable. Just running the Yao household, I don't accomplish anything, let alone help others. Sometimes when I think of it, I feel very depressed."

"And I know about Xiao Hu," I had finally brought up his name. "Lao Yao is too negligent. I've talked to him about it. And you've suffered enough from this matter, Mrs Yao. But I'm certain he will realize eventually, you can rest assured."

She gave a little sigh and hesitated a moment before saying softly: "I don't understand why the Zhao family hates me so much. Why, because of me, do they lead an innocent young boy like Xiao Hu astray? I wanted to be a good daughter to them, a good mother to Xiao Hu, but they won't give me the chance. They treat me as an enemy. People outside the family

don't understand; they would say that, being the stepmother,
I'm in the wrong."

My throat seemed to be blocked by something. I gazed at
those eyebrows, locked tightly in a frown, and couldn't say a
word. Her eyes rested on the wall outside the second gate, as
if she hadn't noticed that I was looking at her.

"Why does the Zhao family hate me like this? I've thought
and thought about it, but I can't make out the reason," she continued. "Perhaps it's because Lao Yao has been so good to me
since I entered the family. From what people say, he treats me
even better than he did Xiao Hu's mother. That's the only thing
they can be unhappy about. But that's not a fault on my part.
I've never said anything bad about anyone in front of Lao Yao.
When I married him, I was only twenty. At home, I was used
to a casual life. My mother was worried that I wouldn't know
how to run a household or bring up children. I was afraid
myself. I was worried so much every day about learning to be
the mistress of such a large household, about being a wife, a
mother. I didn't know anything myself, and there was no one
to teach me. I wanted to treat the mother of his first wife as my
own mother, the child of his first wife as my own son, but
didn't succeed. I don't know what's best to do. And Lao Yao
gives me no help. My courage has been getting less and less."
As she spoke, her head dropped again.

"Mrs. Yao, you mustn't be discouraged. Even someone like
me doesn't look down on myself, so why should you?" I reas-
sured her with sincerity.

"Me? Mr. Li, you're joking with me." She lifted her head
and smiled at me. "How can I be compared with you?"

"You mustn't look at it like that. Perhaps you don't know
that the few words you said last night made me understand so
many things. If in the future I manage to live a little more
actively, more significantly, it will be because of your
strength. . . . You give warmth to people. Why is it that you
yourself can't live a little more actively?"

I felt her bright eyes looking at me directly, eyes that were so gentle. Moreover, I seemed to see tears in them, but before I'd finished what I wanted to say, Lao Yao came back.

"So you're both here! Why don't you go into the room and sit down?" he cried happily.

"We were chatting while waiting for you," she replied, smiling in a most natural way. "We've been standing for ages already. I'm afraid Mr. Li must be tired."

"Yes. You two must rest too. See you tomorrow," I replied.

We went up the stone steps together. From the main hall, they went into the inner courtyard, while I went into the Garden of Repose.

22

I went out the main gate of the Yao mansion at about seven thirty the next morning. Old Man Li, standing under the eaves over the gate, looked at me sadly, greeting me briefly: "Mr. Li." He seemed to want to say something to me, but I just nodded abruptly and hurried past into the street.

Shortly, I reached the Temple of the Grand Immortal. The door was wide open. The Yang boy must be there already, I thought. I hastened into the back room.

There was not a sound to be heard. No one was there. Not only was there no trace of the sick man, there were no blankets, wash-basin, thermos or other things either. The straw lay in a disordered heap on the floor. On it was a scrap of paper held down with a tile. The note said:

Han'er,
   Forget me. Think of me as dead. You will never find me. Let me live out my life peacefully.

Your father

From the roughly pencilled scribble, I could see what kind of man he was. I didn't know the story of this man's "degeneracy", but these brief sentences enabled me to understand the hopes of a loving and affectionate father. I held the piece of paper, lost in thought. The sound of the boy's footsteps approached. I waited for him.

"Hello! Are you here by yourself, Mr. Li?" the boy asked in surprise. "Where's father?"

"I've just got here. Look at this note," I whispered. I handed it to him and turned away, not daring to look him in the face.

"Mr. Li, Mr. Li! Where's he gone? Where are we going to look for him? What do you think we should do?" He seized my left arm with both hands and shook it in a frenzy, crying out in despair.

I bit my lip, keeping down my emotion, and, putting on a false air of calm, I said: "I think we can only do as he says and forget him. We'll never be able to find him."

"No, that's impossible. We're all well-off. We can't let him suffer on his own," he cried in a tearful voice, shaking his head.

"But where are you going to look for him? The world is so large!"

He fell suddenly onto the heap of straw and began to sob broken-heartedly.

My eyes were dry. I stood with my arms crossed, looking upwards. I wanted to ask God: "How can I ease the suffering of this child?" But God in his serenity gave me no answer. Nor could God tell me where the boy's father had gone. I knew only one fact: since his father had taken the blankets and other things, he wasn't going to kill himself. And so, I let the boy weep, giving him no word of comfort. Indeed, there were no words of comfort I could give him.

Eventually, the boy's sobbing ceased. He stood up and said to me beseechingly: "Mr. Li, you've had a lot of experience. Do you think anything can have happened to him? Please tell me frankly. I'm not afraid. Please tell me the truth."

I thought for a moment, but I avoided his gaze, answering him gently: "Don't worry. Nothing can have happened. Let's go and ask Old Man Li. You never know, he might know a bit more."

"Yes, yes. I remember. Last night when I left, he was still talking to my father," the child said as if coming to his senses.

"Then let's go to the Yao house together. Wipe your tears," I said, patting him lightly on the shoulder.

As we went through the front room, I saw the glass bottle still on the altar, but the withered camellia flowers had gone.

23

Old Man Li was standing at the entrance of the main gate, looking in the direction from which we were coming, as if he'd been waiting for us.

The Yang boy ran up to him and, seizing him anxiously by the left arm, asked: "Old Man Li, do you know where Dad's gone?"

"I don't know, young sir," Old Man Li answered, shaking his head sadly.

"You are sure to know. He talked to you for a long, long time last night. Tell me at once. I have to find him," the boy begged obstinately.

"I really don't know, young Sir." Li's voice trembled terribly. He kept his head down as if he didn't want the Yang boy to look at him closely.

"Then what did he talk to you about after I left? Everyone says that you're kind-hearted; you mustn't deceive a child like me. I have to find him. Mr. Li will help me, and we'll get him better first. Afterwards, I can beg my mother and my brother to let him back into the family. This can only be good for him. Why won't you let me find him?. . ." The boy's voice was not loud, but he was agitated as he tried to hold back his tears. His throat became constricted by sobs, and he was unable to speak. He let go Old Man Li's arm, wiping his eyes with his hands.

I was upset, and so went closer and whispered to Old Man Li: "You'd better tell him."

Old Man Li looked up, rubbing his shiny bald head several times with his right hand. I heard him give a long sigh, and then he said painfully: "Third Master really said nothing about going anywhere. Last night, he talked to me for a long time. He said he wanted to move from the temple to somewhere where his son wouldn't find him. I begged him not to bring suffering on himself. He said that he'd seen through everything, only he couldn't bear to leave his younger son. But for his son's good, he had to hide and never see him again. He wanted his younger son to forget him slowly, just as his wife and elder son have, to look on him as already dead. I told him: 'You mustn't do that, sir. You'll break your son's heart.' But he said: 'It's better for suffering to be short than long-drawn out. Otherwise he'll be broken-hearted for too long!' I didn't quite understand his reasoning. I thought it was because he was ill and was just saying whatever came into his head. Then I came back. That's the whole truth. How could I dare deceive you, young sir?" His eyes were red, and the tears flowed unceasingly down his checks.

The boy ran in the gate and sat down on the wooden armchair. Covering his face in his hands, he wept. Old Man Li turned away. His eyes wide open, he looked at him in alarm, with grief and compassion, not knowing what to do.

Going up to the boy, I took him lightly by the hand and said: "Let's go and sit down inside. Don't cry. Crying won't solve anything."

He resisted, unwilling to let me take his hand from his face. And so I repeated what I had said.

"You must find him for me! Give me back my dad!" he cried petulantly through his tears. This time he let me take away his hand. It was the first time I'd heard this young boy, so mature for his age, speak like a little child.

"All right, I'll find him for you. I'll return him to you," I said to comfort him, as if coaxing a tiny child.

Finally, he submitted, became silent, and stood up.

24

I made him sit down in the armchair in my room. I spoke to him for a long time, trying to comfort him. He did not cry anymore. He just kept on agreeing with everything I said. Sometimes he would gaze at me stupidly, his eyes swollen with weeping. Other times, he would just look at the door.

Then, standing up suddenly, he said: "I'll go for a walk outside for a moment."

"All right," was all I said, but I made no move to follow him. I felt exhausted. I sat in the soft armchair with no desire to move.

I thought he would come back, but after over half an hour, when I had not heard a sound from him, I went outside to have a look. There was no sign of him in the garden. He had gone, and must have been a long way off by now.

I had not tried to find out the father's story from the boy. I felt lonely. My mind was ill at ease. But I did not want to go for a walk in the streets. Nor did I wish to sleep. To rid myself of my solitude, I concentrated my attention on my novel.

That day, I wrote a great deal. I was moved by my own story. The old rickshaw puller was beaten up outside the entrance to a teahouse, and, covered with bruises, went to see the blind girl, collapsing in front of her door.

. . . .

"What's happened to you?" she cred in alarm, her voice full of concern, as she groped towards him and seized the hand that he stretched up towards her.

"I slipped," the rickshaw puller replied, forcing a smile.

"Oh, my God, you slipped! Does it hurt?" She bent over him.

"Nothing's broken. It doesn't hurt at all!" The rickshaw puller laughed, wiping the blood from his face. But the tears were already streaming down his cheeks.

. . . .

I seemed to see the two characters before me talking. They were alive, they were suffering. My mind was tormented by

their pain and misery. Just as it was becoming unbearable
to me, Lao Wen ran in to tell me breathlessly: "There's an air-
raid alert on." According to him, it was the second one this
year. I looked at my watch, and saw that it was already ten
past three. I thought that the enemy planes would not likely
fly directly over the city, but I took the opportunity to lay down
my brush.

I asked Lao Wen whether Mr. and Mrs. Yao had left. He
replied that after lunch, they had gone shopping with Mr. Yao's
sister, and were probably at the Shengxi Gardens outside the
North Gate taking tea and listening to traditional music. He
also told me that Master Hu had gone to school in the morning
and had not yet returned. I asked him whether the servants
in the household would all leave town to escape the raids. He
said that after an air-raid was announced, everyone in the mansion, high and low, would flee, and Old Man Li would be the
only one left to look after the place. He would not run away
under any circumstances, and no one could persuade him to do
so.

I chatted to Lao Wen for a while, when suddenly the air-raid
sirens, to which we hadn't heard for a long time, started to
wail.

"Mr. Li, you'd better go," Lao Wen cried in alarm.

"You go first. I'll go in a moment," I replied. I was tired,
and didn't want to go any distance in the sun.

Lao Wen left. The garden gradually became quiet, a quiet-
ness that made me sleepy. I dozed uneasily in the armchair
for a while. When I opened my eyes, there were still no voices
to be heard.

I got up. My tiredness had gone. I went out of the room,
standing for a moment at the door. I noticed the green of
the garden was even greener. I left the garden, following the
stone balustrade.

I reached the main gate. Old Man Li was sitting quietly
in the big wooden armchair. In the street were a few people
in uniform.

"Mr. Li, aren't you leaving?" Old Man Li asked respectfully.

"I'll wait for the emergency signal before I leave," I said as I sat down on the wooden stool opposite his chair.

"If you wait for that, I'm afraid you won't get far. It would be better to go while there's still time," he urged, his voice full of concern.

"Even so, it doesn't matter. I can always get as far as the city walls," I said indifferently.

He said nothing. But I continued: "Old Man Li, please tell me the truth. Why did the third Mr. Yang leave? Why didn't he want us to send him to hospital? Why didn't he want to go home?" This time I came straight to the point.

He was petrified for a moment. I stared at him fixedly while continuing earnestly: "I want to help him. And I want to help your young master. Why are you still unwilling to tell me the truth?"

"Mr. Li, it isn't that I'm not telling the truth. Nothing I told you this morning is untrue." His voice trembled violently. He looked down, avoiding my gaze. I could see that he was about to cry.

I pressed on, not giving him time to think: "But how did he get like this? Why is he bent on destroying himself?"

"Ah!" He gave a long sigh. "Mr. Li, you don't understand. Once a man has taken the wrong road, everything is over for him forever. If he wants to turn back, it really isn't easy. Third Master is like that. Once I tell you what happened to him, you'll understand. Having dissipated all his family inheritance, he felt he couldn't face any of his family. He was so ashamed, and too embarrassed to use his son's money. So he hid, concealing his name, not letting his family know, until he was finally discovered by his younger son. Master Yang kept giving him money, sending him food and drink, picking flowers for him. The flowers he used to pick from our house were for Third Master, for he particularly loved our camellias."

I knew that Old Man Li had not told me the whole truth. He

was hiding at least something from me. But I would not let him off. I kept up my questioning:

"Why don't his wife and his elder son look after him?"

His head dropped even lower. I thought he would not answer me. I sat facing him in silence, my eyes directed towards the street. Some pedestrians carrying parcels or small children passed the gate. I heard a male voice shout roughly: "Hurry up! The enemy planes are coming." In fact, the emergency signal had not yet sounded.

Old Man Li looked up, tears streaming down his cheeks. Some drops of saliva gleamed on his white whiskers.

"I don't understand too well either. The elder son has never got on well with his father. He graduated the year they sold the mansion, and had just come back to Sichuan to work in a bank. His father had been renting a separate establishment for his mistress for several years, and his wife couldn't do anything about it. When the elder son came back, he always sided with Mrs. Yang in quarrelling with Third Master. For some reason or other, the father eventually moved out, and his elder son never tried to find him. Only the younger boy remembered his father, looking for him everywhere. Finally, he ran into him in the street. He was living in the Temple of the Grand Immortal. His son followed him to the temple. There was nothing the father could do. He just had to tell him the truth. . . ."

I did not dare look at the expression on his face. I paid attention only to what he was saying. Suddenly the air-raid alert was lifted. He stopped talking. What he'd said aroused in me new doubts. I wanted to pursue my questioning, but he stood up and, without a word, went out of the gate.

The thought suddenly flashed through my mind: "This man, father and husband, must have been driven from his house by his wife and his son."

Old Man Li had revealed enough of his secrets to me now, so I felt I ought to leave him in peace for a while.

25

Twelve days slowly passed. They went by so slowly and so monotonously. In the mornings I wrote my novel, in the afternoons I wandered about the streets. The novel didn't come easily, and I wrote slowly. Sometimes I had to tear up whole pages of the draft and start again. The suffering of those two unhappy people took hold of my heart. I lost my coolheadedness, and found it more and more difficult to control my brush.

My friend Lao Yao came to see me at least once every other day, talking to me at random on every subject under the sun. He was still just as happy, sure of everything, indifferent to everything, even though he complained from morning to night. At the same time, he boasted of his wife, of his son, and of the happiness of his family.

Mrs. Yao had not come down to my room for a week. She was ill. But I gathered from my friend that she was expecting a "happy event", and so he was not at all depressed by his wife's illness. On the contrary, it made him even happier. But without the sight of her face, my room lost its former light, and sometimes I felt an even greater solitude.

Whenever I wandered down the streets, there was one thought I could not get rid of: the thought that one day I might run into the Yang boy and his father. I not only hoped to unravel the family's secret, I also wanted to do what little I could to help them. But Chengdu was so big, its streets so full of people. Where would I go to catch a glimpse of the father? I hadn't seen even the boy these last few days, let alone the father. I knew I'd be able to get the child's address from Old Man Li. But each time I passed the gate and saw his old, worried face, I thought I had not the right to torture him once more about the Yang family's affairs.

Once when I was coming back from town, as he looked up at me with sad, disconsolate eyes, I suddenly had the feeling

that I understood what he was thinking. He seemed to be asking: "Have you found him?" I shook my head hopelessly, answering with my eyes: "No, not even a trace." The next day, his
eyes questioned me as before, and my eyes gave the same reply.
The third day, the same thing happened. This continued for
many days. Once I almost got angry, and I wanted to say to
him: "You know perfectly well that I won't find him. Why
do you keep asking me?"

But Saturday came. It was exactly three weeks since I saw
the father being beaten up.

That day, I felt dizzy after getting up, as if something heavy
were pressing on my head. I could not do anything, and I
did not want to do anything. I lay on the bed by myself, feeling
quite alone. I hoped that Lao Yao would come and chat with
me, so that I could sit back in my armchair listening to him
talking big. But that day, there was no sign of him. When
Lao Wen brought lunch, he told me that his master had been
invited out to dinner somewhere. I asked about Mrs Yao's
illness. He said that she was much better, and according to
Mrs. Zhou, she was carrying a "little treasure". He also said
that her mother Mrs. Wan and her brother's wife had been to
visit her very early that morning. I did not ask about Xiao
Hu, but he also told me that after going to play at the Zhaos'
the day before, he hadn't come back in the evening. Mrs. Yao
had told the rickshaw puller to pick him up, but Mrs. Zhao had
given him a piece of her tongue, saying that she was keeping
Xiao Hu for a fortnight to protect him from his stepmother's
temper. When the rickshaw man came back, he dared not tell
Mrs. Yao this, for fear of her becoming unhappy. Needless to
say, Lao Wen began immediately to grumble. His views on
the Zhao family and Xiao Hu were much the same as mine. I
also said a few words against the Zhaos. Then he collected
the dishes and left.

I sat in the armchair and dozed off uneasily for a while.
When I woke up, I thought I heard a light cough in the garden.
I got up and went to the door.

I thought at first I was seeing things. What! How could the Yang boy be standing under the camellia tree! I rubbed my eyes. He was definitely there, dressed in his grey school-boy uniform, bare-headed, examining something on the tree trunk.

I went down the steps. The child didn't seem to see me. I went straight up to him. He had his back to me, and didn't even move.

"What are you looking at?" I asked gently.

He gave a start and turned round at once. His face was thinner and seemed longer, his nose curving even further to the left, and his teeth more prominent.

"I'm looking at the inscription Dad made," he answered softly. His eyes turned once more to the tree trunk. There I saw three characters, each the size of a thumb: Yang Mengchi. They were carved very deep, but the strokes were crooked. I looked more closely. Below them were six small characters, carved rather more lightly: Gengshu (1910), 4th month, 7th day. This must have been the date on which they were carved, thirty-two years ago to the day. At the time, his father was only a youth in his teens.

"Have you had any news of him?" I asked softly.

"No." He shook his head in reply. "I've looked everywhere, but I haven't found him."

"I haven't either," I said. My eyes rested on the carved inscription. I thought to myself: What a long road! I began to feel upset.

After a moment, he suddenly turned towards me and implored: "Mr. Li, what else can we do to find him? Where on earth can he be hiding?"

I silently shook my head.

"Mr. Li, is he still alive? Will I ever see him again?" he also asked, his eyes red as he tried to blink away his tears.

I looked at his pale, bloodless face. My heart was bursting with compassion. I urged him with pain:

"You should forget him. What's the use of continuing to remember him? Look how much thinner you've become yourself. You'll never be able to find him."

"I can't forget him! I can't, I can't! I must find him," he said, with a sob in his voice.

"Where will you look for him? The world is so large, there are so many people, and you're only a child."

"Then you must help me. With two of us, we're sure to find him."

I shook my head in pity. "Two of us! Twenty people wouldn't be able to find him. You'd better do as he says and concentrate on studying."

"Mr. Li, when I think of him suffering all alone, how can I have the will to study? If I can't find him, if I can't save him, then what's the use of succeeding in my studies? What would be the point of living on?"

I seized him by the shoulder and said reprovingly: "You mustn't talk like that. You're young, you have your mother at home. Besides, a man lives, not. . . ."

"My brother will take care of Mother, but Dad has only himself. They don't care if he dies outside, . . ." he interrupted with a pout. The tears ran into his mouth, but he did not wipe them away.

"You're all one family. Why are your mother and brother so against your father? You should talk to them about it. They're sure to listen to what you say."

He shook his head. "Even if I talked to them, it would be of no use. My brother really hates him, and Mother doesn't like him either. My brother threw Dad out, and won't let anyone mention his name. . . ."

I had finally learnt the secret. I had already guessed the truth long ago. But now that I had heard the father's unhappy story from the child's own lips, it was like an unexpected blow. I cannot explain my feeling at that moment. I suddenly wanted to hide from him, to look no longer on his thin, pallid face. I suddenly wanted to seize his hand and rush madly out to seek his father wherever he might be. I suddenly wanted to ask him to my room to tell me in detail the story of his family.

I could not decide what I ought to do. I stood with the child under the camellia tree for a long, long time. I did not feel tired. I forgot my dizziness. I seemed to be waiting for something.

Indeed, a sound, the sweet sound of a woman's voice floated over. It did not allow me to hesitate any longer.

"My child, you mustn't be upset. You must tell us all about your father. Mr. Li and I want to help you."

We turned round simultaneously. It was Mrs. Yao, standing in front of the rockery. Her face seemed pale after her illness. She was gazing tenderly at the boy.

"I heard a little of what you were saying. I didn't eavesdrop on purpose." She smiled sadly. "I didn't realize how much you had suffered." Coming over, she took the boy by the hand, and like a mother comforting her child, she said: "Let's go and sit down in Mr. Li's room."

Mumbling something in answer, the child followed her obediently. Walking in front of me, the two seemed like brother and sister. I followed them, gazing as I walked on her slender form sheathed in a pale blue cheongsam of foreign fabric.

26

"When I was small, my father loved me the most. I remember that from the time I was two, it was my father I slept with. Mother loved my brother. My brother has never listened to Dad ever since he was small. Dad was never home in the daytime. He didn't come back till evening. When he came back, he always quarrelled with my mother, sometimes getting really heated. Mother would cry, but the next morning, Dad would say nice things to her, and she would be happy again. A couple of days later, they'd be at it again. I was really afraid of hearing them quarrel. Sometimes my brother would butt in on my mother's side. I would hide in bed, and even if it was terribly hot, I would cover my head with the blankets, not daring to utter a sound and not able to sleep either. Afterwards, Dad would come to bed, pull back the covers and, seeing my eyes still wide open, would ask me whether it was because of their quarrelling that I couldn't sleep. I wouldn't be able to speak and would just nod. He would stare at me, and say that he would never quarrel with Mother again, and I would see the tears roll down his cheeks, so that I would cry too. I didn't dare to cry too loudly. I just cried softly. He would say things to comfort me, and eventually, I would fall asleep."

It was in this way that the boy began to tell his story. He sat in the armchair by the bed. Mrs Yao sat in the other one, while I sat on the edge of the bed. We kept our eyes on him, and his eyes were fixed on the windows. He was not looking at the scenery outside the window of course, for his view was blocked by the pale blue curtains. His eyes, red with weeping, full of unshed tears, seemed to be veiled by a thin mist. He's recalling his childhood, I thought.

"But afterwards, they kept quarrelling all the time. Dad was still away from home all day, and Mother sometimes went to play mahjong. When she lost, she was even more ready to quarrel with Dad. Once, after I'd already fallen asleep, Mother dragged me up, and made me and my brother kowtow to Dad. She said: 'You two hurry and kowtow to your father! Beg him to leave you a few coins to live on, so that you don't make him lose face by becoming beggars! Hurry up! Get down on your knees! Down on your knees!' My brother was the first to kneel. I had no choice but to kneel after him. I saw my father's face redden. He tore his hair in agitation and stammered to Mother: 'Why do you have to do this? Why?' That day, there was nothing my father could do. He was so agitated, he began walking round and round the room. Mother kept urging us: 'Hurry up! Kowtow! Kowtow!' My brother did, but I was so frightened, I burst into tears. Dad stamped his feet and tore his hair, stuttering: 'You, you, you, . . .' Mother pointed at him, screaming: 'Why don't you say anything today? Don't tell me you're embarrassed! They're your sons. Use your authority as their father. Give them a lesson. Tell them that what you spend is money you've earned yourself, and not the money their grandfather left them!' Dad cried: 'Look how you've frightened Han'er so much he's crying. What are you making such a row about? If others hear us, we'll lose face.' Mother became even angrier. Her voice became even louder, and she shouted: 'The other day, it was you who was making a row. How is it you're so frightened today! You can do it, but I have to shut up! Who do you think doesn't know that you've been running around with tarts, and gambling! Who's not laughing at me, living like a widow when my husband's still alive.' Dad immediately covered his cars and cried: 'Shut up, will you! You want me to kneel at your feet, is that it?' Mother butted in: 'I'll kneel to you, I'll kneel to you!' and dropped onto her knees with a thud. Dad stood there without moving. Mother began to weep, pulling at Dad's clothes and sobbing: 'Have pity on the three of us. It would be better to kill us once and for all than to let us suffer like this.' Dad did not say a word, but pushed aside Mother's hand and fled out of the house. Mother called out after him, but he did not turn round. Mother wept, my brother wept, and I wept. Mother looked at us and said: 'You must study hard; otherwise, we'll all starve to death.' I couldn't say a word. I heard my brother say: 'Don't worry, Mother. When I grow up, I'll avenge you.' That evening, Mother let me sleep on my own, for she still thought that Dad would come back. She did not sleep well, nor did I. My eyes stayed open, staring at the lamp, waiting for Dad to come home. The cock crowed several times, but I still saw no sign of Dad.

"He didn't come home the next two nights. Mother was worried, and sent people out to look for him. She also asked my brother to look for him, but Dad was nowhere to be found.

She even stopped playing mahjong, just sitting at home all day crying, blaming herself for quarrelling with Dad. Early on the third day, he came home. Mother chatted and laughed, serving him tea and making him things to eat. Dad also chatted and laughed happily. Later, I saw Mother give him a pair of gold bracelets. Dad was happy. In the afternoon, he took Mother, my brother and me to the theatre.

"I remember this very clearly. I've even dreamed about it several times. For three or four weeks, Dad didn't quarrel with Mother, and we lived very happily. Every evening, Dad came home very early, and every day, he brought us back some pastries. One evening, I whispered to him in bed: 'Dad, please don't quarrel with Mother in future. Look how happy we all are when you don't quarrel.' He swore to me that he would never quarrel again.

"But not long after, he and Mother had another clash. It seemed to be about the gold bracelets. Whenever they quarrelled, Mother always cried, but after a couple of days, she and Dad would make up. Almost every month or two, Mother would give Dad some object of value, and once he got it, he would take Mother and us to the theatre or a restaurant. After another couple of months, they would have another quarrel over this object. It was like this year in, year out.

"They both said that I understood too much for my age. In fact, I understood everything at the time. I knew that money was more useful than anything. I knew that people couldn't tell each other the truth. I knew that everyone looks after only himself. Sometimes they quarrelled so heatedly that it disturbed the neighbours and everyone would laugh at us, but no one was in the least sympathetic.

"Later the quarrels became even more violent, worse and worse each time. After each quarrel, Mother would weep and Dad would sleep away from home. Even my brother and I could see how their feeling for each other diminished with each quarrel. But I never understood why, after quarrelling and weeping, Mother would always happily give Dad something

and let him take it away.   Not only objects, but money as well.
Mother often said to us that Dad would soon squander all the
money.   But she still gave him money to spend.   She also
told us that the money she gave him was left us by her mother,
and that Dad was using it for business.   The money left us
by Dad's father had been spent long ago.

"Whenever Dad got something or got some money, there
would be talk and laughter at home, and he would chat happily
with Mother.   But when he didn't get any money, then he'd
pull a long face all day and not say a word.   In fact, he was
never at home during the day.   We would see him only one or
two days out of ten.

"One day, he took me out shopping.   After we finished,
instead of taking me home, he took me to an isolated courtyard.
There was a very beautiful woman there.   I remember her
face was shaped like a melon-seed and was very heavily powdered.   She called Dad 'Third Master' and called me 'Young Sir'.
Dad called her 'Lao Wu (the fifth)' and told me to call her
'Auntie'.   We stayed there for a long time.   She and Dad were
very intimate.   They talked for a long time.   They didn't speak
very loudly, and I didn't make any effort to listen.   Besides,
I didn't understand what Auntie was saying.   She gave me some
picture books to read, and also gave me a lot of sweets and
cakes.   I sat by myself on a low stool reading the books.   We
didn't go home till after dinner.   On the way home, Dad told
me not to say anything to Mother about 'Auntie'.   He also asked
me what I thought of 'Auntie'.   I said she was very beautiful,
and Dad was very pleased.   When we got home and Mother
saw how happy Dad was, she questioned me for a while, but
then left me alone.   However, my brother didn't believe what
I had said, and dragged me into the garden to interrogate me
about where Dad had actually taken me.   I wasn't willing to
tell the truth.   He got angry, shouted at me for a while, and
left it at that.   Dad treated me especially well that day.   After
I got into bed, he came and told me a story.   He praised me
for being a good boy, and said he would do all he could to

help me with my studies. I had already started primary school at that time.

"The next year, Mother found out about 'Auntie'. She was tidying up Dad's clothes early one morning, when she found a photo of 'Auntie' in a pocket, as well as a letter someone had written to him. Dad had just got up then. Mother questioned him, but Dad gave all the wrong answers. It was only then that she discovered that those valuable things she'd given him hadn't been used as security for business, but had all been given to 'Auntie' to spend. They had a heated quarrel. This time it was really violent, and Dad swept all the cakes, bowls and chopsticks which had been laid on the table onto the floor. Mother, her hair all dishevelled, cried and sobbed. I'd never seen them so ferocious before. Then my mother screamed that she wanted to die, and my brother went to beg First and Second Uncles to come round. First and Second Aunts came with them. My aunts calmed Mother down, and my uncles gave Dad a good telling off, and things eventually quietened down. Dad also apologized to Mother, and promised to get rid of his second household. He didn't go out that day, and by evening, Mother had cooled off.

"That evening, I slept with Dad as usual. It was raining heavily outside. I couldn't sleep, nor could Dad. The electric lamp in the room was very bright. Our house had already been fitted with electricity. I could see the tears in my father's eyes and so I said to him: 'Dad, you mustn't quarrel with Mother again. I'm afraid. You're always quarrelling. What will my brother and I do?' As I spoke, I began to cry. I added: 'You swore before that you wouldn't quarrel with Mother again. You're a grown-up. You shouldn't deceive me.' He took me by the hand and said softly: 'I'm not worthy of you. I don't deserve to be your father. I won't quarrel with your mother again in future.' I cried: 'I don't believe you! In a couple of days, you'll be at it again. You'll quarrel until we're too ashamed to look people in the face.' Dad just sighed.

"I still thought they would stop quarrelling in future. But

after less than a month, I saw once more that Mother and Dad were on bad terms again. Only this time, there wasn't much in the way of quarrelling. As soon as Mother opened her mouth, Dad would go out. Sometimes, he wouldn't come back for several days. Once he came back, Mother would interrogate him, and he'd just give some vague answers and go into the study. She couldn't do anything to stop him.

"Dad's elder brother died. Everyone in the family clamoured to divide up the family property and sell the house. Mother was for it. Dad was the only one against it. He said it was constructed according to designs drawn up by Grandfather, and Grandfather in his will had said that the house wasn't to be sold, but was to be kept as an ancestral temple. Everyone laughed at Dad, and no one would listen to him. His second and fourth brothers both said that Dad had no right to speak like that.

"I can still remember very clearly what happened at the meeting they held to discuss the situation. The Japanese had already attacked Shanghai at the time. Second and Fourth Uncles were arguing with Dad in the sitting-room. Second Uncle pounded on the table, and Fourth Uncle shouted at him, pointing his finger at him. Dad was stuttering, red in the face. I hid outside the door and watched them. Dad said: 'If you want to sell it, then sell it, but I absolutely refuse to sign. I've done too many things unworthy of Father. I'm an unworthy son. I've sold all the land he left me, but I won't sell this house.' Dad absolutely refused to sign. Second and Fourth Uncles couldn't do anything about it. If our branch of the family didn't sign, the house couldn't be sold. Mother came and tried to persuade Dad, but he still refused to sign. I saw Fourth Uncle whisper something in Mother's ear. She went to find my brother. My brother had returned to Sichuan after graduation less than two months before, and hadn't yet passed the exams for working in the post office. He came in and without saying a word to Dad, he went up to the table, picked up the brush and signed. Dad glared at him. But he shouted:

'It's I who've signed. It's I who've given approval for the house to be sold. I'm taking charge of the affairs of our branch of the family. I don't care who objects!' Second Uncle gathered up the papers at once. He was inexpressibly happy. Fourth Uncle and Eldest Uncle's eldest son were also very pleased. One by one, they left the room. Dad was white with anger. After a while, he said, as if to himself: 'He's not my son.' He was the only one left in the room. I ran up to him and seized him by the hand. I cried: 'Dad, I'm your son.' He bent down and looked at me for a long moment. He said: 'I know. Well, I brought all this on myself. . . . Let's go and have a look round the garden. They're going to sell the house!'

"Dad led me by the hand into the garden. The garden at that time was just as it is now. I remember it was close to the Moon Festival. The osmanthus trees were in magnificent bloom, and you could smell their perfume as soon as you went in the gate. I followed him and we walked around the garden for a while. Suddenly, he said to me: 'Han'er, have a good look. In a few days, the garden won't be ours any more.' When I heard him say this, I felt extremely upset. I asked him: 'Dad, we're so comfortable here. Why do Second Uncle and the others insist on selling the house? Why are they all against you, and why won't they listen to you?' Dad looked down and gazed at me for a moment before answering: 'Because of money. All because of money!' Then I asked him again: 'Then we won't be able to come here anymore in the future?' He answered: 'Naturally. That's why I'm telling you to have a good look now.' I asked once more: 'If the house can't be sold, then can we stay?' Dad said: 'You're really a child. When has there been a house that couldn't be sold?' He pulled me over to the camellia tree. It wasn't the flowering season. He wanted me to see the inscription he'd carved in the tree — the words I was looking at just now. Before, we had two camellia trees, but later, when the house was sold to your family, Mrs. Yao," (his eyes turned to rest on Mrs. Yao's face), "the white one died. Now there's only the red one. Dad pointed out the

words and told me: 'They're older than you are!' I asked
him: 'Older than my brother?' He replied: 'Older than your
brother.' Then he gave a sigh and said: 'From his bearing today,
your brother is much more influential than I am. Now I can't
interfere in his affairs, but he, on the other hand, meddles in
mine!' I said: 'He hasn't been very nice to you today. Even
I'm angry with him.' He turned and patted me on the head,
looked at me a moment, and then shook his head, saying: 'But
I'm not angry with him. He's right. I'm not worthy to be his
father.' 'Dad,' I cried, 'he's your son! He shouldn't side with
others to humiliate you!' Dad said: 'I deserve it. I'm not
worthy of your mother. I'm not worthy of the two of you.' I
said at once: 'Then you mustn't visit "Auntie" again. You must
stay at home and keep Mother company, and then she'll be
happy. I'll go and talk to her!' He immediately put his hand
over my mouth, and said: 'Don't talk to your mother about
"Auntie". It's already too late now. Do you see these words?
When I first carved them, I wasn't much older than you are
now. I never imagined that the two of us would be standing
here today looking at them. In a couple of days, this home,
this garden will change owners. Even the inscription which I
carved can't be preserved. Han'er, remember what I say. You
mustn't be like me. You mustn't be like your failure of a
father.' I said: 'Dad, I don't hate you.' He didn't say anything.
He just looked at me, and his tears began to flow. He gave
a sigh, placed a hand on my shoulder and said: 'As long as
you don't hate me and don't curse me when you grow up, I
will die happy.' At this, I burst into tears. He waited till
I could weep no more, then took his handkerchief and wiped
my eyes dry. 'Don't cry,' he said. 'Smell! The flowers of
the osmanthus tree are so fragrant. It'll be the Moon Festival
soon. When I was newly married, I used to come into the garden
with your mother to admire the moon. At that time, there was
no terrace for the flowers, just a pond. Later, after your brother
was born, your grandfather said that, with so many children in
the family, they might fall in, and so he had the pond filled in.

At that time, your mother and I got on very well with each other. Who would have thought that we'd end up like this!' He led me to the goldfish tanks. The water in them was very dirty, with floating duckweed, shrimps and worms. Dad pressed his hands against the tank. I held on to the tank too. Dad said: 'When I was small, I liked to feed the goldfish in this tank. I would come here every day after school, and wouldn't leave until I was called for dinner. The water was really clean in those days. You could even see the sand clearly at the bottom of the tank. I got hold of two flatfish. Your grandfather was fond of them too. He used to come all the time. He came and stood with me in front of the tank many times, just as we're doing today. Then, it was I with my father. Today, it's I with my son. When I think of it now, it seems like a dream.' We went back to beneath the osmanthus tree, and Dad looked up at the flowers. The sparrows were quarrelling in the branches. Many of the flowers were falling. Dad bent down and picked up a whole handful. Afterwards, he went and opened the door of the upper guest room, and we went inside and sat for a moment. We also went and sat for a while in the lower guest room. Dad said: 'In a few days, all this will belong to someone else.' I asked him whether the garden had been laid out by Grandfather. He said it was. He also said: 'I remember, not long before your grandfather died, I ran into him in the garden. He talked to me for a long time, and then he suddenly said: "I don't think I've long to live. When I'm dead, I wonder if this garden, these things will be preserved for very long. I can't help worrying about you all. It's only now that I've realized that without leaving behind a good moral training, leaving property to one's sons and grandsons is of no lasting value. What a fool I've been all these years." Your grandfather really said this. But it's only now that I understand his meaning. But it's already too late. . . .' "

Mrs. Yao covered her eyes with her handkerchief and began to cry. I kept glancing over at her as the child told us the story. I had noticed her eyes filling with glistening tears for some

time. Only when she began to weep audibly did the boy stop
talking, and looking at her in surprise, he cried out affectionately: "Mrs. Yao!" I looked at her in sympathy, my mind
in agitation, but I could not say a word. For a few minutes,
there was complete silence in the room. Tears trickled drop by
drop from the boy's face. Mrs Yao's sobs had already ceased.
The destiny of these two people merged together to move me
deeply. How could there be such suffering in the world! It was
a thousand times worse than anything I could have written
with my brush. What could I do? I could not resign
myself to just watching them placidly! I began to hate myself.
The heavy silence hurt me. I wanted to shout.

The boy suddenly stood up. He wiped the tears from his
cheeks with his hands. Surely he wasn't leaving? Could it be
that he was unwilling to reveal the most important part of his
story? He'd just taken a step, when Mrs. Yao looked up and
said: "My child, you mustn't go. Please go on with your story."

The boy hesitated, and suddenly burst out: "Yes, I will. I
will." He sat down once more in the armchair.

"Just now, I was upset," she said in embarrassment, wiping
her eyes gently with her handkerchief. "Your grandfather's
words really struck home. But I'm amazed. How can someone
as young as you are, remember so many things so clearly? After
all these years, you should have forgotten them."

"I'll never forget anything I know about Dad. I think
about it at night when I can't go to sleep. I even know the
words by heart."

"Are you unable to sleep at night?" I asked him.

"I can't sleep if I think about what's happened to Dad. The
more I lie awake, the more I think. And the more I think, the
more unworthy of him I feel. . . ."

"How can you say that you're unworthy of him? It's he
that's in the wrong. Anyone can see that it's he who's destroyed your family's happiness," I could not help interrupting.

"But afterwards, we were too cruel to him," the child replied. "He was already sorry, and we ought to have forgiven him."

"Yes, you're right, my child. Forgiveness is most important, particularly towards someone in one's own family," Mrs. Yao chimed in with emotion.

"But there's a limit to forgiveness. And besides, with some obstinate people, forgiveness is equivalent to connivance," I interrupted. I was hinting at the behaviour of the Zhao household.

She glanced at me but said nothing, turning instead to the boy to say: "Go on, my child." And she added: "It doesn't hurt you too much to talk about it, does it? Don't force yourself."

"No, no!" The child shook his head emphatically. "Now that I've spoken about it, I feel as if a burden has been lifted from me. I've never talked about Dad to anyone else before. My family treats me like a small child. They rarely talk to me seriously. In fact, I'm not that young, even in years. I'm no longer a child that understands nothing but food."

"In that case, please go on. Let us know a bit more about your father. Let me pour you a cup of tea first." She got up as she spoke.

"I'll pour it myself," the boy said quickly and stood up, but Mrs. Yao had already poured it. The boy accepted the cup of tea gratefully and, lifting it to his lips, took several large mouthfuls.

I got up silently and went to the door, and then to the writing-desk. I moved the cane-chair about four or five paces from the boy, and sat down opposite him. I looked with sympathy at this boy who had matured so young. A child of his age shouldn't have had such a good memory for unhappiness and suffering, nor such a good understanding of it. If I were asked, even I would not have been able to relate his father's story so clearly. Unhappiness had already left such a deep mark on the mind of this child.

27

The child continued the story of his father:

"After a month, the house still hadn't been sold. Outside Sichuan the war raged on. Japanese planes were bombing everywhere, and although we were safe here, the place was rife with rumours. Second Uncle and the others began to worry that they wouldn't be able to sell. Second Uncle, to show his determination, was the first to move out. Then Fourth Uncle followed suit, and so did Eldest Uncle's son. Mother and my brother also rented another place in preparation for leaving, but Dad refused to agree. He argued with them. But in the end we moved out too. Dad said he wanted to stay and look after the house, and so he was the only one who remained behind.

"After we shifted, I would go to the house after school every day to see Dad. I went over a dozen times, but saw him only once. I guessed he must have gone to 'Auntie's, Whenever Mother asked, I always said that I'd seen him, and Mother never suspected.

"Eventually, the house was sold to your family. Each branch of the family got a share, and everyone was very happy. Our share of the money was taken by my brother. Dad was furious, and wouldn't come home, saying that he was moving into a temple outside the East Gate and staying there for a month or so. Mother begged him to come home, but he wouldn't. Later, my brother had a row with him, which made him even more adamant about not coming home. In fact, we'd been keeping a room as a study for him in the house we'd moved to. Our new house had a single courtyard. The rooms were spotless, and just as tidy and comfortable as the old mansion. I begged Dad to come home too, telling him that in any case things at home were much better than outside. But he just wouldn't come. My brother said that he wasn't staying at the temple at all, but was living with his mistress in a separate little house and having the time of his life. According to my brother, she was originally a prostitute from down the river.

"After a couple of months, Dad had still not moved home. He came visiting four or five times, but each time, left after half an hour or so. The last time, he ran into my brother, and they had a row. My brother asked him when he was finally going to come home, but he wouldn't say. My brother cursed him roundly, but he still wouldn't say anything, and just slipped away. When I started to run after him, there was already no hope of catching up with him. After that, he never came again. After just over a month, on the eve of the Lantern Festival, I heard my brother say that Dad was going to move back home. Mother asked him how he knew. He then told us that Dad's whore had run off after plucking him clean of everything of value that he had. Since Dad had no money, he was sure to come back home. I wasn't very pleased to hear my brother talking like this. I didn't think he should be so disrespectful. He was our father after all, and he hadn't treated us badly.

"I didn't believe what my brother said. But according to him, he knew exactly where Dad was, and claimed that he'd seen that 'Auntie' in the street. I couldn't get news of Dad from any other source; I could only grab hold of my brother and ask. But he wouldn't tell me. When I persisted, he got angry. However, I found out a bit, because my brother used to talk about Dad when we were having dinner. I discovered that he was looking for that 'Auntie' everywhere, but without success. But I didn't know where he lived, so there was no way of finding him.

"Eventually one day, Dad came home. I remember it was at the end of the second lunar month. He looked as if he'd been seriously ill. He was all hunched up, his face was even yellower his eyes were sunken, and he'd grown a short moustache. He walked feebly and his speech was full of moans and groans. When he came home, I'd just come back from school, and my brother hadn't yet returned. He was standing in the sitting-room, not daring to go into Mother's room. I went to call her, and she came out of her room and just stood there and said: 'I knew you'd come back.' Dad looked down at the ground. He swayed unsteadily as if about to fall. Mother didn't move. I ran over and took him by the hand, leading him to a chair to sit down. 'Dad, are you hungry?' I asked. Shaking his head, he replied: 'No.' I saw Mother turn and move away. After a while, our maid servant Mrs. Luo brought a wash-basin, poured him a cup of tea and brought some cakes. Dad said nothing. He just drank up the tea and ate all the cakes without looking up. I was so upset that I cried out: 'Dad!' and my tears began to fall. 'Dad, please stay at home. Please don't go out again to look for "Auntie". Look how thin you've become!' He held on to my hand, but said nothing. He just wept.

"At last, Mother came out. She told me to ask Dad if he was tired or not, and whether he wanted to lie down in the room for a while. At first, he didn't want to, but then I saw that he was really exhausted, and so I made him go in. After a while, when I went back into Mother's room, I saw him asleep on the bed, with Mother sitting in a cane-chair beside him. They looked as if they'd been talking. Mother was weeping, her head down. I crept out at once. I thought that this time they'd probably made up.

"We waited for my brother to come home for dinner. That day he was back a bit later than usual. I told him happily the news of Dad's coming home. I never imagined that he would have put on such a sour face. 'I said long ago that he'd come back. If he hadn't, where would he eat?' I was rather angry, and so I answered: 'This is his home. Why shouldn't he come back?' My brother said nothing more. After dinner, when he saw Dad, he put on an air of complete indifference. Dad wanted to say something to him, but he just sat there crossly, saying nothing. Mother spoke to him a little however. After my brother had finished one bowl of rice, he called to Mrs. Luo for more, but Mrs. Luo just happened to be away, so he suddenly got angry, banged on the table, swore, and left, his face black as thunder.

"He gave us all such a fright. 'I wonder what happened to him today that's made him so angry without any reason,' Mother remarked. Dad had been eating, his head buried in his bowl of rice. Hearing Mother's words, he looked up and said: 'I'm afraid it's because I've come home.' Mother looked down and said nothing more. Dad finished his rice and put down his bowl. 'Why are you having only one bowl,' Mother asked. 'Won't you have a bit more?' 'I'm full,' Dad answered in a low voice. He got up. Mother finished eating, and so did I. That night, Dad said very little. He went to bed early. As usual he slept in the same bed with me. I didn't sleep well. I had a bad dream and woke up about midnight to hear Dad crying. I called to him softly, before realizing that he'd been crying in his sleep. I asked him what he'd been dreaming about, but he wouldn't say.

"Dad stayed on at our new home. The first four days, he didn't go out at all, and didn't say much either. Whenever he saw my brother, he would drop his eyes and say nothing. My brother wouldn't speak to him. On the fifth day, he went out after breakfast, and didn't come home till dinner time. Mother asked him where he'd been all day. He just said he'd been to see a friend. It was the same on the sixth day. On the seventh day, he came back when we were just eating. Mother asked him what had kept him out, and why he was so late. Once more, he simply said that he'd been out to see some friends. That day, my brother got angry again, and started shouting: 'Always lying! Seeing friends! Do you think we don't know you've been to look for that tart of yours! When we begged you to come home before, you kept making excuses, saying you had to go to the temple outside town to get better. A pack of lies! It was all to be with your whore. I thought you really didn't want this family, you really didn't want anything to do with us. Who would have thought that Heaven does indeed have eyes? Your "precious jewel" has dropped you to run off with someone else. She's taken everything you've got. And now that you've been left on your own, you come home. This is the family you didn't want.   We're the people you've always detested. But once you get thrown over, it's still we who take you back and see to your comfort here at home. But you're still not satisfied with staying quietly at home.   You still want to go running around outside.   What are you really up to, I wonder? Do you think you can cheat Mother out of some money to go and find yourself another mistress, to rent another flat? I warn you, you'd better not have any such ideas.   I won't let you humiliate Mother again! . . .'

"Dad was sitting in a chair near the wall, his face in his hands.   Mother couldn't bear it, and interrupted, tears streaming down her face.   'Hé (my brother's pet name is Hé), don't say anymore.   Let him finish eating.'   But my brother answered: 'Mother, let me finish.   I've had so much bottled up inside me these last few years.   If I don't speak out, I'll burst.   You're too kindhearted.   Aren't you afraid that he'll deceive you just as he did before?'   Mother answered with a sob: 'Hé, he's your father!'   I couldn't stop from running over to Dad and taking him by the hand, calling out repeatedly: 'Dad!' He let go my hand.   His face was terrible to see.

"Then I heard my brother say: 'Dad? A father should act like a father.   When has he ever treated us as his sons?'   Dad got up, pushed away my hand, and slowly went to the door. Mother called out to him: 'Mengchi, where are you going? Aren't you going to eat?' Dad turned round and said: 'I think I'd better go.   My living here is no good at all for you.'   Mother asked again: 'But where are you going?' Dad replied: 'I don't know yet.   But the town's so big, I'm sure to find somewhere to live.' Mother ran to him weeping, and begged: 'You mustn't go! Let's forget the past.' My brother was still sitting at the table. 'Mother,' he interrupted, 'it's no use talking to him. Don't say you still don't know what he's like.   If he wants to go, let him go!' But Mother said, still weeping: 'No! He's all on his own.   Where do you want him to go?' She turned to Dad once more: 'Mengchi, this is still your home. Please help us keep it as a family.   Surely it's better to stay here than to run around outside!' My brother stormed into his room. I couldn't bear it any longer. I ran and held on to Dad's hand, crying as I spoke: 'Dad, if you go, take me with you.'

"And so Dad stayed. He would go out for a walk every day, but always when my brother wasn't home. Sometimes, he'd even ask Mother or me for a bit of pocket money. I got my money from my brother. Dad told me not to tell him. Since my brother thought that Dad stayed home reading all day, he was a bit more civil to him, and didn't quarrel with him anymore. Dad and I shared the same room. He would mostly stay in the room, reading or sleeping. When I came home from school, he would help me go over my lessons. Mother also got on all right with him. During that month, Dad began to look a little healthier, and he perked up a bit. One day, Mother said to us that Dad would probably reform from now on.

"One Sunday, after my brother and I had had lunch at home, Mother asked us to go with Dad to the pictures, and my brother agreed. We were just leaving when someone came with a letter, and asked whether the third Mr. Yang lived here. Dad took the letter. I heard him tell the messenger: 'I understand,' and saw him fold the letter and hide it away. We went to the cinema. I was absorbed in the film. When it was about to end, I found that Dad had gone. I thought he'd gone to the toilet, and so didn't worry. But when the film finished, he still hadn't come back. We looked for him everywhere, but couldn't find him. I said: 'Perhaps he went home first.' My brother sneered: 'What a fool you are! He thinks our house is a prison. Once out, he's not going to run back in a hurry!' And in fact, there was no sign of him when we got home. Mother asked where he'd gone, and my brother told her about his getting the letter. After dinner, Mother kept some food for him, but he never came back that night. Neither my mother nor my brother was pleased. He came back the next morning. Mother was home by herself. He left before I came back from school. Mother didn't tell me what he'd said to her. It was very much later that I discovered that he'd asked her for some money. He didn't come home that evening, nor the second, nor the third evening. Mother was worried, and wanted my brother to see if he could find out anything. My brother was displeased, and kept saying it didn't matter. On the fifth day, a letter arrived from Dad, saying he'd gone to Jiading on business and had taken ill. He wanted to come home, but had no money on him, and so he wanted Mother to send him money for the journey back. As soon as she got the letter, Mother remitted him 100 dollars at once. It so happened that my teacher had asked for leave that day, so Mother asked me to go to the post office to send the money. I wrote a few words on Mother's letter, asking him to come home as soon as possible. When my brother came home in the evening and discovered that Mother had sent Dad money, he wasn't at all pleased, and grumbled at her, saying a lot of terrible things about Dad. Later, Mother also began to blame Dad.

"After we sent the money, Dad never replied. Nor did he come home. We had no news of him whatsoever. My mother and my brother would get angry whenever he was mentioned. My brother would be the angrier of the two. Sometimes Mother would worry that Dad was still ill, and want to write to him. One day she wanted my brother to write, but he refused, giving her a good scolding instead. After that, Mother didn't dare say anything about writing again. For three whole months, we had no news of Dad, and eventually, we stopped talking about him. One day in the summer vacation, it was raining heavily and I was at home revising my lessons, when suddenly, Dad appeared. He was soaked to the skin. Moreover, he'd come by rickshaw, and didn't even have enough money to pay the puller. He was thinner than before, and his silk gown was dirty and torn, and he had a strange smell about him. He stood on the doorstep, leaning against the pillar, not daring to enter the house.

"Mother got someone to pay the puller, and standing grim-faced at the door of the sitting-room, she said to Dad: 'So you've deigned to come home! I thought you'd died in some distant province.' Dad kept his eyes to the ground, not daring to look at her.   Mother continued: 'It's just as well.   It'll let you see that even without you, we can manage very comfortably, and without bringing dishonour on your family either.'

"Dad's head dropped even lower.   The water dripped from his hair and the rain beat upon his face, but he took no notice. Unable to stand it, I pointed out to Mother that Dad was all wet, and suggested that we let him in to have a wash and change his clothes.   When Mother heard me say this, her face changed. She at once asked him into the house, had water prepared for a bath, and found some clothes for him to change into. Dad didn't say a word.   He was like a mute.   He had a bath, changed his clothes, and had something light to eat.   He did as Mother said, and had a long sleep in my bed.

"When my brother came home and heard that Dad was back, he put on a long face.   I heard Mother telling him to try to be polite when he saw Dad.   My brother muttered something in reply.   When he saw Dad at dinner time, he frowned, greeted him gruffly, and turned away his face.   Dad looked as if he wanted to say something to him, but couldn't get it out.   After he finished one bowl of rice, Mrs. Luo gave him another half bowl.   When he put out his hand, it was trembling uncontrollably, and he didn't hold the bowl properly.   The rice fell onto the ground and the bowl broke.   Terrified, he bent down to clear up the mess.   Mother said: 'Leave it. Let Mrs. Luo bring you another bowl.'   Dad said fearfully: 'There's no need, no need.   This will do just the same.'   Then for some unknown reason, my brother suddenly banged on the table and shouted: 'If you don't want to eat, then get out! I haven't got so much for you to waste.'   Dad got up and left without a word.   Pointing his finger at Mother, my brother said: 'Mother, this is all because of your softness. Our house is not a hotel. How can you let him come and go as he pleases!' Mother said: 'But since he's back now, let him stay here and rest for a few days.'   My brother became angrier and, shaking his head, said: 'No, it won't do! He's done so much harm.   I

won't let him lead a life of ease.   I'll find some work for him
to do.' Early in the morning on the third day, he made Dad go
out with him. Dad followed him, head down, without a word.
From behind them, Mother said, 'With your brother going
ahead of him like that, your Dad looks like his servant.' When
I heard this, I really felt like having a good cry.

"In the afternoon, my brother came back first, and Dad
came later.   When Dad saw my brother, he looked down again.
Whenever my brother asked him anything at dinner, he just
grunted in reply.   Then he put down his bowl, and crept to
his room.   Mother asked my brother what sort of work he was
doing. My brother just said he was a clerk.   I went to ask Dad
in our room, but he wouldn't say a word.

"After four or five days, about four o'clock in the afternoon, Dad suddenly came running breathless into the house.   I
was the only one home.   Mother had gone shopping. I asked
him how he came to be home so early.   Out of breath, Dad replied: I won't do it.   I really can't put up with it. They say I'm
a clerk, but I'm just an office boy.   I don't mind hard work,
but I'm not going to be humiliated like this.' His face was
covered with sweat, which rolled down in drops, dripping onto
his clothes. I called to Mrs. Luo to bring some water to wash
his face.   He'd just done so, and was sitting in the living-room
drinking his tea when my brother came back.   I could see
from the look on his face that he was boiling with rage, so I
tried to side-track him, but he paid no attention to me.   He
went straight up to Dad instead.   Dad stood up as soon as he
saw him, as if wanting to escape.   He seized hold of Dad and
asked him grimly: 'I found work for you.   Why have you quit
after only a few days?'   Dad's head dropped, and he said in
a low voice: 'I can't do it.   If there's any other kind of work,
I can do that.' 'You can't do it,' my brother sneered.   'Then
what kind of work can you do?   Would you like to be a bank
manager? If you're so clever, find yourself a job, but I won't
have you at home here getting free food and lodging.' Dad said:
'I don't want free board, but to ask me to be an office boy, that

really is too humiliating for a member of the Yang family. And
the salary's a pittance.' My brother laughed coldly: 'You're
afraid of losing face for the Yang family! Because of you, the
Yang family had been humiliated long ago! Just reckon up the
money you've spent: the money in your own name, the money
Grandfather left us, not to mention the money Mother gave you!
You've spent it all!' At this point, Mother came back, but he
kept on shouting: 'You've had enough pleaure! You've spent
it all in luxury, in riotous living, on prostitutes and gambling.
You've spent money like water. What do you care whether your
family suffers or not, whether we're looked down on
or not.' Dad whispered in a piteous voice. 'Why do
you have to bring all that up? What's past is past. However
much I regret it, it's not going to bring it back.' My brother
butted in: 'Regret it! If you knew what regret was, you wouldn't
have been so thick-skinned as to come back home. When we
begged you to come home before, you wouldn't come. Now,
we've no need for you. Get out of here! I don't have a
father like you. I don't accept you as my father.' Dad's face
changed. His whole body trembled uncontrollably. He stared
with wide-open eyes. He tried to say something, but the words
wouldn't come. At this moment, Mother called to my brother
to stop. I also cried out: 'But he's our father!' My brother
turned to look at me. He said, tears streaming down his cheeks:
'He's not worthy to be our father. He's never looked after me
properly from the day I was born. It was Mother who brought
me up. He's never carried out his responsibility as a father.
This isn't his home. I'm not his son.' He turned towards
Mother. 'Mother, tell me. In what way does he deserve to be
my father?' Mother said nothing. She just stared at Dad, and
then began to cry. Dad just moved his head to avoid Mother's
gaze. My brother felt in his pocket for a letter and gave it
to Mother, saying: 'Read this letter, Mother. There are things
in it I just can't bring myself to say.' After reading the letter,
Mother said only one word to Dad: 'You!' Then she handed him
the letter and continued: 'Here! It's from a colleague in your

company.' Dad trembled as he read. His face turned a bright red. 'It's not true,' he stuttered. 'I swear it. Most of it isn't true. They're setting me up.' 'Then at least part of it's true,' Mother said. 'I've listened to enough of your lies. I don't dare believe you again. Get out!' She waved him away, turned, and went into her room. She seemed to be very tired, and walked very slowly, wiping her eyes with a handkerchief. Dad called to her anxiously: 'I didn't do it. At least half of them are lies.' But Mother wouldn't listen to him. My brother wiped away his tears and said: 'It's no use arguing. He's a good friend of mine. He wouldn't spread unfounded rumours. I haven't time to talk to you now. You'd better make your plans quickly.' My father tried to argue: 'It's a frame-up. That friend of yours has it in for me. He was involved in a fraud and the evidence is in my hands. He tried to bribe me, but I wouldn't take it. He hates me. . . .' My brother didn't let him finish: 'I don't want to hear your lies. You wouldn't take the money! Who the devil is going to believe that? If you had any concern for face, do you think we'd have had to put up with so much hardship for so many years?' Having said this, he went into my mother's room. Only Dad and I left in the sitting-room. I ran up to him and took him by the hand: 'Dad, you mustn't be angry with him. He'll be sorry after a while. Let's go into our room for a moment and rest.' Dad called my name: 'Han'er!' and his tears started to fall. After a long while, he said: 'It's too late to be sorry now. You mustn't be like me. Remember!'

"At dinner time, it began to rain. When Dad said something at the dinner table, my brother began to argue. Dad added a few words. My brother suddenly threw his rice bowl violently to the floor and stormed angrily into his room. We all put down our bowls, not daring to say a word. Suddenly, Dad stood up and said: 'I'll go then.' When my brother heard this, he leapt out from his room and, pointing at Dad, cried: 'Then go at once! The mere sight of you makes me angry.' Without a word, Dad ran out of the room, down into the courtyard, out into the pouring rain. Mother stood up to call out to him, but my brother pulled her back. 'Don't call him. He'll be back in a moment.' I didn't pay any attention to them. I ran out into the rain all by myself. My hair and clothes were wet through. At the main entrance, I saw Dad's bent back running down the street, a dozen or so paces ahead of me. I ran after him, calling to him. But my voice was drowned in the noise of the rain. My mouth was full of rainwater. I had almost caught up with him when suddenly, my foot slipped and I fell with a splash to the ground. I was covered all over with mud. I felt dizzy, and my whole body was sore. I pulled myself up and ran. I ran to the intersection. The rain was a little lighter. I was only three or four steps from Dad. I shouted to him. He turned to look, saw it was I, and began to run even faster. I ran after him as fast as I could. Suddenly, he slipped and fell. He tried to get up but couldn't. I ran over and helped him up. His face had struck a stone and was bleeding. He stood up slowly, out of breath, and asked me: 'Why have you run after me?' 'Dad,' I said, 'come home with me.' He shook his head and sighed: 'I don't have a home. I don't have anything. I have only myself. I said: 'Dad, you mustn't talk like that. I'm your son. My brother is your son too. We're both your sons. Without you, how could we exist?' Dad replied: 'I'm not worthy to be your father. Let me go. Whether I live or die is purely my business. Go back to your brother and tell him not to worry. I won't bring discredit on you ever again.' I held on to his arm with all my might and cried: 'I won't let you go. You must come home with me!' I pulled him by the arm with all my strength. He was pulled back a couple of steps. He begged me again to let him go, but I wouldn't. Then he gave me a heavy push. I fell onto my back. This time I was stunned. For a long time, I couldn't get up. The rain came down in torrents. My clothes were soaked through. I pulled myself up slowly and stood at the intersection. I couldn't see Dad anywhere. There was only the heavy grey rain all around me. My head was heavy and my legs unsteady. My body was painfully sore all over. I didn't have an ounce of strength. I gritted my teeth and tried to walk a few steps. I'm not clear what happened next. I seemed to trip again, and someone pulled me up. I heard my brother calling me, and I relaxed. He took me home, half-carrying, half-dragging me. I remember it was still not completely dark.

"When I got home, they heated the water for me to take a bath and change my clothes, and boiled some ginger syrup for me. Mother watched over me as I went to sleep. Neither she nor my brother asked me about Dad. In any case, I hadn't the strength to talk. That evening, I ran a very high fever. I had nightmares all night. The next morning, they called a doctor. The more medicine I took, the worse I got, and it wasn't until they finally changed doctors that they discovered that I was being given the wrong medicine. I was ill for over two months before I could get up. Mrs. Luo told me that when I was at my worst and Mother was watching by my bedside, I kept calling out: 'Dad, come home with me!' Mother had wiped the tears from her eyes, and that same day had made my brother go out and look for Dad. My brother really did go, but he didn't find him. However, later, when I was a bit better, at meal times, Mother and my brother would continue to say nasty things about Dad. It was Mrs. Luo who told me that too.

"I recovered from my illness. Mother and my brother treated me so well! But they wouldn't let me mention Dad. I couldn't get the slightest news about him from them. Perhaps they really didn't know. They seemed to have forgotten him completely. When I walked about the streets, I never saw any sign of Dad either. I went to see Old Man Li. I made enquiries from others, but couldn't find out a thing. After the sale of the mansion, Second Uncle, Fourth Uncle and Eldest Uncle's son had never been to our place. They had never once asked about Dad.

"The next year, at the Moon Festival, we had no visitors. During that year, Mother had very rarely accepted invitations from our relatives to play mahjong or to attend other social occasions, and rarely had visitors. The only people who came regularly to visit us were the wife of my mother's brother and her daughter. That day, the three of us were celebrating the festival at home. Mother and my brother were in high spirits. I was the only one who thought about how Dad was going to spend the festival away from home all by himself, and I couldn't help feeling depressed. Shortly after lunch, we heard someone at the door asking for the Yang family. Mrs. Luo brought in a man with a shaven head, dressed in a neat brown uniform. He said he had a letter for Third Master Yang. My brother asked him whom the letter was from. He said it was from the second wife of a Mr. Wang. My brother tore open the letter and then asked the messenger for the account. When the messenger heard that my brother was the third Mr. Yang's son, he took out a red-covered account book and handed it to him, saying: 'This is a deposit-book for 30,000 *yuan*. Would Mr. Yang please write a receipt?' I saw my brother take the bank-book and leaf through a few pages, biting his lips. Then he handed it back to the messenger and said: 'My father's away. He won't be back for a month or so. The total of these deposits is too large a sum. We don't dare accept it. Please take it back and explain to your Mrs. Wang.' The messenger tried again and again to get my brother to accept it, but my brother absolutely refused, and so he had no alternative but to take it back and leave. Just before leaving, he asked where the Third Mr. Yang had gone. My brother replied: 'He's gone to Guilin and Guiyang or thereabouts.' To think my brother could tell such a whopping lie! Mother waited till the messenger had gone before coming out from her room and asking my brother whom the money was from. My brother answered: 'Who else do you think? Who could it be but that precious whore of his? She's now the concubine of some rich fellow. She brought up what happened in the past, claims she acted against her will, says she's infinitely sorry, and asks to be forgiven. She says that now she's a bit better off, she's saved the 30,000 *yuan* to send him as replacement for the amount he lost. . . .' When Mother heard this, she couldn't stop herself from interjecting: 'Who cares for her money! You were right to reject it! You were right!' I'd been standing there all this time, and had no right to interfere. But when I thought of 'Auntie's' heavily rouged face shaped like a melon-seed, I felt she was a kind-hearted person nevertheless. Up till now, she still hadn't forgotten my father. I thought too how wonderful it would be if she knew where Dad was. She certainly wouldn't let him wander about destitute far from home.

"After that, I heard no more of Dad, until one Saturday afternoon last September, when Mother took me to the cinema without my brother. After we came out of the film, Mother waited at the entrance, while I went to call the rickshaws. When I came back with them, I saw that Mother had turned deathly pale, as if she'd seen a ghost. I asked her if she was feeling unwell, but she said she wasn't. She asked me if I'd seen anyone. I said I hadn't. Then she said nothing more. After we got into the rickshaws, I noticed that Mother kept looking round all the time, but I didn't know what she was looking for. When we got home, I asked her if she'd met someone she knew. My brother was still not back, and we were at home by ourselves. Mother's face changed colour and she whispered to me: 'I think I saw your father.' I asked her happily: 'Did you really?' She said: 'It was definitely he. It was his face, only thinner, and his clothes were terrible. He followed us after we left the cinema down quite a few streets.' I said: 'Then why didn't you call to him and make him come home?' Mother sighed, and then began to cry. I didn't dare say any more. After a long while, Mother whispered again: 'When I think about it, I still hate him.' I was just about to say something when my brother came back.

"That evening, I couldn't get to sleep. I lay on the bed, thinking only that the next day, I would be able to find him. I was terribly anxious. The next day, I got up as soon as it was light. Without waiting for breakfast, I ran out to find

Old Man Li to tell him that Mother had seen Dad, and to ask him whether he could help me find him. He told me not to be so excited, but to take my time and look for him calmly. I didn't listen to him. I played truant from school, but after rushing about for three days, I hadn't found any sign of him.

"After another three weeks or so, when we were having dinner, the postman came with a letter for Mother. As she took it, her face changed colour. 'It's from your father,' she said. My brother immediately put out his hand for it. 'Let me see!' Mother drew back her hand, saying: 'Wait till I've read it first,' and tore open the letter. I asked her: 'What does he have to say?' She replied: 'He says he's not too well, and wants to come back home to live.' My brother at once stretched out his hand and snatched the letter from her. When he'd finished reading it, he said nothing. He just put it into the flame of the lamp and set fire to it. Mother tried to snatch the letter back, but it was too late. She asked my brother agitatedly: 'Why did you burn it? His return address was on it!' My brother immediately became angry and shouted: 'Mother, do you mean you're still thinking of writing to invite him back? Well, if he comes back, then I'm moving out straight away. With him to run things at home, you won't need me in future.' Mother frowned, but all she said was: 'I was only asking. There's no need to get angry.' I couldn't contain my anger, and butted in to say: 'But we ought to reply to him!' My brother stared at me fixedly, and said: 'All right, you reply then.' But he'd already burned the letter. Even if I wrote a reply, where would I send it?

"One day, two or three weeks later, shortly after dark, Mother called to me to go and buy something. When I came back, I saw a dark shadow by the main gate and called out to ask who it was. The shadow replied: 'It's me.' 'Who are you?' I asked. The shadow came slowly up to me and whispered: 'Han'er, don't you even recognize my voice?' I saw Dad's thin face and cried out happily: 'Dad, I've been looking for you for so long. But I've never been able to find you.' Stroking my head,

he said: 'You've grown. Are your mother and brother well?' I
said: 'They're both fine. Mother got your letter.' 'Then why
wasn't there a reply?' Dad asked. I replied: 'My brother
burned the letter, and so we didn't know your address.' Dad
said: 'But your mother knew.' 'After the letter was burned,
Mother didn't know either. Mother always listens to what my
brother says,' I explained. Dad gave a long sigh: 'I thought
as much. In that case, there's no hope. I'd better go then.' I immediately seized him by the hand. It gave me a shock. His
hand was icy cold. He was shivering all over. I cried out: 'Dad,
your hand's so cold! Are you ill?' Shaking his head, he said:
'No.' I felt his sleeve. It was already the ninth moon of the
lunar calendar, but he was wearing only an unpadded silk jacket.
I said: 'You're wearing so few clothes. Aren't you cold?' 'I'm
not cold,' he said. I thought of a plan. Telling him to wait outside the gate, I hurried inside to tell Mother about Dad's condition. Mother took out one of my brother's long gowns, a woollen pull-over, and also 500 silver dollars. She told me to give
them to Dad, and to tell him that he wasn't to come again. She
said that she would never change her mind, and he should
have no illusions about it. She also said that, even if she
should change her mind, then my brother would definitely not
relent. I went out. He was still at the gate, waiting for me.
I gave him the money and the clothes, which I made him put
on at once. But I didn't tell him what Mother had said. He
talked to me for a while, then said he had to leave. I didn't
dare hold him back, but I wanted him to tell me where he was
staying so I would know where to find him. I said, no matter
how my brother treated him, I was still his son. The address
he gave me was the Temple of the Grand Immortal.

"Early next morning, I went to the temple, and indeed found
him there. He said he hadn't been there long. He'd moved
there just over a month before. He wouldn't say any more.
After that, I visited him often. Sometimes, I would take him
something. Of course, I didn't dare tell my brother. Mother
seemed to guess something, but she didn't try to interfere. I

told her only that I'd seen him, but I didn't tell her where he was living. But to Old Man Li I told everything. He wasn't far from where Dad was staying, so could sometimes go and see to his needs.

"From then on, I used to come to your mansion often." (The boy turned towards Mrs. Yao and smiled slightly, a little ill at ease. The tears on his face had not yet dried.) "Dad loved flowers. He could never forget the flower garden, and he often talked to me about it. I thought, the garden was originally ours, even if it was sold, and if I go to have a look and pick some flowers, it won't matter. I told Old Man Li what I thought and he let me in. The first time I came in, I didn't run into anyone. I picked a couple of chrysanthemums from the garden terrace and took them to Dad. He was overwhelmed with pleasure. After that, I came many times. Each time, I had a row with your servants. On two occasions, I also ran into Mr. Yao, and got a good scolding from him. Another time, I was beaten by Zhao Qingyun. To tell the truth, I really didn't want to come to your place again, but, when I thought of how happy Dad was when he saw the flowers, I felt I could put up with anything. I didn't care whether your servants beat me or swore at me. I wasn't a thief. I could fight back and shout back. I ran into you, Mrs Yao, only once, but you didn't chase me out. You treated me as a mother or a sister would have, and even picked a pussy willow branch for me. I'd never met anyone outside the family who'd spoken to me so kindly and so gently before. You two are the only ones. My uncles on my father's side and my cousins, all looked down on our branch of the family, and didn't want to have anything to do with us, as if afraid that the moment we saw them, we'd want to borrow money from them. Dad told me once that, not long before, he was walking along the street one day with his head down, when he was knocked down by a private rickshaw. The skin came off his face, and he was bleeding. It was Fourth Uncle's rickshaw. When the puller recognized Dad, he put down his rickshaw at once and ran to help him up. Dad had just got up when Fourth Uncle caught sight of his face and recognized him. He not only didn't greet him, but shouted at the puller for stopping. The puller had to pick up the rickshaw and go. Fourth Uncle spat, and the spittle landed directly on Dad. Dad told me about it afterwards.

"He also told me something else. One afternoon, at the back entrance of the market, he ran into 'Auntie' getting down from her private rickshaw. When she saw him and recognized who he was, she went over to speak to him. At first, he stood rooted to the spot, but when he heard her call out: 'Third Master!' he came to his senses, and immediately ran off. After that, he never saw her again. He said that he saw 'Auntie' two days before he saw Fourth Uncle. I also told him about the money 'Auntie' had sent. He sighed a couple of times, and said: 'To think that it's people like her who are more kind-hearted. . . .'"

After talking for so long, the boy suddenly stopped. He leant back in the armchair as if completely exhausted, covering his face with both hands. And all this time, we, Mrs. Yao and I, had been listening to him, our eyes fixed on him, holding our breath. Now we could relax. I felt my breathing become freer, and saw Mrs. Yao heave a deep sigh. Though she wiped her eyes with her handkerchief, I could see that the tension in her face had gone.

"My boy, I never realized that you had suffered so much. It's really hard. No one else could have endured it as you have," she said gently. The boy said nothing, and didn't take his hands from his face. After a moment, she continued: "What about your father? Is he still in the temple? Ask him to come over and have a chat." The boy's muffled sob could be heard under his hands. I shook my head at Mrs. Yao and whispered: "His father doesn't want to be a burden to him. He's run away."

"Can he be found?" she asked in a whisper.

"I don't think it's possible at the moment. He may even have left Chengdu. Since he's made up his mind to hide, it's not easy to find him," I answered.

Suddenly taking his hands from his face, the boy stood up. "I'm going," he said.

Mrs. Yao said at once: "Don't go. Stay a little longer. Have some more tea and something to eat."

"Thank you, but I'm full. I can't eat anything. I really must go," the boy said.

"I see you're tired. You've been talking without interruption for so long, you must have a rest," Mrs. Yao said with concern.

The boy sighed: "I'm not a bit tired. Now that I've told you all about it, I feel a lot better. These four years, I've recited all this to myself over and over again. I've told Old Man Li only part of it. Today, I've told you everything. . . . I really must go. Mother's waiting for me at home."

"Then from now on, you must come and visit us often. You must treat this as your own home," Mrs. Yao said earnestly.

"Yes, I will. I will. This is our old home!" the child cried, and went out through the wide-open glass doors.

28

"You must come! You must come!" Mrs. Yao cried, running to the door of the room, calling earnestly after the young boy.

"I don't think he'll come," I said, as I stood by her side. I had not heard the boy answer.

"Why not?" she asked, turning her face towards me, her eyes full of doubt.

"This place is full of such painful memories for him. If it were I, I wouldn't come," I replied, feeling a little out of sorts.

After thinking for a while, she said as if to herself, "But there must be many happy memories for him too. I really would like to give him back the garden." She sat down in the cane-chair in front of the desk.

I was amazed. Did she really have such an idea? "Give it back to him? He wouldn't want it. Besides, would Lao Yao be willing?"

She shook her head. "My husband wouldn't agree. In fact, he doesn't appreciate flowers. But I love this garden." After a while, she added: "I think the boy is very nice."

"He's suffered so much, and understands so much. A child as young as he is should have had a better life," I said.

"Only there aren't many people who have a good life. A great many people suffer. Mr. Li, do you think it's worthwhile for such suffering? How much longer will such suffering last?" She gazed at me with her large eyes, waiting sincerely for my reply.

"Who can tell?" I answered without thinking. But the sight of her sad and melancholy eyes made me alert once more. I could not answer her question, for I knew she did not want just empty words. All I could say to console her was: "Of course it's worthwhile. No one has ever suffered in vain. The end will come before long. In a year or two at the most, the war will be won."

A trace of a smile appeared on her lips. She nodded ever so slightly, then lifted up her eyes, but not towards me. What was she looking at so thoughtfully? She must be looking into the distant future. Scarcely opening her lips, she murmured softly: "I think so too. But winning the war is only one thing. We can't expect it to solve everything. But what can a woman like me do? All I can do is wait. I have to wait for everything. None of my ideas can ever be realized. Mr. Li, you really must look down on me." She turned her eyes towards me.

"But why, Mrs. Yao? Why should I look down on you?" I asked in surprise.

"I lock myself up in the house all day doing absolutely nothing. I don't housekeep properly for my husband. I don't look after Xiao Hu's education. Even if I want to, I can't do it properly. I'm completely useless. Yet he dotes on me. He believes in me, but he doesn't realize that I have this bitter pain. I can't talk to him about it much. . . ."

"Mrs. Yao, you mustn't judge yourself so harshly. If you're useless, then what am I? Aren't I also useless? Aren't I also

full of ideas that can't be realized?" I said sympathetically.
Her words made me uncomfortable. I wanted to console her,
but, for the moment, I couldn't think of the right words.

"Mr. Li, how can you compare yourself to me? You've written
so many books. How can you say that you're useless!" she
exclaimed in protest, but giving me a friendly look at the same
time.

"And what's the use of all those books? They're just empty
words!"

"You can't say they're empty words. I remember a novelist
saying that you were like doctors seeking to cure the human
spirit. At least, I've tried your medicine. It seems to me that
you have brought human hearts closer together and enabled
people to understand each other. You help others in their time
of need, consoling them in the midst of their suffering." Her
eyes shone with emotion, as if she were gazing at some distant
hope.

A warm current flooded into my heart. My whole body began
to tremble with joy. I wanted to believe what she said, but I
still differed with her, saying: "All we do is to make black
marks on paper, wasting our youth, wasting some people's time
and arousing other people's hatred. We can't even make a living
from our brush. Look at me, for instance. All I can do is to
live comfortably off you." I smiled, sneering at myself.

She changed at once to a tone of reproach: "Mr. Li," she
said, "you shouldn't talk like that to me. How can you say
you're living off us? You're our old friend. Besides, it's a great
honour for us to be able to look after a guest like you."

"Mrs. Yao, you criticize me for over-politeness, so please don't
use such a word as 'honour'," I interrupted.

"I'm just saying what I think," she said with a smile. But
her smile gradually faded. "I'm not flattering you in the least,
but, for many years now, your books have been like a teacher, a
friend to me. My mother is a kind-hearted but old-fashioned
old lady. My brother is an old-fashioned scholar. At school,
I never came across a good teacher. And since my marriage,

I've had no contact with the school friends of my youth. I have a lot of spare time in the Yao family. When my husband's out, I feel lonely and bored; there's nothing to do but read. I've read a lot of novels, in translation, in the original, other people's, yours. I've read them all. These books have opened up a new world for me. Before, the world I moved in was so tiny: just two families, a school, and a dozen or so streets. It's only now that I realize that there is such a huge universe around me. It's only now that I begin to know what others have in their hearts. It's only now that I understand what unhappiness and suffering mean. I also know what it means to live. Sometimes, I'm so happy that tears come into my eyes. Sometimes, I'm so upset that I burst into stupid laughter. But whether I laugh or cry, I always feel so much happier inside afterwards. Sympathy, love, mutual help: they're not just empty words. My heart beats together with those of other people. When others laugh, I too am happy. When others cry, I too am inwardly sad. I've seen so much unhappiness and suffering in this world. But I've seen even more love. I seem to hear in books grateful and satisfied laughter. My heart is constantly warmed as on a spring day. In the end, to live is such a beautiful thing. You've written something like that, I remember."

"What I said was: To live and work for one's ideals is a beautiful thing," I interrupted, correcting her.

She nodded and continued: "It's nearly the same thing. To live a happy life, to live a meaningful life, you must have ideals! A long time ago, I heard a preacher in a gospel hall. It was an English woman doctor speaking in Chinese. She quoted a sentence from the Bible: 'Sacrifice is the greatest happiness.' I never understood the meaning of this sentence before. It's only now that I understand. To help others, to give one's belongings to others, to bring laughter to those who weep, to satisfy the hungry, to give warmth to those who are cold: aren't the laughter and joy that result the best reward? Sometimes I think it would be much better to go out and be a nurse. In that way, I could help those who are so unfortunate as to be sick:

support this one by the arm, give something to that one, offer medicine to a third to ease his pain, comfort a fourth to dispel his loneliness."

"But you mustn't forget yourself through thinking of others," I interrupted for a second time with emotion.

"In what way am I forgetting myself? In fact, I'm enlarging myself. This is also what I read in a foreign novel. I can see myself in the laughter and tears of others. If only it were possible for me to be a part of others' happiness, a part of their daily life, a part of their thoughts and memories, how wonderful that would be!" The smile on her face sparkled, like the stars on an autumn night. As I listened to her, I thought to myself: "How beautiful!" And I thought also: "Is Lao Yao in this smile?" "Am I in this smile?" I felt in high spirits, as if I had been uplifted by her. My heart beat furiously. I gazed at her gratefully. The starry sky suddenly grew pale. Her tone of voice changed: "But I haven't been able to do anything. I'm like a bird that has been raised all its life in a cage. I want to fly, but I can't. Now I don't even dare to think of flying." At this point, she involuntarily looked down at her stomach, and her face at once reddened.

I did not know what I should say to console her. There was too much I wanted to say, and perhaps she understood better than I did. What she had just said still agitated my mind. As to "enlarging herself", she had already achieved that in me. Perhaps what she wanted was proof and some sympathy.

"Mr. Li, have you finished your novel?" she suddenly asked, turning to look towards my desk.

"Not yet. It's been very slow these last few days," I answered briefly. She had solved my difficulty. There was no need to say anything more.

She turned her head towards me, and, with a sympathetic look on her face, said to me anxiously: "You're too tired. If you write slowly, it'll be all the same."

"Actually, it's almost finished. There's just a little more to do. But these last few days, even when I pick up my brush, I haven't been able to write anything."

"Is it because of the Yang boy's troubles?" she asked.

"Probably," I answered. But I hid the real reason: Xiao Hu, or even more probably, herself.

"If you can't write, then you should simply rest for a while. Why be so hard on yourself?" she said in consolation. Then she turned once more to look at the manuscript piled up on the desk and said: "Do you think you could let me have a look at what you've written?"

"Of course you can. If you like, you can take it now. Just leave the last page behind," I said earnestly.

She stood up and smiled: "Then let me take it and have a look."

I went over and gave her the manuscript. She took it in her hands, and turned over a few pages. "I'll bring it back tomorrow," she said.

"Take your time, it doesn't matter. There's no need to hurry," I said politely.

She said good-bye and left. I stood on the low threshold, gazing at the silent garden. I gazed for a very long time.

29

In the evening, it rained. The monotonous sound of the rain from the eaves, penetrating drop by drop into my very heart, began to drive me mad. I sat there, staring into the vast empty room, not knowing how to ease my mind. I pulled out the screen to break up the immense space, so that the room seemed smaller, and sat quietly in the armchair beside the bed. The light of the electric lamp reflecting the colour of the screen bathed the room in a pale purplish light. Before me, I could see only sadness and desolation, but a voice in the distance seemed to be calling me — a joyful voice, a voice full of life. I glimpsed dimly that smile which illuminated everything. "Sacrifice is the greatest happiness." I seemed to hear that phrase again, hear once more that familiar voice. I waited, expectant. But the voice became silent, and the smiling face faded away. All that remained with me were the dim surroundings and the monotonous sound of the rain.

A mood of irritation seized me. I couldn't stand this quiet. I felt my heart beating wildly. My head began to throb with a dull pain, while the armchair became very uncomfortable. I got up from my chair and folded up the screen. I walked back and forth in the room for a long while, intending to go to bed when I had tired myself out.

But then I began to feel something rise gradually from the inner recesses of my mind. My head was afire. I felt as if my whole body were about to explode. I staggered to my desk, sat down in the chair, spread out before me the page of the manuscript that I had not yet given Mrs. Yao to take away, and then began to continue from where I had left off the previous day. The more I wrote, the faster I wrote. I wrote in a frenzy. The sweat poured down my forehead, but I went on writing without stopping. It was as if someone behind me were whipping me on, so that I could not put down my brush. Eventually, the old rickshaw puller whose leg had been injured so that he could no longer work, was jailed in the Yamen for committing a burglary. The blind woman, accompanied by the neighbour's little boy, came to visit him, and promised to wait for him to come out of prison to be reunited with him.

. . . .

"Six months. Six months pass quickly. They'll be over in a flash!" the old rickshaw puller thought happily. He still had not forgotten how the blind woman had turned to gaze at him with her unseeing eyes. He wanted to smile, but instead, tears streamed from his eyes.

. . . .

I wrote until two o'clock. The rain had still not stopped, but my work was finished.

I put down my brush. My eyes were painfully sore, and I couldn't keep them open any longer. I tottered over to my bed, and without undressing, without even turning off the light, I fell onto the bed and slept.

Early next morning, I was woken by Lao Yao.

"Lao Li, still not up! It's past six o'clock!" he cried with a laugh.

I forced my eyes open, but the room was too bright. My eyes had still not recovered, and I closed them again.

"Get up! Get up!" he urged, coming over to the bed. "Today's Sunday. We're going to visit the Temple of the Marquis of Wu. Zhaohua's going too. She'll be dressed soon."

I opened my eyes again. "It's still early!" I said, rubbing my eyes. "What time are we going?"

"We're going now! Get up, quickly!" he replied. "What! Your eyes are all swollen. You must have gone to bed late again last night. No wonder you didn't even turn out the light. I was talking to Zhaohua about you just now. It seems to us that the way you neglect yourself is no good at all. You don't look too well. You should go to bed earlier at night. In fact, you ought to get married." He began to laugh.

"I've finished my novel. I won't be staying up all night from now on, so you can stop worrying and forget about getting me married," I replied, laughing.

"You'll soon be forty. Even if you're not worried, you ought to be," my friend replied jokingly. But his tone of voice changed immediately as he asked me: "Is your novel finished then?"

"Yes, completely!" I got up.

"I must read what you've written. I forgot to tell you. Last night, when Zhaohua was reading your novel, she cried. She's waiting to read the rest. She never thought you'd finish it so soon. Give me what you've written and I'll take it to her. What happens to the rickshaw puller and the blind woman in the end? Do they both kick the bucket? It seems to me your novels all end like that. That's something I don't approve of. First of all, the trifling events that happen to trivial people, and second, the tragedy. Those two things are not to my taste. But I admire your talent. I myself have one big defect. Big ideas, but little ability! I don't have any talent in that direction. Always boasting, but never getting anywhere."

"Stop making fun of me. How can you admire what I've written? I never thought it would make your wife cry. You can take the rest of the manuscript. And tell her to take her time reading it before giving it back." I went to the writing desk, took the pile of manuscript from the table and handed it to him.

"All right, I'll give it to her." He saw Lao Wen bring in the water for me to wash my face, and added: "I'll go now. I'll be back after you've had a wash and breakfast."

After half an hour or so, he came back into the garden with his wife. I was walking along the patch of ground below the garden terrace. The colour in her face had improved since the previous day. Perhaps it was because today she was wearing make-up. Her air of illness had vanished completely. On her face shone a smile that was brighter than the sun. On top of her pale green cheongsam, so pale that it appeared almost white, printed with tiny dark-green flowers, she wore a grey puff-sleeved woollen jacket.

"Mr. Li, I'm so sorry that Lao Yao woke you up this morning. We didn't know that you'd been working on your novel all night. You can't have had much sleep," she said with a smile.

"Not at all. I had enough sleep. If he hadn't come, I would have got up anyway," I protested politely.

"Lao Li, you're obviously being polite. I had to keep calling you many times before you woke! You were fast asleep," Lao Yao laughed as he stood beside her.

I couldn't argue. I knew that I was looking a bit embarrassed. I saw her give a light smile to her husband as she said: "Let's go! Unless there's something Mr. Li wants to do."

"I'm ready," I said at once. "Let's go!"

Three rickshaws were waiting for us outside the second gate. As usual, I took the one rented from outside. My puller could not run as fast as theirs, so after we had gone along six or seven streets, we fell behind. I saw their rickshaws disappear into another street. Later, we caught up to them again. Mrs. Yao's thick hair, gleaming in the sunshine, appeared before me once more. Lao Yao had just turned his head towards her, speaking to her in his loud voice. Although I could not hear what he was saying, there was no mistaking his air of satisfaction.

Just as we were about to leave the city, my rickshaw dropped back more than half-way down the street again. This slow rickshaw of mine had just reached the intersection when its path was blocked by a group of coolies in short coarse jackets. They were coming from outside the city in pairs, carrying big slabs of stone. They passed in succession directly in front of me. There were about thirty of them. There were also three or four men in uniform, with rifles on their backs and whips in their hands, driving the coolies forward. Their heads were close-shaven except for a tuft of hair left on the top, and their clothes were filthy. They were barefoot, not even wearing straw sandals. I sat in the rickshaw paying no attention as they filed past me. They all seemed to be about the same age, with the same sort of features: sunken eyes, hollow cheeks and greyish faces; walking with their heads down, their backs hunched, their foreheads streaming with sweat. They went past in silence. My eyes strayed by chance onto one face in their midst, and stayed there. I cried out in astonishment. Although my cry had been weak, the face turned back to look in my direction. He was supporting the front end of a carrying-pole. He stood still and raised his head slightly to look at me. It was the same refined face, only thinner, dirtier, and even more ill. In that instant as he looked at me, a faint gleam appeared in his eyes, only to flicker out immediately. His lips trembled as if he wanted to speak to me, but no words came. He just raised his right hand slightly. The fingers of his dry withered hand were covered in sores, some of which were already festering, and with them he scratched his left hand which was resting on the pole. As he did so, I felt my whole body begin to itch.

"Get moving! What the hell do you think you're up to!" a rough voice cursed from the side, and a whip struck him across the face. He gave a cry of pain. The blood was about to burst from the red welt which opened from the base of his ear to the corner of his mouth. He quickly covered the wound with his hand. Tears sprang from his half-dead eyes, but without wiping them away, he lowered his head and continued slowly on.

"Mr. . . ." It was the only word I could get out. Pain blocked my throat like a stone. Only after a desperate struggle was I able to cry out: "Mr. Yang!"

But he had already gone past. He turned back to give me a hurried glance. Then he went on without a single word. I wanted to get down from the rickshaw and drag him back. But it was only a momentary thought. I did nothing. I just let my rickshaw man pull me across the intersection.

30

When my rickshaw arrived at the Temple of the Marquis of Wu, Mr. and Mrs. Yao were waiting for me at the main gate.

"How is it you're so late! We've been waiting for ages," Lao Yao exclaimed laughingly.

"I ran into someone I knew," I replied simply. He did not ask who it was. Just as I was hesitating, wondering whether or not to tell his wife about having seen Yang Mengchi, I heard her say to Lao Yao: "We must tell our own rickshaw puller, next time he should pick a faster one for Mr. Li." The shaven head and face of Yang Mengchi appeared for an instant before my eyes. I thought to myself, it was lucky the puller had been slow, or I would never have run into Yang Mengchi.

I now knew what had happened to the father. But could I tell his son this news? Could I get him out? Even if I could, where would I arrange for him to stay afterwards?

Just as we were about to leave the city, my rickshaw dropped back more than half-way down the street again and had just reached the intersection when its path was blocked by a group of coolies in short, coarse jackets.

And would he be able to turn over a new leaf? As we went into the temple, these questions preyed on my mind. As we walked along the path, the scenery on both sides flashed past me without making any impression on me. We turned into a long quiet gallery, enclosed by a wall on one side, and opening onto a lotus pond on the other. We sat by a tea table near the railing.

The sun had not yet reached the pond, but the green umbrella-like leaves of the lotuses had already spread all over it. The fresh morning air filled the whole gallery. There were only the three of us at the tables placed there. It was so silent all around. Only the shrill chirruping of the birds in the tall trees outside the wall could be heard. The waiter came lazily over, his cloth over his arm. When we ordered our tea from him, he gave the table a quick wipe before ambling off. A few minutes later, he brought the teacups. A feeling of peace and calm gradually pervaded my whole body. I lay back in the bamboo chair and dozed off.

"Look, Lao Li's having a snooze." I heard Lao Yao's chuckle. I did not bother to open my eyes. He seemed to be speaking from a long way off.

"Let him sleep for a while. Don't wake him," I heard Mrs. Yao whisper in reply. "He must be very tired after writing so much last night."

"Actually, he could easily write in the daytime. Writing so much at night is not good for his health. I've told him, but he doesn't listen to me," Lao Yao said.

"It's probably a bit quieter at night. It's easier to think. I've heard that when foreigners write novels, it's usually at night too. They often stay up all night," Mrs. Yao went on. Her voice was so low that I could scarcely make it out. "But now that the novel's finished, he ought to have a good rest." Suddenly, she asked: "He's not going away soon, is he?"

My sleepiness had been driven away by their conversation, but I had to keep on pretending to be asleep, not daring to move.

"Go away? Where would he go? Have you heard him say anything about it?" Lao Yao asked in surprise.

"No. Only, I thought that since he's finished his book, we can't be sure he won't go. We must persuade him to stay another few months. If he leaves, his life's not going to be too comfortable. He doesn't look after himself much. Both Lao Wen and Mrs. Zhou say that he's easy to get on with. Since he's been staying with us, he's never demanded anything from them. He just makes use of whatever they happen to bring him," Mrs. Yao said.

"People used to living away from home are all like that. I like people like that!" Lao Yao gave a chuckle.

"You've travelled about a good bit too. How is it you're not like that?" Mrs. Yao laughed lightly.

"I'm a special case. It runs in the family. Xiao Hu's like that too!" Lao Yao said boastfully.

For a moment, Mrs. Yao said nothing. Then she continued: "Xiao Hu really is like you, but he's changed these last couple of years. If the Zhaos are allowed to keep on spoiling him, I'm afraid he's going to be difficult to manage in the future. I'm only his stepmother, and the Zhao family doesn't approve of me, so there's not much I can do. It's you who ought to teach him what's right."

"I know what you mean. But he's the son of Mrs. Zhao's daughter. She dotes on him. I can't very well interfere. In any case, Xiao Hu's still young. He can easily change. In another couple of years, it won't matter," Lao Yao replied.

"Actually, he's not that young. . . . Let's forget about other things, but the Zhaos always stop him from studying properly. They just teach him about gambling and the theatre. That's not really very good. Besides, there are the end-of-term exams. Do you think we should send someone to fetch him back this evening?" Mrs. Yao asked.

"I don't think it's any use sending anyone. I'd better go myself. But you know what Xiao Hu's grandmother's like.

You can't reason with her. All you can do is plead with her,"
Lao Yao said.

"I know we're in a difficult situation, but Xiao Hu's your
only son. We ought to think about his future," Mrs. Yao said.

"You're wrong there! Xiao Hu isn't my only son now. I've
also got. . . ." He laughed contentedly.

"Sh!" She shut him up softly. "Don't talk so loud. Mr. Li's
here. I'm talking seriously, and you start joking."

"All right, I'll shut up. If we go on, it'll seem as if we
came here especially to have a row. If Lao Li hears us,
when he's writing about the trivial doings of insignificant people, he'll put us into it, and that would be terrible!" Lao Yao
said, purposely making fun of her.

"But you're not an insignificant person! Don't worry. He
won't write about a great man like you," said, Mrs. Yao,
laughing.

I couldn't keep up the pretence any longer. I coughed
slightly, and slowly opened my eyes.

"Did you have a good sleep, Mr. Li? Did we wake you up?"
she asked kindly.

I denied it at once.

"We were just talking about you when you woke. It's
lucky we weren't saying anything nasty about you," Lao Yao
went on.

"I believe you. You wouldn't come to the temple just to
say nasty things about me," I said, laughing at my own rejoinder.

"Lao Li, would you like to go to the main hall of the temple and draw one of the divination slips to see what the future
has in store for you?" Lao Li asked, with a laugh.

"I've no need to. It's you that should go with Mrs. Yao to
try your luck," I said jokingly.

"All right, let's go and try our luck," Lao Yao said to his
wife. He got up and went over behind his wife's chair.

"I'm not interested. I'm not going," his wife said, shaking
her head in embarrassment.

"It's just a game! Don't take it so seriously.   Come on! Let's go!" He continued to urge her to get up.

"It's all right.   I'll stay here and mind the table. You two go.   Since Lao Yao wants to go, you should go with him, Mrs. Yao," I said, joining in on Lao Yao's side to please him.

Mrs. Yao smiled and slowly got up. Turning to her husband, she said: "I'm going only to keep you company," and to me, she added: "Then would you mind waiting here for a moment? You'll be able to have a good sleep." She laughed, picked up her handbag and left, taking her husband by the arm.

By this time, two customers had settled down behind me three tables away.   They were young students, each engrossed in a book.   The sun rose slowly over the pond.   In the eaves opposite, the sparrows were chirping away in conversation.   A quiet air of tranquillity and ease fell over the area.   I was about to close my eyes, when suddenly, a couple of sight-seers walking along the corridor opposite caught my eye.   My fatigue vanished at once.   I looked at them carefully.   The first one I recognized as the Yang boy.   He was wearing his brown school uniform.   Next, I saw his brother, and then, walking behind them, his mother accompanied by a young girl, who was in conversation with Mrs. Yang. The two of them were facing the pool. Suddenly, Mrs. Yang laughed, and the girl laughed in reply.   The two young men in front stopped for a moment, turned and said something to the girl.   Then they laughed too.

Their laughter drifted over to my ears.   I thought I must be dreaming.   Had I not just seen the husband and father? Had I not seen the stroke of the whip with my own eyes? Yet now I was listening to this happy laughter.   They knew absolutely nothing.   They were so close to this man who was carrying the stones, and yet they seemed to be living in another world. I did not know whether they retained any memory of the past, but in my eyes, the love and hatred of the past were linked into a single chain that bound them to that man.   I was a stranger, but I could not forget this bond of theirs.   Yet I knew that I had no right to judge them. Nevertheless, their laughter was repugnant to me. They were coming towards me. The closer they came, the more displeased I felt. I saw the boy's brother accompany the girl through the small gate and go outside. The boy and his mother then turned into the gallery where I was, the boy leading the way. He had recognized me from a distance and, waving to me with a smile, came up to my table to greet me politely: "Mr. Li."

"Are you visiting the temple with your mother?" I smiled as I spoke, for the moment I saw the honesty and goodness in his face, my displeasure faded gradually away.

"Yes. My brother's here too, and my cousin." He smiled as he replied, and then turned and went over to his mother and whispered something to her. She looked towards me, and let him lead her over to me by the arm and introduce her to me: "This is my mother."

I stood up to greet her. She smiled as she nodded in acknowledgement, begging me to sit down. But I remained standing. "Han'er tells me," she continued, "that you've often been of great help to him and given him a lot of good advice, Mr. Li. I really must express my thanks to you."

"You're being much too polite, Mrs. Yang. When have I ever helped him, let alone given him advice?" I answered modestly. "Your son really is a very nice boy. I like him very much." The boy beside me watched me, smiling.

"Mr. Li, you don't know how disobedient he really is," she answered politely, and turning towards her son, she said: "Did you hear? Mr. Li has been praising you to the skies, so you'd better not be naughty in future." Then she turned to me once more: "Please do sit down, Mr. Li. Don't let me disturb you." She smiled, nodded to me again, and then went off with her son.

The boy turned once more to call to me: "See you again, Mr. Li."

I sat down. The image of the mother's face remained with me. An oval regular face with nothing special about it. Not pretty, but her lips formed constantly into a pleasing smile. Her face was lightly powdered, and her thick abundant hair was tied back into a bun. She was wearing a short-sleeved coffee-coloured cheongsam. From her appearance, she seemed to be in her early thirties. In fact, she was over forty. She was moreover a kind and amiable person.

Was it possible? Could the boy's story be true? Was this the woman who had let her elder son drive his father from home? Doubts began to invade my mind. I turned round to look at them. The mother and son had just sat down at the table behind the students. The mother was smiling affectionately at her son. She did not seem at all like a cruel woman.

"Lao Li, marvellous! We picked the best slip!" Lao Yao's voice made me turn with a start. He was coming towards me with his wife, his face beaming. He was only a few steps from the table.

"Where is it? Let me see," I said.

"She's a bit shy, so she's torn it up," Lao Yao said, chuckling contentedly.

"It wasn't important." She blushed as she smiled.

I did not like to ask further. At that moment, the boy's brother came in with the girl. I said to Mrs. Yao: "The Yang boy's brother is here. That's his cousin."

Mrs. Yao looked up, following the direction of my gaze. Lao Yao also turned to look at the pair.

The girl was wearing a pink cheongsam. Her hair was tied behind in two plaits. Her round face was not exactly pretty, but it wasn't ugly either. She could only have been seventeen or eighteen. Her eyes and her lips bore a natural expression. She didn't avoid our gaze, but walked past us with a light step, her face radiant with smiles.

"The two brothers are really alike. The elder one is fairer and more neatly dressed. But he doesn't seem a terrible person," Mrs. Yao whispered to me. "How can he have been so cruel to his father? It's really hard to believe."

"You can't judge by appearances," Lao Yao interrupted.

"Actually, his father was such a good-for-nothing. No wonder he. . . ." I knew from this that Mrs. Yao had already told her husband the young boy's story.

"The cousin's not bad. You can tell at once that she's an honest and nice person. Where's the younger brother?" Mrs. Yao went on to ask.

"At the table over there. His mother's there too," I replied, indicating behind me by a slight toss of the head.

"Yes, I see," she said, nodding slightly. "His mother has a nice kind face." She took a couple of sips of tea, and put the teacup back on the table. She looked again towards their table. After a few minutes, she turned back and said: "They're a very affectionate family. They're so amiable, and seem so easy to get on with. How can such a thing have happened? Can there be some other reason?"

"I've told you, you can't tell from appearances," Lao Yao said. "When judging people, you mustn't go by what they look like. But even judging from the outside, how can you compare the boy with Xiao Hu?"

Mrs. Yao said nothing. I too remained silent. I nearly began disparaging Xiao Hu, but managed with great effort to stifle the words. I bit my lip and turned once more towards the Yang's table.

My feelings had already begun to change. They now changed even further. I thought: What right have I to resent the laughter and happiness of these people? Why shouldn't they laugh? Am I a judge that I can proclaim, "I have the right to revenge!" And must I therefore snatch from them even this tiny drop of happiness left to them?

The intermittent laughter at their table continued to drift over to us. It was the same happy laughter, but now it no longer pierced my heart. Why should I not be happy like other people? Why should I not allow others to be happy? Had I forgotten this one thing: The sound of happy laughter has already gradually become something to be treasured?

No one guessed my mood, for I talked to Lao Yao and his

wife of other things.　In fact, we didn't converse much, because
Lao Yao liked to talk about Xiao Hu, but whenever I heard him
praising Xiao Hu, I felt angry.

At about eleven o'clock, we made a move to the restaurant in
the temple for lunch.　The boy was going out too, and came
past our table.　Just as we stood up, he suddenly came over
to greet Mrs. Yao, and then, pulling me aside by the arm, went
a few steps with me.　He asked me in a whisper, but very
gravely: "Have you had any news of my father?"

I hesitated for a moment.　The words almost sprang from my
lips, and I had to choke them back.　But I very quickly made
up my mind how to answer him.　I shook my head, and said
very calmly: "No." I said it clearly and firmly, without any
feeling that I was lying.

The boy went out with us.　Mr. and Mrs. Yao walked in
front, with myself and the boy following behind.　The boy
remained silent, saying nothing at all.　I knew that he was still
thinking about his father.　He saw us to the door of the restaurant.　When he said good-bye to me, he suddenly leaned
forward and whispered to me, as if telling me an important
piece of news: "Mr. Li, I forgot to tell you some good news.
My cousin is in fact my future sister-in-law.　They were engaged
last week."

A smile flickered over his face, and without waiting for me
to answer, he turned and ran off.

I stood at the door, watching him disappear.　His footsteps
were so light, as if he had never known suffering or sorrow in
this world.　This "good news" had clearly made him happy.

As I thought about this, his cousin's round face appeared
before me for an instant.　It was a young face, set with a pair
of innocent bright eyes, a face not yet deeply stamped with the
experience of life.　I ought to be happy for the boy.　Yes,
indeed.　Didn't he deserve to be happy?

"Lao Li, what are you standing at the door for?" Lao Yao
shouted from inside.

I turned with a start. After I sat down at the table, I told them about the "good news" the boy had given me.

"The girl's really not bad. From all appearances, they'll make a very harmonious family. There are not many families that can say as much. I think they're very lucky to have someone like the elder brother who can support the whole family on his own," Mrs Yao said, her face radiant with happiness.

31

After we arrived home that day, I finally told Mr and Mrs Yao about having seen Yang Mengchi.

They expressed their sympathy and sighed. Then both proposed that we try to find some way of freeing him. Lao Yao said rather self-importantly that he had a way. He knew the place, and someone he knew well even worked there. His wife was the first to encourage him, and I for my part also urged him to do something. For the moment, he was happy, and called for his rickshaw to be prepared immediately so that he could go and see someone about what was to be done. He said it was a "sure thing" that he would find a solution.

After Lao Yao left, his wife talked to me for a while. In her view, once we got him released, we would have to arrange a "quiet and settled" life for him. I proposed that we first send him to hospital, and she said that once out of hospital, her husband could find him a suitable job. Later, when he had been cured of his bad habits, we could find some way of re-uniting him with his family. We were just dreaming, but we didn't know that we were dreaming. We had too much faith in Lao Yao's "sure thing".

That evening, I waited for Lao Yao to tell me the result of his enquiries. But by ten o'clock, I was still listening for the sound of his footsteps. Fatigue began to overcome me. Mosquitoes buzzed all around me, and for the first time that year, I noticed what a nuisance they were. I also saw a fly dancing about under the lamp. My power of resistance failed me, and I took refuge beneath the mosquito net.

That night, I slept without dreams. The next morning, I woke up very late. No one came to disturb me. I had been up a long time before Lao Wen came in with the water.

From Lao Wen, I heard that my friend had come home very late, and moreover had quarrelled with Mrs. Yao over Xiao Hu, and that he had left by rickshaw very early in the morning.

"It's not Mrs. Yao's fault. Master. Hu spends all day gambling at the Zhao's and all night at the theatre. He doesn't go to school, and refuses to let anyone fetch him. Naturally, Mrs. Yao doesn't like it, but Mr. Yao isn't at all concerned. Mrs. Yao sent someone to fetch him, and after two days, they still hadn't brought him home. Mr. Yao said that he'd go and fetch him himself, but instead, he went to the theatre with old Mrs. Zhao and Master Hu, and afterwards, he came home by himself. Mrs. Yao asked him a few questions, and Mr. Yao flew into a rage and made Mrs. Yao cry." Lao Wen related all this to me toothlessly in an indignant voice, while staring at me in vexation.

"And how is Mrs. Yao?" I asked with concern.

"She probably isn't up yet. But this morning, when Mr. Yao went out, he didn't seem to be angry anymore. It's probably all right now. It was Mrs. Zhou who told me."

Not long after I had finished breakfast, Mrs. Zhou came to collect the dishes, and also brought back the complete manuscript of my novel. She said: "It's from Mrs. Yao. She asked me to give it to you and to thank you for it."

Mrs. Yao had bound it together for me, and moreover, had added stiff white covers to the back and the front. It was I who should have thanked her. I told Mrs. Zhou this, and asked her to convey my thanks to her mistress. I also asked Mrs. Zhou about the quarrel. Her story was about the same as Lao Wen's, but in a bit more detail. It had not been a very bad quarrel. They had made up before long. As soon as Mr. Yao had said a few kind words, Mrs. Yao had stopped crying, and had given in. Mr. Yao's going out so early in the morning was on some other business altogether.

Like Lao Wen, Mrs. Zhou knew nothing about the Yang family's affairs. I could not find out from her the result of Lao Yao's rushing about the previous day. But I guessed. The other business Mrs. Zhou mentioned was probably the business of Yang Mengchi. From all appearances, Mrs. Yao was not likely to come to the garden today. I would just have to wait patiently for Lao Yao to return.

It was not until three in the afternoon that Lao Yao finally came to see me.

"Ah, it's no good, no good. There's nothing we can do." As soon as he came in, he shook his head, with an expression of weariness on his face I had never seen before. He came over and collapsed into the armchair.

"You must have found out where he is. Even if it takes a while for us to think of something, it'll be the same," I said.

"But that's just it! I haven't found out where he is! I found the place, but I can't find anyone by the name of Yang. There's absolutely no one there called Yang. If I could find the man, then I could definitely do something."

I looked at his face. I found it strange that that constant free and easy smile of his should have disappeared. I was filled with disappointment, and said: "Perhaps they're purposely trying to get out of it."

"No, it's not possible." He shook his head. "That friend of mine went together with me. They wouldn't dare lie just to get rid of me." He stopped for a moment, raised his hand to scratch the side of his head, and then muttered: "Maybe he's using a false name."

I nodded. "That's quite possible," I said. An idea flashed through my mind. "That's it. It must be that. He's done something he's afraid will disgrace his family, and so has changed his name on purpose. Then we can't be sure that even if we do recognize him, he wouldn't deny that he's Yang Mengchi."

"Then it won't be easy," Lao Yao said. He pulled out a

cigarette case, lit a cigarette, and as he drew on it, fell back into his armchair. As I watched him blowing smoke rings one after another, I thought of his quarrel with his wife. I decided to say something, but I did not know how to begin. After a few minutes, he bent over slightly and said: "There's another thing I can do. You write me a detailed description of him, and in a couple of days, I'll find a way of going there personally and having a look. As long as we find the man himself, it doesn't matter whether he denies it or not. But let's get him out first. Or perhaps I'll get you to come and have a look. You're sure to be able to recognize him."

It was a marvellous idea. I let out a sigh of relief. I felt as if I had just glimpsed a wide road from the top of a steep mountain path. I described Yang Mengchi's face to him in detail relying on my memory. He listened very carefully, as if he were recording every one of my words on his mind.

After we stopped talking about Yang Mengchi, we both felt rather tired. We sat quietly for a while. Suddenly Lao Yao got up and walked about the room for a moment. He looked at me sadly: "Lao Li, I quarrelled with Zhaohua yesterday," he said as he strode towards me.

"What about? It's the first time I've ever heard of your quarrelling." I pretended to be surprised, although I already knew the reason in fact.

He came over and stood before me, scratching his head. He said with a frown: "It was about Xiao Hu again. I went to the Zhaos' to fetch him yesterday, but didn't bring him home. His grandmother wanted him to stay a few more days. Zhaohua thought I was being too lenient with Xiao Hu and complained about me. And so we quarrelled. Later, I gave in, and so nothing came of it. In fact, she misunderstands me. It wasn't that I refused to bring Xiao Hu home. I couldn't get past his grandmother. People with money have a strange temperament. Besides, he's her daughter's only son. So you see, what can I do?"

He threw open his arms as if imploring me to help. But I said nothing, for I did not like his attitude.

He went back to his armchair and sat down as before. "I didn't sleep well the whole night," he went on. "The more I thought about it, the more upset I was. This is the first time we've quarrelled. We've been married for over three years, and we've never quarrelled before. Now we've begun, it's hard to know what will happen in future. Last night, it was my fault. I started it." He took out another cigarette, lit it and drew on it several times.

I was at the end of my patience. I said: "Really, it's your own fault! You simply shouldn't let the Zhaos ruin Xiao Hu in this way. Xiao Hu's your own son. . . ."

"You can't say that the Zhaos are ruining him. They love him even more than I do," he interrupted to object. He threw his cigarette to the floor and crushed it with his foot.

I began to get angry. This time it was my turn to stand before him and speak. I waved my arms and shouted: "You say you're not ruining him! Just think! What sort of upbringing is Xiao Hu getting at the Zhaos'? Gambling, going to the theatre, showing off one's wealth, playing truant. . . . In short, nothing that's good. Do you think that since the Zhaos have money now, they'll always have money? That they'll always be able to look on while others can't even get enough to eat, while they themselves do nothing but buy fields year after year? That their sons, grandsons, great-grandsons, and great-great-grandsons will always have money, will always be able to gamble, go to the theatre, and eat and sleep to their hearts' content? Do you think that for human beings, money is for eating, money is for sleeping, and that we should take money as our mother and father, embrace it and suckle on it all our lives?" I felt myself going red in the face.

"Don't go on, don't go on," Lao Yao waved his hand and said. "You've got me all wrong too. I've never thought about money."

My anger was still not dissipated. I said obstinately: "I

haven't got you wrong at all. Last time I spoke to you, you told me perfectly clearly, that it wasn't as if you didn't have money, that there was no need to worry about Xiao Hu's love of gambling and lack of diligence. Actually, as far as gambling is concerned, it can destroy a kingdom, let alone a family like yours with less than two hundred acres of land. We're old friends. I have to speak up to tell you what I think. The Yangs were once a rich family in this area, but where's Yang Mengchi now?"

"Don't go on. Don't go on." He kept waving his hand as he spoke. He wasn't angry with me, nor would he defend himself. He just lay dejectedly in the armchair.

I had no sympathy for him. I continued to press him with my words. "You ought to think of your wife," I said. "If you behave in this way, what chance has she of being a good stepmother? You should have thought of Mrs. Zhou's character beforehand, and then you wouldn't have remarried. But since you have, you shouldn't just think of Mrs. Zhao. I'm afraid that because of Mrs. Zhao, destroying your own happiness is not going to be enough; you're going to destroy your wife's happiness as well." I thought only of how pleased I was with my own speech, and did not give a thought to his pain. Only when I saw him cover his eyes with his left hand did I stop talking.

After that, we said no more. He took his hand from his eyes, finished his cigarette, said good-bye and left.

The same day, just as I'd finished my evening meal, Lao Yao suddenly came and asked me to go to the cinema. I knew he was going with his wife. I thought, since he and his wife had just quarrelled, I ought to let them have more time together alone, and not get between them to hinder them, so I found a pretext to refuse. I asked him off-hand what film he was going to. He said it was "My Undutiful Son". I was happily surprised. I'd seen the film. It was already quite old, but for them it was new. Moreover, it would be a lesson for Lao Yao, and perhaps be even more effective than my own exhortations. I saw them both off to their rickshaws. Mrs. Yao smiled at

me quietly and happily in her usual way. Lao Yao had a contented look on his face. His previous tiredness had already
vanished.

I hoped that they would live their days in harmony forever.

32

The next day, Lao Yao came to see me before lunch. He was
full of enthusiasm in his praise for the previous night's film.
He'd been moved, and there was no doubt that he had also
drawn a lesson from it. He even went so far as to tell me that
from now on, he was going to make sure that Xiao Hu was
properly brought up.

I smiled with satisfaction. I was convinced that he would do
as he said.

"Did Xiao Hu come back yesterday?" I took the opportunity
to ask.

"No. Zhaohua and I came back too late yesterday, and so
there wasn't time to send anyone to fetch him. But I'll definitely
fetch him back today," Lao Yao replied, laughing and full of
confidence.

Lao Yao had not been talking big. Early next morning, when
Lao Wen came with the water for my wash, he told me that
Master Hu had returned the previous evening, and was now at
school. Later he added that Master Hu had not wanted to get
up in the morning, but Mr. Yao had dragged him out of bed.
Mr. Yao had almost lost his temper, so Master Hu had had
no choice but to get into the rickshaw without a word and be
taken to school.

This news made me very happy. A great burden seemed lifted
from my mind. After I had had my wash, I went into the garden for a stroll as usual, and shortly after breakfast, I began
work.

I was putting the finishing touches to my novel. I had plan-
ned to finish it in three weeks or so, and had never imagined

that I would have to spend so long on it. I had almost broken my word to the old writer. He had already written to me twice, pressing me for the manuscript. I decided to send it to him within the week.

The work of putting the novel into order went fairly smoothly. By the time Lao Yao and his wife came to the garden in the afternoon, I had already finished going through a fifth of the manuscript.

They were going to Mrs. Yao's mother's. The rickshaws were waiting, and they had come to talk to me in passing. But perhaps there was an ulterior motive: to let me see how well they were getting on together again. The weather had suddenly become very hot in the afternoon. The husband was attired in a long gown of white linen, while Mrs. Yao was wearing a sky-blue cheongsam of English linen. Both their faces expressed happiness.

"Thank you, Mr. Li," Mrs. Yao said, smiling when she saw the manuscript lying open on the desk. "I like the way you've changed the ending."

"It's for me to thank you, Mrs. Yao. It was you who saved them," I replied contentedly.

"In fact, this novel of yours should be called *Garden of Repose*, since you wrote it here in our 'Garden of Repose', "Lao Yao interrupted from beside her.

"Yes, that's right," Mrs. Yao agreed. "Mr. Li can use this title as a reminder of his stay. In the book, there's a teashop where the blind woman used to sing. The rickshaw puller used to wait for customers at the door of the teashop every day. Sometimes he would see the blind woman going in, and sometimes coming out. Once he even gave her a ride. It was there they got to know each other. Later, the blind woman's voice deteriorated, so she couldn't sing in the teashop anymore. There was a garden in the teashop. Mr. Li called it the 'Garden of Light'. If he decides to change it, it would be nice to call it the 'Garden of Repose' instead." This speech was delivered to her husband, but she also intended that I hear it.

When I heard her talking with such familiarity about my novel, I was extremely pleased, and was ready to do this small thing she had suggested.

"That's right, that's right! Calling the teashop 'Garden of Repose' is perfect! In any case, no one's going to come to our place for tea. Lao Li, what do you think?" Lao Yao asked in high spirits.

I agreed to their suggestion, adding also: "Since you don't mind, what should I be afraid of?" I picked up my brush and at once wrote the characters "Garden of Repose" on the cover.

When they left, I saw them out. The two new pots of gardenias on the green porcelain stands below the balustrade were just beginning to blossom. A heavy fragrance filled my nostrils. We stood for a moment before the balustrade.

"Mr. Li, please don't go out the day after tomorrow. Spend the Dragon Boat Festival at home with us," Mrs. Yao said, turning towards me slightly.

I smiled in reply.

"Oh, I forgot to tell you," Lao Yao cried suddenly, slapping me on the shoulder. "Yesterday, I met that friend of mine. I've arranged it all with him. We'll settle the matter of Yang Mengchi after the festival. He's not only agreed to go with me, but will see someone in charge and smooth things over first. I think it's seventy or eighty percent resolved."

"That's excellent. When everything's settled, and Yang Mengchi's health has recovered, and we've found him a fixed job, then we can let his family know. At least his younger son will be very happy. Only I'm still a bit worried about how long it'll take for him to correct his bad habits," I said, smiling.

"Don't worry. After he comes out, you can leave everything to me," Lao Yao said, waving his hand contentedly.

"Mr. Li, are there many mosquitoes in your room?" Mrs. Yao interrupted. "I told Lao Wen yesterday to buy some mosquito coils. Has he lit them for you?"

"No, there aren't many mosquitoes. It's all right without the coils. Besides, there are the window screens," I replied politely.

"That's no good," Lao Yao exclaimed. "The window screens aren't enough. You must have the coils lit. Lao Wen must have forgotten. I'll tell him again later."

When we came out of the garden, we saw the rickshaws waiting at the second gate. Lao Wen was standing in the courtyard talking to the pullers. Before getting into the rickshaw, Mrs. Yao spoke to Lao Wen about the mosquito coils. I heard Lao Wen admit that he had forgotten about them. An apologetic smile appeared on his wrinkled face, but no one reprimanded him.

When I went back to the garden, my mind was calm. I read the part of the manuscript I had corrected that morning once again from the beginning and, following Mr. and Mrs. Yao's suggestion, changed the name of the teahouse to the "Garden of Repose".

I worked right through till it was dark, but didn't feel at all tired. Then Lao Wen brought the mosquito coils. I didn't like the smell but let him light one and put it in a corner of the room. I shut the door. The screens stopped the mosquitoes from flying in. The room was very quiet and comfortable. I turned on the light, and continued working without a break until three o'clock in the morning when I finished reading the whole manuscript.

After I fell asleep, I had a series of strange dreams. I dreamed I was a rickshaw puller taking Mrs. Yao to the cinema. But when we reached the cinema and I put down the rickshaw, the occupant had changed into the Yang boy, and the cinema had been transformed into a prison. I followed the boy inside, and ran into a warder escorting Yang Mengchi out. The warder looked at me and said: "I'm handing him over to you. From now no, I wash my hands of him." No sooner had he finished speaking, than he disappeared. Even the prison vanished. There were just the three of us left standing in a huge courtyard. Yang Mengchi's legs were in fetters. We wanted to get them off, but had no way of doing so. Suddenly, an air-raid warning sounded. Enemy planes soon came. We could hear the roar of the bombs. In my panic, I woke up. The next time, I dreamed that I myself was locked up in prison, with Yang Mengchi and I sharing a cell. I did not know why I had been imprisoned, and he said he did not know what his crime was either. He added that his elder son was trying to arrange his release, and indeed, his son did come and see him that day. He was as pleased as could be. But when he came back from seeing his son, he told me that his son had told him, that his sentence had already been passed: Death, and that there was no way of saving him. Then he said that, in any case, since he was to die, suicide was the best way, and with that, he ran his head against the wall. His head split open, and smashed into smithereens with blood and brains spattered everywhere. . . . I cried out in terror. When I woke, my head was bathed in sweat and my heart thumping madly. Outside my window, the first birds were singing. Day was beginning to break.

Eventually, I fell once more into a deep sleep and did not get up until after nine o'clock.

I lost confidence in this novel of mine. When it was time to seal it up for posting, I began to hesitate, not daring to waste the time of the older writer. That day, I read it through again in detail, and put it aside once more. The day after the Dragon Boat Festival, I took out the manuscript to read it yet again and made corrections once more, spending two days on the job. Finally, I made up my mind, wrapped it up, sealed it and took it to the post office to send it in person.

When I came back from the post office, I ran into Lao Yao's rickshaw parked outside the second gate. Leaping down hastily from the rickshaw, he exclaimed as he seized me by the arm: "You're back just in time. I've got news for you."

"What news?" I asked in surprise.

"I've found out where Yang Mengchi is," he answered briefly.

"Where is he? Can you get him out?" I asked him happily, surprised. I didn't notice the expression on his face.

"He's already out."

"Already out! Where is he then?"

"Let's talk in your room," Lao Yao said, frowning as he

spoke. As we went, I began to wonder: "Surely he can't have escaped!"

We went into my room. Lao Yao sat down in his usual armchair, while I kept my eyes on his lips, waiting for him to begin.

"He's dead." Lao Yao uttered these three words and then was silent.

"It's not true! I don't believe it! He can't have died so soon!" I cried out in pain and bitterness. The shock had been so sudden. "How do you know it's he who's dead?"

"It's definitely he who's dead. I made the most careful enquiries. Didn't you describe his face to me? Everyone remembered him. His face was exactly as you described. He changed his surname to Meng and his personal name to Chi. If it wasn't he, who was it? I found out what his crime was too. They say he was up for attempted robbery and that he was a hardened thief. They also said he was involved in a case of theft. He'd been in prison for just over a month. . . ."

"How did he die?" I interrupted.

"He took ill and died. According to them, one day after coming back from carrying stones with a fellow prisoner, he wouldn't go to work the next day under any circumstances, and so they beat him up. That same day, he pretended to be ill. But they really did send him to the sick ward. Actually, there wasn't anything seriously wrong with him, but he caught cholera while he was there, and no one looked after him. Within three days, he was dead. The corpse was wrapped in a bamboo mat, taken out and dumped. No one knows where. . . ."

"Then where can they have buried him? If we can find his body, we can buy a piece of land and re-bury it, and put up a stone for him. I've sent my novel already, so I'll have a bit of money. I can pay half."

Lao Yao shook his head with finality. "I'm afraid only his spirit knows where he's buried. I thought of that too at first. But I couldn't find out where his body was. Who dares get close to the body of a cholera victim? Needless to say, as soon as they've got rid of the body, that's it. According to them, they always throw the bodies into a public burial ditch outside the East Gate, where the stray dogs eat everything except for a few bones. Even if we found the place, we wouldn't be able to tell which bones were whose."

I shuddered and clenched my teeth. After a moment, the feeling which had attacked me gradually subsided.

"Well, so this is the end of the former owner of the 'Garden of Repose'! Who would have imagined it? That camellia tree of ours is still engraved with his name." Lao Yao gave a long sigh of sympathy.

He was dead. And so that was how the boy's story ended. Could all this be possible? Surely, I was dreaming? What difference was there between this and the nightmare I had had the other night? I suddenly remembered the note he had left his younger son: "Consider me as dead. . . . Let me live out my life peacefully." And was this the way he should have lived out his life? I could not say I sympathized with him. But when I thought of what had happened in the Temple of the Grand Immortal, my tears began to fall.

Lao Yao stood up. "I'll go and tell Zhaohua," he said as if to himself, his voice slightly hoarse. He sighed briefly once more and left the room.

I sat there unable to move, gazing stupidly at his back. An overwhelming fatigue pressed down on me from head to foot. I closed my eyes in submission.

33

I passed the next week or so in a kind of daze. Every afternoon, I ran a temperature, suffered from dizziness, lost appetite and felt weak in all my limbs. I refused to admit I was ill. Sometimes, I still went out to see a film. Now there was no need for me to stay bent over my desk writing. On fine days,

I would go for a walk in the garden a couple of times a day. I drank masses of boiled water and slept continually.

Lao Yao came to see me once a day to chat. He did not know I was not well. He just thought I was tired out by my writing, and so was not looking very energetic. He advised me to rest as much as possible. He himself was in high spirits. He seemed to have completely forgotten that unhappy affair. All day his face displayed his smile of unconcern about everything, and his hearty laughter was often to be heard. His wife also came frequently. She would always sit for a while before leaving with her husband. In the end, it was she, attentive as usual, who noticed that I was ill and begged me to take some medicine. She asked the cook to prepare me some rice gruel. Her calm smile showed her inner contentment. I observed the couple's happiness as a spectator. I saw that they were both still as much in love as when I had first met them. Xiao Hu also came to my room a couple of times. He had not looked me directly in the face for a long time. Now he was a bit politer towards me. When I talked to him, he would answer briefly, but politely. From Lao Yao's own lips, I knew that Mrs. Zhao had taken her grandson and granddaughter for a visit to a member of the family in another county, and probably would not be back for another couple of weeks. Xiao Hu had no one to pass the time with, so could only go to school and study obediently, and revise his lessons when he got home. He was even willing to do as his father told him.

And so the family must now be enjoying a happy life. I was delighted for their sake, and indeed secretly gave them my blessing. One day when I was talking to Lao Wen about Xiao Hu, I mentioned that Xiao Hu had now greatly improved. Lao Wen snorted: "He'll never change! Don't you believe him, Mr. Li. In a few days, as soon as Mrs. Zhao returns, he'll revert back instantly. Mr. and Mrs. Yao are too honest, and so are taken in by him. We all know what he's up to." I did not believe what Lao Wen said. I thought that his prejudice against Xiao Hu was too deeply rooted in him.

My illness stopped suddenly.   I suffered no longer from fever and my appetite returned.   My friend and his wife came to ask me out.   I saw they were in good humour, and so I went out with them the next three days.   On the third day, we came back rather early.   Their rickshaws were back first.   My puller couldn't run very fast; besides, when we were turning at an intersection, he collided with a rickshaw coming from the other direction.   The two pullers put down their rickshaws, started shouting at each other and almost came to blows, but restrained themselves.   After cursing each other thoroughly, each took up his rickshaw and left.   When I was back at the Yao mansion, I unexpectedly ran into the Yang boy inside the main gate.   He was sitting on a wooden stool talking to Old Man Li.

"You've finally come back, Mr. Li! I've been waiting for you for ages!" The child leapt up happily when he saw me. "Mrs. Yao and the others have been back for quite a while."

"You haven't been here for a long time.   Have you been all right?" I asked, smiling at him kindly.

"I've been here twice, but didn't run into you either time. I've been a bit busy recently," the boy replied affectionately.

"Let's go in and sit down.   The moon is beautiful tonight," I said.

He followed me in.   As he took my hand, he said in a voice full of happiness: "Mr. Li, my brother's being married tomorrow."

"Are you pleased?" I asked him.   I needed all my strength to repress another feeling that rose within me.   I was afraid of saying something that I ought not to say at this time.

"I am," he said, nodding.   "Everyone's pleased," he continued in explanation, "and so am I. I like my cousin very much. When she becomes my sister-in-law, she's sure to be even nicer to me."

By then we had already reached the gallery in the garden. Beyond the balustrade, the moon was shining through the leaves of the trees. The rockeries were patterned with intermingling moonlight and shadows.

"You've never come here at night," I said to the child, bending my head slightly.

"Never," he answered briefly.

We followed the stone balustrade to the front of the lower guest room. The scent of gardenias wafted over and filled my nostrils.

"I won't come in. I'll just stand here awhile and then go," the child said.

"Are you in a hurry because you have to get back to help with your brother's wedding preparations?" I asked with a smile.

"I have to get up as soon as it's light tomorrow. There are so many guests. I'm afraid with a family as small as ours, we won't be able to manage," the child replied.

We went down the steps and stood beneath the osmanthus trees. The shadows of the trees in the moonlight formed a pattern on the child's body. He lifted his head and his eyes peered through the spaces in the leaves of the two trees, gazing at the cloudless sky above.

"If I were to attend your brother's wedding, would I be welcome?" I asked, half-joking.

"Of course, of course!" the child cried happily. "Mr. Li, you must come!" Before I could reply, he went on: "There'll be so much bustle tomorrow. There's only one person missing. If only Dad were there, the family would be complete." His voice changed, and became a whisper, as if he were speaking to himself. Suddenly he turned his face towards me and, raising his voice, asked: "Mr. Li, have you still had no news about my father?"

I was at a loss for words for a moment, but then said firmly: "None." Then I added immediately: "He doesn't seem to be in Chengdu."

"That's what I think. I haven't been able to find him for so long. Old Man Li hasn't had any news of him either. If he were still here, someone would definitely have seen him. With all of us looking for him everywhere, we'd be sure to have found him. He must have gone elsewhere to work. Maybe he'll come back someday."

"He'll come back," I answered mechanically. I was not in the least ashamed of my lie. Why should I destroy even this hope of his which could never be realized?

"Then I can come here with him to look at the words he carved himself," the child said, as if in a dream. Then he went up to the camellia tree, stretched out his hand and felt it for a moment. Just then, his head was hidden by a large shadow, so that I could not see the expression on his face. He did not speak. Only the cry of the insects calling to their companions could be heard in the garden, imbuing it with an atmosphere of loneliness and solitude. A breeze rose momentarily. The shadows formed by the moon trembled slightly, then all was still again. Two or three mosquitoes bit me on the cheek. The silence enfolded my heart in a vague feeling of grief. Suddenly, that long thin dirty face floated into my brain, and there appeared before me those clear eyes, those trembling lips and the right hand covered with sores. I had not forgotten my last glimpse of him. What had he wanted to say to me? Why had I not given him the chance? Why had I not allowed him one drop of comfort in the moment of his approaching death? But now it was too late.

"Mr. Li, let's go over there, shall we?" the child suddenly suggested, his voice tinged with tears.

"All right." I was startled back into reality. The moonlight shone all around us. Thick shadows covered only the spot where we were standing. I peered into the darkness to try to look at the child. Our eyes met, and I turned away my glance. "I'll come with you," I said, as my heart began to fill with pain.

We walked in silence along the crooked path between the rockeries. He walked very slowly, and when we were almost under the paper windows of the upper guest room, he suddenly stopped, and leaning his hand on a corner of the rockery, he explained: "I slipped here once and knocked my forehead on the rocks. There's still a scar."

"I've never noticed," I said absent-mindedly.

"It's here, hidden by my hair. You can't see it if you're not told about it." He rubbed the scar with his right hand. I followed his hand with my gaze, but I still couldn't see it.

We followed the wall, from the magnolia trees to the side of the goldfish basin. Putting his hand on the edge of the basin for a moment, he said as if to himself: "I still remember this basin. It's even older than I am." After two or three minutes, he went towards the garden terrace. Then we arrived back at the osmanthus tree.

"Let's go and sit inside for a while," I proposed, for I was tired from standing.

"No, I have to go back," the child replied, shaking his head. "But thank you, Mr. Li."

"All right. I know they're waiting for you at home, so I won't keep you. When you've time, you must come and see me."

"I will," the child answered with affection. He hesitated a moment, and then continued: "Only I hear that my brother will be transferred to be head of a department in another district. I hope it's not true. Otherwise the whole family will have to move. Then when Dad comes back, he won't be able to find us." His young voice betrayed his anxiety. I was so moved that I was unable to say a word for a long time. During this pause, the boy said good-bye and left. But before going, he didn't forget to invite me. "You must come tomorrow, Mr. Li. Old Man Li knows where we live,' he said.

I could only murmur my acquiescence.

I went into my room, turned on the light, and saw a registered letter on my desk. I tore it open and read it. It was from that old writer friend of mine. Enclosed in his letter, was a money order of 4,000 yuan in part payment for my novel. In his letter he also wrote: "Come soon. There are many of your friends here waiting for you. Together, we can accomplish something. . . ." He mentioned the names of several people. Among them were two who really were old friends of mine whom I hadn't seen for over three years.

That night, I could not sleep. I lay on the bed, tossing and turning, thinking for a very long time. I thought about having to leave. I really ought to leave. My novel was completed, Yang Mengchi's story was finished, Lao Yao and his wife's "misunderstanding" had been cleared up. My old friends were waiting for me elsewhere. What was I doing staying in the Garden of Repose? I couldn't stay there as a long-term sponger.

The next day, when Lao Yao and Mrs. Yao came to see me, I spoke to them of my intention to leave. I saw surprise and disappointment on their faces. Naturally the two of them tried in turn to hold me back. They spoke sincerely and earnestly, but I maintained my refusal. I had my reasons, they had theirs. In the end, we found a compromise: I would come back the next year, while they promised to let me go in a fortnight. Then I put the buying of a bus ticket in Lao Yao's hands.

That day, Mrs. Zhou brought the food, since Lao Wen was minding the gate for Old Man Li. It seemed that he had asked for leave to visit his relatives. I knew that he must have gone to the wedding in the Yang family in order to help his old masters out for the day. But when he came back, I said nothing to him about it.

34

Ten days passed quietly. On Wednesday morning, Lao Wen told me a piece of news: Old Mrs. Zhao had already come back to Chengdu, and the previous afternoon, had sent someone to fetch Master Hu. Moreover, she'd made it quite clear that he was to stay for several days, and told Mr. Yao not to keep on sending rickshaws to fetch him back home. When I heard this, I frowned in displeasure. I thought: Why has she come once more to disturb the peace of another's household?

In the afternoon, Lao Yao came to tell me that he had already reserved a ticket for Saturday. He also gave me a letter of introduction that I needed for buying the ticket, and told me that on Friday afternoon, he and his wife were inviting me to a farewell dinner at a restaurant. From what he said, I gathered that his wife was not well that day, and discovered that he was going to Mrs. Zhao's shortly. I asked whether Xiao Hu was going to stay at the Zhaos' for long this time. At first he said that, as Mrs. Zhao had just come back to Chengdu and was inviting Xiao Hu to keep her company, it didn't matter if he stayed a few extra days. In any case, school had already broken up for the summer, so there was no need for him to go over his lessons. Then he said that he was going to fetch Xiao Hu back the day after tomorrow to see me off. Finally, he also added: "It's got rather warm these last couple of days. It won't be comfortable in the bus. You'd better stay till autumn, when it will be cooler."

Naturally, I couldn't do as he suggested. He left. When I thought of old Mrs. Zhao's strange temper, I felt a little worried for Mrs. Yao, for the happiness of the whole family. But it seemed that Lao Yao himself hadn't thought about this problem at all.

That day, it really was very hot. I didn't go out into the streets. I moved a lounge chair to beneath the window alongside the stone balustrade and sat there with a book, allowing the monotonous song of the cicadas to float over me like a lullaby, and in this way, I passed the whole afternoon. At nine o'clock in the evening, heavy rain began to fall and the weather turned cooler.

The rain beat down for quite some time. When I woke at midnight, I could still hear the sound of rain and thunder. I worried that the roof tiles might be broken by the rain, and that the flowers and plants in the garden would be knocked down by it too. But when I opened my eyes the next day, the room was flooded with sunlight.

At about four o'clock in the afternoon, Lao Yao was chatting with me in the garden. He brought out the cane chair I usually sat in and set it at the bottom of the steps beside the flowerpots. He sat there, leisurely and carefree, listening to the strident call of the cicadas, while drinking freshly brewed Longjing tea. Suddenly, Zhao Qingyun rushed in, his face tense, his voice trembling. "Mr. Yao, sir! Old Mrs. Zhao has sent someone to beg you to go over at once. Master Hu has been washed away by flood."

Lao Yao was just about to take a mouthful of tea. "What!" he cried out in alarm, throwing his cup to the ground and leaping up from his chair. The teacup was smashed to pieces, and the tea splattered onto my feet.

"Master Hu and some of his cousins went out of the city together to go swimming. They'd gone there yesterday as well. Today, the water was up, but Master Hu didn't pay any attention, and there was an accident. The water was very swift, and no one knows where he's been swept away to," Zhao Qingyun explained in agitation.

Lao Yao's face had turned a bright red. Sweat poured from his brow. His eyes were fixed in a stare, and he kept running his hand through his hair scratching his head. After a while, he said hoarsely: "I'll go at once. I won't go in. Go and tell Mrs. Yao I've some business to attend to. You mustn't let her know about Xiao Hu. Wait till I've come back."

"Yes, sir," Zhao Qingyun answered at once, and went out first.

I stood up and patted Lao Yao lightly on the shoulder, trying to comfort him. "Don't worry. Perhaps it's not as. . . ."

"I know," Lao Yao interrupted with a frown. "But I'm also to blame. I'm going. If you come across Zhaohua, you mustn't say anything to her about Xiao Hu." In just a fraction of a moment, his face had turned ashen. He looked at me vaguely and, saying nothing more, left.

I followed him out the garden gate and saw him into his rickshaw. I did not say another word to him. A strange feeling came over me. I mulled over what he had said: "I'm also to blame." His words had been sincere. He really did bear the responsibility. But my peace of mind had been disturbed by this unexpected incident and never recovered the rest of the day.

When Lao Wen brought me my evening meal, I could see a gloating expression on his face. His tiny eyes squinted as he said: "Mr. Li, God has seen clearly. He has been just. It is a clear punishment." I looked vaguely at the wrinkled face which seemed to smile and yet was not smiling. He continued as if in explanation: "The Zhao family tried every day to harm our mistress. Instead they've brought retribution on their own grandson. And whose fault is that? If the master had been willing to listen to his wife, this would never have happened. The mistress has suffered for years, and at last she can hold up her head."

If he had said this to me a few days later, I might have listened contentedly. But to hear it now disgusted me. I did not want to argue with him. I just warned him coldly: "But this is your master's only son!"

Lao Wen looked down at the ground and said nothing. I lifted up my bowl to eat, but my eyes kept turning to look at his face. I saw him slowly lift his head, turn, look towards the window and surreptitiously wipe his eyes. He went to the door and stood there for a moment. When he came over again to collect the dishes, he said in trepidation as he wiped the table: "If only we pray to God for Xiao Hu to be safe, all will be well." From the tone of his voice, I knew that these words came from his heart.

"Perhaps it's nothing serious," I answered briefly. I said this purposely to calm him. In reality, like him, I knew that everything was already over. The only hope left was to find Xiao Hu's body.

35

Our hope was not realized.

Early next morning, I took Lao Yao's letter of introduction

to the bus station to buy my ticket. At first, I was too early, next I couldn't find the place, and then I couldn't find the person. It took me until half past eleven to complete all the formalities and get my ticket. By then I was thoroughly exhausted.

I remembered that there was a place near there where one could rest. It was a teashop which also served meals. The building was by the side of a small stream, the roof was covered with thatch, and there was a fence woven from the branches of trees. Flowers and plants grew in the courtyard, while along the bank of the stream stood several weeping willows. A small clump of bushes flourished at the gate, and a narrow path led to the entrance. Seen from the outside, it had the air of an abandoned garden. I had been to this teahouse once before. The seats were clean, and the customers few. It was the kind of place I liked.

I sat down at a small table by the fence beneath the shade of one of the willows by the stream. I had two bowls of noodles, and was leaning back in my bamboo chair dozing, when suddenly, raucous voices woke me with a start. I did not know what had happened. All I could see was some customers rushing out excitedly. Several people were also standing by the fence looking towards the opposite bank along which ran a crooked earthen path. Beyond the path was a ricefield, and on the other side of the rice-field was the glistening white surface of another river of which the stream in front of me was a branch. The villagers and children watching the excitement were strung out in a line running from the earthen path towards the river.

After a good while, I saw a waiter come over, and so, pointing to the people standing by the fence staring, I asked: "What's going on? What are they looking at?"

"Someone's been drowned," the waiter replied, quite unconcerned, as if it were a daily happening. He looked in the direction that I had pointed, and added disdainfully: "How can they see anything from there?"

Another drowning! Why did I meet disaster everywhere?

Surely it couldn't be to remind me continually that I was living in the midst of suffering.

A plump woman, a handkerchief hiding her face, went past with muffled sobs. Behind her came an old nurse and a man who looked like a rickshaw puller. They had come from the riverside.

"It's his mother. She was sobbing her heart out just a while ago," the waiter explained, pointing to the woman. "She's a widow. The two branches of the family had only this son."

"When was he drowned?" I asked.

"Yesterday afternoon, a good many miles from here. He was about seventeen or eighteen. They say it was a bet. Someone dared him to swim across to the other side. He accepted the dare and dived in at once, regardless of the consequences. The water was very high yesterday. He didn't care. When he got to the middle, the water divided into two whirlpools and he'd had it. His body was washed down to here and caught by the pillars of the bridge. It was found early this morning. When his mother learned about it, she rushed down here and sobbed her heart out. Now she's probably gone to make the funeral arrangements." The waiter spoke as if he were relating a story from ancient times, with no sympathy and no compassion.

I did not ask him any more, but lay my head back in fatigue against the cushion in the bamboo chair and closed my eyes. I had no desire to sleep. I was just thinking quietly about Xiao Hu.

After about half an hour or so, everything had returned to its usual peaceful calm. I got up to pay, and went out the front gate. I had not gone a hundred steps when I saw, on my way, the bridge which the waiter had mentioned. There were still five or six people standing at one end. Curiosity drove me to go over.

The bridge stretched silently between the banks. It was not wide. To the left end of the bridge at which I was standing grew a weeping willow tree, its leaves almost touching the surface of the water. Near this willow tree, underneath the bridge, the body of a youth, completely naked, floated on its back. His left arm was stretched upward, tethered by a belt to the bridge post, while his right arm hung limply at his side. His long regular face was a dark grey in colour, the eyes and lips tightly closed. It was as if he were lying in deep slumber. It was not at all like a corpse.

"He looks just as if he were alive!" I exclaimed to myself in surprise.

"It looked better before. The face was so rosy," a villager beside me commented. "After his mother came and wept for him, his face changed colour instantly."

"Is that really so?" I said, unbelieving.

"I saw it with my own eyes. How can it be false!" he retorted, glaring at me.

I looked down and silently examined the peaceful sleeping face. Gradually my sight blurred. I seemed to see Xiao Hu sleeping there. I gave a start and almost cried out loud, but then I hastily rubbed my eyes. It was after all the sleeping face of a stranger beneath the bridge. So this was death! So swift, so simple and so real!

36

When I came back to the Yao mansion, I saw Lao Wen at the main gate talking to Old Man Li. I asked them if they'd heard any news of Master Hu. They replied that they hadn't. They also told me that Mr. Yao had gone out very early, taking Zhao Qingyun with him, and still had not returned. Lao Wen also told me that Mr. Yao had asked him to tell me that my farewell banquet was being held at home instead.

"Actually, there's no need. After what's happened to Master Hu, with Mr. Yao away from home and Mrs. Yao not well, why continue to be so polite?" I said to Lao Wen apologetically.

"Mrs. Yao says that they're Mr. Yao's instructions. He also said he was coming home for dinner," Lao Wen replied respectfully.

"Can he get back in time?" I asked without thinking.

"Mr. Yao said to start dinner a bit later, and to wait for him to return." At this point, Lao Wen added immediately, "To keep you company, sir."

Lao Yao did indeed get home before seven o'clock. He came with his wife to the lower guest room, wearing a white jacket of grass-cloth and long trousers, while his wife wore a white linen cheongsam with blue edging. The table was laid in the middle of the room. The wine jug and the dishes of food were already on the table. They made me sit in the seat of honour, while they sat on each side. Lao Yao poured me some wine and filled his own glass as well.

There was a variety of elegant appetizing courses. The wine was Shaoxing wine of the best quality. But none of us had any appetite. We did not talk much and we scarcely ate. Lao Yao and I kept proposing toasts, but I took only small sips. It was as if the wine had become bitter. A sad atmosphere descended over the table. All three of us were reluctant to say the slightest word, to eat the smallest tidbit, or even to cough. The faces of husband and wife expressed sadness, especially Mrs. Yao's. She tried to hide this sorrow but this only made it the more apparent. Her brows were tightly knit, her face was pale, and her eyes were down cast. Her husband's face was sombre, his bushy eyebrows drawn together in a frown. His eyes, ringed with dark grey circles, kept resting vaguely on one spot as if he were looking at something, and then as if he were looking at nothing. I could not see my own face, but I thought, it couldn't have been a pleasant sight.

"Mr. Li, please help yourself to the food. Why aren't you eating?" Mrs. Yao looked at me and smiled. But her smile seemed to me to have a bitter touch, quite unlike her usual smile.

"I'm eating, I'm eating," I answered at once, and immediately took a couple of mouthfuls. But after that, I stopped again.

"Actually, you should stay here until it gets cooler in autumn, then go. After you've gone, the place will be even quieter. And besides, Xiao Hu's accident happened." She spoke slowly. As soon as she spoke of Xiao Hu, she dropped her head.

Up till then, I had not asked Lao Yao anything about what had happened to Xiao Hu. It was not that I did not want to know, it was simply because I was afraid of reviving his pain. Now, hearing Mrs. Yao speak Xiao Hu's name, I gave him a swift glance. His head was lowered as he drank his wine. I couldn't stop myself from asking his wife: "What about Xiao Hu? Have they found him?"

She lifted her eyes slightly to look at me and shook her head. "No. Lao Yao has been to look, but the current was so swift. We don't know where he's been swept away to. At present, they're dredging all along the river. He didn't sleep at all last night . . ." she said, her voice choking. Tears glistened in her eyes. She lowered her head once more.

"Can he have been saved by someone?" I asked, simply to console them, though I knew myself that my words were meaningless.

Mrs. Yao said nothing. Lao Yao suddenly turned to look at me, raised his glass, and in a hoarse voice said: "Lao Li, let's drink," and in a single mouthful, downed over half a glass of wine. Mrs. Yao watched him in silence and with concern. He immediately filled his glass to the brim again.

"Lao Yao, let's not drink so much today. I'm not a natural drinker, and you're not a good drinker either. Besides, it's no good drinking on an empty stomach. . . ." I said.

"Don't worry, I won't get drunk," he interrupted. "You're leaving. We don't know when we're going to meet to drink together again. What does it matter if we drink a few more glasses today? Have some more to eat." Then he picked up his chopsticks as a hint for me to follow suit.

"It's so hot, it's better not to drink so much," his wife put in from the side.

"No," he said, shaking his head. "I feel out of sorts today. I must have some more to drink." He turned towards me again. "Lao Li, just drink as much or as little as you like. I won't force you. I just want to drink. I don't feel like talking. Zhaohua will talk to you." His eyes were dry, but the look on his face was even harder to bear than tears would have been.

"It doesn't matter. You don't need to bother about me," I answered. "Actually, I've been staying here so long, I don't feel like a guest anymore."

"It hasn't been even a few months. How can you call it so long? Mr. Li, you must come back next year," Mrs. Yao said.

I was just going to reply, when Lao Yao suddenly stretched out his right hand to me and cried: "Lao Li." His face was completely red. I put out my right hand too. He grasped it firmly and, gazing at me earnestly, stressed the two words: "Next year!"

"Next year," I replied with emotion. Only then did I notice that two wine bottles were already empty, but I had not finished even one glass.

"That's a real friend!" he cried. Then he withdrew his hand, raised his glass, and drained it dry. Afterwards, he looked at his wife, and said with a forced smile: "Zhaohua, open another bottle. Get Lao Wen to bring one."

"You've had enough. You can't drink any more," his wife replied. She turned and gave Lao Wen a look. Lao Wen stood at the door waiting for their decision.

"No, I haven't had enough. I'll go and get it myself." He pushed aside his chair and stood up. He was unsteady on his feet. He swayed once or twice before leaning on the table for support.

"What's wrong?" his wife asked in alarm, getting up at once. I rose too.

"I'm drunk," he said with a bitter laugh, and sat down again.

"Then you'd better go back to your room and lie down,"

I urged him. I saw also that his eyes were bloodshot. He didn't answer me. Suddenly, he seized his hair in both hands and in a hoarse voice cried out in pain: "I've never done anything wrong. I've never hurt anyone. Why can't they find Xiao Hu's body? Surely we won't have to leave him to lie in the water forever! I'm his father. How can I ever bear it?" He covered his face and burst into uncontrollable sobs.

"Mrs. Yao, go back with him," I whispered to his wife. "He's drunk. He'll be better in a while. He's tired himself out these last two days. You must be careful too. You've only just recovered. You should both go to bed early."

"We won't keep you company then. Next year. . . ." At this point, her dark glistening eyes gazed at me, full of regret at parting.

"I'll definitely come and see you next year," I said, a little emotionally. I saw a sad smile creep slowly across her face. Her eyes seemed to say: "We'll expect you." She stood by her husband's side, bent down to look at him, wanting to speak to him.

Lao Yao suddenly stopped sobbing. He took his hands from his face, stood up, and slapped me on the shoulder with his large hand, saying in a firm voice: "I'll see you to the station tomorrow morning. I've already given instructions to have the rickshaws ready for us tomorrow at daybreak."

"There's no need to see me off. I haven't much luggage, and I've already bought the ticket. I can go by myself without any trouble. You've been so exhausted these last two days."

"I must see you off," he said obstinately. "I'll definitely come and see you off tomorrow morning." He let his wife take him by the arm, and he left the room, staggering as he went. I asked Lao Wen to follow them, for I was worried that he might fall on the way.

I sat all alone in the vast empty room, ate a bowl of rice, and drank up my glass of wine. When Lao Wen came to collect the dishes, he told me that Mrs. Yao had already agreed that he should come to the station with me. I thanked him for his consideration. But I couldn't listen to his long conversations as usual, for my brain and nerves were dulled; the wine had begun to take its effect on me.

Then the wine calmed my nerves. I slept very well. I didn't think about anything. In fact, I was incapable of thinking.

When Lao Wen came to wake me, the sky had just started to lighten, although the darkness of the night was still lurking in the corners of my room. He brought me water for washing my face, and also served me breakfast. By the time I had finished packing, it was past five o'clock. I decided not to wait for Lao Yao to come before setting out for the bus station. I had just told Lao Wen my intentions, when I heard whispers outside the window, followed by the sound of footsteps. I knew who was coming, and went out to meet her.

As I stepped across the doorway, I saw Mrs. Yao and Mrs. Zhou approaching.

"Mrs. Yao! Are you up already?" I asked, my voice happy with surprise and excitement. I also thought: "Lao Yao will be here soon."

"We were afraid we wouldn't make it," she said, smiling warmly. As she accompanied me into the room, she added: "Lao Yao can't see you off. He drank too much last night and was sick several times. He can't get up this morning and sends his deepest apologies."

"Mrs. Yao, why are you so polite?" I smiled as I spoke. "Is he all right?" I then asked.

"He's fast asleep now. He'll probably be better after today. Only he's suffered such a blow. You know how much he loved Xiao Hu. And on top of that, he's been running round for two whole days. It's difficult for him to keep up his spirits. If by chance you have time, I hope you will write to him to encourage him, persuade him not to dwell on the past, but to look to the future."

"Of course. I'll definitely write to you both."

"Thank you so much. Don't forget now, you must write!"

She smiled at me and turned to ask Lao Wen: "The rickshaw's ready, isn't it?"

"It's been ready for a long time, Mrs. Yao," Lao Wen answered.

"Then Mr. Li must be going, I suppose."

"I'm off then." I looked at the letter in her hand? I had noticed it when I had first seen her outside the door. I asked her: "Mrs. Yao, do you want me to deliver a letter for you?"

"No, it's our wedding photo. I got it out the other day. My husband said he's never sent you a photo, so I've got it out for you to take with you." She handed me the envelope. "You mustn't forget we're your friends now. Any time you come back, you'll be very welcome." She smiled again. This time, I found once more her usual sparkling smile.

I thanked her, and put the photo into my coat pocket without taking it out of its envelope. Then I shook the hand she held out to me. "See you again then. I can't forget all you've done for me. Please give Lao Yao my regards."

The four of us went out of the garden gate together, with Lao Wen carrying my baggage and with Mrs. Zhou following Mrs. Yao.

"Please go back in," I begged as I went down into the courtyard, turning to face Mrs. Yao.

"I'll see you into the rickshaw. I'm seeing you off on his behalf," she said, coming with me right up to the second gate. Just as I was getting into the rickshaw, I suddenly heard her sigh softly: "I really envy your being able to travel freely everywhere."

I knew that this was only a momentary feeling of hers. I answered briefly: "In fact, everyone has his own place in the world."

The rickshaw took me and my luggage; Lao Wen would follow. He was going to hire another rickshaw. As my rickshaw turned towards the main gate, I glanced behind me and saw Mrs. Yao still standing at the inner gate talking to Mrs. Zhou. I waved to her feeling rather reluctant to leave, and a moment later, the Yao mansion disappeared completely from my sight. The characters "Garden of Repose", as big as hand-basins, still looked proudly down from above the gate. They had watched me arrive, and now they watched me depart.

"Mr. Li!" a familiar voice called from behind. I turned round and saw Old Man Li running towards my rickshaw. I called the puller to stop.

The old man ran up breathlessly, and when he stopped, he ran his hand over his bald head.

"Mr. Li, you must come back next year," he stammered, his face turning red, his white beard trembling slightly in the early morning light.

"I'll be back next year," I replied gratefully. The rickshaw rolled forward again. We passed the gate of the Temple of the Grand Immortal, where Lao Wen was getting into the rickshaw he had rented. As for the temple, there is something I must add here: The place which I had visited so frequently had begun to be demolished four or five days before. They said it was to build a memorial of some kind. But at that moment it was still under demolition, so that when my rickshaw went past, all I could see was a heap of broken tiles.

Epilogue

At the time I began to write this novel, a newspaper in Gui-yang announced that I had renounced literature for business. I should have followed the advice of these gentlemen, but if I did not, it was not because I think that men of letters are nobler in spirit than businessmen. The sole reason is that I am not enamoured of money. Money can add nothing to what I already have. What enables me to live better is ideals. Besides, money is like snow in winter. It accumulates slowly, but melts away rapidly. As in this novel, huge mansions and beautiful gardens are indeed often as impermanent as their masters. Who has seen private property maintained for a hundred or several hundred years? What is maintained are things which people regard as vain and empty — ideals and faith.

This novel is my creation. But there is nothing new or marvellous in it. My heroes express only what others have expressed before them:

"Provide people with a little more warmth, wipe the tears from every eye, and bring happiness and joy to everyone."

"My heart beats together with those of other people. When others laugh, I too am happy. When others cry, I too am inwardly sad. I've seen so much suffering and unhappiness in the world, but I have seen even more love. I seem to hear in books grateful and satisfied laughter. My heart is constantly warmed as on a spring day. In the end, to live is such a beautiful thing. . . ."

I do not know how many people before me have said such things, nor how many times. But I am glad to have been able to say them once more in this novel, so that the people I men-

175

tioned at the beginning of this epilogue will know that man does not live by cheques alone. Apart from making money, he has more important, far more important things to do.

Ba Jin, July 1944

Preface to the French Translation
of *Garden of Repose*

I am delighted that my novel *Garden of Repose* has also been translated into French, so that readers of *Family* may see even more clearly how Chinese feudal landlord families went on their way to ruin and destruction.

When the first edition of *Garden of Repose* appeared in 1944, I wrote the following synopsis:

> "This novel, through the history of a rich mansion, tells the tragic story of two successive owners in the old society. . . . The acquisition of wealth without working for it is the cause of the family's destruction, and provides the context for the degeneracy of the sons and grandsons. A rich parasitic life leads to a youth being drowned, brings about the death in prison through illness of a rich spoilt son of another household, and causes a son to drive away his father and a wife to reject her husband. After the fall of the Yang family, the original owners of the Garden of Repose, the new owners, the Yao family, begin their downward descent. Even the kind-hearted woman who wishes to 'wipe the tears from every eye' will, in the future, suffocate in this mansion, unless she has the courage to break out and escape."

I was bron in this mansion. What I have written about is life as it really was. The third son of the house, Yang Mengchi, is none other than Gao Keding of *Family*. His death is based on what actually happened. I have been criticized for "showing sympathy for the leading characters, for being compassionate towards them, for feeling resentment on their behalf, yet . . . not a single one of these characters rises up to fight to change his destiny". There is indeed no one in the *Garden of Repose* who dares to fight. My novel is a dirge for an old society in the throes of death.

However, all this has finally passed, like a nightmare. My country and my people, including my readers, are today striding towards a future of unlimited brightness. The bitter memories of the past and a comparison of the old with the new society can only strengthen their courage and confidence as they move forward.

If from this melancholy story, my French readers and friends can visualize the old society in which we used to live, if they can come to understand better both the vigorous spirit of the Chinese people after having shaken off the fetters of the past, and their will and determination to achieve modernization rapidly, and if they can warmly grasp the hand of friendship that we stretch out to them, then, as a novelist, I have nothing more to ask.

May 3, 1978

On *Garden of Repose*

A short time ago, someone wrote an article pointing out the shortcomings of my novel *Garden of Repose* and of my other writings, and so today, I would like to say something in favour of these works. It's not easy for someone to identify his own illness. That's why he calls in a doctor to diagnose and prescribe. I do not understand even the simplest principles of medicine, so I cannot even take my own pulse to see how I am. I am an author who loves to chatter away, so that sometimes, I cannot resist the impulse to tell my readers about my own work. But I have absolutely no idea of blowing my own trumpet or of advertising my works. I have only one purpose, and that is to say a few "words in confidence" to the people who have read my writings, to tell them how these works were written. This could be considered a kind of professional secret, I suppose. But it seems to me that I shall just be imparting a personal "secret" to people I feel close to.

In relating confidences or imparting secrets, it is difficult to avoid the mistake of speaking too freely. Besides, as time passes, things change, and the memory grows weaker, so that it is even harder to avoid lapses of memory and errors of fact. But if I don't say anything now, then, later on, I might not even know where to begin. Take *Garden of Repose,* for instance. I still seem to see before me, the scene of myself in an upstairs room of a Guiyang hotel, beginning the first page of the novel, but, in a flash, seventeen years have passed. I cannot remember the name of the hotel. What I remember is that the major part of the novel was written in Huaxi, outside Guiyang, in the "Huaxi Rest-house". I took the unfinished manuscript to Chongqing and finished it there. If I had spoken about this novel fifteen or even ten years ago, I could have said much more about it, and perhaps said it more clearly. It is only now that I have become so deeply aware of how precious memory is.

To write *Garden of Repose,* I made use of a stack of Western lined letter-writing paper. I got used to writing with a fountain pen long ago. It was not that I did not like writing with a brush. Quite the contrary. I enjoy it very much. It's just that when I was young, I did not practise my calligraphy seriously (over the last few decades, I've been kicking myself ever since), so that my Chinese writing is really an embarrassment. With a fountain pen, I cannot only hide my inadequacies, but write faster. And so, nearly all my works have been written with a fountain pen, the only exceptions being two of my short novels, *Garden of Repose* and *Ward No 4.* Some of the first pages of *Bitter Cold Nights* were also written with a brush, because brush writing was clearer on the lined paper from Jiale I was using. Later, when I found some paper of rather better quality, I gave up the brush. When I was writing *Ward No 4*, I didn't seem to have any paper at hand that was even up to the standard of Jiale paper, and so I used ordinary cheap wide-lined paper. I was able to write more freely, and moreover, I enjoyed myself. Unfortunately, this kind of paper soaks up fountain pen ink. Even the tiniest drop spreads rapidly into a big black blot. And so, to write on it, I just had to use a brush dipped in thick Chinese ink. Of course a fountain pen would have been better for the Western letter-writing paper that I used for *Garden of Repose*, but at that time, it was not convenient to travel around with a bottle of ink. I just kept in my leather bag an ink-stick, a fine-tipped writing brush, and a pile of letter-writing paper. When I reached some destination and settled in there, if I could borrow a saucer, there would always be water available. I could then take out my ink-stick, and grind it in the saucer, ready for me to sit down and write. If I could not find a saucer, then I would use the lid of my teacup, and if there wasn't a lid, then the best I could do was to turn the cup upside down and grind the ink in the tiny space at the bottom of the cup. The whole novel was written in this way, in the hotel in Guiyang, in the rest-house at Huaxi, and in little inns on the road from Guiyang to Chongqing. When I eventually reached Chongqing, I did not settle in straightaway. I went to several other places as well. I remember one night in a hotel in Beibei, when I was continuing *Garden of Repose*, the electric light would not work. I found a small candlestub, but it burnt out before I had exhausted my train of thought. I wanted desperately to find a candle or an oil lamp so that I could go on writing at my ease. But it was not easy to find a ray of light on a dark night like that. . . . Those days are gone, never to return.

I began writing *Garden of Repose* in May, 1944. I had only just begun the novel, when I had to go into hospital. About the life in the hospital I later wrote very frankly in *Ward No 4*. I came out in June, staying first at a China Travel Service guest-house, and then for a short period at the Huaxi Rest-house. Every day, I would write from morning to night, going for a walk or resting only after my two meals. In the Travel Service guest-house, the electric light was bright, the tea easy to get, the courtyard quiet, and it was not far from the main street. When I was tired of writing, I would brave the light rain and go to the Guansheng Restaurant for a bowl of soup noodles or a bowl of pig's liver gruel, together with a couple of stuffed steamed bread rolls, and this would count as one of my meals. When I stayed at the Huaxi Rest-house, I had to take a half-hour's walk into town to find a restaurant, whether for a snack or for a meal. The "rest-house" was a beautiful garden villa in Western style, situated in an immense park. It was only one storey, and had a magnificent spacious reception room. Although the "rest-house" served as a guest-house for outsiders, there were very few guest-rooms and even fewer guests. I stayed there less than a week, and most cf the time I was the only guest. It was quiet in the daytime and even quieter at night. Even in the daytime, it was rare to hear the sound of human voices. But there was the sound of water day and night. The water flowed swiftly and noisily, never ceasing, the monotony never changing, so that once I became used to it, it was as if there were no sound at all. In short, it didn't interfere with my writing. There was no electric light in the rest-house, so I had to rely on the feeble light of a lamp which burnt ordinary vegetable oil, and write with my head close to my work. Here too, I wrote from morning to night, apart from the walks I took twice a day to town to eat. Sometimes, I felt so tired that I would go for a walk in the park. Frequently I had trouble with my eyes. Writing so much under the weak light of an oil lamp can cause your vision to blur, so I used to go to bed quite early, but I didn't get up late at all. At the time, I was in the prime of life. Every day, I would bend over my desk for over ten hours, without ever feeling my train of thought drying up. In a few brief days at the "rest-house", I wrote quite a lot. When I write, I am rather like the author of *Ordeal*. Once I think of a detail and sit down to write, this detail gradually draws out the whole story. Alexy Tolstoy has written in this way about his own writing: "When I'm working most intensely, I do not know what the characters are going to say five minutes later. I just follow them in amazement." In the past, that was the way I wrote most of the time. When I began *Garden of Repose,* I had in mind only a very simple story of the third Mr. Yang, together with some details of the "I" of the story returning to his home town, meeting an old friend in the street and being invited to stay in the garden of his home. To tell the truth, after I had written the first part, I still did not know how I was going to fit the third Mr. Yang's story in, or where I was going to put it. But I went on writing calmly, and all the problems solved themselves. The characters spoke, acted and strove of their own accord. Whatever I needed, flowed out quite naturally, as if from a fountain.

I'm not making things up, and I am not trying to say that creative writing is all a mystery. I am just explaining how I personally work. Every writer has his own way of doing things. It's said that Leo Tolstoy used to work only in the mornings. He thought that in the evening, it was easy for a writer to pour out loads of rubbish. Our woman writer Bing Xin has said: "I like writing in the morning, because then the brain is clearer. In the evening, I can't write a thing." Someone has also said that one of the reasons for Dostoevsky's "verbosity" is that he worked at night, while drinking endless cups of tea. In that case, my garrulousness can also be explained: I nearly always work late into the night, and if I have a cup of tea in my hand, I feel even more contented.

Let's go back to *Garden of Repose*. My idea of writing the story of the third Mr Yang goes back to January, 1941, when I went back to Chengdu for the first time. I left home at the age of eighteen, and after being away for eighteen years without a break, I came back and stayed for fifty days. "Everything seemed changed and yet unchanged; so many people had died, and so many families ruined; so many loved ones buried beneath the soil, and so many newcomers to succeed them in acting out these unnecessary tragedies," just as I have written in one of my short pieces. During those brief fifty days, I was besieged by many thoughts and feelings. Two things in particular left the deepest impression on me. The first was the death of my father's fifth brother. I had been back in Chengdu only a few days when I heard the news of Fifth Uncle's death through illness. That very evening, one of my relatives had invited me to a simple meal at a restaurant. Everyone had just seated himself when one of my cousins rushed upstairs into the room where we were, and without a word, fell onto his knees before me and started kowtowing to me. I was astonished, but in less than a minute, it suddenly dawned on me. It was an old rule of etiquette, a long-standing custom. Previously, when my mother and father died, how many times had I kowtowed to others! It never occurred to me that such an abominable feudal custom would have been preserved so unchanged. At the time, I kept on talking and laughing as if nothing had happened. Fifth Uncle's death drew from me not the slightest feeling of grief or sorrow. I had never thought much of him at any time. To me, he had been dead long ago. Around the dinner table, the laughing and talking continued without a break. My cousin also joined in the laughter and the chatter. I'd heard it said that he and his mother had together driven his father out. The facts were probably as follows: His father, having dissipated most of his wife's fortune, had abandoned his home, not caring what happened to mother or son. But finding no way to support himself, he was so thick-skinned that he had the nerve to return. The wife and son refused to welcome back a husband and father who'd already become a confirmed thief. Because of this, some people perhaps condemned my cousin, but I for my part approved of what he had done. Why should we not allow people like Gao Keding to taste the bitter fruit of the trees which they have planted with their own hands? Apart from exploitation and extravagant living, what have people like him ever done in their lives? Only after he had been driven out, only after he had been locked up, did he work with his hands for a very, very brief period. But not long after, by pretending to be ill, he caught an infection and really did become ill, dying a senseless death. According to some relatives, my fifth uncle had been arrested by the police that very winter and locked up. He had not committed any crime at the time, but he was a well-known petty thief and opium addict, involved in all kinds of larceny, and during the winter clean-up, it was even more likely that he'd be up to a little private trading. The police authorities thought that they might just as well lock him up for the winter. At least it would save them a lot of trouble. Of course, he was not the only one that was locked up like this. Later, he was forced to go out with his fellow-prisoners to do coolie work and other heavy labour. He was afraid of losing face if he were seen by relatives or friends, and so he pretended to be ill, refusing to go

out into the street. Because of this, he used to sleep with the
inmates who were really ill. It's possible that he caught an infectious disease, or it may be that the craving for opium overtook him without there being any way of overcoming it. In any
case, it was not long before he was dead. His wife and son collected back the body, had a coffin made, and laid him out in a
broken-down temple. I went there one afternoon. It was a cheap
coffin in a small room, with an old altar on which was placed a
spirit tablet representing the soul of the deceased, together with
some cheap joss sticks and candles. It was all rather dark and
gloomy. I gave a bow, which my cousin standing on the other
side returned. There was no sound of weeping. No one shed a
single tear for the dead man. I and the person who came with
me (probably a niece or perhaps another cousin about the same
age as I) exchanged a few casual remarks that had nothing to do with the deceased, and then calmly left. I was not
in the least upset, for I really felt that all this had happened
long ago, and I had not the least feeling of surprise. I went to
the temple, not to pay my respects to the dead man, but simply
to witness the end which he had deserved

That evening, when my sisters-in-law, sisters and nieces and
I came to talk about what I had seen and heard in the temple,
no one expressed any sympathy for the dead man. It was as if
we had closed an old book which we were tired of reading.
Late at night when all was quiet, as I lay in my old-fashioned
bed, I suddenly thought of the time several years back when I
was thirteen or fourteen. Fifth Uncle had dragged me out, wanting me to spend a few cents to buy him a copy of *Two
Years in the Qing Palace*. At first I just thought it was good
for a laugh, but eventually, I took it more seriously. I hadn't
meant to think much about him, but once I began, there was
no stopping. The many things that my sisters-in-law had talked
to me about all came to my mind. My fifth uncle was the only
son of my grandfather's second wife. He grew into a delicately
handsome youth, and was clever moreover, so that he was my

grandfather's special favourite. At the time, if anyone criticized
him, even if it was only a word, this would draw Grandfather's
ire. And so he grew up in an atmosphere of praise and flattery.
It was this kind of love that ignores all principle, and the environ-
ment of a feudal-bureaucratic family that ruined the life of this
young man. Later, he also got into bad company. Some of his
friends were rich, spoilt sons like himself, while others were
hoping to get something out of him. In short, in order to lure
him, people indulged him in every kind of pleasure that could
not be found at home, and he leapt into the trap gladly and
willingly. His mother died young. His doting father believed
blindly whatever came from his smooth glib tongue. When
bystanders tried to give sincere advice, it had no effect on
either his father or himself. Within a very short time, he
learnt a great many things: whoring, gambling, drinking —
there wasn't one in which he was not an expert. His father
did not believe that he could handle money, and so had not
given him a monthly allowance to do with as he liked. So he
ran through his wife's money first, converting into spending
money the jewellery she'd brought with her as a dowry. Later
he resorted to stealing, then cheating, then borrowing. As
long as he could get money, there was nothing he wouldn't
stoop to. He borrowed a substantial amount of money from
outsiders on his father's name to hire an unlicensed prostitute
whom he called "Saturday", and rent a small villa for her.
In the "evening of his rendezvous" he would write a long-
winded epistle full of oaths and pledges of love, as if he
wanted to inform the gods and future generations: on such
a day, in such a month and in such a year, Chan Ying'an had a
rendezvous with Fang Wen at such a place. His writing was
not really too bad. I picked up a draft by chance in the reception hall of our home. I don't like this kind of flowery language,
and so had no intention of keeping the paper for him, so
after glancing through it I either returned it to him in
person or threw it in the waste-paper basket. Now, all I
can remember is the incomplete phrase above. Chan Ying'an

was a name my fifth uncle had adopted, while Fang Wen was the name of his paramour. A name like "Saturday" was of course unsuitable to appear in such high-flown epistles as these, and so he'd chosen for her the much more elegant name of Fang Wen. After the little villa was all set up, his expenditure outside was even greater. Before long, because he'd cheated his wife of her jewellery, and had no way of making it up, heated quarrels broke out between them, which ended with giving the game away to my grandfather and revealing things as they really were.

The scene I described in *Family* is completely true. Much more happened in real life than in the novel. Many happenings I could never have thought up. In short, my grandfather's eyes were opened, and he saw things he did not want to see. The truth shocked him, and angered him, but it did not wake him up, nor could it make him realize his own mistake. All he recognized was that, in not behaving well, his son had let him down. He never, at any time, thought that it was he himself who had ruined his son. He thought that since he had piles of money, money was all powerful. When he finally discovered that money could not solve every problem, he changed to his other weapon: abuse. And not just abuse. He ordered Fifth Uncle to kneel on the ground, and alternately box his own ears. Fifth Uncle was capable of any ignominious action, and would do anything his father ordered him to, as long as he could get out somehow of the difficult situation he was in. Finally, he swore to high heaven that from that day on, he would remain at home studying diligently, and not seek the company of his dubious friends again. Grandfather surprisingly believed his oaths, but nevertheless ordered Father to watch Fifth Uncle and not allow him to go out.

Everyone knew that Fifth Uncle's oaths were not to be counted on. In less than three days, he had slipped out secretly. It was just getting dark, and I happened to be at the main gate, so even if he'd gone like the wind, he couldn't

have escaped my notice. I often went to the porter's lodge
to talk to the men-servants, or to the main gate to chat with the
gateman, Old Man Li. In fact, it was to get each of them
to tell me about their past. At the time, I was only ten. They
all liked me. There was no need for them to have any reserva-
tions in front of me, and there was nothing they wouldn't talk
about. I was genuinely fond of them too, for I gained an
enormous amount of knowledge from them. Amongst them
were some who smoked opium. Most of the older sedan-
chair bearers smoked opium, because they weren't strong
enough and they had to have a stimulant, knowing full well
that it was like drinking poison to quench one's thirst. But
there was no other way. I would often lie beside the opium
lamp of an old bearer (in fact, he was only forty, but was
already old and feeble), and listen to his unending stories of
the hardships of this world. I was very close to these people,
I was fond of them, and I felt that I could see clearly into
their very hearts. I did not understand my father's younger
brothers in the slightest, and there was no way of getting
close to them, except after my father died and Second Uncle
began to care for us. Even if it was only a general kind of
concern, that for us was already surprising. As for Grandfather, the whole family, old and young, had to go to his
room every morning and evening to ask after him. When
my brothers and I saw him, we felt constrained, and did not
dare say anything more than necessary. So none of us liked
Grandfather. But in the six months before he died (about
two years after the death of my father), he suddenly softened,
and to me, he showed the greatest solicitude. It was only
in this brief period that he spoke to me some words of affection and kindness. Before long, his mind started to become
confused, and his health went from bad to worse until he
finally died. There were not many moments when his mind
was completely clear. But I still remember him, sitting in a
sedan chair, asking to be borne round and round the courtyard. I still remember him sitting in the upper guest

room one morning and calling me over. He was writing a scroll: "I sit in the guest room freezing with cold, calling on Messrs Shao and Fang to save me." He was about to write "save", when suddenly, he asked me in all seriousness how the character "save" was written. . . . His madness had a good deal to do with Fifth Uncle's behaviour. That Fifth Uncle had revealed his real nature was one of the heaviest blows Grandfather had to bear. Needless to say, there were others. When Grandfather died, I wept, heart-broken. However, even then, I knew that the wrong was on his side. Of course, a fourteen-year-old of forty years ago doesn't think like a fourteen-year-old of today. Besides, I was also the rich son of a landlord family, and so all I thought was: A man should rely on his own labour to live. To leave money to one's sons and grandsons so that they can live a parasitic life is the stupidest thing, and it is because of this, that the feudal families have been unable to bring out worthy men of character. I was very naive, and understood very little, but I despised those who lived on their inheritance. I despised those who reaped but did not sow. Naturally, it was impossible for me to have a good opinion of Fifth Uncle.

This has been a long digression. Let us come back to Fifth Uncle's slipping out of the house. Since I saw it take place, I couldn't of course keep quiet. I went in and told my father. Father was worried but he did not go out to look for Fifth Uncle, nor did he dare tell Grandfather. He just waited until Fifth Uncle crept back quietly, then got hold of him, and gave him a serious talking to. Fifth Uncle could not care less about what Father said, and after a couple of days, slipped out again. However, the days he was outside, he did not stay very long. He seemed to have managed with sweet words and blandishments to persuade Fifth Aunt into not saying a word. My grandfather, as usual, acted as the awe-inspiring master of the household, but did not know what Fifth Uncle was really up to. Before the month was out, to everyone's surprise, Fifth Uncle suddenly disappeared. Nobody could find him. Not that they tried very hard. The main thing was not to let Grandfather know. After some time, a telegram arrived from Shanghai, sent to my father by Fifth Uncle. I was by Father's side while he was deciphering the telegram. A child like me who liked to poke his nose into everything couldn't miss an opportunity like that. There were two sentences in the telegram that I still haven't forgotten today: Remember brotherly affection. Remit 300 yuan immediately.

Needless to say, the money was sent as requested, and he finally came home. Fifth Uncle may have received a big scolding. Or perhaps, because of the various ways in which his brothers covered up for him, Grandfather never found out about this journey. It's possible even that he never left Sichuan at all, but simply made use of some friends to help him play a trick. I'm not able to say now, for, when all's said and done, a man's memory is limited. To cut a long story short, Fifth Uncle became more and more daring, he got up to more and more tricks, and his deeds became cleverer and cleverer. Lying, deceiving people, stealing money and goods, cheating at mahjong — there wasn't one at which he was not skilled. And it was all to indulge his personal life of pleasure. But there comes a time when money obtained without working for it runs out. "Saturday" finally left him and ran away. (She eventually became the concubine of some warlord or other, and when she heard that Fifth Uncle was out of money, she even sent him some.) His wife's money was nearly all spent, but he was still unwilling to change his style of living. It seems that it was at this time, that wherever he went, he would make a point of walking off with something. He became unwelcome not only at all his relatives' homes but also at his own home; even his wife and son loathed him, hated him, and finally drove him out. Yet even at this point, he refused to drop his lordly airs to become a new man by relying on his own hands to earn his living. He kept on as before, stealing, cheating, drifting along aimlessly, and adding begging to his activities. His standard of living dropped lower and lower, until finally he became a real confirmed thief, and was put in prison for the winter. From malingering, he became really ill and eventually, having utterly lost face, died of illness in prison. Now that he was dead, it could be said that he was a man who throughout his life had never done anything of benefit to another person, a man who lived solely for himself. He'd been raised and fed for decades to no purpose. There could be no waste greater than that.

I lay on this broken-down bed which had seen so many vicissitudes, thinking of my fifth uncle's shameful life. It was not through any nostalgia for the past. I had anticipated how he would end long ago. But I could not help feeling indignant, for in Chengdu society at that time, I saw everywhere the ghosts of the past. In the circle of our relatives, there were still people who continued to follow in the footsteps of my grandfather and of my fifth uncle. Some were landlords, relying on exploitation to become richer and richer, abusing their power and riding roughshod over others with even fewer scruples. For quite a number of people, money was still an all-powerful treasure. For its sake, they were even willing to sell their souls. I had written in *Garden of Repose* the following words: ". . . Do you think that since the Zhaos have money now, that they will always be able to look on while others can't even get enough to eat, while they do nothing but buy fields year after year? That their sons, grandsons, great-grandsons and great-great-grandsons will always have money, will always be able to gamble, go to the theatre . . . ? Do you think that for human beings, we can eat money, sleep on money, and we should take money as our mother and father, embrace it and suckle on it all our lives?" Actually, I was really excited as I wrote these words. For, they were not the words of "Mr. Li" to Lao Yao, but my own in talking to many of my relatives. At the time, I had long ago stopped being a rich young master in a landlord family. The level of my thinking was a little higher than when I had been a youth of fourteen. But even if I had wasted my life by writing, without a penny to my name, I still couldn't say that I wasn't a petty bourgeois intellectual. That's why I was able to create the story of the third Mr Yang out of Fifth Uncle's death.

My first version of the story of the third Mr Yang wasn't at all like the one I finally wrote. Moreover, at that time, I was thinking of incorporating it into a short novel to be called *Winter*. As I conceived it, late at night while lying on a canopied bed that winter, *Winter* was to be a sequel to *Autumn*, the epilogue of my trilogy *Torrents*. My idea of writing *Winter* did not just vanish like a flash of summer lightning, but stayed with me for a long time. Something else even helped me think of some concrete situations for the plot. This is the second thing I mentioned above. One day, towards evening, I passed the gate of our old family home in Zheng Tongshu Street.

I passed the old home I had left eighteen years ago. The street had changed in appearance, and so had the home. But when I saw them, I looked on them still with great warmth. I recognized them. It was like meeting old faithful friends. The stone paved street was now just an ordinary road, the pair of smooth-backed lions had been driven away by the lofty gates and walls, while the threshold in its iron sheath held by copper nails had been sawn away. Nor could I find the two rectangular stone vats filled with water, in case of fire, that used to stand at the bottom of the low stone steps on the side of the pavement in front of the gate. When I was seven or eight, I often used to sit astride the stone lions underneath the wooden boards inscribed with the couplet: Honour to the Family, Long Life and Prosperity. At dusk, my cousins and I would often stand beside the stone vats, chatting or eating some fruit or Chinese chestnuts fried with sugar that we had just bought. We dubbed the vats the "Vats of Universal Peace". But in 1917, when the warlords were engaged in street fighting in Chengdu, a young man-servant from the house opposite (or perhaps it was next-door) was shot just to the right of the vat and died. I saw only the tiny spots of blood after the body had already been carried away. It seems that he was busy talking with someone when a bullet hit the middle of the street, ricocheted and struck him. He just gave a weak cry, clutching the bullet wound as he fell. I had no particular feeling for the Vats of Universal Peace, but I did wish I could see the pair of lions in their original place. I could not help laughing at this childish desire of mine, for I knew very well that they had been removed long ago, not long after I left home, when the streets in Chengdu had been tarred. That was the first change. I had seen a photo, taken not long after my second uncle died. The gate looked brand new. But there were people burning paper money and other burial objects in front of the gate. The sight irritated me. In fact, the designs on the gate were neither Chinese nor Western. It was neither simple nor in good taste, but gaudy and brightly coloured, not at all like a high-class mansion. The couplet "Honour to the Family, Long Life and Prosperity" had disappeared. Even the door-frame had been changed and Westernized, while the two characters "House of Bliss" over the doorway gave it the air of a pretentious teahouse. The high walls on each side of the gate had also vanished, replaced by two shop fronts that could be rented. I heard that one of our family's chief cooks had run a restaurant there. When I came to the gate that day, I did not know which set of alterations I was looking at. Some-one told me that the mansion had been used to house some secondary school or other. One of my nieces had gone to school there. My aunt had also been in to visit, shedding tears as she stood in the garden before the camellias and the cassia trees. But what I saw was no longer the "House of Bliss", but had been transformed into the "Li Pavilion". Moreover, some armed soldiers were on guard at the gate. The shop fronts were no longer there, replaced once more by high un-scalable walls. The new owner was the head of the Peace Pres-ervation Office, and he wanted to use his own name to firm-

ly establish his right of ownership. His guards glared ferociously at everyone who approached. I could not stand at
the gate for more than a moment and had to go back
twice. The gate was open. I saw the original wall-screen,
still inscribed as before with "To be long enjoyed by future
generations" in decorative characters in seal script. It was
exactly as it had been when I saw it eighteen years before.
They called up my memories. As I gazed attentively at the
wall-screen, my eyes filled with nostalgia. Then I lifted my
head and left. I did not care about the two characters above
the doorway. I was sure that the next time I came, someone
else's name would be there. After over a year, I went
there a second time, but the same characters still hung
above the gate. After some sixteen years, I went once
again. It was still the "Li Pavilion", but the tyrannical owner
had been toppled, and I was finally able to go in and have
a look. Another four years passed, and I went to this street
again. Not only had the characters "Li Pavilion" vanished
without a trace, but even the gaudy multi-coloured gate and
the coloured glass doors had been demolished. The clean
simple tasteful Western-style gate gave me a feeling of fresh-
ness; On the board was nailed a board bearing the words,
"The Standard-bearers' Troupe". The sight of this new ad-
dition filled me with pleasure. Having found an appropriate
new owner, even this old dwelling had finally undergone a
thorough transformation. Of course, this is what happened
later. At the time, as I walked along, I thought of the inscription "To be long enjoyed by future generations", words that
drew me to that partly thought-out novel *Winter*. My confidence increased. About ten days later, I left Chengdu. At
that time, I wrote an essay "Elka's Lamplight" in which
I said: "Riches cannot long be enjoyed by future generations if one does not provide them with a skill in life and
does not point out a right way to them. The small circle of
the 'family' can only stunt the development of a young spirit
if it does not at the same time open its eyes to a wider world;

riches and wealth can only destroy lofty ideals and an honest disposition if they are expended solely on personal interests." It was precisely this view that I wanted to put in *Winter*. It was this idea that I more or less followed in *Garden of Repose* later. When young people of today read these words I have written on the "family" and on "money", they may think it laughable, but some years ago, many of my relatives could not accept even that much. Our branch of the family relied on our own labour to live, but met with only contempt and bullying by the new lords and masters, young and old, who grew fat on the wealth inherited from their forebears. I returned to Sichuan twice, in January, 1941 and in May, 1942, and each time, I saw the airs of money, and watched the shameful comedy of money chasing money, interest pursuing interest, played by actors who sat idle and ate. Chengdu was the cosy nest of parasites and exploiting monsters, a warm nest nurturing spongers and hangers-on of every description. Rich landlords, collecting rents which they could not use up, bought up more and more land. The cleverer or greedier masters did a bit of speculation under the cover of "business," for they saw that people who set up get-rich-quick businesses in gold, rice or opium, made money come in even faster, and besides, their lavish display of gold as if it were dirt, made them real subjects of envy. Even the warlords, big and small, who made their money relying on the barrel of the gun, were, in the eyes of the rich landlords truly to be envied. But they couldn't learn or do as they did. For the warlords could buy up the land of a whole county, could set up water dungeons privately in their own houses, and do exactly as they liked in their own area of jurisdiction. The landlords, on the other hand, had to live the life of exploiters hidden in their houses, relying on their hired thugs to do their errands for them. Although they had a host of ideas and high hopes, they lacked ability and daring, unable to accomplish anything other than depending on their forebears for food (of course, that meant living on the peasants). In other words, they were good-for-nothing trash. Nevertheless, in the old society before Liberation, they lived their days in the greatest comfort, strutting about and giving themselves airs, as if no one in the world could equal them. They thought that their family property would last for ten thousand generations. In fact, anyone with a clear head could see that they were already on the verge of destruction.

The first time I returned to Chengdu, I stayed for fifty days. Later, I went back there again to write the second volume of *Fire*. The second time, I went back to Chengdu from Guilin, staying there for over two months, before returning to Guilin to write the third volume of *Fire*. During this period, I also wrote other things. But as for *Winter*, I had not yet written a single word. In the beginning of May, 1944, I went from Guilin to Guiyang, and in the train and the bus, I was thinking of this and that, when the thought of the novel I'd still not begun crossed my mind. For the next few days (of course, not throughout each day), my thoughts turned back and forth on some workings of the plot. This fifth uncle of mine kept appearing before me, connecting together the strands of the plot. A story with a beginning and an end took form: the story of the third Mr Yang. But his name Yang Mengchi came to me only later. Apart from this, I thought of two other people: the novelist, Mr. Li, who went back after an absence of fifteen years, and his old friend, Mr. Yao.

When I reached Guiyang, I happened to buy three pads of Western writing-paper. In the rear area in those days, this was considered very good paper. I ran my fingers through the sheets several times, extremely happy, and decided that I had to make the best use of it. How was I to do so? I did not need to think about it for very long. I already had an idea. I was going to begin my novel shortly. I had even thought of the title: *Garden of Repose*, for I'd decided to take as the setting the tiny garden of my old home. How many years of my youth had been frittered away there! One year, after the warlords had been fighting among themselves, we heard that soldiers were going to billet themselves there. (At first, an officer's bodyguard, accompanying the wife of the company commander, came to look for rooms, but was turned away. He went off in a huff, saying he would bring soldiers to be billetted, and sure enough, the same day, a whole platoon came. But they stayed only one night. Everyone in the family was afraid that the soldiers would come back.) My second uncle wanted me and my third brother to move temporarily to the garden and stay there. The two of us lived in the so-called "lower guest room" for over a fortnight. But the soldiers didn't return. Order was gradually restored to the provincial capital. Since there was no need for us to stay in this cold, cheerless guest room we moved back to our own rooms. I have described the visit of the company commander's wife in Chapter 23 of *Family*. As for life in the lower guest room during that fortnight or so, it became very useful for Mr. Li, the novelist in *Garden of Repose*. It was because of this that I had Mr. Yao invite him to live in the Garden of Repose. And so, not only was I able to ascribe to him things that I myself had seen and heard in the past, and which I myself had experienced, but, since I was so familiar with the Garden of Repose, and had such a great affection for it, once I began writing, I was able to wield my brush with ease, writing without restraint. "Garden of Repose" was in fact the name of the garden in our house. Later, I was to describe it in the novel as follows: "The row of doors to the right were tightly shut. At the top of the steps beside the hall was a small double door, above which was pasted a strip of paper, once more in seal script, in deep black characters, with the words 'Garden of Repose' . . . ." This was just what the entrance to our garden was like. Not only this entrance, but the whole garden, from the upper and lower guest rooms and from the wall-screen inscribed with "To be long enjoyed by future generations" to the main hall with its row of doors painted in gold — all were described as they appeared when I left home at the age of eighteen. It is much easier for a writer such as I to follow a model than to create something out of nothing. Only the three private rickshaws in the hall were my own invention. In my day, they were sedan chairs. I also changed the main entrance and the gates. In describing them, I followed the appearance of either the "Li Pavilion" or the "House of Bliss", because, if I hadn't removed the threshold, then the rickshaws couldn't have been pulled in. The two multi-coloured gigantic gate gods armed with two huge swords were also out-of-date, and so it wasn't convenient to leave them standing there. But I didn't like the gaudy gates, and so I described them simply as: "Huge lustrous gates in black lacquer set in a high wall of grey brick. The words 'Garden of Repose', written in seal script in large red characters the size of hand-basins, looked proudly down from the lintel." I've said already that there was no inscription above the gate of our old family mansion. Nevertheless, a residence with the majestically written characters "Garden of Repose" did indeed exist. It was the mansion built later in Yuhuangguan Street by my third uncle. The characters were written by Third Uncle himself. I visited the house for the first time in January, 1941. At the time, two of my cousins, brother and sister, were living there. It was a one-storey house, situated in a narrow alley. The grounds were small and there was no garden. There were just a few rooms in all. I didn't like the house much, but the words "Garden of Repose" stirred in me many memories. What I want to say is that if I had not gone to that Garden of Repose several times during those two years, my novel would probably not have been so named. There was no need to change the setting, for even today, I can remember the garden very clearly, but the characters over the lintel, although I have not forgotten them, do not keep coming to my mind. The house is still in Chengdu. One morning, this January, I wandered as far as Yuhuangguan Street and turned into the alley. I saw the characters "Garden of Repose" still on the grey wall above the gate. But the owners of the house had changed long ago. The person living there now must be the right sort of owner.

As for my third uncle, I'd heard all kinds of stories about him.
Briefly, people did not seem to have a very high opinion of
him. It seems that after squandering his share of the inheritance (perhaps it was only the major part of it), he racked his
brains and, giving full rein to his talent for exploitation,
grabbed back something with which to build this new house.
He died in the Garden of Repose reciting the Buddhist scrip-
tures, leaving a young concubine. He had spent a lot of money
buying her in December, 1925, when she was only fifteen.
He was sure that his spirit tablet would be honoured here
for a long time to come. But the first time I entered the small
courtyard of the Garden of Repose, I already had the feeling
that my two cousins would not be there for long. It is not
that I am a prophet. The reason was very simple. Anyone
could see the coming social revolution. It was something
that no one, no force could stop. In fact, my cousin himself
seemed to know that he was simply a guest in the Garden of
Repose, that he was dragging out his days there. All my relatives thought him muddle-headed and naive. He was two
years younger than I. I'd sympathized with him since I
was small, for I had seen him grow up under the whip of his
father with my own eyes. I mention just the whip, but I am
covering things up for his father. When his father was
angry, he would take to beating people, especially him. It
didn't matter whether he was in the wrong or not, and moreover, his father did not choose his weapons. Sometimes, his
father would use a cudgel, and if there wasn't a cudgel, a whip
or something similar at hand, he would even throw a chair or
a stool at his son. So that when I was at home, my cousin
had only to see his father put on a stern expression he would
begin to tremble. Nevertheless, even a father as strict as that
couldn't make his son inherit his own abilities. His mind was
permanently impressed with his father's whiplashes. Although
he was working, he did not earn enough to support such a
large family, and was well on the way to exhausting his fortune. But Liberation saved him. Today, although the place

he lives in is not up to the standard of his previous home, and he is gradually becoming old and feeble, nevertheless, his mind is at ease, he has no mental worries, and moreover, his sons and daughters have one by one taken the right road. They all have a bright future before them. But that, of course, is a later story.

I have been chatting away non-stop about all these trivialities of the past, because I think they all have something to do with my novel. When I began to write it, even though I had thought out only the story of the Yang family and some incidents, and only in a simple way at that, nevertheless, when I started writing, the work went without a hitch, because I had beside me another inexhaustible storehouse. I seemed to have a conveyor belt leading from it directly to my desk, sending material in an unending stream to the tip of my brush. I took my manuscript with me on my journey on the long-distance coach from Guiyang to Chongqing. It was inevitable that my work would frequently be interrupted. Nevertheless, I never at any time had difficulty in writing or felt any depression as a result of having to put down my brush to cudgel my brains. On the contrary, I had the feeling of being led along by my brush. The characters themselves were alive. They grew and matured, and frequently overturned my original plan. There were times when I also had to struggle. I had to struggle with my own weakness, with my own soft-heartedness, for I was moved. I fell in love with the characters in the novel. I thought about Mrs. Yao and the Yang boy too much. I became even more partial to the Yang boy because he was so forgiving to his father. My first version of the story of the third Mr. Yang wasn't like that at all, but when I started to write, it came out differently. I should have been more severe in condemnation of him and lashed him more stingingly. But in this struggle, I was not victorious. Some people may say that this is a question of political stand, and my explanation is meant to exonerate myself. I don't deny it. I did not take a proletarian stand. This is something that every reader of the period knew. Otherwise, I wouldn't have allowed my brush to lead me on, and even less would I have allowed my reason to give way to my feelings. I've often said that what I was castigating was the system, but other people would think I was letting people off. Because of this, some readers are unable to make out where my intention as an author lies.

The narrator of the novel, Mr. Li, is perhaps I, and then again, perhaps he is not I. At the time, I had written about "trivial events and insignificant people". I had previously also lived off my friends as a "sponger". In November, 1934, when I went to Japan, I changed my name to Li Derui, and after I came back to China, continued to use the name from time to time. The novel expresses my own feelings, my own loves and hates. For instance, I have already mentioned earlier my ideas about money. Then there is what Mr. Li says about his "rich uncle" and about "selling the house". All these things I had talked to people about before. In the novel there is the sentence: "They have destroyed the only thing that reminds me of my childhood." When I returned to Chengdu for the first time twenty years ago, it really did sadden me that I couldn't see the places in which my childhood was buried. Although I had written with a clear understanding of what I was saying: "This will be the last time that I look with nostalgia at the home where I was born", yet, when I began to write *Garden of Repose,* I still could not say that I had no feelings for the past. And so, each time I re-read this novel, I have the feeling that "Mr. Li" is indeed myself in January and February, 1941, and from May to July, 1942. I knew that *Garden of Repose* would be sold, that the third Mr. Yang would die a tragic death, and that Lao Yao would not be able to keep his son or his mansion, but I felt that that was how things ought to be. But in speaking of these things, I cannot help feeling a little sorry for them. This feeling is wrong. I thought so in the past, and today I cannot but think so even more.

I just said that "Mr. Li" was myself. Now I must add that

he was not I. Even twenty years ago, I could not have been so soft-hearted as he was, to the extent of yielding to the pure-hearted Yang boy, and being willing to lift the burden from the shoulders of a parasite, whom no medicine could cure, onto his own back. I have said repeatedly that my life and my writings are full of contradictions. These contradictions are easily seen in *Garden of Repose*. Although "Mr. Li" expresses many things on my behalf, he also speaks and acts in ways I do not approve.

Mr. Li's friend Yao and his wife are fictitious characters. Yao's given name is Guodong, because his father hoped he would become a pillar of the state. He considers himself to be above the common herd, has grandiose aims but little ability. He prides himself on being more above politics and material pursuits than anyone else, yet relies on the hundred-odd acres of land inherited from his father to pass his days in idleness. He likes to keep making a few harmless complaints, criticizing others while being lenient towards himself. He has been overseas, served as an official, taught in a university, made an unpublishable translation of part of a novel, but has never seriously done anything that could be of benefit to another person or to society. Of course he cannot openly maintain that money will solve every problem, but he destroys the life of his only son, precisely because he believes that money can guarantee everything. To tell the truth, when I came to write about his son's death and about his tears, I felt happy. I felt satisfied. I've already said that at that time I was too tenderhearted, and so I could not write about this man with too much hatred. But there were many things I did not like about him. I did not like his attitude toward other people. In particular, I hated his mother-in-law, old Mrs. Zhao, and all her family. These people never make their appearance at any point in the novel. "Mr. Li" does not even have chance to hear them speak. But they are like an evil shadow hanging over the whole of the Yao mansion. In fact, these evil shadows are still conjuring up demons to make trouble not only here, but in other places, and it is only since Liberation that these devils have been caught and received their just punishment. In 1941 and in 1942, during my two visits back to Chengdu, I came across such evil people. I do not mean just "old Mrs. Zhao". In those days, people like old Mrs. Zhao included men as well as women, and their numbers were by no means small. I felt the air was polluted by them. They stank so of money that people were suffocated and could scarcely breathe. But when I went back to Chengdu in 1956, the air was much purer, for the demons had vanished. Yao Guodong also felt the shamefulness of his parasitic life, and was working honestly and conscientiously to earn his living. But this is only the first step. As to whether "Mr. Yao", the former lord and master of the past, can truly change or not, I still have no way of giving a definite answer.

Mrs. Yao, or Wan Zhaohua, was also a fictional character. She is beautiful and intelligent, gentle-natured and kind-hearted. She herself describes clearly the small circle in which she has lived for twenty years: "The world I moved in was so tiny: just two families, a school and a dozen or so streets." She is like a hot-house flower. She has seen the wide world and the complexities of life only in books. It was in books that she "came to recognize so much unhappiness and suffering". She realizes that she is "like a bird that has grown up in a cage". She even wants to fly into the outside world. She wants to "help others, to give her belongings to others, to bring laughter to those who weep, to satisfy the hungry, to give warmth to those who are cold". But her kind-heartedness is in vain, for she lacks courage. In the end, she has to admit that she cannot fly and that now she dare not even think of flying. In fact, is she not indeed just a small bird in the cage of the Yao mansion? Is she not indeed a "toy"? If there is no great social revolution, family disaster or individual tragedy, it is very likely that she will either die peacefully or wither away in this cage, after having lived her life to no purpose. How many women in the old society must have died in solitude like her! When I wrote *Garden*

of Repose, the fate of these well-intentioned women was truly to
be pitied. I even thought bitterly, if they had lived in another
society, lived under another system, their youth could have
blossomed into a beautiful flower, their intelligence and talent
would have had the opportunity to develop and mature. In
short, they would not have lived out their lives as parasites
as they did in the old society. In reality, what was impossible
in the old society has been accomplished in the new society.
After Liberation, I saw with my own eyes, many such "tiny
birds" fly from their broken cages. Women like Wan Zhaohua
left the small circle of their families and, changing their way
of living, began to do things of benefit to other people and
even of benefit to society. From October last year to February
this year, I stayed in Chengdu for four months. I thought for
a moment of writing a sequel to *Garden of Repose,* to write of
the changes in some of the families, to write of Wan Zhaohua's
transformation.

Of course, the Yang boy was also completely fictional. I
created him solely for the purpose of helping the third Mr.
Yang. All I mean by this is that, with a boy like him, it was
even easier for me to bring out clearly Yang Mengchi's character. Without a supporting actor as a foil, it is difficult to bring
out many of the special characteristics of the main character.
My fifth uncle could never have had a son like this. He didn't
even have a son like Han'er's elder brother! And I'd never
seen anyone like him in any of the families that I knew so well.
Needless to say, many of his characteristics appear in other
children too. That a son should love his father is perfectly rea-
sonable. But Han'er's reluctance to leave his father, his forgiveness of his father, his fond hope that his father will come
to his senses, his determination to change his father's destiny
— can we say that all these stand to reason? Yet I cannot say
that this declining landlord family could not have given birth
to a Han'er. Quite the contrary. It was very possible, but
seldom seen. For my own part, I liked this child's stubborn-
ness. But I didn't like the way he was so forgiving to his father.

All the same, I wanted the father to be punished as he deserved, and so I didn't condemn the elder boy very severely for driving his father from his home. During the Qing Dynasty, this would have been a terrible crime against morality. If my novel had been written at the height of the Qing Dynasty and published (which of course would have been impossible), I would certainly have been brought up before the literary inquisition and dragged others to their death with me. Even around the time of the May Fourth Movement, there was still a minority of people who believed that "if a father wishes a son's death, to refuse to die is unfilial". Some "heads of households" really did wilfully destroy the life and happiness of young people. From what I know, in 1932, there was a father who tried to force his daughter to commit suicide, because, having fallen in love with someone else, she disobeyed her parents' wishes and broke off her previous engagement. But the girl did not use the knife or rope her father gave her. Instead, she fled with the man she loved to another region, and lived a settled and happy life. And in that year too, I also saw elsewhere, a young girl go mad because her father interfered in her marriage. One resisted her father's orders, refused to recognize her father's authority and found happiness; the other endured pain and suffering through following her father's will, and eventually went mad. Although I am too lenient with the third Mr. Yang in my novel, there is a bit of veiled criticism when Yang boy speaks of his brother's attitude towards his father. But his brother continues to live and work happily in his small circle. This shows that times had definitely changed. Feudal influence was then only a "paper tiger"; it could not force the majority of young people to sacrifice everything that was most precious to them in the foolish name of loyalty and filial duty. But even I cannot believe that it is possible to say that a young man like this brother would have been able to work and live in happiness forever. On the eve of the collapse of the old society, to still think that working in a place with the right conditions and being competent in one's work would enable one to maintain

a life of temporary ease, was simply a dream. Unless he
went forward, there was no future. In fact, he had the pos-
sibility of honestly accepting transformation. But he was like
my cousin (my fifth uncle's son), continually harbouring resentment because his father had sold all the lands and property
handed down from his forebears, so that he himself could not
live a life of ease. After Liberation, he must however have
thanked his father for not leaving him this inheritance, for
today he can at least earn his own living by working with his
own hands. Otherwise, he would have had to follow in the
footsteps of my other cousin. He was one of my distant cousins,
two years younger than I was. When his father was alive, he
was a spoilt playboy. On his father's death, he left him quite
a bit of land and property. When Chengdu was liberated, he
was already over forty. But apart from spending money, he
didn't know how to do anything. When I was at home,
when he was only fifteen or sixteen, I heard people talk about
what a loose character he was outside the house. And indeed,
after many years of marriage, he and his wife didn't manage
to produce a single child. After paying back his mortgages
during the Land Reform, he and his wife had no way out. To
earn a living, he had to depend on selling loose pipe tobacco and
running round the teahouses. His wife, unable to stand the
hardship, had a nervous breakdown. He could not bear it
either, and quietly threw himself into the river and drowned.
At the time I wrote *Garden of Repose*, he was living very
comfortably, and there was even a small number of relatives,
who, because he had money, would follow him around and
flatter him. At the time, he was intoxicated by the wonderful
dream of the omnipotence of money, and had absolutely no
thought that, ten years later, things might end as they did. I
have not the slightest compassion for his death, for it was a
road he chose for himself, a road chosen for him by his father.
As you sow, so shall you reap. This is but just. However, as
a person, he was several points better than his two brothers. He
wasn't as cunning as they were. He didn't have the same

thought of harming people. But they had sons and daughters, and so could continue to hang on to their parasitic life. . . .

At this point, perhaps some people may ask: "What about Yang Mengchi?" Readers can easily see that I took my fifth uncle as the model. But the Yang Mengchi I described is not exactly the same as the person I had in mind. My brush added some things to him. I made him better than my fifth uncle, for, in the end, he did finally feel concern for another human being. My fifth uncle, on the other hand, from beginning to end, thought only of himself (it was he of course who squandered all his share from the proceeds of the house). If I had followed my fifth uncle's character exactly, then Yang Mengchi's story would have been shortened by half. It frequently happens to authors that characters run on of their own accord, transforming the story and breaking through the framework imposed by the author's mind, forcing his brush to follow as they run. It is called "the characters' rebellion". Even some writers who follow an outline when they write come across this situation. What about a person like me then, who is used to writing at random, going wherever my brush takes me! In fact, there is nothing mysterious which cannot be understood. A writer's thoughts, feelings, political stand and point of view play a very important role here. My shortcomings are revealed without my being able to hide them. The only thing I regret is that my story has the air of a dirge.

Everything must come to an end, and so must this long personal soliloquy that I have written down. In any case, it is impossible to tell everything. Some people think that authors should not say anything outside their works, in which case, what I have written is just a lot of superfluous nonsense. But even nonsense has a limit and comes to an end. Please allow me, before I "shut my trap" to say a little about Old Man Li and Lao Wen. There is not much to say, but the memory I cherish of them is very deep. I wrote about them as they really were. And this "as they really were" was limited only by my view at the time. I admit that my understanding was shallow.

But I loved them. I truly thought of them as good friends, and even today, I still think of them. Although they are long dead, when I close my eyes, I still seem to see them before me. There are times too when a writer writes for himself. In writing about these men, you could say, that I was writing something for myself, as a souvenir for remembrance. I thank them with all my heart. They have brightened the memories of my childhood, and the memory of kind-hearted people can never fade. These people are dead now. The rubbish of the past, the refuse of the old society has gradually been swept away. Today, when the bright sunlight of the new society shines onto my desk, people like Old Man Li still live on in my thoughts. But that is not necessarily of concern to my readers.

November 12, 1961

BITTER COLD
NIGHTS[1]

1946

---

[1] The title has also been translated as *Cold Nights* or *Frosty Nights*. The translation *Bitter Cold Nights* will recall to English readers the opening scene of *Hamlet*, in which Francisco exclaims:
". . . 'tis bitter cold,
And I am sick at heart." — *Tr.*

I

It would soon be half an hour since the air-raid warning had sounded. The throbbing of the planes could be heard faintly in the distant sky, but the streets were quiet, without a gleam of light. He stood up from the stone steps in front of the iron gates of the bank and walked down to the footpath, looking up at the ash-grey sky stretched out like a piece of faded black cloth, but apart from the dark shadows of the tall buildings opposite, he could not see a thing. He stood there looking up for a moment, his mind a blank. He was not looking for anything in particular, but appeared simply to be passing the time. But time seemed purposely to obstruct him, passing with slow deliberation. And not just slowly. It felt to him as if it had even stopped. As the chill night air seeped slowly through his thinly-lined gown, he shivered suddenly. Only then did he look down and give a painful sigh, murmuring softly to himself: "I can't go on like this."

"Then what are you going to do? Do you have the courage? A harmless 'good sort' like you!" a voice retorted in his ear. He was startled. Looking all around, he suddenly realized it was his own voice. He answered angrily: "Why shouldn't I have the courage? Am I going to go on being a 'good sort' forever?"

He looked round involuntarily, but there was no one beside him, no one to contradict him. The white beam of a torch gleamed in the distance like a quick glance from an old friend, and a feeling of warmth rose suddenly within him. But the light went out again immediately. He was enveloped once more in the still not quite total darkness. The chilly air continued to pierce him to the bone. He shuddered. He walked a couple of steps along the footpath, rubbing his hands, and then a few steps farther. A black shadow slipped past him. Instantly vigilant, he turned to look, but all he could see was the shadowy darkness as before. He did not know what his eyes were seeking. The torch came on again, this time quite close to him. Then it flashed on and off several times in succession. The man carrying it came closer and closer, until he passed him and disappeared. He was wearing a grey over-coat. He was not very big or tall, a very ordinary person that you could meet on a street anywhere. He did not even look at his face as he passed. He could not have seen it clearly anyway, but he kept staring in the direction in which the man had disappeared. What was he looking for? He did not know himself. But suddenly, he stood still.

He was not aware of just when the noise of the planes had stopped. It was only at this instant that he remembered having heard them. He listened intently for a moment. But then he thought, perhaps there had not been any sound of planes at all this evening. "I must be dreaming," he said, unwittingly speaking aloud his thoughts. "Then I can go back," he thought straight afterwards, and as he did so, he found that his feet were already taking him along the road that led to his home. Without being conscious of his actions, he turned into another street, walking slowly, his thoughts caught and enmeshed in a tangled net.

"I've sold five packets of rice wafers and two cakes. That's all the business I've had!" Turning his head slightly, he saw a black shadow squatting in a corner of the wall from which the hoarse voice rose.

"I haven't had a single sale this evening. It's not nearly as good as it's been in other years. They won't let us into a lot of the shelters. Before, I could go into all of them," a younger voice replied.

"I wonder where they're bombing tonight. Is it Chengdu again? It's been so long now, but they still haven't lifted the alert." The first speaker did not seem to have taken in what his companion had said, and kept muttering to himself as if meditating as he spoke.

"Last night, the alert didn't end till the third watch. It might be even later tonight," the other voice put in.

It was the completely trivial conversation of two pedlars, but he was suddenly startled. Last night . . . the third watch! . . . Why did the unknown voice have to remind him!

Last night, at the third watch . . . what in fact had happened? After the alert had been lifted, he had left the air-raid shelter with everyone else and gone home.

But at that time last night, he had not been alone. He had been with his 33-year-old wife, his 12-year-old son and his 52-year-old mother. They had gone home laughing and chatting, or at least, on the surface, they had been.

"But afterwards?" he asked himself.

After arriving home, as soon as his son had gone to bed, he and his wife had begun chatting casually. At dinner that evening, someone had brought a letter for her, and so he had asked her what it was about, never suspecting how angry she would become. She began to quarrel with him. He became agitated, lost control of his tongue and said things he did not mean. In his heart, he really wanted to give way, but the thought of his mother sleeping in the next room made him think about the need not to lose face. He and his wife were quarrelling in the larger room, while his mother had taken their son with her to sleep in the smaller room. Throughout their quarrel, not a sound issued from his mother's room, the door of which was shut tight. Actually, the quarrel had been very brief. It could not have lasted more than ten minutes. Then his wife had rushed out of the flat. He had thought she would come back. At first he had felt so wronged that he had not cared, but then later, he had run downstairs to look for her. He not only went out the front door of the building. but also walked down two or three streets. But there was not even one woman's figure to be seen, let alone hers. Even though it was the centre of the wartime capital, there were only a few stray

pedestrians at this time of night. The shops on both sides of
the street had locked up, and only the lamps of two or three
small eating-places were still burning brightly. The places were
more than half empty. Where was he to find her? He would
never be able to cover such a huge city of hills in a single
night. She might be in any of the streets, and then again, she
might be in none of them. In that case, where on earth was
he going to find her?

Yes, indeed. Where was he to find her? That was what he
had asked himself last night. That was what he was asking
himself now, this evening. Why did he still ask? Had she
not sent someone with a letter today? But all it contained
were a few brief sentences, their wording curt and cold,
telling him only that she was staying with a friend, and asking
him to hand her personal belongings to the messenger. He
had done as she had asked, and replied in a note that had been
even briefer and colder, saying nothing about having run out
to pursue her, and making no mention of wanting her to come
home. His mother had stood beside him watching him write
the letter, but had said nothing the whole time. As for his wife's
"running off" (in his mind, he thought of it as "running off"),
apart from a few brief remarks she had made at breakfast in
commiseration, she had merely frowned and shaken her head
slightly. This 52-year-old woman, in poor health, her hair almost
grey, usually so full of worries, loved her son, loved her grandson, but detested her daughter-in-law. And so, although for her
son's sake, she was upset at her daughter-in-law's "running off",
inwardly, she was rather pleased. Her son was not yet aware
that his mother felt this way, and was waiting for her advice.
She had only to say the word, and he would write another
letter, a warmer one, begging her to come home. He wanted
very much to write such a letter, but he did not. Instead, his
letter expressed indifference as to whether his wife returned or
not. The letter and the suitcase had gone, and the estrangement
between them became more acute. Now, unless he changed his
attitude and wrote to his wife's place of work (he did not want

But at that time last night he had not been alone.

to go there to find her), it would become even harder for them to make up.   And so, up till now, he was still asking the same question, and still unable to find a satisfactory answer.

"I wonder if Xiao Xuan can help me," he suddenly thought. He felt a little more relaxed, but only for a moment.   Then he told himself: "It's no use.   She doesn't care about Xiao Xuan, nor he about her.   There doesn't seem to be much affection between them."   Actually, Xiao Xuan had gone back to school early that morning.   On leaving, the child had not asked about his mother, as if he knew what had happened yesterday.   In any case, when he said good-bye to his father, Xiao Xuan should have asked about his mother.   But he had said nothing!

In his despair, he could not help exclaiming petulantly: "What kind of family have I got!   No one really cares about me!   Everyone thinks only of himself.   No one is willing to give way!"   It was only a cry from the heart, heard solely by himself.   He did not realize this and, thinking that he had cried out loud, turned at once to look all around him. All was utter darkness and complete silence.   He had left the two pedlars far behind long ago.

"What am I standing here for?"   This time, he spoke rather loudly, for his thoughts were concentrated solely on himself. That was why he asked.   The question startled him.   Then he answered in his thoughts: "Am I not sheltering from an air-raid? — Yes, I'm sheltering from an air-raid. — I'm cold, and I'm walking about. — I'm thinking about my quarrel with Shusheng. — I want to ask her to come back —" Then he quickly asked (still in his thoughts): "Will she come back? If I can't even find her, how can I get her to come home?"

No one answered.   Again, he answered himself in his thoughts: "Mother says she'll come back of her own accord. Mother says she's sure to come back."   And then: "Mother seems very calm, as if she doesn't care in the least.   How does she know that she's certain to come back?   Why doesn't she urge me to go and fetch her?"   And then: "Where's Mother now?   Has she taken the opportunity to go there while I'm out? Perhaps they're sheltering from the air-raid together. Then everything will be solved. If I go home slowly after the alert's over, when I get back, I'll find them waiting for me at home, laughing and talking. — What shall I say when I see her?" He hesitated. "If first I just say something to please her, after that, the words will come of themselves."

At this thought, his face lit up with a smile. He felt as if the burden on his mind had been completely lifted. He experienced a moment of relief, and quickened his footsteps. But when he reached the intersection, he turned back.

"Look! There are two red lights now! Does that mean the alert will be over soon?" It was not his voice, but that of one of the pedlars beside him. They had never stopped talking, but he had ceased paying any attention to them long ago, although he had passed them several times. He at once looked up towards the warning platform on the top floor of the bank opposite. Two brightly lit lanterns hung from the pole. The quiet atmosphere around him was abruptly broken by a rush of human voices.

"I must get home before they do. I must meet them at the front door!" he suddenly said excitedly to himself. He looked up at the signal pole again. "I must go home at once. The alert will be over any minute now." Without further hesitation, he strode forward in the direction of his home.

The streets began to come to life. Though his mind was elsewhere, he could not help noticing the activity. The beams from countless torches were already breaking through the dark net of night that still hung over the streets. And so, on one corner, someone was lighting the carbide lamps. It was a stall specializing in "Jiading spicy chicken". A waiter was busy cleaning the table, another lighting a fire, while a group of people were gathered around the table, as if attracted by the brightness of the lamp. He turned his head slightly to glance at the place, but he had no idea why he wanted to look. Then he walked on ahead.

He had gone half-way down the street, when the lights on

both sides came on again, and everything ahead of him burst suddenly into brightness. Some children clapped, shouting in glee. A wave of happiness filled his heart. "A dream! A nightmare! It's over at last!" he thought with relief, quickening his pace.

Soon after, he arrived home. Mr. Fang, the manager of some shop or other, who lived on the first floor, was talking to his large-bellied wife, while the cook and the nursemaid went back and forth through the swing doors. Solely for the sake of politeness, Mr. Fang remarked: "They must have bombed Chengdu again this evening." He forced himself to mutter something in reply, and went hurriedly inside. He crossed the passageway and went up the stairs, running up the two flights in one breath. From the pale yellow light of the electric lamp in the corridor, he could see that the door of his flat was still locked. "Too early!" he thought. He was the only one on the second-floor landing. "No one's back." He stood for a moment outside his flat. Someone was coming up. It was Mr. Zhang, a civil servant who lived next-door. He was carrying a one-year-old boy in his arms. The child was already asleep. The man smiled at him kindly and asked: "Isn't your mother back yet?" Not wanting to go into details, he merely replied: "I came back first." Without asking any further, the man went over to the door of his own flat. Then Mrs. Zhang came up. She was wearing a faded black woollen overcoat. Not only was it old-fashioned in style, but the wool had been worn smooth and shiny. Her face was always so thin, pallid and meek, her forehead lined with a few wrinkles, her lips dry and pale. But her features were regular. She was a woman of twenty-six or twenty-seven, but still not at all bad-looking. She was puffing as she came up. Seeing him standing there, she greeted him before going directly to her husband's side, whispering something to him as she bent to unlock the door. Having opened the door, the two entered, full of affection for each other. His eyes followed them with a look full of envy.

Then he turned away to gaze first at his own door, then at

the staircase. He could not see anyone coming. "Why are they still not back?" he wondered, and began to worry. In fact, he had forgotten that when his mother went to the air-raid shelter, she usually came back a little later than everyone else. She was not in very good health and had to walk slowly. She would go out in great haste, but come back taking her time. Once home, she would fall into the cane chair in his room and lie back and rest for ten minutes or so. Sometimes his wife came back with her, sometimes with him. But where was she now? . . .

He decided to go down and meet his mother outside. He was desperate to see her. No, what he wanted was to see his wife returning with his mother.

He turned and ran down the stairs all the way to the main entrance. He looked up and down the street, but could not see clearly whether his mother was among the pedestrians or not. Two women were approaching from a distance. In fact, they were not so far off. They were passing the wine-shop. The taller one resembled his wife and was wearing a dark-blue woollen overcoat like hers. The shorter one, in a black cotton gown, looked like his mother. It must be they! He broke into a smile and walked towards them, his heart beating furiously.

Only when he had nearly reached them did he discover that it was a man and a woman. The one he had mistaken for his mother was an old man. How could he possibly have taken him for an old woman! His eyes were playing ridiculous tricks on him!

"I shouldn't make mistakes like that," he scolded himself, stopping in disappointment. "There wasn't the slightest resemblance."

"I'm too agitated. That's no good. When I do see them in a moment, I might say the wrong thing as well. — No, I mightn't even be able to say anything. — No, it can't be so bad that I'll be tongue-tied in front of her. I've done nothing to her that I need apologize for. No, I'm afraid I'll be so happy

I'll get flustered. — But why should I? I really am useless!"

He kept talking to himself in this way, arguing with himself, but unable to come to any conclusion. As he arrived back at the main entrance, he heard someone call his name: "Xuan!" He looked up. His mother was standing before him.

"Mother!" he cried, happy and surprised. But his joyful expression soon vanished, and he continued: "How is it that only you. . . ." He choked back the rest of his words.

"Do you think she's coming back?" his mother answered softly, shaking her head and looking at him with compassion in her eyes.

"Then she hasn't come back?" he asked in surprise and bewilderment.

"Come back? It seems to me it's better if she doesn't." She glanced at him as she replied, her voice tinged with contempt. "Why don't you go and look for her yourself?" She had no sooner administered this rebuke than she noticed the anguish in his eyes. Her heart softened, and changing her tone of voice, she added: "She'll come back, don't worry. Quarrels between husband and wife aren't all that serious. We'd better go inside."

He followed her in. They both had their heads down, not saying a word. He let her carry the rather heavy cloth bag as far as the foot of the staircase before taking it from her.

They unlocked the door and went into the flat. That evening, the room seemed emptier and untidier than usual, the light from the electric lamp even dimmer. A chilly draught struck him in the face, a draught filled with the stench of coal and other suffocating smells. He coughed two or three times, unable to stop himself. While his mother went into her room, he put the bag on the little square table, and stood there alone, staring vaguely at the whitewashed walls, seeing nothing. His thoughts seemed to float about everywhere like cotton fluff. His mother called him from the inner room, speaking to him, but he heard nothing. Eventually, she came out to see him.

"Why haven't you gone to lie down?" she asked in surprise. "You're tired enough for today." She went over to him.

"Oh, . . . I'm not tired," he replied, as if waking from a dream. He glanced at her vaguely.

"Aren't you going to bed? You still have to go to the office in the morning," she said with concern.

"Yes, I have to go to the office," he muttered in a kind of daze.

"Then you ought to go to bed," she repeated.

"Mother, you go first. I'll go shortly," he said, frowning as he spoke.

His mother remained standing where she was, gazing at him in silence for a moment. She wanted to say something. Her lips trembled, but in the end, she said nothing. He still did not move. She stood for a few more minutes, and then all at once, sighing softly once or twice, she went into her room.

He was still standing by the table, seeming not to notice that she had gone. He stood there thinking, thinking. His thoughts flew rapidly, racing about in confusion, collecting themselves, and then becoming so entangled that they could not be unravelled. The more he tried to disentangle them, the more knotted they became. He felt as if a huge stone had been stuffed into his head. Unable to bear it, he staggered over to the bed and fell onto it, exhausted. Without turning out the light or pulling the covers over himself, he fell into a heavy sleep.

It was not a sound sleep, but a restless unconsciousness.

2

One dream followed another. Of course, he did not know he was dreaming.

His wife and he were living in a quiet little town. Their life was not particularly happy, for they were always quarrelling over trivialities. They did not get on too badly as husband and wife, but there was never any understanding between them. She was always losing her temper, while he was often disgruntled. That day, they were arguing over some trifle again. He remembered it was about his mother. His wife was especially bad-tempered that day. They were still eating, when his wife suddenly gave the table a push, tipping it over and breaking all the bowls and plates. His mother was not at home, and the child took refuge in a corner, crying. He was so angry that he could not get a word out, but simply beat himself on the head, muttering curses to himself.

Just at that moment, he heard a sudden noise like a thunderclap. They could not tell where it was from, but their room was shaken by two violent jolts.

"What's happening?" he asked in fright, though his mind was comparatively clear.

His wife stood speechless by the door. The child's sobbing ceased.

"I'll go and see," he said, turning towards the door intending to go downstairs.

"Don't go, or if you go, let's go together. Whatever it is, it's best to stay together." His wife was no longer angry. Her attitude had changed to concern, as she stopped his going out.

He did as she said, and remained standing in the corridor outside the door. But he said nothing. He looked rather remorsefully at the broken crockery and the bits of food on the floor, waiting for her to speak.

She said nothing. He stayed there, waiting. Suddenly, a cannon (it must be a cannon, he thought) sounded once, twice. Then all was quiet once more. The child began crying again. His wife let out a scream.

"The enemy's here," he murmured to himself in alarm. "Mother!" he cried immediately, and ran along the corridor to the top of the staircase.

"Xuan!" his wife called after him. "Where are you going?"

"I'm going to look for Mother!" he replied without even turning his head, and rushed down the stairs in one breath.

His wife ran down after him, dragging the child behind her "You can't go off by yourself. You can't leave the two of us behind. Even if we die, we're coming with you," his wife sobbed.

"I have to find Mother. We can't leave her behind. If anything should happen, what will she do on her own!" he said as he threw open the front door of the building.

From outside came a hubbub of voices. The road was full of people, and he could see the heads of the thousands milling about. Everyone was fleeing the city in terror. Some had young children in their arms, some were carrying bundles and some supporting the elderly. The children were sobbing, the women calling their husbands, and the men urging on their companions.

The southern sky was completely obscured by the thick billowing smoke which soared into the sky. Explosion followed explosion, each more deafening and more terrifying than the last. He knew that danger was facing him, but his first and only thought was "Mother!" He ran down the stone steps at once. He wanted to cross the patch of grass in front of the door onto the road. He wanted to go into the city to look for her.

"Where are you going? You can't leave us behind!" his wife began to shout, sobbing as she tried to drag him back by the arm. "If you're going to flee, you can't flee by yourself, not caring whether the two of us live or die!"

"I'm not fleeing! I'm going to bring Mother back. She's still in town!" He stopped to defend himself.

"You want to go into town to look for her!" his wife scoffed. "Doesn't she have eyes or legs? Can't she walk by herself?"

"You go in quickly and get things together. When I've brought Mother back, we can all leave together. Even if we're going to flee, we still need to take something with us," he said, pulling himself impatiently from her grasp.

"Isn't that your mother over there?" his wife exclaimed, pointing to a clump of creepers by the ditch at the side of the road. His eyes followed the direction in which she was pointing. His mother was standing under the creepers (which were climbing up an old tree), her hair dishevelled, her face deathly pale. There seemed to be blood on her forehead. Her eyes were wide open, as she looked around in all directions, obviously looking for him. He lifted his head and shouted: "Mother!" gesturing to her as he did so. But it was no use. He wanted to dash across. But he would have to cross the road in front of him. It was so packed with people that not even a drop of water could have trickled through. He ran to the edge of the road. No one would let him through even a crack. He seemed to hear his mother calling. He called too. But a hand caught hold of his left arm. It was his wife. She had a small leather suitcase in one hand, while the child followed behind her.

"Let's go. Forget about her," she said impatiently.

"I can't. I have to get across to fetch her," he replied angrily.

"You want to get her at this time? You must be mad. I ask you, don't you care about your life? I'm not waiting for you!" his wife said harshly, her face stern.

"Let me go. I must go and get her. She's right in front of me. I can't abandon her and think only of my own safety," he said, pulling his left arm free.

"All right then, go and get that precious mother of yours. I'm taking Xiao Xuan, and we'll go our own way. But don't blame me afterwards!" she declared resentfully. He felt her lift her eyes, look at him directly and glare at him. He had never seen eyes like that in anyone before! Involuntarily, he shuddered.

She did indeed turn and walk off with the child. Her expression revealed no sign of sorrow, none at all. On the contrary, she had looked at him with that haughty air of hers.

But he still thought she would come back, back to his side.

Or perhaps he could catch up with her later. But in a flash, her figure had vanished. People seemed to press in on him from every side, as if countless hands were pushing him. He felt himself swaying and staggering as if he were standing on a boat tossed by the waves. He felt dizzy as if having a fever. He pushed once more with all his might, trying to squeeze his way through.

Then he woke. When he woke, he was still pushing with his hands.

But it was only a dream. That night he dreamt still other dreams, all as absurd as this one.

3

It was already daylight when he opened his eyes. There was not a sound in the room. His mother's door was open. He was lying peacefully in bed, but his heart was pounding furiously. Terrifying images rose indistinctly before him. A feeling of bewilderment, of weariness weighed him down. He lay there without moving, without thinking. Slowly, his eyes moved as he forced himself to open them wide. But he could not see anything clearly. Which was the dream and which the reality? Was it the present or the past? He did not know. Nor could he grasp his present situation. He felt only that something was wrong. His head ached. Not badly, but it ached. He was struggling, but against what? He could not make it out. He remained in this befuddled state for some moments.

Suddenly, a thought shot through his brain. With one bound, he was out of bed. He stood in the middle of the room (let's call it the middle since he was not near any of the furniture) and looked around in stupefaction. Scratching his head vigorously, he muttered in despair: "What shall I do?" He remembered the events of yesterday, recalled those of the day before.

"It's all my fault. I should have gone in person yesterday and explained to her, apologized to her. It was I who started it all. No wonder she was angry," he continued.

"Why did I have to write that letter yesterday? Why didn't I tell her frankly? Why didn't I go to her myself? Why? ..." At this point, he made a decision: "I'll go now."

But his mother came back, a basket of vegetables over her arm. Seeing him still in the room, she asked in surprise: "Why haven't you gone to work? It's half past nine."

Half past nine! He ought to be at work. But he had forgotten all about it. He was over half an hour late already. What was he to do?

"You still haven't washed? You look terrible. Don't you feel well? Then you'd better ask for a day off. Write a note and I'll take it for you," his mother said with concern.

He gave a start, and said in confusion: "I'm fine. I'm just going."

He did not want to listen to her anymore. He took the wash-basin, filled it with cold water from the tub in the corridor, carried it back into the room, and had just put it on the table, when she asked again: "Why are you washing with cold water? That won't do at all! Go and get some hot water, quick! I left some for you in the pot. I'll go and get it for you," she said as she stretched out her hands to take the basin.

"I've finished already, Mother," he answered quickly. His mind had become much clearer the moment he had wiped his face with the cold water. He wrung out his face-cloth and hung it on the back of a chair. Without emptying the basin, he hurried out of the flat. He had not even brushed his teeth, and as well, forgot to put on his old felt hat. From his anxiety to leave, it was clear that he did not much want to talk to his mother.

"What a useless character! Because of a quarrel with your own wife, you go around like a zombie!" his mother scolded from inside the room. But he was already out of earshot.

He went down the stairs into the street. There were so many

people, and so much dust. It was a fine day, neither too hot nor too cold, a day such as was rarely seen in this city of hills.

"Where shall I go first?" he asked himself as he stood on the pavement.

"First, find her!" was his initial answer.   Following this idea, he started walking in the direction of her office. After a few steps, he stopped, thought for a moment, then went on a few more steps.

"No, I must go to the office first," he finally decided, and made an about-turn. "That damned office! They dock your pay even if you take a couple of hours off."

Before long, he reached his place of work, the head office of a semi-government stationery and publishing company. His desk stood in a corner on the first floor. The sign-in book on the ground floor had already been taken away. It was the first time he had been late in three and a half years. He went quietly up the stairs. Mr. Zhou, who was head of the editorial department and a manager as well, was in his office. He looked up suddenly, glanced outside and saw him, but said nothing, allowing only an expression of disdain to pass over his face. But he did not notice this at all, for his mind was concentrated on one person: her! always her!

He began work, the same monotonous, depressing work. The pile of proofs on his desk (he saw them lying there as soon as he entered) was no higher than yesterday's. The partly-legible, partly-illegible handwriting and the galley-proofs that still seemed to smell of ink, were no more sickening than usual. His eyes, his hands, his brush moved mechanically, making copious corrections on the proof sheets . . . without his ever lifting his head.   They had an old-fashioned wall clock in the office.   He heard it strike ten . . . eleven . . . twelve. He could not remember a single word of the proofs.   But he heard the clock striking clearly, especially the last twelve firm strokes. He knew what they meant.   It was time to stop work.

He stood up, at least, it could be said that he stood up, for he did so without realizing it. But the others were faster than

he, and had all left their desks already. He folded the
proofs and manuscripts that remained to be read and put them
to one side. He stood before his desk, gazing vaguely towards
the windows that looked out onto the street. They were all
shut, the glass covered with a thick accumulation of dust. He
had not given any thought to what he was expecting to see. He
was thinking. No, he could not even say he was thinking. His
thoughts had come to a standstill, were bogged down by one
word — "her"!

The bell had rung long ago, but he had not heard it. Moreover, it never occurred to him that it was time to go downstairs
for lunch. The others seemed to have forgotten his existence
too. No one came up to call him. No one even thought that he
might still be upstairs.

But his mind finally became active. He woke up, left his
desk and went downstairs.

Some people were still in the dining-room, eating at tables
scattered with dishes.

"What! Were you upstairs?" a colleague exclaimed in surprise, looking at him with a pitying air.

He muttered something in reply, thought for a moment, but
instead of sitting down to eat, walked out of the dining-room
towards the main entrance of the building.

He seemed to hear the scornful laughter of his colleagues.

"They must know about me," he thought, feeling his face
redden and his ears burn.

He was not hungry. He hadn't thought about being "hungry"
or "full". One idea obsessed him: to find her!

But he had not gone a dozen steps before he suddenly
thought: Will they follow me? By "they", he meant his colleagues. The thought made him slow down. He felt hesitant.
But he did not stop walking, nor did he look around. He was
beginning to imagine what it would be like when he saw her
— the expression on her face, her first words of greeting.

"She'll forgive me," he repeated to himself twice. Then he

smiled with tenderness, feeling that it was her he was smiling at. His courage rose.

Before he knew it, he had arrived at the place where she worked.

4

She was a clerk in a commercial bank, the Bank of Sichuan, which stood in the middle of a street in the vicinity. He saw her coming out just as he reached the street corner. She was not alone, but was accompanied by a young man of about thirty. They were coming directly towards him. It was definitely she. She was still wearing that thin dark-blue overcoat of hers. The only difference was that she'd had her hair permed, with the front combed very high. The man looked to be a colleague from the bank. He was, you could say, not bad-looking. He was hatless, and his hair was combed till it was smooth and shiny. He was about half a head taller than she and was wearing a brand-new autumn overcoat, which, you could see at a glance, had just been brought in from Calcutta.

The man was laughing and talking effusively, while she listened attentively. They didn't see him. He felt his heart sink. He didn't dare continue walking towards them. Just as he was thinking to avoid them, he saw them step off the footpath and cross to the other side of the street. He changed his mind and followed them across. They were walking rather slowly, close to each other. He could see that the man was purposely brushing his shoulder against her, but that she, whether consciously or not, was avoiding him. At first, he did not dare go too close to them, in case she discovered that he was trailing her. Then he suddenly plucked up courage, and followed closer behind. The man said something or other that made her burst into clear and melodious laughter. The familiar sound stabbed him to the very heart. He went pale, and was unable to go on. He stood there, staring stupidly at her back. Her shapely figure seemed more seductive than ever, aggravating his pain. As he stared, his view was cut off by other pedestrians. All at once, he moved forward again, blushing furiously, his heart beating wildly. He wanted to stretch out his hand and seize her, or to call out loudly to her. But he did nothing. She went with the man into a high-class coffee-shop that had only recently opened.

He stood in front of the door, not knowing what to do. He thought: Should he go in to talk to her? No, that would be no good. It might make things worse. Then, should he go back to the publishing company and wait for another chance to seek her out and talk with her? That would be no good either. He couldn't stop worrying. He had to find a time to make up with her as soon as possible. Then, should he stay at the door and wait for them to come out? No, that wouldn't do either. It might embarrass her. And besides, what if she ignored him? Suppose the other man helped her against him? If the worst happened and a quarrel developed, he had no rights over her. They were only living together. They were not officially married. In the beginning, he had been against a wedding cere-mony, but now he regretted having so lightly thrown away the only weapon he could have used. And so, she was completely free. When he thought of this, he could only go back dejectedly to his own office.

All the way back, he kept seeing the figures of his wife and the young man together in intimate conversation. From time to time, he could hear her laughter as well. He was so pre-oc-cupied that he was almost knocked down by a rickshaw.

When he entered the book company, two of his colleagues were sitting at a desk downstairs reading the newspapers.

"What's the matter, Lao Wang? You don't look too well today. You didn't even have lunch. Is there something on your mind?" a young man by the name of Pan asked mockingly. He must know about me, he thought.

"It's nothing. My stomach's playing up," he answered at

once, making up a lie on the spot and forcing himself to smile.

"If your stomach's playing up, you should take some medicine for it. You shouldn't work this afternoon. You should ask for a half-day's sick-leave, old man," another colleague by the name of Zhong said. He was a man of about fifty, stoutly built, and completely bald on top. The flesh of his cheeks hung heavily down, making his face square in shape. His nose was especially large, and bright red at the tip. He was an amusing man, always smiling, and got on well with all his colleagues. He loved to drink and loved to talk. He had no family here, and no relatives either. His colleagues called him affectionately "Zhong Lao" or old Mr. Zhong, and admired him because he knew how to "live", how to "enjoy himself" and how to "arrange his life".

"It's really nothing. I'm fine," he (it's time I gave you his full name: Wang Wenxuan) answered perfunctorily, and started to go upstairs.

"Lao Wang, stay downstairs for a moment. It's not time to start work yet. What's the point of going upstairs now?" the man named Pan urged with a smile.

"You've lost weight recently. You should get more rest. It's not worth it, working yourself to the bone just for this pittance of a salary," old Mr. Zhong said, looking at him with concern.

As he sat down on a stool, he could not stop himself from sighing softly.

"What's the matter? What's the matter?" Mr. Zhong asked in surprise, patting him lightly on the shoulder. "You young people should look on the bright side of things. Don't take things so seriously. Who's really happy these days! The most important thing is still to keep in good health."

"On a salary like this, you can't even keep a wife! How can you think about looking after your own health!" he replied dejectedly.

"Oh, I see. You've quarrelled with your wife again," Mr. Zhong said, realizing the truth.

"No, no," he said, shaking his head in denial. But it was obvious from his face that he was lying.

"There's no need to deny it, old man," Mr. Zhong said with a smile. "It's natural for a husband and wife to quarrel. If it's a real quarrel, just give way a little. Then your wife will be even more considerate towards you. There's no need to take this kind of thing to heart!"

He said nothing. He thought about it to himself, nodding mechanically.

"I don't agree with Zhong Lao's theory· If you keep on giving in, you'll just end up being hen-pecked," Xiao Pan laughed. "In a quarrel between husband and wife, the man should never give way. What can the woman do except cry and shout abuse? You don't think they can beat us up, do you?"

"Oh, shut up! Everybody knows that you're scared of your wife!" Mr. Zhong said, throwing up his hands in laughter. "Come on, we're all friends here!"

Xiao Pan went crimson, and turned away without a word. As he looked up and glanced at Xiao Pan, Wang Wenxuan's lips trembled as if he were about to say something. But in the end, he said nothing.

"There's a proverb in these parts: Good advice is half the battle. These days, everyone's having a tough time, so what's there to quarrel about? Women can't stand it as well as the men, and sometimes they can't overcome their depression, and so they complain a bit. That's also a common human failing. Just let her get it off her chest. Don't take any notice of her, and there'll be nothing to worry about. The best weapon for dealing with a wife is silence."

"Zhong Lao is speaking from experience, I see," Xiao Pan cried in laughter. Wang Wenxuan was startled. He seemed to understand what Xiao Pan said, and yet didn't seem to take it in. He stood up abruptly, muttering to himself: "I'm going to see her again." Then he went towards the street door.

"Lao Wang, where are you going?" Xiao Pan called after him.

"I'll be back soon," he answered quickly and, without turning his head, went out.

"What's he gone to do?" Xiao Pan asked with curiosity.

Old Mr. Zhong shook his head without a word, and then, a moment later, let out a soft sigh.

5

When he reached the Bank of Sichuan, it was not yet time for work to begin. The front doors were still locked. But he did not have the courage to go in by the side door. Suppose she wasn't back yet? Suppose she refused to see him, or if she did see him, refused to smile at him, or refused to answer him with a single word of tenderness? What would he do then? Would his clumsiness with words allow him to express his feelings? Would he be able to make her understand his mental suffering, understand what was in his heart? Would he be able to persuade her, to move her, to reconcile her to coming back home with him?. . . As he thought, his determination wavered. His courage deserted him. He hesitated, not knowing whether to go forward or to turn back. He stood by the side door for two or three minutes, then turned away crestfallen, and left.

He had already gone a dozen steps or so, when the sound of high heels on a pair of leather shoes made him look up. She was there in front of him, dressed as before. As she came towards him, she recognized him and stopped. She looked at him in surprise, her lips parted as if she were about to say something, then she turned her face away abruptly, and went on without a word.

"Shusheng!" he cried, summoning up his courage, feeling his heart beat more wildly as he waited for her reaction.

She turned to look at him. In her eyes was a look of astonishment, but she said nothing. He called out once more, his voice shaking. She came towards him.

"What is it?" she asked coldly. Even her eyes were cold.

"Can you spare me a quarter of an hour? I've something to talk to you about," he said, looking down at the ground, his voice still quivering slightly.

"I have to start work," she said briefly.

"I've something important to talk to you about," he said, his face reddening, like a child who has just been scolded.

She relented and, after a moment's pause, said gently: "Then you'd better come and meet me at the bank at five o'clock."

"All right," he agreed, tearful in his gratitude.

She glanced at him again. He watched her figure disappear through the side door of the bank.

He'd been separated from her for only just over a day. How could she be so distant? — The question suddenly crossed his mind, and he waited, hoping that someone would give him an answer. He waited. His head felt so heavy, as if something hard had been stuffed inside it. A shoulder bumped against him, and he tottered uncertainly, almost falling to the pavement. "Oh!" he cried softly, as if waking from a deep dream. He steadied himself at once. He could see people coming and going, the cars and the rickshaws throwing up the dust as they raced madly to and fro. He thought: "I have to go to work too," and strode purposefully ahead.

Along the way, he continued to think of his problem. When he reached the door of his company, he suddenly said to himself: "It's all my fault. I must apologize to her this afternoon."

He returned to his desk upstairs. The manager, Mr. Zhou, was not there. Two senior members of the staff, the secretary, Mr. Li, and the head of the proof-reading section, Mr. Wu, were there smoking and chatting. They were laughing quietly together, and cast him sidelong glances. They must know about him and his wife, he persuaded himself. He felt his face burn, and buried his head in the proof-sheets, not daring to look up at them.

He was correcting the proofs for a translation by a famous author, a biography, but the translation read like a Buddhist sutra, full of strange words and phrases. Unable to grasp the meaning of a single sentence, he simply corrected mechanically, one word at a time. As his colleagues' laughter grew louder and louder, his head bent lower and lower. The stench, to which he was so accustomed, today was nauseous to him, but there was nothing to do but to put up with it.

Mr. Zhou arrived. For some reason or other, he was in a foul temper. No sooner had he sat down than he began berating the office boy. An employee went to see him to discuss a rise in salary, explaining that his present salary was really not enough to live on, and that for a low-level clerk, things were especially difficult.

"It's decided by the government. What can I do? Even if they didn't work here, they'd still have to eat!" Mr. Zhou shouted angrily in reply.

"In that case, you needn't pay them anything at all. Wouldn't that be even better?" Wang Wenxuan thought angrily to himself. "When you share out the bonuses at the end of the year, you get two to three hundred thousand. What do you care whether we live or die? If it weren't for your meanness, why else would Shusheng have quarrelled with me?" He had to struggle to keep down his breathing, not daring to utter a sound, in case Mr. Zhou's attention should be drawn to his inner discontent.

It wasn't easy to hold on until five o'clock. He didn't dare leave early, waiting till the bell rang before getting up. Then he locked the proof-sheets in his drawer and went hurriedly downstairs. Zhong Lao called after him, wanting to speak to him, but he didn't hear.

When he reached the Bank of Sichuan, the front doors were already shut, but the side entrance was still open. He'd just reached it, when he saw her turning from her office into the lane. When she saw him, a faint smile crept over her face, and she nodded slightly. His courage increased. All at once, the world around him grew bright, as if spring had suddenly come. He went over to her, his face wreathed in smiles.

"Let's go and sit down at the International," she suggested softly.

"All right," he answered gratefully, not realizing that the International was the coffee-shop where she'd been with the other man only a few hours previously. He felt inwardly relaxed, as if the millstone that had been weighing on his heart these last two days had been lifted.

She walked on his right, not too close to him, but as she walked, she said nothing, coughing lightly just three times. "Aren't you well?" he could not help asking with concern. He looked up at her face, but there was no sign of illness.

"It's nothing," she said briefly, shaking her head slightly, and became silent once more.

He lost the courage to question her, and remained mute. After a while, they entered the lounge of the International.

It was the first time he had ever been there. The lounge was beautifully decorated, he thought, especially the sky-blue curtains which were so restful to his eyes. The furnishings were all new, and although the narrow lounge was full of customers, the noise of conversation was subdued. The only empty table was far from the door, facing the street. He followed her over and sat down.

"It's the first time I've ever been here," he remarked, unable to think of anything to say.

On her face appeared an expression of sympathy. "With a salary like yours," she answered in an undertone, "how can you always be going to coffee-shops!"

He felt as if a needle had stabbed his heart. He looked down, and said as if to himself: "I used to go to coffee-shops quite often once."

"That was eight or nine years ago. We didn't live like this in those days. Everyone's changed these last couple of years," she said, also as if speaking to herself. And then she sighed softly. She would have continued to speak perhaps, but the waiter came over and interrupted what she was about to say. She ordered two coffees from him.

"It's hard to know how much worse it'll be later. Before, when we were in Shanghai, even in our worst dreams, we would never have imagined that things would turn out like this. At that time, our minds were filled with ideals. There was our teaching, the classroom to which we tried to give a rural, a family atmosphere." He smiled, as if lost in thought, but continued a little resentfully immediately afterwards, frowning as he spoke: "The strange thing is, it's not just our living conditions. It seems to me that we ourselves have changed, and I can't say how it came about."

The waiter brought two cups of coffee. He lifted the cover of the glass sugar bowl and put a spoonful of sugar into her coffee. She glanced up at him kindly.

"The past is really a dream. We had ideals, and had the courage to work for our ideals. And now,. . . In fact, why can't we live as we did then?" she asked. The sound of her voice lingered for a long time, for her words were clearly spoken from the heart. He was moved. He felt the distance between them shrink. His courage suddenly increased enormously. He said, his voice still trembling:

"Then come home with me today."

She did not answer, but simply fixed her eyes on him, partly in surprise, partly in joy. He could see her eyes shining, but a moment later, the light faded. She turned to look out the window, then turning back again, she sighed, her eyes red with tears: "Haven't you had enough of that kind of life?"

"In the past, it was all my fault," he said, bowing his head in an attitude of guilt. "I don't know why my temper has become so. . . ."

"You're not to blame," she interrupted impatiently. "Who can keep his temper these days? It's not just you who are in the wrong. My temper's been bad too."

"I'm sure things will get better in the future," he said, plucking up courage.

"The future is even more uncertain. It seems to me, life is really not worth living. To tell you the truth, I really don't want to go on working at the bank. But if I don't, what am I going to live on? Someone trained in education like me, working in a bank as a petty clerk, letting myself be pushed around, it's really shameful!" At this point, her eyes became red with tears once more, and she looked down slightly.

"Then what about me? I spend all day correcting articles that seem to make sense but don't. Shusheng, you mustn't talk like that. Forgive me this once, and come back with me today. I promise never to quarrel with you again," he begged, losing control of himself.

"Calm down! People are watching us!" she whispered in warning, leaning her head towards him. She lifted the cup to her lips, and began to slowly sip her coffee.

He felt as if a ladle of cold water had been splashed over his head, and even his heart froze. He too lifted his cup to drink, but today the coffee was particularly bitter. "Good," he thought to himself. "The bitterer, the better," and he drank the coffee to the dregs.

"You mustn't be upset. It's not that I can't come home with you. But just think. What will it be like when I'm back? Your mother is so stubborn. She can't stand a daughter-in-law like me, and besides, she's not happy that anyone should share her son's love. As for me, I can't stand her temper. In the end, we'll spend the days quarrelling as before, and life will only be worse for you. In any case, it's so costly to live. With me there, it will only increase your expenses. You ought to understand that even if we do separate in this way, we can still be good friends. . . ." She spoke calmly, but her voice revealed a bitterness that she was doing her best to restrain.

"But Xiao Xuan —" he said painfully.

"Xiao Xuan gets on well with his grandmother. He has his grandmother's love, he has his father's care and protection. It's the same. In any case, he's not with me often, and he's not young any longer. He doesn't need a mother like me." She spoke distinctly, enunciating one word at a time.

"But I need you —" he continued, still pleading.

"Your mother needs you even more. I can't chase her away. As long as she's there, how can I come back!" she persisted.

"Then what am I to do? I might as well be dead!" he cried wretchedly, clutching his head in both hands.

"We'd better go. You have to be back for dinner," she said gently, sighing briefly. Then raising her voice, she called the waiter over to pay. She was the first to stand up, putting a note on the table as she did so. She pushed the chair aside and began to leave. He was forced to get up too, and followed her without a word.

Outside the coffee-shop, night had already fallen. The cold air hit them in the face. He shivered.

"Well, good-bye," she said gently, and turned away.

"No," he cried. The word came out in spite of himself. When he saw her turn back, he could not restrain himself, and finally blurted out the question that had been haunting him all day:

"At least tell me frankly, is it because there's someone else? And I don't mean my mother."

Neither her face nor her attitude seemed to change. Nor did his question anger her. It merely aroused her sympathy, for she understood what he meant. She smiled sadly.

She nodded. "There is and there isn't. But please don't worry. I'm thirty-four this year. I won't do anything silly." Then she left him, and went off determinedly in the other direction.

He stood stupidly where he was, gazing at her back. But he saw nothing. In his mind was only one image: that of her, accompanied by the young man in the smart overcoat, walking in front of him, forever in front of him.

"You've failed. After all that talking, you've achieved nothing," he told himself. "I really don't understand what's in her mind. What shall I do?" he thought, seeing only blackness all around him.

"You'd better go home," he seemed to hear his own voice whisper in his ear. He turned and went off disconsolately.

"Home! What kind of home have I got!" he kept repeating
to himself as he walked.

6

He arrived home. The main entrance of the building was like
a black cavern. Today, it was their district's turn to be without electricity, but there had been no kind-hearted soul to light
an oil-lamp at the door. After he had groped his way across
the darkness of the passageway, he turned to go up the stairs,
climbing up to the first floor, and then to the second.

The door to his flat was slightly ajar, letting through a little
patch of light. He pushed it open and went in. His mother was
sitting bent over the square table, eating her evening meal. On
hearing the door creak, she looked up and cried happily:
"You're back!" He nodded. "Come and eat, quickly! I waited
till now, and then I thought you wouldn't be back for dinner,"
she went on garrulously.

"I had something to do, so I'm a bit late back," he answered
listlessly. He went over to the table and sat down on a stool
opposite her. She stood up, filled a bowl of rice and placed
it in front of him.

"Quick! Eat while the rice is still hot," she said, smiling at
him as she sat down again. "This afternoon, Mr. Fang on the
first floor gave me a *jin* of meat from his share, and so I've
made a bowl of pork braised in soy sauce. I know you like it.
I put it in the pot of rice to keep it warm, and I've just taken
it out. It's still hot. Try it and see. It's your favourite dish."
She hurriedly ate up the rice in her own bowl.

As he listened quietly to his mother's kindly words, his eyes
lingered for a moment on the dish she had prepared. He saw
some odd grains of rice stuck to the side of the bowl, and felt
a moment of desolation. He wanted simply to fall on his bed
and weep bitterly, but he kept his head down, assenting per-

functorily to everything his mother said. Though he had no appetite, he just kept swallowing mouthful after mouthful, picking up the braised pork with his chopsticks, one piece after another. In the presence of his mother, he was as ever the obedient child.

"Aren't you feeling well, is that it?" his mother asked solicitously, for this interminable silence of his made her uneasy.

"It's nothing," he replied, shaking his head. "I'm fine," he added. Then he looked down again without another word.

His mother looked at him anxiously. She hoped he would say something more to her, but he did not even glance up at her. Unable to bear the silence, she remarked: "The food's not cold, is it?"

"No," he answered mechanically, still not lifting his head.

She was disappointed. She had waited all day for him, and now that he was home, he treated her so coldly. She understood. He must have that woman on his mind. She watched him closely. He put down his bowl and chopsticks, and silently stood up.

"Have you had enough?" she asked gently, repressing the anger that was beginning to rise in her.

"Yes," he replied, and began to clear the table.

"You had only one bowl," she went on.

"I've just had coffee with Shusheng," he admitted frankly, without thinking.

Her anger at once flared up. It was that woman again! Here she had been cooking the meal at home, waiting for him to return, while he'd been having coffee with that woman. They knew how to enjoy themselves! That good-for-nothing son of hers! He'd gone chasing after that tart! He had bowed down before that shameless bitch! It was too much. She would not put up with it.

"How can you still run after her? . . . How can she have the face to see you?" she cried.

"I asked her to come home," he answered weakly.

"Huh! She still has the nerve to come back!" she sneered.

"She wouldn't come, but I think perhaps she may think it over and change her mind after a few days," he ventured timidly.

"She might come back? You really are in a dream! If I were you, I'd put a notice in the papers divorcing her. In any case, you can't get water back once you've thrown it out," she retorted, her face flushing with anger. "I married into the Wang family over thirty years ago when I was eighteen. When I became a daughter-in-law, I was never like her! I've never seen a woman like her before!" She was helpless with rage, knowing that her son would never listen to her, knowing that he would never forget that woman, so much that even now, she could not get the better of her. He still pronounced the name of Shusheng with such affection.

"I think she also has her difficulties, only she's not willing to speak about them, — " her son said, as if he had not heard his mother's words. Only his own worries concerned him, so that his words were directed at himself, but he had only half-finished before he was interrupted by his mother.

"You still stick up for her. You really are hopeless! She has boy-friends behind your back, she writes them love letters, what problems does she have to talk about!" his mother exclaimed, standing up and waving the forefinger of her right hand before the tip of his nose.

"They may not be love letters," he countered.

"If they're not love letters, then why is she afraid of showing them to you? Why does she elope —" At the word "elope", she could not go on. She was his mother after all. She just stood there before him, staring at him.

"Mother," he cried imploringly, his eyes already filled with tears. For a moment, he could not continue.

"Go on," she said kindly, after a moment. His tears had won her sympathy, and her anger subsided. She looked at him with tenderness, as if he were still her child of long ago, who had been wronged by outsiders, and had come home in tears to complain to his mother.

"Mother, you don't understand Shusheng at all. She hasn't eloped. She's simply gone to stay with a friend for a few days. She'll be back," he said in anguish.

"Huh! I don't understand her?" she sneered. "To tell you the truth, I understand her better than you do. She can't put up with living in poverty with you forever. She's not that kind of woman. I saw through her long ago. It's time you should understand. Your mother's the only one who'll never leave you, whether you're rich or poor. You say I don't understand her. Was it she who told you that?"

He saw that his mother was getting angry again, and so he didn't like to answer this last remark of hers truthfully. He simply shook his head and said: "No, she didn't say anything."

His mother stared at him, and then after a moment, gave a long drawn-out sigh. "You'd better go and rest," she said. "Leave me to clear up. You're tired enough for one day."

"It's nothing. I'm not tired," he answered dejectedly. In reality, he was exhausted, but he managed finally to hold on, and help his mother wash the bowls and chopsticks and put them back in the cupboard.

She placed the earthenware candle-holder on the square table in the centre of the room and told him: "I'm going to do some mending. If you've nothing to do, you'd better lie down for a while." She went into the little side room, took out a boy's overcoat, then sat down by the table and began to mend it by the light of the candle. Her head bent very low, although she had put on her glasses. The candle flame flickered violently, and after a while, as the light became dimmer, her head seemed to bend even lower.

He went to his bed, intending to lie down and sleep for a while. But instead, he just sat for a moment on the edge of the bed, then got up and went back to the table, standing there without a word. His eyes rested on his mother's head, which looked as if it had been sprinkled with salt. Only then did he realize how old and feeble she had become. Her hair had completely changed colour. All at once, she put down her glasses, and gave her eyes a hard rub before putting her glasses back on again and continuing with her work.

"Xiao Xuan is to be pitied too. He's worn this overcoat for three years now. Even if it hasn't fallen to pieces by then, he'll be too big to wear it next year. By rights, we ought to have had a new one made for him this year, only his father's so poor. It's already hard enough just paying for him to go to school. . . . Ah! the candles are getting worse and worse. Thirty *yuan* each, and they're like this. There's no light at all, and it's bad for my eyes. I'm getting old after all. I'm really no use at all. Even this little bit of sewing takes me so much time. His mother doesn't bother about him. It's just his bad luck to have landed in a family like ours." She went on muttering to herself, as if she had not noticed that he was standing beside her, watching her.

"Mother, you shouldn't work in the evening. Your eyes have got worse recently. You have to take care of them," he said aloud, his voice full of emotion and pain.

"I'll have finished soon. Just a few more stitches," she replied, lifting her head to look at him. "Where will I find the time if I don't do it at night? I have to do the shopping and the cooking during the day. There's no other use for my eyes, so why would I want to take care of them?" Her right hand was quivering as she plied her needle and thread shakily back and forth through the overcoat. "I can't compare with his mother, always as fresh as a flower, unable to do this, and unable to do that. She's so concerned with dressing up beautifully that she doesn't have time to look after her son. She's supposed to be a university graduate, with a higher education, doing important things in a bank, but I've never seen her bringing any money back for the house."

"Mother," he interrupted, "just Xiao Xuan's tuition fees and meals make a big hole in her pocket, without talking about her helping out with the household expenses. This term already, it's cost over twenty thousand, and it'll soon be thirty thousand."

"Well, didn't she bring that on herself? She absolutely had to send him to that posh school. His schoolmates are all sons of the rich. He's the only one from a poor family. He can't keep up with anyone in anything. And she won't give him any more money to spend. Xiao Xuan's always complaining," she said.

He could not continue to listen to her. No matter how exhausted he felt, he was terribly upset. He could not sleep quietly, and he could not work quietly. Even less could he quietly watch his mother working. The room was so cold, so dark. His mind seemed to float about in empty space, unable to find a place to rest. He felt that he had not yet suffered enough pain, enough bitterness. He needed to cry out, to sob out his heart, perhaps to suffer greatly, to be cruelly beaten. But he could not stand calmly at his mother's side.

He strode towards the door, threw it open, and went out. "Xuan! Xuan!" he heard his mother call from the room. Without even bothering to reply, he dashed down the stairs. In the darkness, he knocked his right temple, and though it became swollen, he felt no pain. He simply thought: "I've let everyone down. I ought to be punished!"

7

He reached the main entrance. On the footpath opposite, the carbide lamps of the fruit stalls and portable noodle stands glimmered in the darkness like stars. A feeling of coldness made him shudder. "Where shall I go?" he asked himself. Finding no answer, he strode off down the street.

He wandered aimlessly for three blocks, and was nearly knocked down by a rickshaw speeding down the hill. The puller cursed him roundly, but he did not take it in, for i was as if an immense distance separated him from everything around him. In his heart was a vast emptiness.

He went on for another block, still not knowing where he should go. The street ahead of him was brightly lit. How many electric lamps were there, he wondered. The two streets were two different worlds! He headed towards the lights.

He had just reached the corner of the street when a voice suddenly called his name: "Wenxuan!" He turned in astonishment. He found himself standing before a wine-shop. The man who had hailed him was a middle-aged man in a Western suit. He had stood up from a table near the door.

"You've come just at the right time. Sit down and have a drink," the man said in a loud voice. He recognized him as someone he had known at secondary school. They had not seen each other for some six months. How greatly he had aged. At any other time, he would have exchanged a few words at most and left. But now, he went over to the table in silence, pulled out a stool, and sat down opposite his school friend.

"Bring a bowl of *hongzao*!" his friend shouted, turning towards the counter.

The man at the counter acknowledged the order, and then brought over a bowl of sweet-smelling liquor made from fermented yeast.

"Bring me another bowl," his friend commanded, drinking up the rest of his own wine in a single gulp, his face reddening as he banged on the table.

"Baiqing," he said, "I remember, you never used to drink. When did you pick up the habit?"

"It's not a habit, and I haven't picked it up. I just want to drink. I have to drink," his friend explained loudly, shaking his head. "You drink up first."

He looked at his friend without answering. After a while, he lifted the wine bowl, and without a word, gulped down a large mouthful. As he put the bowl down, he gave a long sigh. A stream of warm air rushed up his throat. Unable to hold it back, he hiccupped.

"Drink up! Drink up! You haven't drunk up yet! That won't do!" his friend kept urging him, gesturing with his hands.

"All right, I will," he said, becoming excited, and he did indeed drink the rest of the wine in one gulp. He felt his heart throbbing violently, and his face began to burn.

"Another bowl," his friend shouted, pounding the table, at the same time picking up a piece of dried bean-curd from the china saucers in the middle of the table and seizing a handful of peanuts which he placed before him.

"Here, eat!" he said.

"I can't drink any more," he answered, waving his hand in refusal.

"What are you afraid of, old chap! What does it matter if you get drunk? It's much better to be drunk than sober," his friend said. The wine had already been placed before them.

"But you can't be drunk forever. You have to sober up sooner or later," he answered with a lonely, sad smile. He looked at his friend's face. He noticed that this young man of thirty had aged at least ten years in the last six months. His forehead was lined with wrinkles, his cheeks were sunken, his eyebrows knitted in a perpetual frown, while his eyes had completely lost their lustre, the two pupils staring at him lifelessly. For a moment, he was upset. Then he added: "But when you sober up, isn't it even worse?"

His friend said nothing. He lowered his gaze and took a mouthful of wine, then looked up again to stare at him before taking yet another gulp. "I really can't stand it," he said as if to himself, shaking his head.

"But if you can't stand it, why do you come here to drink? Wouldn't it be better to go home earlier? I'll go with you," he offered with concern.

"What's there to do apart from drinking? If I drink too much, all that can happen is that I'll make myself ill and die. I don't care. I might just as well be dead," his friend said miserably. "I'm finished. Everything is over for me."

"You don't realize it, but your situation is much better than mine. If I can bear mine, why can't you bear yours?" he said sympathetically. As he looked at the thin face, he felt his own wounds revive, and a momentary pain stabbed his heart, almost bringing tears to his eyes. "How's your wife? Is she still in the countryside?" he asked, changing the subject. He thought of the child-like face of his friend's wife. The wedding reception had been held in the Longevity Restaurant a year ago. He'd attended the simple ceremony with Shusheng. Afterwards, he'd been a guest in their house in the countryside. How sweet the smile of this young wife was. Shusheng had liked her too. When he thought of his own misery, his thoughts had turned to Shusheng, and from there to his friend's wife.

"She's passed away," his friend whispered, turning his face from him.

"She's dead? What of?" he asked, stunned. He almost leapt up, as if he'd sat on the point of a needle.

"She wasn't ill," his friend answered without emotion, shaking his head. His face was terrible to see. It was hard to make out what he meant.

"Then, she —" When he got to "she", he stopped abruptly. He was afraid to hear his own question. Suicide? A tragic death? A sledge hammer seemed to be driving its way into his heart.

His friend said nothing. He said nothing either. The silence became unbearable. The drinkers at the other tables seemed no happier. Some were going on about their hardships, and some were arguing with their companions about something or other. At a table in the corner, on the right, a middle-aged customer who had been drinking dejectedly by himself with his head down, suddenly got up to pay for his wine and left. After he had gone, the waiter told a pale-faced client that it was an old customer who came unfailingly every evening. He didn't like to talk, but also never overdrank, eating only two pieces of dried bean-curd with his wine. He always came at the same time and left at the same time. No one knew who he was, or what he did for a living.

Wang Wenxuan was irritated by what he heard. He looked up and sighed, remarking sourly: "There's nowhere where there's no suffering!"

His friend looked at him in surprise. Then his tears fell, drop by drop. "It's the seventh day today since she died." After a moment's pause, he continued: "Ten days ago, she was still perfectly well. There wasn't the slightest thing wrong with her. The child she was carrying was due. I went with her to the hospital for an examination, but the doctor said it wasn't yet time, and that it would be at least another fortnight, so he wouldn't admit her to hospital. I couldn't stay in the countryside for another two weeks. I don't get on with the head of section at my place, and he purposely made things difficult by refusing me leave. So I came back to town. On the third day, my wife's labour began. She was in pain most of the day, but there was no one to look after her. It was only when a woman living in the same courtyard finally discovered her that she was taken to the hospital. When she'd had the examination, they'd said it would be an easy birth, and that there'd be no problem at all. But when she got to the hospital, the child wouldn't come out. The doctor delivering the baby tried everything on her, and it wasn't until midnight that they got the baby out. But it was already dead, and the mother's condition was bad too. My wife called my name all night. She must have cried my name over a hundred times before she died. They told me her cries were so heart-rending that even the people downstairs could hear them. Her sole wish was to see me once more before she died, to beg me to avenge her. But I was in town. How was I to know! When I got the phone call, I went down straightaway. The body was already stiff. Her belly was so frighteningly distended that we could not even close the coffin. Now I'm all alone, just as I was before I married. I buried my wife. The first thing I did when I got back to town was to ask for long leave.

I do nothing all day. All the time, at home or in the street, I hear my wife's voice calling my name. Listen to her calling: 'Baiqing! Baiqing!'" The speaker drummed two fingers on his right temple. "Yes, it *is* her voice. Her cries are so heart-rending! . . . That's why I only want to drink. I just want to get drunk. The best thing is to drink myself into a stupor. That's the only way I can stop the sound of her cries. To live, to go on living, really isn't easy! From now on, apart from wine, what do I have to keep me company?" Covering his face with his right hand, he sobbed softly, but briefly, becoming silent as if he had fallen asleep.

After Wang Wenxuan had heard the man's story, he felt as if a huge hand had seized his heart in its tight grasp. His mouth was full of an unbearably bitter taste. He felt a cold shiver run up his spine. His ability to control himself was at the breaking point. "You can't go on like this." It was only because he was trying to resist the pressure which became stronger and stronger that he spoke out like this. He became even more upset, and so he added: "You have a master's degree in literature. Do you still remember your literary am-bitions? Why don't you take up your pen?"

"My books have all been sold. I had to live. Writing's not my line." His friend took his hand abruptly from his tear-stained face. His eyes glistened agressively. "What do you think I ought to do? Should I get married again, get another child and drive another woman to her death? I won't do it. I'd rather destroy myself. The world isn't for people like us. We're honest and law-abiding. It's the others who become rich and powerful. . . ."

"And so we should drink for all we're worth!" Wang Wen-xuan interrupted, almost shouting. He had finally crumbled. It was no use trying to restrain himself. The dam had broken, and the water had to flow somewhere. His grief and indigna-tion had reached their limit. He needed to forget everything.

Naturally, to get drunk became his only way out. "Wine! Wine!" he shouted. The waiter brought him another bowl of wine. He looked at the sweet-smelling liquid and thought in-wardly: What kind of a world is this! He lifted the bowl, took a huge mouthful, clenched his teeth, and swallowed it. A wave of warm air rushed up his throat. He couldn't stop himself from hiccupping. "I can't finish the wine," he said apologetically. I'm really good for nothing, he thought. I can't even drink. I shall always have to accept the bullying of others. Then, as an act of bravado, he drank up the rest of the wine, gulping it down, one mouthful after another.

"Your face is as red as Guan Gong's[1]. Are you drunk yet?" his friend asked kindly.

"Not yet, not yet!" he replied energetically. He felt his brain solidifying into something heavy and hard. As soon as he made an effort to speak, his head would ache. His face was afire, his body floating in air. He tried to stand up, but couldn't remain steady, and fell dejectedly back again.

"Hey! Be careful!" his friend cried.

"I'm not in the least drunk," he said, wanting to smile, but he couldn't even manage that. He just wanted to cry. He felt as if all things sad had surged into his heart. He couldn't make out what they were. He was exceedingly dizzy and extremely upset. He couldn't bear it. It seemed as if his friend's eyes had multiplied into countless pairs, spinning in front of him; he peered to look more closely, but saw the same thin, grief-stricken face. But after a while, the countless pairs of eyes appeared again, and even the light from the electric lamps began to revolve. He struggled, and finally stood up, holding on to the table. "I'm drunk," he said, admitting defeat. He nodded to his friend and lurched out of the wine-shop.

He staggered crookedly along the footpath for a block or so. The thought of his home came suddenly to him, and he seemed to see his own body bathed in light. He sobered up a little. "How can I be like this?" he thought with vexation.

---

[1] Guan Gong: a hero in the Ming Dynasty novel *Romance of the Three Kingdoms* — Tr.

He turned and went off in the direction of his home. He had just gone a couple of steps, when a huge black figure coming towards him ran straight into him with such force that he saw stars before his eyes. One side of his face began to throb with pain and burn. He tottered and swayed, and almost fell.

The man cursed him roundly several times, but he did not hear what he said. He continued to stumble along. He wanted to walk quickly, but he was too upset, and his stomach seemed to be full of something boiling up inside him. He tried to hold it down, but in the end, he opened his mouth, and the meal he had taken at home earlier that evening spurted out like a fountain.

When he had vomited all he could, he did not even wipe his lips, but continued forward on his way. He himself was disgusted by the stench of the wine. He just wanted to get home as quickly as possible, but the more anxious he became, the slower his feet moved. When he was over half-way along the street, he threw up again. This time, the vomiting gave him no relief. It seemed as if the rice and vegetables he hadn't vomited were stuck in his throat. His chest was burning. He continued to vomit as he went. Some of the passers-by eyed him curiously, but their stares aroused in him no distaste. Nothing around him concerned him. At that moment, if someone had dropped dead at his side, he would not have turned to give him a glance.

But just at that moment, two women chatting together came out from the dazzling lights of a restaurant specializing in East China style cuisine. His eyes strayed involuntarily onto their powdered faces. He was startled and turned his face away at once. But he was not quick enough. The older of the two women had already recognized him. "Xuan," she called.

Without answering her, he strode off into the darkness. But he had not gone far before he found himself unable to control his movements. So he stood on the edge of the footpath, bent over and vomited. He did so noisily, but little came out. He felt as if he were under torture. His mouth was filled with a bitter taste. Slowly, he straightened up, panting as he leaned against a lamp-post.

"Xuan," he heard a soft, gentle voice call. He turned involuntarily, his eyes blurred with tears. She was standing with her back to the light. He glanced at her hastily, seeing only the outline of her figure, but he had already recognized her as Shusheng. "What's the matter?" she asked in alarm.

He gazed at her, gasping for breath, feeling that he had so many things in his heart he wanted to say to her, but not knowing where to begin. In fact, he could not get a word out.

"Are you ill?" she asked with concern.

He shook his head. His breathing became more natural, but his tears began to flow once more. The tears had first come when he was vomiting, but now they were tears of both gratitude and grief.

"Why don't you go home? You're vomiting so terribly!" she continued.

"I got drunk," he replied regretfully.

"What on earth did you go drinking for? You've never been able to drink. Hurry up and go home to bed, or you'll really become ill," she urged anxiously.

"At home, Mother doesn't understand me. I was fed up, and so I came outside for a walk. I ran into an old school-friend and he dragged me along for a drink, and so I got drunk," he explained, as if apologizing. "Thank you. Good night." He felt a little better, and left the lamp-post and began to cross the street, still swaying unsteadily.

"Be careful! You'll fall over," she shouted in warning from behind, and at once followed him, walking beside him for a while. "I'll see you home," she said, and then moved forward to take him by the left arm.

"You're really going to see me home?" he asked, his voice shaking. He looked at her timidly.

"If I don't see you home, you might go and have more to drink," she said with a smile. He felt a glow of warmth, and his heart was greatly comforted.

"I won't drink any more," he promised like a child, and let her help him home.

8

When they reached the main entrance and he saw the vast black cavern, he frowned and hesitated, unwilling to enter.

"You can't see properly. Be careful. Go slowly!" she enjoined solicitously. She not only did not leave him, but pressed closer to him, supporting him firmly by the arm.

"What about you? Aren't you coming in?" he asked anxiously.

"I'll see you up the stairs," she replied, whispering into his ear.

"You're so good to me," he said gratefully. He wanted so much to embrace her and weep tears of joy. But he just glanced at her, looked down in silence and then began to move through the main entrance, stepping onto the steps which were so familiar to him. "Be careful," she kept urging from beside him, continuing to support him firmly. But her help only made him all the slower.

"Go upstairs," she told him again. He muttered something briefly in reply, hiding his secret joy.

Finally, they reached the second floor, and had just stepped off the last steps of the staircase, when they saw the wife of the civil servant next-door come out, a candle in her hand.

"You're back, Mrs. Wang!" The pale-faced woman broke into a smile as she greeted them. Her look betrayed an air of astonishment, but it was full of goodwill.

She smiled as she nodded to the docile woman, and asked politely: "Are you going out, Mrs. Zhang?"

As she answered, Mrs. Zhang looked at him in surprise. Then she asked gently: "Is Mr. Wang not well?"

He stood beside his wife, hanging his head, unable to reply.

She answered for him: "No, it's not that. He's had too much to drink."

"Mr. Zhang's drunk too. I'm going to buy him some mandarines. Mrs. Wang, you'd better take Mr. Wang inside. He'll be much better after he's had a sleep," the little woman advised, smiling cordially. There was nothing forced about her smile, but when she smiled, the wrinkles on her forehead did not disappear, nor did her eyebrows relax from their frown. "Poor little woman! Life is really too hard on her." This sympathetic thought came to Mrs. Wang every time she saw her. The little woman went slowly down the stairs. The two of them were able to reach the door of their flat by the light of her candle.

The door hadn't been bolted. It opened wide the moment he pushed it. The room was still just as dark, the candle on the table still alight, his mother still sitting beside the table, her glasses on, mending clothes. She looked so old and feeble, her back so hunched. Not the slightest sound came from her. The charred end of the candlewick had grown longer and longer, but she had not bothered to trim it. She looked as if she hadn't stirred for a long time.

"Xuan, where have you been? Why didn't you say something to me first? Did you go to look for that woman again? You should.... I tell you, it's better to forget her. These modern women, how can they put up with hard times like these for long!" his mother said, continuing to sew as she spoke, without looking up. She thought that her son had returned alone.

"Xuan, don't be upset. It's better if that woman's gone. In the future, when the war's won, you'll be rich one day. You won't need to worry about not having a woman then!" Not hearing an answer from her son, she looked up in surprise. She was blinded by the golden light, and could see nothing. Her eyes were dry and sore. She put down her needle and thread, took off her glasses, and rubbed her eyes several times.

When his mother had pronounced the words "that woman", he had frowned, wincing in pain. At the same time, he had reached out to squeeze his wife's hand firmly in his own, afraid that she would begin quarrelling with his mother. But his wife said nothing throughout. He could bear it no longer. "Mother!" he implored, his voice filled with distress.

"What is it?" his mother asked, startled. She took her hands from her eyes. This time, she saw. "That woman" was standing before her!

"I saw him home," Shusheng said, purposely pretending to be cool and calm.

"Wonderful! How clever you are! You've managed to get her to come home," his mother sneered, and turned back to her sewing again.

Shusheng looked at his mother and smiled, before saying finally: "It wasn't he who got me to come back. He got drunk somewhere, and was throwing up all over the street. I ran into him and brought him home." She spoke like this intentionally to anger his mother.

"Xuan, why didn't you say something to me before creeping out to drink?" His mother was so startled, she almost jumped out of her chair. Dropping the clothing and the needle and thread onto the table, she went up to her son and examined him carefully. "You can't hold your liquor. Why did you run out and drink all of a sudden? Have you forgotten that your father died of drink? I've never let you touch alcohol since you were small. How can you still go out and drink!" she protested bitterly.

"He was upset. You'd better let him sleep," Shusheng interrupted.

"I wasn't talking to you!" his mother retorted, turning angrily towards her.

Shusheng snorted, but piqued, refused to answer.

"Xuan, tell me how you came to be drinking," his mother said tenderly, as if talking to a child she doted on.

His head dropped in fatigue. He made no answer.

"Tell me. What's on your mind, tell me!" his mother urged. "Tell me frankly. I won't blame you."

"I was upset. I thought it would be better to be drunk," he answered candidly, forced to the point where he no longer cared what he was saying.

"Then when did you run into her?" his mother pursued, refusing to let go. Her feeling against his wife made her blind to her son's pain.

"You should let him go to bed," Shusheng interrupted once more, unable to contain herself.

His mother ignored her, still waiting for an answer from her son.

"I — I —" It needed all his effort just to get these two words out. His mind was in a turmoil. A force was welling up in his stomach. He tried with all his strength to suppress it, but finally, losing control, he opened his mouth and vomited. The mess splattered over both himself and his mother.

"Quick! Sit down," his mother cried in alarm, thrusting her questions to the back of her mind.

He continued to stand where he was, bending over and vomiting, while his wife rubbed his back, and his mother went to fetch a stool. He didn't bring up very much, but his eyes ran copiously. He sat down on the stool, gasping for breath, his hands pressed on his knees.

"Was it really worth it?" his wife said, feeling sorry for him as she stood behind him.

His mother finally relented, and giving way to her daughter-in-law, said: "You'd better see him to bed. I'll go and get some ashes and clean up."

After his mother left, the wife supported her husband to the bed. She silently took off his shoes, socks and outer clothing. He had never enjoyed such happiness for many years. He obeyed like a child.

Finally, when he got into bed, she tucked him in. She was about to turn and go, when he suddenly stretched his hand out from under the covers and, grasping her hand, held firmly on to it.

"Have a good sleep," she said to calm him.

"You mustn't go. . . . It was all because of you. . . ." He looked at her beseechingly with wide-open eyes.

She did not answer. She was thinking. She stood beside him for a long moment, tears trickling from the corners of her eyes. Before long, he fell asleep, but his hand never relaxed its grip.

That evening, she stayed. And so, in this simple way, his difficulty was resolved without his knowing it.

That night, he slept soundly, waking only when it was broad daylight. His wife was sitting by the desk near the window, putting on her make-up.

"Shusheng," he called happily. She turned to look at him, her face bursting into a bright smile. She said to him gently:

"Are you better? Do you want to get up?"

He nodded, stretched himself lazily and said contentedly: "I'm better. I'll get up."

She turned away and continued with her make-up. The curls of her perm were so fresh, so beautiful. She coughed lightly.

She was home. Then it was not a dream. It was real.

9

They spent the next ten days or so leading a life of peace and tranquillity. Both went to work punctually, and both came home punctually. His wife said no more about leaving, and even had her suitcase brought back from her friend's place. The evening it was brought back, the husband took his wife to the Cathay Cinema to see a film. They went again a second time, but this time, the projection stopped after they'd seen about two-thirds of the film, because the red air-raid warning balloon had been hoisted.

His mother stayed most of the time in her own little room. She seemed to be avoiding her daughter-in-law deliberately, but if the two did happen to meet, she did not put on a sour face or say anything sarcastic. She just said very little, that was all.

Early on Sunday morning, Xiao Xuan came home, going back to school the same afternoon on the last bus. When the grandmother saw her grandson, she was overwhelmed with joy. She naturally gave him the overcoat she had repaired with her own hands to try on. Because of this, her daughter-in-law even gave her a smile and said a few words in thanks.

The weather remained cloudy during all this period. Sometimes, it would rain lightly, at other times not at all. The road was never completely dry. At times, it was so slippery because of the mud that it was not easy to keep your footing when you stepped on it. The footpath was muddy too. A fortnight soon passed. One morning, when Wang Wenxuan was going to work, he slipped and fell just as he reached the intersection, taking the skin off his left kneecap. He hobbled as best he could to the main entrance of the building where his office was, arriving there before it was time to start work. Old Mr. Zhong was sitting at his desk, watching the passers-by in the street.

Seeing him come in, he asked: "What's happened? Did you slip?"

He nodded instead of answering and, after signing in, turned towards the stair-well.

"You should ask for a day's leave. You don't want to ruin your health!" Mr. Zhong suggested solicitously.

He stood at the bottom of the staircase, turned, and with a smile of helplessness, answered lightly: "You know, how much of my salary I can afford to have docked!"

"In times like this, you still think of your salary being docked! You still want to work yourself to death for the sake of the company! You know how much longer the company is going to feed us!" old Mr. Zhong exclaimed resentfully and a little excitedly.

"What can I do? We depend on them for our daily

bread," he answered wearily. He wanted to laugh, but no sound came.

"Depend on them? They're not going to keep employing us forever," old Mr. Zhong snorted.

He was astonished, and going over to Mr. Zhong's desk, he whispered: "Have you heard something?"

"The Japanese have reached Guilin and Liuzhou. They're advancing with terrifying rapidity. I heard that the chief manager has said that if the Japs enter Guizhou, he's going to move the company to Lanzhou. He's already wired Lanzhou to find rooms. If they really move to Lanzhou, we've had it. The likes of us had just better beat it," old Mr. Zhong said querulously.

Could such a thing happen! He stood there, stunned. A veil of darkness descended before his eyes. He shook his head wearily: "That's impossible. It can't happen."

"I'm not so sure. People like them are capable of anything. Take the company for instance. Some people do absolutely nothing and draw huge salaries, while others like you work your fingers to the bone all day for a miserable pittance." Mr. Zhong had still not finished when he saw Mr. Zhou come striding in. He broke off and whispered: "Why's he here so early today!... You'd better go up and start work."

He went despondently up the stairs. As he passed the desk of Mr. Wu, his section head, Mr. Wu suddenly glanced up and looked him up and down so minutely that he felt his skin tingle. He went over to his desk in trepidation and sat down. He opened up the long translation that needed never-ending correction, intending to bury himself in the black mass of printed words. "I really am spineless. They can't even write properly, yet I'm afraid of them!" he muttered to himself in self-reproach. But he continued to carry on meticulously with his work.

His leg kept hurting. He could not concentrate and had no idea what he had done the whole morning. He thought of his home, he thought of his situation at work, he thought of what old Mr. Zhong had just said. He had not read the newspapers for days, for his own personal suffering had occupied his whole mind. Nothing outside himself had aroused any interest in him. Previously, when fighting had broken out in northern Hunan, when Changsha had fallen, when fierce battles had raged at Hengyang, and Quanzhou had been taken, none of it had added not one jot to his suffering. The burdens of everyday life had pressed so heavily upon him during these past few years that he had not taken one breath in happiness. But what did the events around him have to do with him? People were always telling him that the world situation was getting better daily, but his own life became daily more difficult.

The bell for lunch woke him and rescued him from the thoughts in which he was entangled. He lifted his head and sighed heavily. Just then, a colleague came over to him. "Here, sign this," he said, spreading a sheet of letter-writing paper on the desk before him. He looked at it in astonishment. It was a subscription list drawn up by his colleagues for Mr. Zhou's birthday. One thousand *yuan* was written beside each name. One thousand *yuan*! It was not a small sum by any means. He hesitated a moment. His colleague eyed him disdainfully and coughed. Intimidated, he at once picked up his brush and signed. He colleague smiled and went off. He stood up. Not only did his left knee hurt, but his whole body ached. Forcing himself to bear it, he proceeded reluctantly down to lunch.

At the lunch tables, his colleagues were discussing excitedly the fate of Guizhou and Liuzhou and the enemy's likely movements. He buried his head in his rice, neither taking part in the discussion nor listening to their conversation. He felt his whole body go cold. He suspected it was an attack of malaria. Putting down his bowl, he left the table. Old Mr. Zhong noticed and came over to him, saying: "Aren't you well? You look terrible. You shouldn't work this afternoon. You'd better go home and have a rest."

He nodded gratefully and answered: "Then, will you ask for half a day's leave for me? I really don't feel well." He went out the door. A rickshaw was just passing the entrance, and the puller's eyes strayed towards him. "You'd better go home by rickshaw," Mr. Zhong urged from the doorway.

"It doesn't matter. It's not far. I can walk slowly," he answered, turning his head. Then, pulling himself together, he stepped onto the road to cross to the other side.

He walked very slowly, his body swaying unsteadily. His head was inordinately heavy, and from time to time, felt as if it would sink down into his neck. As he walked, the bruise on his knee continued to hurt. He just had to grit his teeth and go on, head down, stopping every few steps. In this way, he managed to cover quite a long distance. Ahead of him was the International. Suddenly, he heard a woman's voice. It was clearly his wife speaking. He looked up in surprise. It was indeed she. She was standing before the glass display windows admiring the goods there, together with the young man in the smart overcoat, whom she followed almost at once into the shop. She had not seen him, and would never have suspected that she had been within only three or four steps of him.

He caught a view of her back. Today her body seemed more alluring than ever before. Her full figure looked so young, bursting with the vigour of life. They were the same age, but when he thought of his own thin, frail body and his unsteady gait, not to mention his weariness of spirit, he felt there were too many differences between them. They did not seem to be of the same generation.

These thoughts aroused in him an acute feeling of wretchedness. The stalwart young man worried him. She seemed even closer to this man, the distance separating them even less. When she was standing beside him, anyone seeing them would have noticed what a harmonious couple they made. He was uneasy. He had already passed the coffee-shop, but he turned back now to stand in front of the windows, looking to see what was displayed there: large iced cakes, American coffee, chewing-gum, chocolates, goods of every kind. What had they been looking at? — He wondered about it. Two English words in red, "Happy Birthday", stood out amid the red flowers and green leaves of an iced cake. He suddenly remembered that her birthday was in just over a fortnight. Was the birthday cake what they'd been looking at? Was the young man thinking of presenting it to her for her birthday? And what about himself? What present did he have to give her? He put his hand involuntarily into his coat pocket and pulled out a handful of notes. He bent over and counted them. One thousand and just over one hundred *yuan*. It was his complete capital. And tomorrow night, he would have to fork out a thousand *yuan* for his share of the boss's banquet. He saw the white price-ticket beside the cake: "41b iced cake, 1,600 *yuan*". He sighed. He could not afford even one pound. How shameful! He turned away furtively, as if to hide, thinking as he did so: "He certainly can afford it." By "he", he meant the young man inside. Turning back once more, he went inside the front doors and stood at the glass counter, pretending to look at the cakes and sweets on display inside. In reality, he was stealing a glance into the coffee lounge. Shusheng had just lifted her cup to her lips and was sipping her coffee, her face covered in smiles. Jealousy seized his heart. Afraid she would see him, he dared not linger, and quickly slipped out the door.

On the way, he could only feel his heart beating and his head burning. He was afraid of slipping on the sloping, muddy road. He managed to endure it till he finally reached home.

His mother was standing by the square table, her apron on and her sleeves rolled up, washing the clothes. Looking up in surprise, she asked: "Have you had anything to eat?"

"Yes," he replied wearily. He stood reluctantly at his mother's side for a moment.

"Why have you come home so early today? You look so terrible! Aren't you well?" she asked in alarm, taking both hands out of the basin, and drying them on her apron. "Quick! Go and lie down, lie down!" She half-supported, half-pushed him to the bed.

"I'm not ill," he tried to explain. But when he got to the

bed, unable to hold out any longer, he collapsed onto it without even taking off his shoes.

"Take your shoes off. It'll be more comfortable," his mother said as she stood by the bed.

He tried to struggle into a sitting position, but at once fell down again, groaning with pain at the same time.

"You have a good lie down. I'll take them off," his mother said, and did indeed bend down to untie his shoelaces. He stretched out on the bed and closed his eyes. After taking off both his shoes, his mother straightened up and looked at him with sorrow and concern. "I'll get you a blanket," she then said, and unfolding the blanket at the foot of the bed, spread it over him.

Opening his eyes to look at her, he said weakly: "I'm afraid it's a bout of malaria." His face was as white as a sheet, and even his lips were grey in colour.

"Go to sleep. You just go to sleep. I'll bring you some quinine in a moment," his mother said comfortingly. The wrinkles on her face seemed to have multiplied. There did not seem to be a single strand of black in her hair. It was not at all like this when she had first come back to Sichuan. Now she did the cooking herself, the washing herself. These last few years, she had had hardships aplenty. And it was all his fault. But she had continued to care for him all along. She had never left him. "She really is a good mother," he thought approvingly to himself.

Later, his mother brought him three quinine tablets to take, and then placed the cup with the rest of the boiling water on the table.

"Mother!" he called out in gratitude, tears springing from the corners of his eyes. He looked at her, and for a moment, was unable to speak.

"What is it?" she asked, coming back to the bed and bending over him affectionately.

"You're so kind,.... You're too good to me,...." he stammered disjointedly.

"Go to sleep. We can talk about it when you're better," his mother said kindly to console him.

"It's nothing serious," he said, shaking his head weakly. Seeing that she was paying no attention to his words, he went on to explain: "I've just asked for half a day's leave. Tomorrow, they're giving a dinner for Mr. Zhou's birthday. I have to be there."

"You asked for only half a day's leave?" his mother said disapprovingly. "But you need another whole day's rest. There's no need to worry about your salary being docked."

"I have to go tomorrow; otherwise they'll look down on me and say that I'm too mean, and just want to get out of a few cents," he explained, his face red with the effort to speak.

"Whether you're mean or not is your business. What's it got to do with them? Mr. Zhou's not that much of a big shot!" his mother retorted angrily. Then she asked abruptly: "Have you seen Shusheng?"

"I've just seen her," he replied without thinking.

"Why didn't she come home with you then? She could have asked for leave to come back and look after you. 'Flower vase' like her don't care about having their salaries docked." Her jealousy and her hatred had been aroused once more by what he had said. She thought only of giving vent to her anger, and not at all about how her words might wound him.

He stared at his mother blankly. It was some time before he smiled (and what a pained smile!), saying softly, as if to himself:

"She, she's an angel. I'm not worthy of her!"

His mother heard only the last phrase clearly, and interrupted in anger:

"You're not worthy of her? It's obvious that she's not worthy of you! She claims to work in a bank, but she spends all day making herself seductive. If she's not an escort-girl of some kind, then who knows what she's up to all day!"

Instead of replying, he simply sighed in misery.

10

He slept uneasily all afternoon, dazed and confused, not waking until nearly seven. He lay back on the bed, drained of all strength. His singlet, soaked in perspiration and icy cold, clung to his back. Becoming conscious that he'd been sweating profusely, he moved slightly, thinking to loosen his singlet from contact with his flesh. He thought about getting out of bed to change into fresh underwear, but the moment he tried to move, his whole body ached so much, as if his bones had lost their joints, that he could not prevent a groan from escaping him.

His mother came to the bed and asked: "Are you awake? Aren't you well?"

That evening, the electricity had not been cut. The pale yellow light of the electric lamp diffused over his mother's face, making her look ill too. Moreover, she seemed so alone, so frail.

"It's all right," he replied. He opened wide his eyes, searching every corner of the room. "Isn't she here?" he asked in disappointment.

"She? You mean Shusheng?" his mother asked contemptuously. "She went out first thing in the morning and hasn't been back since."

"She ought to be back," he said after a moment, sighing.

"Yes. Has there been one day when she shouldn't have been back early?" his mother interrupted angrily. Seeing that he did not answer, she changed the subject and asked: "Would you like something to eat?"

"I don't feel like eating. I'm not hungry," he answered.

"What about some rice gruel? I've made some for you. There are some preserved eggs to go with it," his mother suggested.

"Perhaps I might manage a bowl," he agreed submissively, forcing a smile.

His mother turned happily to the crockery cupboard, took

out a bowl, and ladled the gruel from an earthenware pot on the brick stove by the door.

"In the long run, one's own mother is the best," he murmured to himself. His mind was no longer a blank as before. Just as he was gathering the strength to pull himself out of bed, his mother came in with the gruel and the preserved eggs. "Don't get up," she said. "Just sit up in bed and eat. I'll hold the saucer for you." She waited for him to sit up, gave him the bowl and chopsticks, while she herself sat at the bedside holding the saucer with the eggs, keeping watch over him eating.

But he had no appetite at all. For his mother's sake, he forced himself to eat one bowl of the gruel. When he had finished, his mother brought him a towel with which to wipe his face and said: "You'd better lie down again. Don't get up today."

He did as she suggested, and lay down again. But he did not like to undress, hoping to stay awake and await Shusheng's return.

Ten minutes or so after he had lain back down, there was a knock at the door. His mother answered. A man's form slipped in and a rough voice asked: "Is Mr. Wang back? Miss Zeng has a letter for him." He gave a start. He heard his mother ask: "Who's it from?" But there was no answer. The bearer of the letter had already gone.

He saw his mother, letter in hand, standing blankly in the middle of the room, as if she did not know what she ought to do. He could not bear it. "Mother!" he called. She came over at once and said with an air of indifference: "She's sent you a letter. I wonder what it's about now." But she did not give it to him, being more concerned with her own thoughts, muttering:

"Miss Zeng? With a child of twelve, she still has the nerve to call herself 'Miss'! She has no shame!"

"Let's see what she's written," he said, putting his hand out for the letter. So she had to hand it to him.

He seized it, tearing it open in apprehension. It was in Shu-sheng's own handwriting, and read:

"Xuan,
A friend of mine has invited me to a dance at the Victory Mansions this evening. I may be very late back. Please don't wait up for me, and please don't bolt the door. Don't let Mother know I've save having to listen to all her old-fashioned moralizing tomorrow.

Your wife
This evening."

After reading it, he said nothing. He stared at the ceiling, the letter still in his hand, as if meditating on something.

"What does she say?" his mother asked, unable to restrain her impatience.

"She's gone to dinner with an old school-friend. She says they've got things to do, and she'll be back a little late," he answered, his voice perfectly calm.

"What kind of thing? If it's not the theatre, then it's mah-jong or dancing! What serious things do you think she can have to do! When I was a daughter-in-law, when did I ever dare to behave like her! Her child's nearly a grown man, and she still pretends to be a 'Miss', running wild all over town. And she has the nerve to boast that she's a university graduate, and in education at that!" his mother muttered resentfully.

"She doesn't play mah-jong." He did not understand his mother's mood, and was concerned only with defending his wife. He certainly had no idea that his defence would merely add to her ill-feeling against Shusheng.

"Not play mah-jong? Well, she plays cards, doesn't she? You're ill, and she doesn't even come home to see how you are. She doesn't understand the simplest duties of a wife!" his mother continued.

"She doesn't know. Otherwise, she'd surely have come home early. In any case, this doesn't count as being ill," he said, continuing to speak up for his wife. The image of her smiling face seemed to float before him.

"You're too weak. She treats you so badly, yet you continue

to stick up for her. I'd say that she's the way she is because of you. If I were you, I'd give her a good talking to when she comes home this evening," his mother shouted, pointing her finger at his forehead.

"It's not good for a husband and wife to quarrel too much. Squabbling over little things eventually leads to fights over bigger things," he replied, almost in a whisper.

"What are you afraid of? You're not in the wrong. It's clearly she who's in the wrong. She doesn't carry out her duties as a wife. She runs around with boyfriends —"

He could not repress a groan of pain. Startled, his mother at once swallowed the words she was about to utter, bent down over him and asked with concern: "What is it?"

He shook his head. After a while, he said weakly: "Mother, she really isn't a bad woman."

When his mother heard this unexpected reply, she did not quite know what to make of it at first, but then it suddenly dawned on her. She cried angrily: "She's not a bad woman! Then it must be I who's bad!"

"Mother, you've misunderstood what I meant," he pleaded anxiously. "I'm not making excuses for her."

"Who said you were!" A smile spread slowly over his mother's face and her anger gradually subsided. "It seems to me, she's bewitched you."

"It's not that at all," he explained earnestly. "You're both good people. It's I who am no good. I'm no use. I've made life hard for you both. Who'd have thought that we would end up living like this, with you doing all the cooking yourself . . . washing the clothes. . . ." He felt his nose twitch, and then his tears began to fall. He began to whimper, unable to continue.

"Don't talk anymore. Have a good sleep. It's not your fault. If it weren't for the war, we wouldn't be as poor as this!" his mother said gently. She also felt upset. She did not dare look at him any longer. His face was so terrible, the two cheeks so sunken. When they first arrived here, he was not like that at all. She remembered clearly: his face had been full, his cheeks rosy. "I hear that the war will be won next year. That will be a good thing finally. Otherwise, everyone will —" She had been speaking at random, meaning only to comfort him. But without waiting for her to finish, he interrupted:

"Mother, are you talking of winning? By the look of things, the Japs are fighting their way towards us. It's not at all certain that we won't be refugees before long. . . ." At this point, he became suddenly worried.

"Where did you hear that?" his mother asked, startled, though not at all afraid. "It can't be as bad as that, can it? Everyone says that in Hunan and Guangxi, they were interested only in pillaging. They can't hold the places. They'll withdraw of their own accord."

"That's all right then," he answered rather wearily. His mother's words soothed him, for he had no clear point of view of his own, and her words were comforting to hear. "I can't make it out," he added, "but someone at work said that the situation was so bad that the company was thinking of moving to Lanzhou."

"Lanzhou! So far! Short of being condemned to exile, who would be willing to go there! We're all right; why should we want to move? It's the people with money who don't have the courage of a mouse. These last couple of years, the Japs have been bombing till they don't dare bomb anymore. How would they have the gumption to attack us here!" His mother thought only of her grumbles, as if she wanted to redirect her dissatisfaction with her daughter-in-law (half of which she had to bottle up inside her because of him) onto another target.

"That's what I think too, but it's difficult to say in these matters," he answered, his eyes resting on his mother's face, as if seeking support in the midst of his solitude and hesitation. "Mother," he said gratefully, "you should rest for a while. You work too hard."

"I'm not tired," she answered tenderly, changing her tone and sitting on the edge of the bed.

"Are you all right now?" she asked him.

"Much better," he answered. But he felt exhausted, though not at all sleepy.

"We've managed to get through the years so far. It's hard to know what life is going to be like in the future. What worries me is Shusheng —" she murmured to herself, lowering her eyes. At Shusheng's name, her voice became so low that, apart from herself, no one could have heard what followed. But he certainly heard the name "Shusheng". For a long time, he said nothing. Then suddenly, he gave a little sigh, and was silent again.

After sitting on the edge of the bed for a short while, she stood up and gazed at him for a minute or two. She saw that his eyes were closed and that he was not making a sound. Thinking he'd fallen asleep, she tiptoed out of the room. Shortly afterwards, she came back in again and closed the front door, but instead of bolting it, blocked it with a chair before turning off the light and returning to her own little room.

In reality, he had not yet fallen asleep. He had closed his eyes simply to allow his mother to stop worrying and go back to her small room to rest. He could not sleep. His thoughts were fiercely active, flying back and forth over so many things, and in their midst, one woman's face kept appearing and reappearing, sometimes laughing, sometimes crying, sometimes angry, sometimes sullen. He was so tired. His head began to ache, and he began to sweat all over. But all the time, he was listening intently for the sound of one person's footsteps.

The room was dim but not completely dark, for a tiny ray of light filtered out from his mother's room. He could clearly see the chair blocking the door of the flat. Why didn't she come back? Mother was coughing. She was still not asleep! The old lady had such a hard life. It must be getting late.

Yes. From the street, he heard the clapper sound the second watch. She must surely be back soon. He listened intently to the sounds outside the door, for sounds there were. They were of rats running along the corridor. There was one in the flat as well. It seemed to have run to the foot of his bed, waiting. What was it doing? Was it eating his leather shoes? These shoes which he had worn for five months had already been attacked twice. Their openings had been chewed till they looked like the chipped edges of a bowl. If the rat called him again, there would be no way in which he could wear them in public. Every evening, just before he went to sleep, he put his shoes on top of the old suitcase under his bed. Today, he had forgotten, and now he could not lie there calmly and do nothing about it. He pulled himself up at once, stretching out his hand to pick up the shoes. The rat was off like a puff of smoke. He wondered whether the shoes had really been chewed or not, but he put them carefully on top of the suitcase nevertheless.

He lay down again. I must sleep, he told himself. But he had just closed his eyes when he heard the sound of high heels coming up the stairs. He opened his eyes at once and cocked his ears, listening. Nothing. Why was she still not back?

Eventually he fell asleep, but he did not sleep soundly. He would lie in a confused state for ten minutes or so and then wake up. There was no sound of a woman's footsteps. He would fall asleep again, but would wake up again not long after. He had bad dreams. Once he woke up whimpering softly, and then could not get to sleep again. By that time, the light in his mother's room was already out, and he had no way of telling how early or how late it was. The streets were exceedingly quiet. An old man was calling in a dreary voice: "Puffed rice and sweetened water!" It was a sound he was long accustomed to. The old man called out his wares the whole night long, regardless of how cold the weather was. This time he shivered, as if the voice of that feeble old man had sent a draught under his quilt.

It was then that he heard the familiar sound of her high heels. "She" had returned at last!

She pushed open the door lightly, came into the room humming a Western tune, and turned on the light.

The light was blinding. It hurt his eyes, but he opened them slightly nevertheless to peer at her. On her face was a smile of excitement. Her lips were as red as before, her eyebrows as delicate, her face as soft and fair. She stood in the middle of the room for a moment, thinking of something or other. Suddenly, she turned to look at him. He quickly closed his eyes, pretending to be asleep.

She came over slowly as far as the bed. He caught a breath of her powder and perfume. She bent down to look at him and arrange his bedcovers for him. Finding that he had not taken off his outer garments, she called to him softly. He was forced to open his eyes, pretending that he had woken from a dream.

"You went to sleep without undressing. Were you waiting up for me?" she asked with an affectionate smile.

Not knowing how to answer her, he simply nodded silently.

"I told you not to wait. Why did you then?" she asked, but her expression was one of gratitude.

"I slept for a while too," he replied awkwardly. There were so many things on his mind, but he did not have the courage to say them.

"You didn't let Mother see my letter, did you?" she asked, her voice very low.

"No," he answered, shaking his head.

"She didn't say anything?"

"She doesn't know," he answered. Then he asked: "Did you have a good time at the dance this evening?"

"Marvellous," she said contentedly. "It's so long since I've danced. That made it especially wonderful for me. I changed at my friend's place. There wasn't time to come home." She tilted her head upwards, and pirouetted lightly once.

"Whom did you dance with?" he asked, forcing a smile.

"With several people. But mostly with the departmental head, Mr. Chen," she answered happily. But she did not tell him who Mr. Chen was.

"Ah," he exclaimed briefly. Mr. Chen was probably the

young man who had accompanied her to the International Coffee Shop, he thought, as he looked, full of misery, at her body so full of life.

"You'd better undress properly and go to sleep. You're too good to me," she said with a tender smile, comforting him. Then she bent down and kissed him lightly on the lips, pressing her soft cheek for a moment against his left cheek. Then she went and sat down at the desk, brushing her hair in front of the mirror.

He touched his left cheek lightly and took a deep breath, inhaling the perfume she had left behind her, and gazing fondly at her thick black hair. After a moment, he thought: "She hasn't changed towards me. She's right. She ought to be happy. These last few years with me have been too hard on her." As he thought this, he turned over to face the wall, briefly shedding tears of shame.

I I

The next morning, he got up earlier than his wife. His mother wanted him to stay in bed another day, but he refused, claiming that he was fine, and in any case, he had to attend the banquet for Mr. Zhou's birthday that day. If he did not turn up, the others in the office would despise him even more, thinking him either too poverty-stricken or miserly. And so she gave in. He sat with her and ate a bowl of gruel left over from the previous night, leaving with her when she went out to shop for the vegetables. Shusheng was still sitting at the desk putting on her make-up.

As they emerged from the main entrance, his mother looked at him closely. What did she have on her mind, he wondered. They had gone part of the way together and were about to separate, when she called to him, her voice trembling: "Xuan, you can't go on like this! . . . You're sacrificing yourself for the family."

He frowned. It was a moment or two before he said in an undertone: "What else can I do?　Don't you suffer just as much?"

"But what about her? She's enjoying herself. She has to get herself up in the latest fashion just to go to the office. You'd think she was off to a wedding banquet," she burst out, unable to control herself.

He cast his eyes down, saying nothing.

"Xuan, I tell you, she's not like you or me. Sooner or later, she's going to go her own way," she continued.

He waited for a long moment before answering: "But we've been married fourteen years already."

"What kind of marriage do you call that?" his mother asked contemptuously.

The words grated on his ears, but though displeased, he simply pressed his lips firmly together and said nothing.

His mother said no more either, and they went their separate ways.

When he reached the office, it was old Mr. Zhong again who greeted him. "Why didn't you rest for another day? And you've come so early too!" Mr. Zhong said, rubbing his shiny bald head with his plump chubby hand.

"There's nothing much wrong with me. I'm fine," he answered with a smile.　He could see the sympathy in Mr. Zhong's eyes and attitude, yet he felt no humiliation at the old man's pity. After exchanging a few casual remarks, he went upstairs.

The tedious work began once more: forever, that seemingly comprehensible yet incomprehensible translation, the oddly used vocabulary and the bizarrely constructed sentences.　He had no authority to change them; he had simply to correct the misprints word by word. He had been sitting for barely an hour, when he felt his back run cold and his head burn with fever. He paid no attention. "Just for the sake of a few pence!" he muttered wretchedly to himself from time to time, and forced himself to go on working till twelve o'clock.

He did not feel like eating, but he told himself: "I should at least take a bowl of rice. After all, I'm not ill." Then he went downstairs, sat down at a table, and indeed, finished a bowl of rice. Normally, it was not too hard to get the cheap half-polished rice down, but today it was rather difficult to swallow. He put down his bowl, went to stand at the entrance and look out at the scene in the street. After a while, he lost all interest and went back upstairs to his desk.

He sat at his place casually leafing through the documents, tidying up the proofs he had already finished. An office-boy delivered him a letter. He could see from the handwriting that it was from Xiao Xuan, posted from school. Somehow, he felt comforted and slowly relaxed. Then he tore open the letter:

> ". . . the teacher says that with prices going up, the library and dining-room fees this term don't cover everything. Everyone has to pay another 3,200 yuan. He says that if there's any leftover, they'll refund it later. Many of the pupils have already paid up. I know that you're not well-off and don't have much money, and so I don't like to ask. But the teacher keeps pressing me, and pressing very hard. He says that if the money's not paid, then I can't take part in the the term exams. So I have no choice but to ask you and Mother. Please send the money to me at school within three days. . . ."

Even his last piece of comfort vanished as his eyes rested on these few lines of childish handwriting. "We've already paid over 20,000 and they want more. Where's the money to come from!" he muttered resentfully. No one paid him any attention.

"A school's not a business. How can they think only of money! And China relies on people like that to run her education! No wonder things are the way they are!" he protested angrily under his breath. The letter lay impassively before him, giving him no answer.

"I must talk with Shusheng to see if she can do something," he thought. "I'd better go now."

Then he changed his mind. "It's not a good time now. I'd better wait till the evening. She mightn't be at the bank, and I'm tired. I don't feel like moving."

In the end, he folded the letter, and returned it to its envelope.

before carefully putting it in his coat pocket. The afternoon's work began once more.

It was the same stumbling translation. "What language was it written in?" he wondered. The words and phrases wound themselves around his brain like a long hempen rope. He was so very tired. But he could not throw it aside. He felt his whole body begin to ache. He wanted so much to close his eyes, to forget everything, just to lay his head down on the desk and sleep. But Mr. Wu's eyes were fixed all the time on his face (or so he thought), so that he did not dare laze for one moment. In the end, he did not even dare look up.

"Heavens!" A silent protest formulated in his mind. "How can I have become like this! I put up with everything. Anyone can push me around. Surely I'm not going to let my life be wasted by this incomprehensible rubbish! To think I have fallen so low just for this tiny bit of money!"

But it was no use. He had protested like this a hundred, no, a thousand times before. But no one had ever heard him. No one even knew that he had ever harboured any resentment. Whether to his face or behind his back, everyone liked to call him a "good sort". He even thought of himself in this way. It had been like this for years.

"It's only been these last few years. I wasn't like that before. We didn't use to live like this, Shusheng and I, my mother and Xiao Xuan. It's all over. My happiness, my whole life has been snatched away by the war, by the way we live, by all the high-sounding insincere speeches, not to mention the official proclamations posted up all over the streets." His eyes continued to move unceasingly over the proof-sheets, but his thoughts were elsewhere.

"What am I thinking about! How did I change to this extent, clinging to life, afraid of death, thinking only of myself," he continued in self-reproach. But after a moment, he could not help thinking: "If the war's won soon, I ought to be able to find some way of improving our life. . . . But the Japs have

already penetrated deep into Guangxi. . . . They even say they
may storm and capture Guizhou. . . ."

He did not dare continue this train of thought. In fact, he
could not go on thinking. His head ached terribly. He felt his
forehead with his left hand. He was still feverish. A fever, what
did it matter? These last few years, he had often felt feverish in
the afternoon. He was used to it already. In any case, he was
not going to die so soon. Moreover, he had no time to spare
to consider the question of life and death. Those stern eyes
continued to watch him ferociously. "Why do you bully me like
this? At the most, I can stop depending on you for my living.
In what way am I inferior to you?" He had had such thoughts
before. But if he left this place, on which his living depended,
where would he go? In this city of hills, he had no friends or
relatives in high places or powerful positions. Even this insignificant job had been obtained through the influence of someone from his home village. That was when he had been out
of work for three months, and had been living on his wife's
salary. The villager who had been so good to him had already
moved to another province, and so even this last hope had gone.

"I have to put up with things just to survive." How often he
had stilled his protests with these words, and now he had recourse to them once more to solve his insoluble problems.

It was not easy to get through till five o'clock. He stopped
work, leaned back against his chair to relax, and then got
ready to go to the Guangzhou Restaurant for the banquet. Mr.
Zhou was a Cantonese, which was why his colleagues had
chosen a Cantonese restaurant. Mr. Zhou and the others were
already there when he arrived, but had not yet seated themselves, explaining that they were waiting for the Chief Manager. They were all standing under the bright lights of the dining-
room, talking and laughing in noisy joviality. Only two people
did not join in the conversation. He was one, of course. He hid
in a corner, hunched up in a chair, looking vaguely at the
crowd of people, while taking an occasional sip from his cup
of tea.

After half an hour or so, the Chief Manager arrived by car. In the course of the year, he had not had many chances of seeing this great personage, who was so thin that he resembled a monkey. When the Great Man made his solemn entrance, sporting a cane, the crowd rushed forward like a swarm of bees to welcome him, while he hovered rather timidly behind them. The Chief Manager apologized with a smile: "I'm so sorry to be late."

"No, no. Not at all! We've only just arrived!" a chorus of voices sounded in unison. He said nothing. He had no desire to talk to the Great Man, who did not even glance at him. His colleagues also seemed to have forgotten his existence, abandoning him in his corner as before.

There were two tables set. Before seating themselves, everyone kept politely offering seats to one another, while he stood silently in the background. Even the members of staff on about the same level as himself laughed and chatted away as they settled themselves. It was old Mr. Zhong who eventually called him over, having kept a place for him.

The others ate and drank and were in excellent spirits. The Chief Manager and Mr. Zhou were at the other table. The staff members at his table had all been over to drink their health, and he was the only one who had not yet done so. Apart from old Mr. Zhong, no one paid him the least attention, not even Xiao Pan, who did not deign to utter a word to him the whole time. He could not stand the way they all fawned on the Chief Manager and Mr. Zhou. The base flattery nauseated him. He was out of place in these surroundings, especially at this time, when what he needed most was peace and quiet. They certainly did not need him, nor he them. Yet no one had forced him to be present. But he had looked on attendance at the banquet as his duty. He had come of his own accord, and having come, there was not a second when he did not regret it. He thought of leaving, but did not stir.

He just kept his head down, drinking his wine. Old Mr. Zhong would say a few words to him once in a while, to which he would mutter some answer or other. Since wine was prohibited at that time, the waiters poured the Shaoxing wine into teacups, pretending it was tea, so as to avoid trouble from the police. And he really did drink his wine like tea. No one urged him to drink, but of his own accord, he drank a great many cups, knowing that his capacity was not large, but wanting to get drunk, wanting to cloud his brain. But right up until the banquet ended, he remained stone cold sober. Mr. Zhou, however, was so drunk that all he could do was giggle fatuously, saying things incompatible with his position. While everyone was shouting away in confusion, apparently over preparations for a programme of entertainment to follow, he took the opportunity to slip out on his own.

After coming out of the restaurant and reaching the quiet of the street, he felt a little chilly, but breathed much more freely. He stepped forward with great strides.

He hurried home anxiously, telling himself with relief: "I thought I was going to be ill today, but it's all right." He went up the stairs. The door of his flat was slightly ajar. His mother was sitting at the table making clothes, waiting up for him on her own. Shusheng was nowhere to be seen.

"You're back already?" his mother asked, looking up with an affectionate smile.

"Yes, Mother," he answered, his eyes still seeing someone else.

"You haven't been unwell today, I hope. I've been worried all day. It seemed to me you weren't looking too well when you left first thing this morning," his mother said, putting the things in her hand down onto the table, and taking off her glasses to rub her eyes.

"I'm fine. Mother, why don't you rest? Why do you have to work at night?" he said.

She picked up what she had just put down and showed it to him. "I'm making you some underwear. When I was tidying up the trunk today, I found a piece of cheap white cloth. Your singlet and underpants are in such unspeakable tatters, it seems to me, that I thought I'd make you two sets while I'm still capable of plying needle and thread."

"Mother, you mustn't tire yourself out. It doesn't matter if you leave those things until a little later," he said with feeling. "I can still wear my old ones for another three to five months yet. After that, I can buy new ones."

"Buy new ones? With a pitiful salary of a few pence like yours, what will you buy them with? You haven't bought even a pair of socks these last two years. And you're too good-natured. If I weren't such a burden to you, you wouldn't be so hard up. You never think of yourself. You've got so thin these last few years. To look at you, anyone would think you were over forty. You've got quite a few grey hairs already," his mother said, tears filling her eyes.

"Mother, you shouldn't keep thinking about such things. These days, who doesn't live from day to day? As long as we stay alive, that's enough," he said, heaving a sigh. "Hasn't she come back?" he asked abruptly.

"She? You mean Shusheng? She came back and went out again, saying she had something to do at the bank, and is sure to be back at ten," his mother replied. But she at once changed her tone and added: "You see. She's the only one who's having a good time. She doesn't do a thing around the house. She spends all day socializing around town." She looked at him suddenly and said with concern: "You've been drinking again today. I hope you didn't take too much. You're not strong enough to drink much."

"I didn't have much," he replied, and sighed once more. He felt extremely unwell. His head was dizzy, and something seemed to be scratching at his heart and at his throat. He decided to pour himself a cup of boiled water, and had just taken one step, when his body swayed for a moment to the right, as if he were about to fall. He steadied himself at once, but his body continued to sway uncertainly for a moment.

"What is it?" his mother cried, leaping up in alarm.

"I had two cups of wine." He forced a smile as his mother

ran over to support him. He turned away, shaking his head.
"It's nothing, nothing at all," he added. "I'm not drunk."

"Then you'd better go to bed early," his mother advised.

"No, I'm not sleepy. I'll wait up for her," he said, sitting
down in the cane chair by the desk.

"Wait up for her? Do you know when she's coming back?"

"Didn't you say she'd be back at ten?" he objected.

"You can't believe what she says. You'd better go to bed."

"All right, I'll go to sleep. I could do with a short lie-down,"
he said, standing up.

Dong-dong, dong-dong, dong-dong. The air-raid alert
sounded.

"It's the air-raid alarm. Mother, you'd better go down to the
shelter. I don't feel like going today," he said, going over to
his bed and sitting on the edge.

"If you don't go, I'm not going either. You'd better lie down
for a while. In any case, the actual attack signal hasn't sounded
yet," his mother said calmly.

The whole building, which had been very quiet, erupted
suddenly into activity. Voices and footsteps, accompanied by
the slamming of doors, could be heard everywhere. In the street,
some people were running about, but even more were shouting
and talking.

"X X, aren't you coming?" someone next-door shouted.

"I'm not going. The Jap planes aren't going to come, why
go to all the bother?" another voice replied.

"They nearly reached Guizhou the last couple of days. You
can't be sure they won't come and give us one good bombing,
if only to frighten us. I heard from some banking people
yesterday that they gave Guizhou a terrible pasting. The newspapers didn't even dare report it. I tell you, it's better to go
and shelter."

"Oh well, a walk might do us good. Let's go together then."

There followed the sound of a door slamming and of footsteps. Although separated from the speakers by a corridor, the

conversation transmitted through the very thin partitions was clearly heard by mother and son.

"Mother, it's better for you to go," he pleaded.

"There's no hurry. It's only a warning at present," his mother answered slowly.

A few minutes later, the attack warning suddenly pierced the air.

"Mother, go!" he urged.

"I'll wait till the urgent warning sounds," she replied, still sitting there calmly.

"I think you'd better go early. If you leave too late, you mightn't get into the shelter," he said, a little worried. She didn't answer. All at once, he stood up. "All right, let's go then," he said.

"It's not certain that the enemy planes will come. It takes too much energy to go. I still think it's better to wait for the urgent signal before we go," his mother stubbornly persisted. He did not answer. "Even if we're bombed," his mother continued, "it won't matter. The way we have to live, we'd be better off dead anyway."

"Mother, you mustn't talk like that. We've never robbed anyone, stolen from anyone or harmed anyone. Why shouldn't we live?" he cried with impassioned indignation, sitting down again on the edge of his bed.

The door was pushed open. A woman entered. "Haven't you gone yet?" Shusheng cried, happy in her surprise.

"Why didn't you go and shelter? What are you back here for?" he asked, getting up to welcome her.

"I came to give you your pass for the air-raid shelter. I don't know how it came to be in my purse. I've just discovered it, and dashed back especially to give it to you," she explained, smiling as she opened her purse, took out a card and gave it to him.

He gave her a smile in thanks, put the pass into his pocket and drew out a letter. "To tell you the truth," he said, "the pass never entered my mind. Anyway, if the urgent warning doesn't sound, we won't need to go to the shelter."

"Let's go now," Shusheng urged with a smile. "The earlier we get there, the better," she added, glancing at his mother.

"I'm not going. I don't believe I'm going to be killed by a bomb," his mother said testily, her face hardening.

The rebuff stunned Shusheng for a moment, but she instantly put on a smile and said: "And you? Aren't you afraid to die either?"

"I'm tired. I don't feel like going," he answered wearily.

"Then I'll go on my own," she said, still pretending to smile, and turned abruptly away.

"Shusheng," he called, thinking of the letter in his hand.

She turned to look at him. He held the letter out, saying: "It's from Xiao Xuan. His school wants him to hand over another three thousand two hundred yuan. You read it."

She came back, took the letter, pulled it from its envelope and read it. "All right," she said lightly. "I'll send him three thousand five hundred yuan tomorrow." Putting the letter in her purse, she turned to go.

"It won't cause you any difficulty?" he asked briefly.

"Not at all. I can borrow it from the bank. In any case, it's easier for me to find a way out than for you," she answered carelessly. Then she asked again: "You're not coming to the shelter?" Seeing him hesitate, she ran quickly out on her own.

"You see. Look what she's like! And you put up with it!" his mother exclaimed irately. The sound of Shusheng's high heels was already echoing down the corridor.

"But we depend on her for Xiao Xuan's school fees. If it weren't for her, Xiao Xuan would have had to leave school long ago. I'm useless as a father," he sighed.

"If it were I, I'd rather Xiao Xuan stopped school," his mother said between her teeth.

Feeling some phlegm stuck in his throat, he coughed hard, trying to dislodge it.

"Wait on a minute. I'll get you a glass of boiled water,"

his mother cried. But by the time she brought it, he had already coughed the phlegm up onto the ground. Not only onto the ground. The back of his left hand was splattered with it. In it he saw traces of blood, and for a moment, his heart went cold. He instantly wiped the back of his hand on his clothes, at the same time rubbing the phlegm into the floorboards with his foot.

"Oh, well. It'll be better now that you've coughed it up," his mother said consolingly, offering him the glass.

He took it from her, gulped down a few mouthfuls, and then, forcing himself to smile, answered: "Yes, I feel much better now." Putting the glass down on the table, he said: "I'm terribly tired. I think I'll sleep for a while."

"Then you'd better not undress in case the urgent warning sounds. It'll be easier to get away," his mother instructed.

He gave a perfunctory answer, having already reached his bed and lain down in his clothes. In that single moment, his spirit and his physical strength had been completely sapped. His mind in a blur, he felt his mother come and cover him with a cotton quilt.

12

He did not want his mother or his wife to know that he had coughed up blood, and so, in spite of everything, he forced himself to go to work the next day. He had been in very low spirits the night before and had slept badly. Now he had to endure as before the same tedious work, the same indecipherable translation, Mr. Zhou's detestable expression, Mr. Wu's hostile look, and his colleagues' impassive faces. Time dragged on and on. His mind was not on his work. He could not have told himself how many errors he had actually found. On hearing the lunch bell ring, he put down his brush, breathing a sigh of relief, like a criminal just pardoned. He still had no appetite, and so he ate very little, while saying nothing at all. Everyone at the table seemed to be eyeing him with compassion, but it gave him no comfort. It was as much as he could do to finish his bowl. Then, catching his breath, like someone who has just been rescued, he left the lunch table, not daring to glance at anyone around him. No one paid him any attention anyway.

He went back upstairs and sat down once more before his desk, but without looking at his proofs. It was not yet time to start work. There was no use his wasting what limited energy remained to him. He looked vaguely around, but seemed to see nothing but an indistinct blur. He was exhausted. His brain became more sluggish than usual, his eyelids gradually closed, and his head became heavier and heavier. He slept.

The laughter of his colleagues woke him. He sat up abruptly, his brain still filled with the strange figures that had inhabited his dreams of joys and sorrows, reunions and partings. A feeling of despondency and perplexity remained with him.

It would soon be time to begin work. Since Mr. Zhou and Mr. Wu were not there, his colleagues continued to joke and laugh in animation. Then, when one of them brought up the subject of the war situation, another responded by bringing up the previous night's news. The atmosphere at once became tense. The Japanese were continuing to advance unopposed. It was said that they'd already reached Yishan.

"There's nothing about it in the papers, you know! They can't possibly have advanced so quickly!" Wang Wenxuan protested in silence, not daring to speak his thoughts aloud.

"It's not possible. How come you're so well-informed? The newspaper says the situation at the front has improved these last few days," Xiao Pan interrupted.

"You believe the newspapers! Do you know how much news the censors delete every day?" the well-informed colleague retorted.

"That's right! These last two days, the situation really hasn't been all that marvellous. I've a relative who's been living in

Guiyang for four years, and now, he's going to move the whole family here," another colleague interposed.

"That's nothing! I've a friend who's already booked his plane ticket and is moving his family to Lanzhou. If you're going to run away, you might as well be thorough about it," another colleague added.

"That's why our office is moving to Lanzhou. That's being thorough," the well-informed one said.

"Are you going?" Xiao Pan asked.

"Who, me? I'm afraid the firm's not going to want small-time clerks like us. You're not still banking on that, are you?" the well-informed speaker scoffed, though he, in fact, could not be considered a small-time clerk, for he had been in the publishing section for a long time, earning a basic salary that was far higher than Wang Wenxuan's.

"Well, if they don't want us, they'll have to give us redundancy pay. An extra three months' pay will be all to the good," Xiao Pan said nonchalantly.

"Three months! I should think it would be two months at the most! But what's the use, even if you do get the money? It's not enough to run away with, and it's not enough even if you don't run away. Besides, a semi-government organization like this...." Just then, footsteps were heard on the staircase, and the well-informed colleague shut up at once, making a face at the same time.

Mr. Zhou entered. The whole floor was instantly hushed. Xiao Pan slipped quietly back downstairs. The afternoon's work began.

Wang Wenxuan sat before his desk without making a sound. He felt as if he were still dreaming. He could not see the proof sheets spread out before him. His whole mind was occupied by his colleagues' conversation. Run away ... redundancy,... wouldn't this mean his ruin and the ruin of his family?... from the lips of others, he had heard all about the trage dies that had taken place during the retreat from Hunan and Guangxi ... and what was more, he was so useless! ... if the day really came when.... He shuddered. He did not dare go on thinking about it, but he could not stop himself. The more he thought about it, the more confused he became. He turned over a couple of pages, but not a single word penetrated his brain. He did not care about work anymore. As for Mr. Zhou's expression and Mr. Wu's look, he did not care about them either. He seemed to hear a familiar voice whisper: Annihilation! A death sentence had been pronounced on him, yet he had no thought of appealing to a higher court.

He passed the next half-hour in a daze. His whole body began to ache, his head began suddenly to burn, and he began to feel rather dizzy. A few minutes, ten minutes, half an hour, an hour later, his fever had still not abated. "It must be TB," he decided, "since I coughed up blood last night. It doesn't matter, I'll die anyway," he consoled himself by saying. This calmed him down a little, so that he was no longer as afraid as before. Then he was seized by another chilling thought.

"If I die, I shall die alone, in such solitude," he thought. He wanted desperately to run home, to embrace his mother, to embrace his wife, to embrace his son, and weep his heart out.

By the time work stopped, his fever had died down, and he made his way home, feeling a little more cheerful.

His mother had finished the cooking and was waiting for him. She asked him affectionately about his day at work and, while eating, brought up the subject of Shusheng again, pouring out her load of grievances once more. He mumbled in agreement, feeling that his mother was in the right, yet conscious at the same time that Shusheng was not in the wrong.

When his mother was collecting the dishes, she could not stop herself from speaking her mind. "Since she doesn't have dinner at the bank, she should come home to eat. You can see for yourself! How many days in a month is she at home? If she hasn't gone to meet her lover, what else can she be doing?"

He said nothing. He did not accept what his mother said, but her words made him wretched: always these same accusations, this same hostility. "Why don't you give me some peace? Since you love me, why can't you love her too? You know how I can't do without her!" he thought. But he did not dare speak his thoughts aloud· "I can't do without her!" The words hurt him, making him feel so alone, a loneliness intermingled with anxiety and unease. He stood up without a word, and paced about the room, biting his lip lightly.

"If you've nothing to do, would you like to see a film? We're educated people after all, and no matter how poor we are, we still need some relaxation," his mother suggested, coming over after she'd finished what she was doing.

"I'm terribly tired. I don't feel like going out," he replied lethargically. After a long pause, he added with a sad smile: "Today, people with education are the lowest of the low. Only opium-dealers, rice-speculators and the like can afford to throw money away on the cinema and the theatre."

The door was pushed open, and Shusheng entered.

"Have you eaten?" he asked, in delighted surprise.

"Yes," she answered, smiling. "I had originally intended to come back in time to eat, but one of the people at work insisted on inviting me out, and she wouldn't take no for an answer. Something very interesting happened at the bank today. I'll tell you about it later."

"Her smile is so radiant, her voice so clear and melodious!" he thought, while his mother just muttered something vague, and went into her tiny room.

While she was changing her clothes and her shoes, the lights suddenly went out. He quickly looked for the matches to light the candle.

"This place is disgusting. They're always cutting the electricity," she complained crossly in the darkness.

Once the candle was lit, its pale light filled the room with flickering shadows. He continued to stand before the table. She came over and, leaning against one edge of the table, sat down. She said as if to herself: "I'm afraid of the dark, afraid of the quiet, and afraid of the solitude."

He turned to look down at her in silence. After a few minutes, she suddenly looked up and said: "Xuan, why don't
you talk to me?"

"I was afraid you were tired. You'd better rest for a while,"
he answered, putting on a false smile.

She shook her head. "I'm not tired. The work at the
bank's not heavy, and we're comparatively free. The boss has
been very nice to me recently, and the people I work with
aren't too bad. It's just that —" She hesitated for a moment,
frowned, and then abruptly changed her tone of voice. "When
I'm away from here, I keep thinking of home. But when I'm
back home, I always feel so cold, lonely and empty inside. And
then lately, you haven't wanted to talk to me much."

"It's not that I don't want to talk. I'm afraid you may not
be in the mood," he explained timidly. But it was not true.
In reality, he was afraid that by talking too much, he would
make her unhappy, and besides, they saw so little of each other
every day.

"You really are an inoffensive 'good sort'!" she said reprovingly. "I'm always in good spirits, much more so than
you, and yet you worry about me! That's just like you, always
thinking of others and forgetting about yourself."

"No, I think of myself too," he objected awkwardly.

There was no sound from his mother's room. The candle
flickered alarmingly. The corners of the room became even
darker than before. From the first floor came the coughing
and the crying of a small child. From outside the window came
the soft sound of a light drizzle.

"Let's play a couple of hands of bridge," she proposed in
sudden animation, jumping up from her seat.

He was tired, and did not feel like playing. But he agreed
at once, even going to get the cards and placing them on the
table. He sat down, shuffled and dealt.

He could see that her enjoyment was diminishing as they
played. He felt even less inclined to play. Just as they finished
the second game, she stood up abruptly and said with lassitude;

"Let's stop. It's no fun with only two people. Besides, we can't see properly."

He put the cards back into the packet in silence, and sighed softly. He noticed that the candlewick was drooping to one side, and that the candle wax had dribbled into a big lump on the table. Having found the scissors, he trimmed the wick down.

"Xuan, I really do admire you," she said, her voice suddenly trembling as she stood by the table watching his actions. He looked up at her in surprise, not understanding her meaning. "You're so patient. You can put up with anything," she continued in a peevish tone of voice.

"If I don't, what else can I do?" He smiled desolately.

"But how long do you intend to put up with things?"

"I don't know."

"I get so exasperated. Xuan, how long will we have to wait before we can stop living like this? How long will it be before things get a bit better?"

"I'm sure that a day will definitely come, when the war's won. . . ."

She didn't let him finish, cutting him short with a wave of her hand. "I don't want to hear about when the war's won. If we have to wait till then, I'll probably be old already, or dead. I haven't any ideals left. While I'm alive, I just want to enjoy life to the full, to live more comfortably." She was so excited that she even seemed a little angry. She paced back and forth about the room.

It was only after a long pause that he said briefly: "It's all my fault. I'll just never get anywhere." He said this dispiritedly, in a tone of apology.

"What's the use of blaming yourself? I'm to blame for having been blinded in the beginning," she said in annoyance. The words were no sooner out of her mouth than she softened, but it was too late to take them back. Each word pierced his heart like a sharp needle. Grasping his head in both hands, he silently tore at his hair with his fingers. She ran over to him at once, and said with tenderness: "Forgive me, I'm so confused." She took his right hand from his head and for a long moment, squeezed it tightly between her two palms. But all at once, overcome by a wave of despair, she released him, went over to the window, and heaved a long, long sigh.

13

He continued to live a miserable life of mediocrity and monotony. What force sustained his sick body, he did not know himself. Every afternoon, he developed a light fever, and every night, he broke into a cold sweat. Not that he sweated a lot. It was the phlegm that he coughed up that worried him. Twice more, it had been streaked with blood and he had hidden it from his family. His mother noticed only the pallor of his face, and would say: "You don't look too well today." And he would reply as usual: "But I feel fine." She would look at him sadly, but say nothing more. She could not know what was in his mind. Once, his wife, overhearing his mother's comments on how he looked, interrupted drearily: "When in the last two years has he ever looked well?" It was true what she said, but she did not know what was on his mind either. Deep concern, compassion — that was all they had to offer him. His mother seemed more concerned about him than his wife. She seemed to think less of herself, yet even she could not alleviate the suffering that he felt.

"Is it better to live or to die?" he often thought secretly to himself, especially in the office. He felt that "Death" was lying in wait for him. Mr. Zhou's expression and Mr. Wu's look seemed to be whipping him towards "Death". When he arrived back home, his mother's concern and his wife's compassion gave him no great comfort. His mother liked to pour out her woes, while his wife was always flaunting before him her rich vitality and the youth she had as yet not lost. He was beginning to fear his mother's worried expression and his wife's **face** glowing with health. He became more and more taciturn. **A** whole world seemed to separate them from him. When they gazed at him with concern or talked to him with tenderness, he would think to himself: "You don't understand." And indeed, they did not. Perhaps they felt that he sometimes looked at them oddly, but this did not seem to worry them particularly. His mother worried perhaps, but her constant instructions and enquiries (instructions to be careful of his health and enquiries as to whether he was ill) simply aggravated his fear, his pain and his suffering. "She's going to find out," he warned himself, and became even more on his guard. Once when his mother brought up his health, his wife promptly added: "Get him to go to the hospital for a check-up," and turning towards him, she implored him fervently with her eyes: You should go once and see! "I'm fine, I'm fine!" he replied in confusion. "If you go for a check-up, we can at least feel more sure," his wife said. He did not answer directly. Only after a moment did he murmur, as if to himself: "A doctor, medicine, the hospital, they all cost money these days. People like us can call themselves happy if they get enough to eat. They say that thousands of refugees have died of starvation on the roads from Hunan to Guangxi."

His mother sighed, aggrieved and resentful. His wife pondered for a moment before saying: "There's no knowing that we won't end up like them one day. But while we're still alive, we should try to think of some way out." She frowned. A shadow crossed her face briefly, but instantly disappeared, leaving not a trace of anxiety.

"Think of a way out? I don't think there's anything we can do until we end up dead. They said the year before that things would be better the next year, and last year they said things would improve this year. Well, what about this year? It just gets worse from year to year!" his mother finally began to complain from beside them.

"You can blame that on our man being too good-natured," his wife said, rather sarcastically.

His mother quickly retorted, her face changing colour: "Xuan is absolutely right! An upright man sticks to his principles. I'd rather starve to death otherwise!"

His wife snorted derisively, and after two or three minutes, said, as if to herself: "It seems to me that you can be upright without being naive. What's the point of making things tough for yourself!"

"I live like this willingly and gladly," his mother said, her anger rising. "In any case, it's better than being just an 'ornament'!"

"Mother, don't go on. Shusheng's views are actually no different from yours," he interrupted at once, trying to smooth things over. He was terrified of having to listen to them quarrel again.

"They're different! There's a world of difference!" Shusheng cried vehemently, her face going crimson. "To abuse someone by calling her just an 'ornament', that was out-of-date ages ago."

"Shusheng, don't go on about it. It's all my fault for dragging you all into this life of hardship. You can't blame Mother," he begged his wife anxiously, pulling her aside and whispering in her ear: "Mother's old. She doesn't see things straight. Give her a little leeway."

"What do you mean she doesn't see things straight! It's clearly you who don't!" she hissed angrily at him, without raising her voice, and then sat down on the edge of the bed, saying no more.

"Of course, people today are so thick-skinned, they don't mind what they do," his mother went on, continuing to sneer and rail.

He was just going to calm her down, when he heard someone call: "Mr. Wang! Mrs. Wang!" He looked in surprise towards the door of the flat. Standing there was Mrs. Zhang from next door, her face pale.

"Come in and sit down, Mrs. Zhang," he called instantly in welcome, while his wife and mother greeted her in turn.

"Mr. Wang, do you think it's safe to stay here? I'm terrified. If we have to flee, then people like us from outside Sichuan simply won't know what to do," Mrs. Zhang began as soon as she'd settled herself, her eyes wide-open in fear.

He did not answer, but his wife replied for him: "I don't think there's anything to worry about. There are lots of rumours about, but I don't listen to them."

"Rumours? What rumours have you heard?" he asked in surprise, his heart suddenly beginning to pound.

"They say the Japanese have reached Nandan already, and are approaching Guizhou. Everyone at the bank says so," his wife replied, perfectly calm.

"I heard they'd already entered Guizhou. Mr. Zhang's place is getting ready to move office. But junior clerks like us won't be able to go. What are we going to do? Mr. Wang, you're a local. You must look after us!" Mrs. Zhang implored in a terrified, anxious voice.

He thought: You come to me when I don't know what to do myself! But he replied instead: "Yes, of course. I'll certainly help."

"We thought of going to the countryside to hide for a while, and that it would be best to go wherever you go," Mrs. Zhang added.

"You mean to flee now? It's too early! Mrs. Zhang, don't be afraid. When the time comes, we're sure to think of something." His wife smiled comfortingly at the sickly-looking young woman.

"I'm just saying that if we should have to flee. . . . Thank you very much, Mrs. Wang, Mr. Wang and you too, Mrs. Wang. Thank you all so much. I'll tell my husband. Once he hears, he'll stop worrying." Mrs. Zhang stood up, a smile spreading over her face as she spoke these words of gratitude.

"Stay a little longer," his wife urged, trying to keep her.

"No, I won't stay. I must go," Mrs. Zhang said, moving towards the door at the same time.

After their guest had left, the three of them sat silent for two or three minutes, until his mother suddenly asked: "Xuan, is it true that we'll have to flee?"

His heart gave a violent leap, but he did not dare answer.

"Impossible," his wife said quickly, smiling with apparent calm.

But the next day, after she came back from work, she said to him with a frown: "The news today hasn't been at all encouraging. They say that even Dushan's about to fall. It's even said that there are air-raid warnings in Guiyang every day."

"Then what are we going to do?" his mother interrupted in alarm.

"Apart from waiting for the Japs to come, there's nothing we can do," he said, as if there were no question about it, and giving a despairing smile. But he was not afraid. It was more a feeling of uncertainty and doubt. Death, life, disaster — what difference did it make to him? What was to be, would be. He had no strength to resist it. And if it was not going to happen, then it was even more pointless to fear.

"We can't just wait to be killed," his mother said anxiously.

His wife scoffed disdainfully: "It won't come to that! If a time comes to flee, then we'll manage somehow. Today, one of the people at work asked me to go to the countryside with her and take refuge there for the time being. She's afraid there's going to be heavy enemy bombing. But I didn't accept."

"Of course, you can pull more strings than we can," his mother said with angry sarcasm.

"Perhaps you're right. When I feel like going, I'm sure to be able to," his wife replied, deliberately assuming an air of self-satisfaction.

"And Xiao Xuan! What about Xiao Xuan! You can forget about Xuan and myself, but Xiao Xuan's your own son. You can't just abandon him!" his mother protested loudly, going red in the face.

He looked in turn at the faces of the two women. He wanted to say: "I'm about to die, and yet you go on quarrelling!" But he did not dare.

"Xiao Xuan has his school to look after him. There's no need for you two to worry about him," his wife said coldly.

"Good. So that way, you'll be able to run off with your boy-friend. I've never met a mother like you in all my life!" his mother hissed between her teeth.

"I'm sorry, but I'm not like you. And I have no desire to live to be as old as you," his wife screamed in reply, her face beginning to change colour.

Unable to bear it, he shouted out in pain: "Shusheng, let Mother say what she likes. We're all one family. Why do we have to be like this! You never know, in a couple of days, if things get really bad, we all may be —" He felt his head aching violently, pressed his lips firmly together, gritting his teeth.

"It's not I who wanted to quarrel. It was your mother who started it. Why don't you tell her to stop?" his wife retorted, turning her head, unintimidated.

"I don't want to listen to your fine speeches," his mother screeched, pointing at his wife.

"Go on, then, quarrel! Go on quarrelling," he muttered irately to himself. Their voices clashed and jangled inside his head until he felt that it was about to explode. Unable to bear it any longer, he went towards the door of the flat in silence. They paid no attention to him. He went out the door, and ran down the stairs in a single breath.

He walked along the footpath, his brain in a complete turmoil. The chill night air began to wash against his face, gradually clearing his mind.

"Where shall I go?" he asked himself, but he had no answer. He wandered about aimlessly until he arrived once more at the wine-shop.

"You must make yourself forget everything," a voice seemed

to whisper in his ear. He looked inside the tiny shop. All the tables were occupied by customers. Only a square table right at the back was partly empty. Seated there was a single customer, long-haired, with a dark, lean face, dressed in an old cotton gown. He was drinking his wine, with his head down, taking no notice of anyone around him. "I'll go and find myself a place," he said under his breath. Then he went in, pulled out a stool from the table and sat down opposite the man.

"A bowl of *hongzao*!" he shouted. When the waiter brought it, he picked it up and downed it in one gulp. As the wine entered his stomach, a wave of warm air surged up. Unable to hold it back, he hiccupped.

Suddenly, the customer opposite him looked up and, seeing him, called his name: "Wenxuan!" He looked up in blank amazement at the dark, lean, sickly face, failing for the moment to recognize who it was.

"Don't you recognize me? Are you drunk, that even an old school-friend —" The man gave a bitter smile.

"Baiqing! How did you get like this!" He cried in astonishment, his eyes opening into a stare as he interrupted the man's words. His friend's face had changed completely, his voice rasping, his cheeks sunken, his eyes bloodshot and his lips framed by a growth of short black whiskers. "What have you been doing? It's not even a month!" he demanded, his flesh tingling.

"I'm finished. I'm already dead," the man replied in his grating voice, forcing himself to smile, but his smile was tense, revealing teeth that were a deathly yellow.

"You mustn't talk like that, Baiqing. Have you been ill?" he asked solicitously, forgetting his own troubles.

"My illness is here," the man said, tapping his forehead with his fingers.

"In that case, you shouldn't drink. You'd better go home at once and rest," he urged anxiously.

"I want to drink. I feel happy only when I drink," the man

replied, grinning hideously, but leaving the bowl in front of him untouched. It was still more than half full.

"Then you'd better drink up quickly and go home," he urged anxiously.

"Home! Where do I still have a home? Where do you expect me to go?" the man cried with a grim smile.

"Where do you live? I'll see you back," he said.

"I have nowhere to live. I have nothing, nothing at all," the man replied angrily, then lifting his bowl suddenly, drank the wine down in one gulp. "Marvellous! Marvellous!" he shouted. "After wasting my whole life reading books, this is what I've come to! Who would have thought it? Do you know where I live? Sometimes I sleep in a little tavern, sometimes on the road. Once, I even slept outside the main entrance of your building. . . ."

"You're drunk. Don't talk anymore. Let's go," he interrupted. At the same time, he stood up and called the waiter over to pay the bill. He pulled the man by the arm, urging him over and over: "Let's go, let's go."

"I'm not drunk, I'm not," the man kept repeating, shaking his head, unwilling to move.

"Then let's go and find somewhere to have some tea," he suggested.

"All right." The man stood up, swayed for a moment, and sat down again. "You go first. I'll sit here a bit longer," the man said despondently, glancing at him miserably.

"Then come to my place. Shusheng thinks of your wife all the time," he said gently. But no sooner had he spoken the word "wife" than, realizing his mistake, he was silent again and said nothing more.

"Look at the way I am! How can I go to your home!" the man exclaimed, his cheeks twitching slightly. Then he looked down at his own chest. Patting the front of his old filthy gown with the fingers of his right hand, he added: "With clothes like this," and rubbing his chin, continued: "and a face like this!" He shook his head. "No, I'm not going. Your old friend

Tang Baiqing is already dead. Why should I worry about all this? What's it got to do with my friends what clothes I wear, or where I live? If my friends ignore me, so much the better. In any case, I'm dead already, dead." Finally, he forced a smile: "You'd better go home. Don't worry about me. Ah, just now you said you both missed my wife. Since you remember her, how can I forget her!"

Wang Wenxuan averted his eyes and looked all around him. At several tables, the customers had all turned their glances in the direction of his friend. He blushed.

"Quick, let's go! They're all looking at you," he urged in a whisper.

"Looking at me? Then let them! We're all in the same boat." The man looked up at him, his eyes gleaming with a kind of madness. "People who come to a wine-shop to drink, and that includes you, are none of them happy." At these words, Wang Wenxuan suddenly shuddered. He continued to urge in a whisper: "Don't talk now. Let's go."

"Snobs! Snobs! There's no one who's not a snob!" the man said, absorbed only in himself. "I've seen through people. All those old friends of mine, who came to the wedding reception when I got married a year ago, now they all ignore me when they run into me in the street. Huh! Money, money!" His face twisted in a contemptuous sneer. "There's no one who doesn't worship money! A poverty-stricken wretch like me! If you're going to die, you might as well die early. What's the use of my living! Good!" He stood up suddenly. "I'll come with you to visit your wife. When my wife was alive, she said we must go to your home to pay our respects to our elder sister-in-law. Now...." Unable to continue, he began to sob.

Wang Wenxuan left the wine-shop, dragging his friend by the arm. The two of them had gone only a few steps along the footpath, when his friend stopped abruptly and said: "I'm not going."

"Then where will you go?" he asked.

"I don't know myself. Don't worry about me," he answered doggedly.

"Baiqing, it's no use like this. Come and stay with us for the night," he urged sympathetically, pulling him by the arm.

"No, no!" the man said, shaking his head.

"Baiqing, you can't go on like this. Remember the aspirations you used to have. Pull yourself together," he shouted miserably. But all he wanted to do was weep.

They went on for another few steps. Just as they were about to turn into the street where he lived, the man suddenly cried stubbornly: "No, I'm leaving." Then: "Let me go!" he shouted, wrenching himself free from Wang's grasp, and ran down the street towards the other side.

"Baiqing! Baiqing!" he called in despair. He was about to run after him in pursuit, when he heard a rumbling noise, followed by a terrifying screech. His eyes blurred. He seemed to see an enormous lorry fly past him.

People began running madly towards the intersection, at which a large crowd gathered, jostling one another. He followed in a daze, but was unable to see anything, his view obstructed by the people in front of him. He felt as if a terrifying black shadow was hovering above his head.

"Horrible! The head was crushed to mincemeat. It made me sick to look at it," he heard a voice beside him say.

"In my opinion, they should absolutely forbid lorries from driving at places like this. A lot of people have been run over here just this month. A young married woman was run over at a minor intersection the day before yesterday. So tragic! The car not only didn't stop, but even knocked over and injured a policeman," another voice said.

He woke from his stupor. He understood what had happened. He tried to cry out in terror and pain, but no sound came. He was so distressed and upset that he began to shake all over.

He stepped away from the crowd without a word to make his way home. No one paid him any attention. But a voice accompanied him on his way, a familiar voice crying over and over again: "I'm finished, finished."

He pushed open the door of the flat. The light was blinding. His wife was sitting alone at the desk, reading. As she put down the book and looked up, a happy smile of surprise appeared on her face. She asked him affectionately: "Did you go to the wine-shop again?"

He nodded. There was a long pause before he managed to say with effort: "I had a dream, a horrible dream."

"Xuan, you're back!" his mother called, hurrying from her room.

"What was the dream? Are you all right? You'd better rest for a while," his wife said gently.

He wanted to reply. But the terrifying screech still echoed in his brain. He was drained of all energy. He seemed on the point of physical collapse. He made an immense effort to keep control. Two pairs of eager, solicitous, tenderly affectionate eyes gazed at him, waiting for an answer. His heart was on fire. In his anguish, his lips quivered, and before he could answer, sputum spurted from his mouth.

"Blood! Blood! You've coughed up blood!" the two women cried out together in alarm. They dragged him over to the bed and made him lie down.

"I'm finished, finished." He mumbled these terrible words in a dazed stupor. The shrill screech still echoed in his brain, and his tears fell like rain. Feeling he had no more strength to fight back, he closed his eyes in submission.

14

He was haunted the whole night by a succession of terrifying dreams, waking the next morning weary and feverish, his limbs weak, and his mind uneasy.

His mother and his wife no longer quarrelled, but both alike looked after him with affection. In the afternoon, the doctor came to examine him. It was a doctor in traditional Chinese medicine who had been called by his wife. She was a believer in Western medicine, and had suggested that they call the medical consultant of the Bank of Sichuan, but his mother had insisted on getting a Chinese doctor. Since he did not wish to offend his mother, his wife had had to give way. She had gone first to the office of the publishing company to ask for sick leave for him, then to the Bank of Sichuan to ask for a day's leave for herself, and finally to call the doctor, Zhang Boqing, a distant relative of his mother's who had been practising medicine in this city for three or four years and had acquired a certain reputation. Each time he called at their flat, he would refuse payment for the consultation, accepting only his rickshaw fare. Because of this, Wang Wenxuan himself approved of calling the Chinese herbal doctor. "Western medicine is so expensive! It's best not to spend too much! Where would I get the money?" was his thought.

The doctor was a genial old man, who carefully examined his pulse, asked how he felt, and in a gentle voice, comforted both the patient and the family, assuring them that it was a case of excessive heat in the liver aggravated by fatigue, definitely nothing to do with the lungs, and that after a few days' rest and care, he would gradually recover.

His wife did not much believe what the doctor had to say, but his mother had implicit faith in him, while he himself hovered between doubt and belief. At any rate that the doctor brought comfort to the three of them, and he gradually came to feel that Chinese medicine did have its principles. "For thousands of years now, we Chinese have diagnosed and prescribed in this way. How can one say that there is no basis to it?" he cheered himself up by thinking. In this way, he perceived a ray of hope, and the dark shadow of death receded a little.

When his wife came back from buying the medicine, his mother took it and brewed it for him. After drinking it, he slept for a while. But he slept badly, finding it difficult to breathe.

Towards evening, his temperature rose, and he was again caught in a terrible web of nightmares. Immense black figures kept flickering before his eyes: they were countless images of the thin, dark face and bloodshot eyes of Tang Baiqing. They surrounded him, each face opening its mouth to repeat: "I'm finished, finished." In his terror, he fled, first walking, then running. He was so exhausted, but his legs refused to stop. Suddenly, he was running up a barren hillside. There was no one to be seen, nor did he know where he was going. Night fell. He groped about in the dark· What an exhausting journey! All at once, he saw a light. Suddenly, the trees all around him burst into flames. There were flames everywhere, burning fiercely, coming closer and closer, until they scorched his clothes. Unable to bear it, he cried out hoarsely: "Help!"

He woke up. He was lying on his bed, covered by his cotton quilt, his body bathed in sweat, groaning in pain.

"Xuan, what is it?" His wife was sitting on the edge of the bed, bending over him, calling to him. "Are you in pain?" she asked gently.

Gazing at her, he sighed, but made no reply. After a moment, he asked in a whisper: "How long have you been back from work?"

"I asked for a day's leave today. Didn't I tell you?" she exclaimed in surprise.

"I forgot," he replied. Then he added in explanation: "My dreams confused me." After a while, he again spoke: "I dreamt ... I thought ... my old school-friend was run over by a lorry."

He was deceiving himself, mistaking the reality for a dream.

"Your old school-friend? Whom do you mean?" his wife asked in surprise, stretching out her hand slowly to feel his forehead. It was covered in sweat, but the fever had subsided.

"Tang Baiqing. We went to his wedding banquet at the

Longevity Restaurant. His wife died in childbirth. I told you about it a few days ago," he said with effort.

"Yes, you told me. I remember. You mustn't talk too much. You mustn't think about other people's tragedies. You're not well, and you've been running a fever. You'd better go to sleep again for a while," his wife said gently to console him.

"I'm afraid to sleep. I might have more nightmares," he complained like a whining child.

"You won't. You mustn't think about anything. Just forget about everything and go to sleep. I'll be here beside you to keep you company. You won't have any more bad dreams." His wife smiled at him in answer.

"Where's Mother?" he then asked.

"She's cooking. You go to sleep. In a while, you'll have to take your medicine," she said, turning away and not looking at him again.

After a long pause, he suddenly asked: "Please, can you get me some tea?" Not that he really wanted any tea. He simply wanted to talk to his wife.

She poured him over half a cup of hot tea, holding it for him as he lifted his head and took three sips. "Thank you," he said, letting his head fall once more.

"You can go back to sleep for a while," his wife said, standing up to put the teacup on the table.

No sooner had he closed his eyes than he opened them again, stealing a look at his wife without letting her notice. But after ten minutes or so, unable to restrain himself, he called her name and began talking to her again.

"Shusheng, I don't think I'm going to recover," he said.

"You're talking nonsense again," she said in gentle reproach, her smile showing her affection. "Didn't the doctor say you'd be better after a couple of doses of medicine and a few days' rest?"

He paused for a moment before saying: "But you don't believe in Chinese medicine."

For a moment, his wife did not know what to say. Finally,

she answered: "But you mother believes in it firmly. Besides, he's related to you. He wouldn't lie to you."

"Who doesn't lie these days!" He laughed bitterly. "I know what's wrong with me. I won't last till the war's over. It's just as well perhaps. Alive, I'm not only of no help to you, I'm a burden to you all." He had seemed at first to be speaking to himself, then his tone had changed, and finally, he abruptly stopped. Noticing that his eyes were filled with tears, his wife too became uneasy, but she said only: "You shouldn't say things like that," and forcefully bit her lip.

"And then Mother's old now. Her life is hard, her temper's getting worse, and sometimes she complains all the time. I hope you can forgive her. She means well," he continued imploringly, drawing out the words slowly, unlike in his previous excitement.

"I know," was all she said, looking down at the ground, stretching out her right hand to squeeze his left hand and also wanting to weep.

"Thank you. I'll go to sleep now," he said, as if relieved.

The weak rays of the electric lamp, scarcely stronger than candlelight, shed their desolate, sickly yellow light over the room, making the room even more dreary. He lay there with his eyes closed, his mouth half-open. His thin face, seemingly smeared with wax, stirred such pity in her.

She remained seated on the edge of the bed, continuing to hold his hand, not letting go, looking around her with an air of desolation. His sympathy for her made her suffer, but another inexpressible feeling was tormenting her.

"Why do we have to live like this?" a resentful voice inside her demanded.

She felt how weak and feeble was the hand she pressed in her right hand, and how cold the fingers. She wanted to protest: "This is his reward for putting up with things! I can't — "

She glanced at him in surprise. He was breathing regularly. He seemed much more comfortable now. No nightmares seemed to be troubling his sleep. She gently released his hand, and put out her hand to feel his temples. Then she stood up and stretched lazily.

From next-door came a buzz of voices, while from the street could be heard the monotonous sound of car-horns. The mice, squeaking intermittently, gnawed at the floorboards, their activity seeming never to cease. All this threw her thoughts into even more disarray. The chill night air, working its way through the wooden floorboards and partitions from every direction, made her shiver. For no reason at all, she stared at the electric light bulb, but its dull red filament could not warm her heart.

"This is what our life is like. It will never light up, and never die out, but drag on endlessly like this. In the last two or three years, we had some ideals, we had some hope, and we could hold on. But now . . . if she didn't quarrel with me every day, if he weren't so weak, I might still. . . ." she murmured to herself, and this time, she frowned. She felt even more irritated, not knowing how to calm her spirit. She began to pace about the room, but stopped after a few steps, afraid that her footsteps might awaken him.

The half-closed door of the flat was suddenly pushed open as his mother entered with the rice-pot.

"She suffers too," she could not help thinking when she saw his mother's drawn face.

"Is he asleep?" his mother whispered, a trace of a smile appearing on her thin, pallid face as she turned to look towards the bed.

She nodded, answering quietly: "He seems to be sleeping better this time."

"Then, let him sleep a bit more. He can take the medicine when he wakes," his mother said. "We can eat first."

She ate a bowl of rice, sitting opposite his mother, who had little appetite. While at the meal table, she felt lonely, uninterested, and had to force herself to say a few words to his mother.

"She can put up with anything. She seems to have settled

down to this kind of life. Why can't I?" But her inner reproaches did nothing to alleviate her feeling of loneliness.

"Why am I always dissatisfied? Why can't I sacrifice myself?..." She became even more agitated, reproaching herself mentally a second time.

But finally, the night passed in calm.

From the next day, his condition began to improve slightly. Shusheng went back to work at the bank as usual, but left rather later in the morning and came home in the afternoon straight after work. For the moment, she broke off all social engagements with her colleagues. She helped his mother prepare the meals, sometimes even seeing to it that he took his medicine and ate his breakfast and dinner. After dinner, if he did not feel like sleeping, she would chat with him, talking about the many things that happened at the bank. She would discuss everything, except the current political situation.

The Chinese medicine seemed to be very effective, for his health improved daily. When his mother sang the praises of Chinese medicine in front of his wife, instead of arguing, she would just smile vaguely. In fact, the really effective medicine was the change in his wife's attitude, for what he needed was precisely rest and consolation.

"Where have the Japanese in fact got to?" When he felt his health improve, and his mind was able to concentrate, this was the question he often wanted to ask, but he did not dare, for fear of hearing catastrophic news. Sometimes he would examine her face attentively, hoping to guess from her expression whether the military situation was good or bad. But it was of no use. During these days, she presented him constantly an expression of gentleness and happiness. If by chance he caught her in deep thought, she would at once cover up with a smile. She no longer quarrelled with his mother. Sometimes, he even saw (of course, with closed or half-closed eyes while pretending to be asleep) the two of them sitting together chatting. "I only hope they get on better from now on. Then my coughing up blood will have been worth it," he had even thought with a sense of solace.

One day after coming home from work, his wife said to him in great excitement:

"I've some good news for you. The bombing of Guiyang was all rumour, and so was the fall of Dushan. The Japanese haven't entered Guizhou at all."

She was radiant. How he loved to see her smile like this.

"Truly?" he cried happily, looking at her with relief in his eyes. "I really would like to go out and have a look round tomorrow," he said slowly.

"You've rested only five days. You need to stay in bed at least ten days to a fortnight," his wife urged. "You should think only of getting better, and forget completely about everything else."

"And what about money?" he asked.

"I can manage. You don't need to worry about that," she replied.

"But it's not right to be using your money all the time. You've so many expenses of your own, and Xiao Xuan is also costing you a lot," he said apologetically.

"He's my own son, isn't he? Do we have to divide things into yours and mine? What difference does it make whether the money's mine or yours?" She gave him a reproachful smile.

He said nothing, for he could think of no argument to counter her.

"The last few days, there's been a lot of talk about salary adjustments. Eventually it died down because of the military situation in Hunan and Guangxi. Now they're talking about it again, and intend to do something after the situation improves. After the adjustments, my salary may go up by a third, so that a little extra spending isn't a problem," she continued in explanation, smiling, when she saw him become silent and thoughtful.

"But I still don't think it's very good. It embarrasses me. To think I've reached my age, and still can't support even myself," he grumbled.

"Why are you so old-fashioned! You can't grasp even this little point! When you're better, once the situation's improved and the Japanese have withdrawn, you'll be able to manage. Do you think I like working at the bank? At present, there's no other way. In the future, I want to work with you to realize our ideals. I want to help you in education," she said, her voice gentle and comforting.

"Yes, when the Japanese have been forced to withdraw, I'll be able to manage," he murmured to himself.

His mother came in with the pot of rice.

"Mother, let me." She went towards his mother, intending to take the pot from her hands.

"Quickly! Go and keep an eye on Xuan's rice gruel. Don't let it burn. I can manage this by myself," his mother replied, shaking her head. But she insisted on unfolding an old newspaper and spreading it on the table for his mother to put the pot on.

As he watched the figure of his wife disappear through the door, he thought to himself how lucky he was: "She's still good to me. No matter how useless I am, she's still good to me. What a kind-hearted woman she is! But it embarrasses me to use so much of her money. She'll despise me. One day, she'll despise me. I must pull myself together." He thought for a moment, and could not help repeating aloud what she had just said: "When the situation has improved, and the Japanese have been driven out, then I'll manage. I'll go back into education."

"Do you want something, Xuan?" his mother came over to ask, thinking that he was talking to her.

"I didn't say anything," he said, shaking his head, as if suddenly awakened from the dream-world he had just entered. What hope could this dark, bitter cold room give him?

His mother remained standing by the bed. Stretching out

her hand to feel his forehead, she asked softly: "How do you feel now?"

"Fine," he replied. "I think the medicine's working very well."

"We'll get the doctor to came again tomorrow," she said.

"There's no need," he said. "I'm already better." But to himself, he thought: "Where do I have the money for a doctor, or for medicine? Do you really want me to live off Shusheng?"

His wife came in to feed him his rice gruel. All at once, the lights went out. "Why is there a power-cut again tonight?" he cried in disappointment. "They never let you have any light," he added querulously.

"Light? You want light as well now?" his wife asked. He didn't know whether she was commending him or laughing at him.

After lighting a candle, his mother went out again. The room was bright once more, but the unsteady flicker of the dismal yellow candlelight seemed to smear a depressing layer of colour on everything. Two mice raced each other across the room, while downstairs, a woman's dreary voice was calling to the soul of her sick child.

"Light? How can I dare nurse such a hope?" he sighed in resignation.

"Don't be so pessimistic. Just concentrate on getting better You've still got one dose of medicine to take. I'll go and pre pare it for you. After you've taken it, you can go to sleep ear lier," his wife's gentle voice said comfortingly.

"No, you'd better have your own meal first. In fact, i doesn't matter whether I take the medicine or not. I know yo don't believe in Chinese medicine anyway. It might be jus as well if you give it to me after you've eaten. Perhaps it doe work. I feel much better this evening. I don't like taking i much, it's so bitter. But they say, the bitterer a medicin is, the more effective it is. Mother believes in it. Her worl revolves around Xiao Xuan and myself, and I'm absolutel no use at all." He gave a half-hearted smile. "You hurry up an eat. Why hasn't Mother come in? Is she making another dish? She must be preparing my medicine. She's really too good to me. You'd better go and see what she's up to, and both hurry up and eat. I can shut my eyes and sleep for a while." He smiled once more. "Go on, hurry up! I'm very happy today. The war's going better, and so we won't have to flee. Otherwise, my health would be a hindrance to you all."

His wife went out the door. His eyes wandered listlessly about the room. The candle flickered alarmingly. He could see nothing clearly among the dim shadows that filled the room. He sighed in pain and suffering.

The next day, his wife came home early. She came into the room wearily, her brows locked in a frown, greeting him and his mother with an unenthusiastic smile, before sitting down in silence at the desk.

"Why are you back so early today? It's not time to stop work yet," his mother asked.

"There was nothing to do at the bank. It was so exasperating sitting there that I left early," his wife replied dispiritedly.

"Don't you have any social engagements today?" his mother asked in spite of herself.

"No." His wife shook her head. After a while, she added: "The news is not good today. No one had the heart to work."

"Why, what's happened?" his mother asked, changing colour.

"They say that Dushan's fallen already. They also say that the Japanese have passed through Dushan and will soon be at Duyun."

"Then what are we going to do? And Xuan is so ill!" his mother cried in panic. "Do you think they'll reach Sichuan?"

"I think perhaps not. But if they do, all we can do is flee. I can go with the bank, but there's the problem of Xuan — " his wife muttered, frowning. But his mother interrupted her.

"Of course, you'll manage all right. But what about me and

Xuan, and Xiao Xuan! Where are we going? How can we flee completely empty-handed? And Xiao Xuan hasn't been home for a whole fortnight now, because he says he's so busy. And Xuan is so ill! It worries me to death!" His mother, concerned solely with pouring out her grievances, had the piteous, hesitating look of someone with no one to turn to.

"Mother, I'm almost completely better. I can move about; you don't need to worry. And the firm is sure to make some arrangements for us." He could not help interrupting, raising his voice. What he said about the firm was a vain hope spoken simply to calm his mother. No sooner were the words out than he saw suddenly before him Mr. Zhou's icy countenance and severe glance, and his feelings cooled considerably.

"Your firm will make arrangements! You're too naive! What can you expect from them? That Mr. Zhou of yours is not a very nice type, if you ask me. He has the eyes of a thief. Disgusting!" his wife exclaimed, her voice tinged with anger. "If I could do anything about it, I wouldn't let you work for him."

He knew that she was right. But the truth of her words, spoken out like that in front of his mother, hurt him and aroused his antagonism. "Why shouldn't I work under him? At least I'm living off my own labour!" he protested.

"What you say is true. But does he give you enough to live on? You should remember what kind of life you're living! To accept humiliation from people like that just isn't worth it!" his wife exclaimed.

"What's the use of remembering! In any case, what's past is past," he said with a sigh.

"But there's still the future, Xuan. You shouldn't lose heart," his wife continued, her voice suddenly gentle, her eyes filled with tears.

Surprised at her tone, he gazed gratefully into her eyes.

"Mr. Wang! Mr. Wang!" The voice of Mrs. Zhang, their neighbour, calling from outside, made him turn his eyes away from her to the door.

"Come in. Please come in," his mother called promptly in greeting.

Mrs. Zhang pushed open the closed door and came in. "Mrs. Wang, you're home early today!" She had not expected to find Shusheng there. "You're a bit better today, I hope, Mr. Wang." Then, turning to his mother, she asked: "Mrs. Wang, you must be so hard-worked these last two days!" Then she added: "Mr. and Mrs. Wang, and you too, Mrs. Wang, we have to ask your help. If we have to flee, please let us go with you. There're my husband and I, and our two-year-old child. We're not from Sichuan, and have no relatives here. We've nothing to flee with, no money and no transport. We can't be sure that my husband's office won't be disbanded at any moment. They won't take us with them. If by chance the Japs arrive, you must do a good turn and save us. Being from Sichuan, you can escape to the countryside, or even to another county. In other words, is it all right if we come with you?" she begged, with the air of a helpless orphan.

"Things can't be as bad as that," he said, in a display of calm, forcing himself to smile.

"It's said that Duyun has already fallen. The Japs are only twenty or thirty miles from Guiyang," Mrs. Zhang said in a grave whisper, as if afraid of being overheard. "And some people say that there's also a road to Sichuan that by-passes Guiyang. Mr. Wang, Mrs. Wang, you absolutely must help us!"

"Don't be afraid, Mrs. Zhang. They're all rumours. Things can't be as bad as that," Shusheng said gently.

"These last two days, everyone around's been thoroughly alarmed, and because he doesn't know where to turn, Mr. Zhang just drinks. You can see why I'm so worried! Well, thank you all so much. I'm afraid the baby might wake, so I'd better go back. If there's anything, I'll come back again. Thank you all again." A smile appeared on Mrs. Zhang's pallid face, but her brows remained fixed in a frown and her forehead covered in wrinkles. She tiptoed quietly from the room.

"Then your news was right, Shusheng," he said in a low

voice to his wife, showing no emotion, as if the matter had nothing to do with him.

"I'm not sure, but our department head, Mr. Chen, urged me to leave," his wife replied indifferently, as if it were of no concern to her either. But in reality, the news had thrown her mind into a turmoil.

"Leave? Leave for where?" he asked, lowering his voice to a whisper.

"He's angled a promotion to Lanzhou. It was announced to-day that he's to be the manager, and he wants to transfer me," his wife said, lowering her voice too, and purposely averting her eyes to avoid looking at him.

"Then, are you going or not?" he asked, raising his voice considerably, but unable to hide his agitation.

"I don't want to go. If there's a way of not going, I won't go," she murmured in reply.

"But if the bank transfers you, can you refuse to go?" he went on to ask.

"Of course I can. I'm still a free agent. At the worst, all I have to do is resign!" she answered, raising her voice too.

"If you go off on your own, then what will happen to Xiao Xuan? And what about Xuan?" his mother suddenly asked, her face becoming hostile.

"I haven't agreed to go. In fact, I don't want to go," his wife replied calmly, unperturbed by his mother's words.

"But you haven't refused him either," his mother persisted, unwilling to let go.

"But I told them I have a family, so it's not easy for me to go. Besides, whether the transfer will be made is still not cer-tain. At present, it's just words." His wife's voice showed a hint of exasperation, but she managed to keep calm neverthe-less.

"You intend to abandon us all, and run off by yourself. You think I don't know what's in your mind!" his mother con-tinued to insist.

Without replying, his wife went over and sat down on the

edge of the bed. Bending over slightly to look at him, she saw
the tears in his eyes. Silently, she took his hand in hers, and
after a long pause, she finally forced herself to say: "I won't
go."

"I know," he said with emotion, nodding his head. "Thank
you!" After a long while, he said in a low voice: "But you ought
to go. What's the good of staying with me all your life? My
life is as good as over."

"You mustn't speak like that. The circumstances we're in
aren't your fault. You've had your share of suffering these
last two years. The first thing is for you to get better," his wife
said soothingly to comfort him.

"If it's not my fault, then whose fault is it? Why does everyone else manage?" he asked, unable to hold back his self-re-
proaches on hearing these words of comfort from her.

"Because you're too good a sort," his wife said, smiling, her
eyes filled with love and compassion.

Too good a sort! The words made him wince imperceptibly.
He had heard this remark made of himself so often that he was
sick of it. But she had no thought whatever of being sarcastic.
He said no more, thinking over the problem he had never been
able to solve. "I don't want to be a good sort!" "But what do
I do to stop being a good sort?" "There's no way out. I'm like
that by nature." All these thoughts succeeded in reducing to
nothing any idea of injustice or revolt. The last few years of
his life had been wasted on this problem. . . . And so, he just
sighed softly.

"What is it? You're unhappy again?" his wife asked, taken
aback.

"It's not that," he said, shaking his head. Only then did he
notice that his mother had already retired to her tiny room.

"Then you'd better have some more sleep. I'll stay home
and keep you company. I won't go off by myself, so you don't
need to worry," his wife said gently.

"I know, I know," he said quietly, nodding his head.

Standing up, she went slowly to one of the windows, and

looked down at the scene in the street. Below the window, which was set in the right brick wall of the building, was a tiny straight street (actually, it was only an alley). This building was taller than the surrounding buildings, so there were no walls or roofs to obscure their view. Directly opposite her, she could see the upper section of the main street which was cut out of the hillside. Several rickshaws were racing down the hill one after another, so fast that the pullers' feet seemed scarcely to touch the ground, becoming a blur in her eyes.

"They're all busy," she remarked to herself without thinking, her voice so low that it was audible only to herself. This comment, so seemingly trivial, was yet full of significance. Her mind was crowded with images, and yet seemed totally empty. She was not looking for anything in particular, yet she remained at the window staring at the dust flying over the road. She felt that time was like a stream flowing past her, slowly but relentlessly, carrying away her blood in its current.

"Surely I'm not going to spend the rest of my life like this, in quarrelling and in misery?" an inner voice demanded. She sighed, unable to answer.

Suddenly, two knocks sounded on the door. She turned in surprise. An office-boy from the bank pushed open the door and entered.

"Miss Zeng, here's a letter for you from Mr. Chen," he said, handing her the letter.

Ripping it open, she read through the few scrawled sentences inviting her to the Victory Mansions for dinner, then, without a word, she tore the letter to pieces.

The office-boy stood before her, waiting for her reply. "All right, I know. You can go back now," she instructed.

"All right," the office-boy answered obsequiously, closing the door as he went out.

She rolled the torn pieces of the letter into a ball in her hand, and stood for a moment leaning with her back to the window. The room began gradually to dim, but the night was like a brush, painting the corners of the room here and there. The

face of the invalid began to blur as he lay on the bed, taking
urgent, gasping breaths. "What was he dreaming about?" she
wondered. Not a sound came from his mother's tiny room.
They had all abandoned her, leaving her alone in her loneliness! She felt her blood draining away, ebbing unceasingly
away. An uneasiness began to steal over her. A doubt suddenly
arose in her mind. "Must I then simply wither away like this
and die?" She paced briefly about the room, uncertain of what
she should do. She did not want to accept Mr. Chen's invitation. She'd even forgotten the ball of torn paper in her hand.

His mother came out of her tiny room and turned on the
light, the same exasperating, dirty yellow light. "Ah, haven't
you gone yet?" she asked provocatively.

"Gone? Gone where?" she asked in surprise.

"Didn't someone just deliver a letter inviting you out?" his
mother sneered.

"It's still early," she answered vaguely. She glanced at the
ball of paper in her hand. A vindictive smile suddenly lit up
her face. She had decided.

"Have you been invited out to dinner again today?" his
mother asked, persisting with her question.

"Someone from the bank," she answered curtly.

"Is it to see you both off?"

At the wound inflicted by his mother's words, she flushed
and her eyebrows rose, but she repressed her anger at once, and
deliberately assuming a nonchalant smile, she nodded and said:
"Yes."

She changed her dress and re-touched her make-up. She
wanted to say a few words to him, but he was fast asleep. She
glanced at him, and then, affecting an air of content, went out
of the flat, leaving his mother muttering something behind her
as she went rapidly down the stairs.

"The more you talk, the more I'll show you. I hadn't intended to go originally," she muttered to herself, her lips pursed
in anger.

15

She took a rickshaw to the Victory Mansions, where she found Mr. Chen waiting for her at the entrance. He accompanied her to the restaurant upstairs, where he had already booked a table. After helping her off with her overcoat, he pulled a chair out for her to sit down and seated himself opposite, gazing and smiling at her until, to cover her embarrassment, she spoke first:

"Did you manage to get the plane ticket?"

"Yes. For three days from now," he answered, his expression becoming rather tense.

"Wonderful! Then au revoir! You'll be back next year, I suppose?" she said with a smile.

He could not tell from her smile what her real feelings were, but it encouraged him. He gazed at her intensely and whispered: "Shusheng." It was the first time he had called her by her first name, having till now always addressed her as "Miss Zeng". She was startled by it and blushed slightly. "I've just received some reliable news," he continued. "The Japs have already reached Duyun, and it seems that the situation there is untenable. There are rumours that Guiyang can't be relied on to hold out either."

"It can't have happened so fast, can it?" she exclaimed, shaking her head, desperately trying to hide the terror she felt inside her.

"It's been very rapid. Simply unbelievable!" He grimaced in incredulity. Just at that moment, the waiter arrived with the soup. He quickly stopped talking, bent down and took a couple of spoonfuls of soup. "What do you intend to do?"

"Who, me? Where can I go? I'll have to stay here, of course!" she said, deliberately smiling at him.

"And what will you do if the Japanese come?" he then asked.

"Wait till they come first. If there's time, I'll run away. If not, we can take refuge in the countryside," she replied, purposely affecting a couldn't-care-less attitude. She bent over and drank her soup.

"That's no good. When the Japanese come, they'll be out in the countryside on the look-out for pretty girls. It's better for you to leave now. There's no problem with the bank. I can wangle a plane ticket for you on the black market. You can come with me in three days' time," he said gravely.

"Three days is too soon. I can't make it," she said, lifting her eyes to look at him and then lowering them again.

"You think it's too early? The Japanese may be here even earlier!" he exclaimed anxiously. "This is a rare opportunity. If you miss it, it won't be so easy to find another one. Everything I tell you is true. The situation at present is very, very serious. You have to make up your mind fast."

But she still said nothing. She was thinking. Her husband's sickly, anaemic face, his mother's eyes burning with hate and jealousy, the everlasting gloom of the flat . . . the stories of the refugees on the roads from Hunan to Guangxi, the enemy atrocities ... all these crowded into her mind. She was so thoroughly confused that it was impossible for her to decide. She could not go on pretending. Putting down her soup-spoon she looked up and sighed: "How can I possibly leave now!"

"You can't leave? You must realize, this is the time to leave! Your family is a simple matter, isn't it? What else is there you can't leave behind!" he cried. He knew that she had a husband who was always ill, a mother-in-law that she did not get on with, and that she was not happy in her home life. But he did not know that she had a twelve-year-old son, and certainly did not know that it was the husband who was always ill that she could not "leave behind".

"It's too soon. Let me think about it," she said, shaking her head, hoping that he would not continue to press her like this. She did not want to decide such an important question so quickly.

"Then I'll wait for your answer first thing tomorrow morning. After tomorrow, plane tickets will be difficult to get hold of," he said.

"Let me think about it," she murmured in reply, but almost immediately, shook her head again. "No, I think it's better if I give you an answer now. I'm not going," she said, smiling.

"This is your last chance. You can't let it go," he said, changing colour slightly. "You shouldn't sacrifice yourself for your family. They don't care about you. Why should you worry about them?"

The soup-plates had long been cleared away and changed for fried fish. She looked down, saying nothing.

"Shusheng, think it over again. You can't sacrifice yourself like this for nothing. It's better for you to come with me," he begged.

"But what will they do?" she said, as if talking to herself.

"They can look after themselves. It's not going to do them any good if you don't go. Whereas if you do, you can leave them quite a bit for household expenses."

"But he —" She wanted to say "he's ill", but at the word "he", she suddenly stopped, halted by the image of that thin, sickly, pale face. She did not want to talk about her husband to this man who was two years her junior. That would be too humiliating.

"You still think of others at a time like this! You're too kind-hearted," he went on quickly. "But what's the use of being kind-hearted? You just sacrifice yourself for nothing. It's not worth it!"

She found what he had to say rather disagreeable. "If I don't go, it's not certain that I'll be killed," she said coldly.

"Shusheng, you don't realize how serious the military situation is. I'm not joking with you," he said anxiously.

"I didn't say you were," she said, smiling slightly. "But there are thousands upon thousands of people here. Why are you concerned only about me?" she continued.

"Because I — " he replied. But afraid of hearing the rest,

and knowing what was in his mind, she interrupted, blushing, and abruptly changed the subject.

When the time came for coffee, they suddenly heard someone at the neighbouring table say: "I've decided to move the whole family to the countryside. What about you? You have to make plans early."

"I've only just got here. I'm so exhausted already, what else can I do?" another voice replied. "People like us from East China have nowhere to flee to now, even if we wanted to."

"Did you hear what they said?" Mr. Chen whispered, drawing her attention to them. "It's obvious that the situation's serious. You can't not come with me!"

"It's not that easy even if I did want to go. I've got a lot of things unfinished," she said, saying the first thing that came to mind. She was rather afraid, and a struggle was going on within her.

"You worry about that at a time like this! Stop talking about it anymore. Just get ready to leave in three days," he said in agitation.

"To hear you talk, anyone would think you were forcing me to go with you," she said with a smile, deliberately hiding her own hesitation and doubt.

"Of course. Because I care for you," he said, his voice tremulous as he reached out his hand to take hers.

She looked down, saying nothing, but slowly withdrew her hand. After a few minutes, she abruptly stood up, saying in a low voice: "I have to go back."

"Wait a few minutes. I'll see you home," he said at once. She sat down again without a word.

After paying the bill, Mr. Chen accompanied her down the stairs. As they stood by the entrance of the mansions, several cars blowing their horns arrived simultaneously at the empty space before them. In a hubbub of voices, beautifully dressed young women, aristocratic ladies and tall, stalwart foreign army officers poured from the cars, and followed one another into the ballroom next-door.

"It doesn't look as if it's time to flee. It seems to me, all that talk was just rumour," she said doubtfully.

"Rumour! You still don't believe me?" he said, taking exception to her words. "I'm willing to bet that within a week, those people will have disappeared without a trace!" In his mind, the future of the city was one of utter darkness. No matter how he tried, he could see nothing but destruction ahead.

"But there are plenty of people who can't run away. Those who can flee, are in the minority after all," she said, aroused by a feeling of pity for her husband.

"But whatever you say, those who can flee are all going to," he said.

After picking their way slowly between the cars, they walked slowly out of the lane.

"It's really rather early to go home now. What about going for a walk?" Mr. Chen suggested.

"I'd like to get home early," she replied in a low voice.

"A little later won't matter. Another half-hour won't make any difference. I think it must be very lonely for you at home," he said.

She felt the last sentence strike a tender nerve. She wanted to reject his proposal, to argue that her home was not lonely, but her honesty prevailed. She bit her lip, saying nothing at all, and followed obediently in his footsteps.

Although it was not yet very late, the air was bitterly cold. The street lights were dim, and most of the shops were closed, except for a few eating-places, which, though not dead, were not as alive with activity as usual. A cold wind overtook them by stealth. Pedestrians and rickshaws were all hurrying along as if trying to avoid the biting cold.

"Look, how everything's changed," he whispered in her ear, in a voice tinged with a sense of foreboding. "In a couple of days, it will be even more bleak and desolate."

She said nothing, concentrating solely on following him, her eyes fixed to the ground. Before her still floated the faces of the young women and aristocratic ladies of the Victory Mansions. "They're all happier than I am," she thought resentfully.

When they reached the street where she lived, she even forgot to look up at the building which was her home. They walked towards the riverside, taking the road that twisted down the hill towards the bank of the river. They began the descent. Half-way down, at a place where the opposite bank could be seen, they stopped. They leaned against the stone balustrade, looking across to the lamps twinkling like stars on the opposite bank. On the surface of the river, lights rose and fell, sparkled and faded, like countless blinking eyes, like numberless stars in secret conversation.

Also leaning against the balustrade on this part of the road, about twenty steps away from them was a young couple, apparently lovers, chattering away in a ceaseless conversation.

"I've lived in this damned place long enough. I have to get away," he said, as if to himself.

"While you're here, it seems terrible. But who knows what it'll be like elsewhere," she said, after a long pause, also as if to herself.

"In any case, it's bound to be better than this damned place. The weather in Lanzhou's nice. It's famous for it," he added.

"If I go to Lanzhou, there won't be any problem about my work, will there?" she suddenly asked.

"None at all. I guarantee it!" he said excitedly. "Then you've decided!"

"I've still decided not to go." She paused for a moment before replying. He could not make out whether she was serious or joking.

"We'll talk about Lanzhou tomorrow. Let's drop it for tonight," he said, suddenly changing the subject. "Look how tranquil it is tonight. I feel like writing a poem."

His last words almost made her laugh out loud, but she managed to contain herself. She asked with a smile: "Do you write poetry as well, Mr. Chen?"

"I like reading poetry, both ancient and modern. Sometimes I write a few verses in secret, but they're not very good. I'm afraid you'd laugh if you read them," he replied, a little flustered, but rather pleased with himself nevertheless.

"It never occurred to me that you were a poet as well, Mr. Chen. I hope you'll do me the honour of letting me read your poems, Mr. Chen."

"You must stop calling me Mr. Chen. Call me by my name. Call me Fengguang," he begged.

"But we're so used to calling you Mr. Chen, it's difficult to change. It's easier to go on calling you Mr. Chen," she replied with a smile. She felt herself becoming excited, and began to fantasize, though what her fantasy was, she herself could not have said.

"But you'll have to change later in any case," he said, pleased with himself for having thought of this double meaning. He deliberately waited for a moment before adding: "At Lanzhou, I'll be the manager." He smiled.

"In the future, when we've fled to Lanzhou and have to come begging to you for a bowl of rice, I hope you won't put on a surly face and refuse," she said, purposely making fun of him.

"In the future? Aren't you leaving in three days' time?" he asked, half-jokingly.

She shivered slightly. She felt the warmth of his breath against her cheeks and moved a little away. "I still haven't decided." Then she added quickly: "I can't abandon them and run off by myself."

"You can't give up the plane ticket. Besides, you shouldn't sacrifice yourself for others. Besides, if you leave first, they can follow after. Besides, . . ." In his agitation as he spoke, he suddenly put out an arm and lightly encircled her waist. She wanted to move away, but it was too late. She felt her face flush and her heart beat quickly. There was no time to analyze her feelings at this moment. Exerting all her self-control, she broke into what he was saying: "Look at the bank opposite, look at the river, look at everything around us. How quiet and tranquil it all is. Everyone is so calm and peaceful, why should we alarm ourselves? You have a job, and of course you must go, but why should I go?"

Summoning up all his courage, he whispered excitedly into her ear: "Because — because I love you!"

Although the words were not a complete surprise to her, she was startled nevertheless. She flushed all over, and the throbbing of her heart became even more rapid. A strange indescribable feeling swept over her. Not knowing how best to answer him, she bent even further forward, peering out at the dark surface of the water.

"Now that you know what is in my heart, will you still not come with me?" he said in a rapid whisper, his lips still close to her ear.

She saw the weeping face of her sick husband, the angry countenance of his hateful mother, and the grave expression on Xiao Xuan's pale face (so out of character for a child). Shaking her head, she repeated wretchedly: "No! No! No!" He thought she was refusing to go with him, but she herself had no idea of the real meaning behind the three "no's".

"Why do you still say 'no'? Surely you believe me?" he asked softly, his arm still round her waist. He bent down, trying to see her expression, but just as his head was approaching her face, he caught the fragrance of her powder and perfume, giving him the courage to place his lips on her left cheek and kiss her. At the same time, his right arm around her waist clasped her even more tightly.

"No! No!" she whispered in alarm, slipping at once from his grasp and retreating a few steps, her face crimson. He came to her side, still wanting to speak to her, but he got no further than "I", when she abruptly waved him away, saying:

"I'm so confused. You'd better see me home." She was ashamed yet excited, but also in agony. She was filled with perplexity; she seemed to be standing at a crossroad, unable to decide which way to go.

"But you still haven't answered me," he protested softly.

She said nothing. Her face was still flushed, her left cheek especially was burning. Not only was her heart beating wildly, it seemed to swing from left to right inside her. Her brain was quite numb, and she had no idea of what to do. A white, misty fog hung over the river. She had not noticed when it had begun to form, but now she could smell it, a suffocating stench capable of rotting a man's lungs. The night began to turn white as the fog spread to the shore. She was enveloped in it, unable to see anyone but him, for the young couple had long been swallowed up by it. She was troubled. She seemed to hear a familiar voice whisper: "I'm only a burden to you." She shivered. "We'd better go back," she proposed once more. The romantic feelings aroused in her a moment before had vanished.

"But it's still early. Let's find somewhere else and sit down for a while," he suggested.

"I'd rather go back earlier," she said briefly. "I'll meet you at the Guansheng Garden Restaurant tomorrow morning at eight."

"Then you must give me a definite answer tomorrow," he insisted gravely. He was happy, for he was sure that she would give him the answer he wanted to hear.

"All right, tomorrow," she nodded in reply, putting her left arm through his right arm as they stepped off the footpath into the thick fog that enveloped the centre of the road.

After walking in silence for a while, he suddenly asked with concern: "Is there anything wrong at home? You don't seem very happy today."

"It's nothing," she said, shaking her head, continuing to clasp him by the arm as they walked through the fog. Overcome by a vague mixture of fear and disquiet, she felt the need to grasp hold of something, and so she clung to his arm even more tightly.

"I really can't help worrying, leaving you behind like this," he then said. "You can't have much of a life here."

His words brought new thoughts to her mind. A feeling of

pain and resentment rose within her, attacking her so suddenly that she was powerless to resist. She wanted to cry, but managed to suppress her tears. A home without warmth; a sick husband, good but weak; a selfish, pig-headed, old-fashioned mother-in-law; quarrels and hostility; solitude and poverty; a youth lost in the midst of war; a vain search for personal happiness; a grey future . . . all these rushed like a floodtide into her mind. He was right. How could she say that she was living well?. . . She was only thirty-three, still brimming with energy. Why shouldn't she make the most of life? She had the right to pursue happiness. She ought to rebel. Finally, she spoke up: "Perhaps it would be just as well to leave. In any case, things can't stay like this for long." Her voice was very low, as if she were conversing with herself.

"Then make up your mind and take this plane! Once we get to Lanzhou, everything can be fixed easily," he cried, surprised and happy.

"No!" she protested, as if waking with a start. But then she added: "I'll let you know tomorrow."

"Tomorrow? How long this night will be!" He sighed in disappointment.

"I'll have to go back and think about it carefully, but this time, I'll definitely make up my mind," she said, but she felt neither the happiness of love nor that of being loved. She was still hesitating at the crossroads, trying to decide which road to take. But still, she could not make up her mind.

"Then you won't refuse tomorrow," he concluded, hoping still that all was not yet lost. "I'll wait for your answer tomorrow morning at eight in the Guansheng Garden Restaurant."

"Tomorrow, I may decide to leave," she said. "I really can't stand the fog here. It seems to have corrupted my spirit. These last two years, I've had enough." She was distraught. She wanted to resist. But before her eyes stretched only a white expanse of fog. In the distance, she could see nothing at all.

16

And so she was back home again. Once through the front door of the building, it was as if she had entered another world. Everything was so familiar, yet she could not help frowning. An unseen hand seemed to drag her into the float.

A light was on in his mother's room, but no sound issued from it. Her husband was lying quietly on his bed, not yet asleep. Seeing her coming in, he called: "You're back!" His voice was so affectionate, so lacking in resentment, that she felt ashamed. Approaching the bed, she asked him gently: "Aren't you asleep yet?"

"I was waiting for you to come back," he replied.

"It's your health that's important. Why do you think only of me?" she asked, moved.

"I slept a lot during the day, so that I can't sleep at night," he replied affectionately. "Mrs. Zhang came by again tonight to say that the outside of our main entrance is piled with luggage, apparently belonging to refugees from Guiyang. She's heard that even Guiyang can't be held and she's urging us to leave early. What do you think?"

"The front entrance seemed pretty deserted. I didn't notice anything. It can't be that bad," she answered, her mind elsewhere.

"That's what I think. Things can't have happened that fast. Actually, for people like us, with no money or influence, it's no use running away anyway. Even if something did happen to us, our lives are not worth a candle. It's not obvious that it's better to be alive than dead. Now that I see this, I'm not worried anymore. I've been waiting for you to come back because I wanted to have a talk with you." He carefully lowered his voice. "I can't get through to Mother, and I don't dare discuss things with her too much anyway. You understand more than she does, and better. I've been looking forward to your coming back, so that I could talk things over with you seriously."

"What about? You mean about getting away?" she asked offhandedly.

"Yes, that's exactly it," he replied, looking at her intently. "I think that this time, it's eighty to ninety per cent sure that something's going to happen. I can't get away, because I can't move. I'm not afraid either. But you ought to get ready early. You don't have to stay to look after me. If you can take Xiao Xuan with you, and find a place for Mother where she can be safe, then my mind will be at ease." His voice was shaking slightly, but there was no hint of sentimentality.

"I'm not leaving," she said simply. She had not expected him to speak like that, and he seemed at that moment so magnanimous that she felt her conscience reproach her. "He wants me to leave," she reflected to herself. "He's actually asking me to leave!" But the thought only made her more unhappy.

"When the time comes, you can't not leave. You mustn't think only of me, because I can go with the firm then," he explained anxiously. "We men, after all, have more ways out. Didn't you say the bank was thinking of transferring you to Lanzhou? Just now. . . ." He paused for a moment before continuing: "I've been chewing it over all day, and I think it's best if you agree to go. It's not an easy opportunity to come by."

"I don't want to go," she replied briefly as before. As she sat on the edge of the bed, his expression of genuine concern made her even more uncomfortable, so she turned away to avoid looking at him.

"Shusheng," he called, his voice shaking slightly. She was forced to turn back towards him. "My idea can't be wrong. I've thought about it quite dispassionately — "

"Is it because Mother said something to you?" she interrupted abruptly.

"I didn't say anything! I never talk behind people's backs," his mother unexpectedly shouted in protest from her tiny room.

Shusheng said nothing, but was so angry that she bit her lip. He raised his voice in reply: "Mother, no one accused you of saying anything behind Shusheng's back. Please don't be so sensitive!"

"I know what's going on. I know everything," his mother continued. "She won't stay with us in the long run. Let her go, the earlier the better."

"I certainly won't go! Just see what you can do about it!" Shusheng muttered, feeling herself wronged. But her voice was so low that his mother did not hear her properly.

"Mother's like that. Don't take it to heart. Just let her have her say," he urged in a whisper.

"I've had enough these last few years. You can see for yourself," she murmured in reply.

"Then you get away on your own first. Take Xiao Xuan if you can, but if not, leave by yourself first. You mustn't be so hard on yourself," he said softly but distinctly, his voice intentionally low so that his mother would not hear.

"Is this really what you've decided?" she asked without emotion, doing her utmost not to reveal her own feelings.

"It's the best thing to do," he replied frankly and earnestly. "It's the best for everyone."

"You aren't trying to chase me away, are you? Is that why you want me to go by myself first?" she then asked.

"No, of course not! I've no such idea," he protested anxiously. "Only the situation is so bad, you must save yourself first. Since you have the chance, why give it up? I can find a way to leave too, and we'll meet up again very soon. Do as I say and go first. We'll follow you eventually."

"Follow me? But what if by some chance you can't leave?" she said, still as impassively.

He waited for a moment, before whispering in reply: "At least *you* will be saved." He had finally blurted out his real motive.

She suddenly buried her face in his chest, tears welling up

in her eyes, her heart torn apart. She wanted to weep her fill, to choose her road and to hesitate no longer.

"Xuan, go to sleep. Why don't you ever think of yourself?" She sighed as she stood up, wiping her eyes.

"I'm not important. I don't count," he quickly answered.

"But I can't do this," she said, as if to herself, pacing about the room. "I won't go. If I go, we all go together!" she said, her decision made. But the decision gave her no joy.

Early the next morning, the answer she gave to the departmental head, Mr. Chen, was brief. "I'm not going."

Mr. Chen's face changed colour instantly. It was a moment before he was able to force a smile and ask: "Is that really what you've decided?"

"I've thought about it very carefully, and I've decided to stay."

After a few minutes, he said softly to her, looking very serious: "I don't want to deliberately frighten you, but I'll tell you a piece of news. Last night, the bank had a wire from the Guiyang branch to say that they're in the process of closing down. You must make up your mind."

"I've already made up my mind," she said coldly.

"Think about it again. The situation today's even worse. There are far fewer people having breakfast here than usual, and look how jittery they all are. Disaster is staring us in the face, and even if it doesn't strike at once, it's only a matter of a few days," he said.

"Have you got your plane ticket?" she interrupted to ask, not wishing to listen to him continue in this strain.

"Not yet. I'm going to enquire again this afternoon," he replied, rather out of sorts.

"You'd better go early. Aren't you afraid that someone else might get the ticket?" she asked in mock concern.

"If they do, it's all the same to me. For myself, I don't really care whether I go or not," he said as if to himself, purposely trying to look at her with sorrow in his eyes. Just at that moment, the waiter brought a bowl of Cantonese rice broth that he had ordered. He looked down, dipped his spoon into it and began to drink.

Feeling that there was nothing more to say, she lifted her cup to her lips and sipped her tea. She gazed at him briefly. She felt sure that he was not striking a pose or showing off, that his sorrow and disappointment were real. She began to sympathize with him. She began to doubt her own decision. If I promise to go with him, she thought, what will be the result? Her determination wavered.

"You go first.   I might follow later."   She had not intended to say this, but the words came simply because she wanted to cheer him up.

"Later! But you can't afford to wait till later!" he said in agitation. His wide-open eyes stared at her as if in reproach: why can't you understand! His words stung her, and she answered huffily:

"Then you can come back later and give us a decent burial!"

"I tell you, I'm not going," he said, scowling.

"You're not going? But isn't it a post you've been after for a long time?" she asked, taken by surprise. "You've even managed to get a plane ticket."

"I've had in mind right from the beginning that you would go too," was all he said in reply. She reddened instantly. She understood completely what he meant. She had not wanted to hear him say this, but consciously or sub-consciously, she had forced him to do so. This time, she did not dare answer. Her resolution had never been firm, and now she was afraid that he would shake it. He said nothing either, simply gazing at her in silence. This stare of his, this deep silence made her uncomfortable. The fire in his eyes seemed to scorch her face. She could not bear it. "Let's go," she whispered, but she sat there motionless. He seemed not to have heard, and so, after a moment, she went on to say: "If the bank insists on transferring me, then I may perhaps go." She had already given way a little, but he was not yet aware of it. But then, neither was she.

After leaving the Guansheng Garden Restaurant, he saw her to the entrance of the bank building before separating. She thought he was going to the airline office, but he himself had no idea of where he should go. Finally, he decided to kill time by going to the International Coffee Shop.

When she entered the bank and saw the office desks, the glass tops, the abacuses, the account books, the heads of the clerks (it seemed that nothing here would ever change), she was suddenly overcome by a feeling of solitude. She wanted to run out and call him in, but she took no step towards the main door, for she did not even know what she wanted him for. She went in silence to her own desk.

The new chief accountant, an older man of about fifty, old-fashioned and inflexible, had already arrived. He looked at her curiously several times in succession, then silently shook his head.

She sat at her desk, her mind a blank. It was long past the time for starting work, but the quiet, happy atmosphere that usually reigned had vanished. Her colleagues hurried nervously in and out, talking and whispering with their heads together, abandoning their schedule of work. Noticing suddenly that two of the desks were empty, she wondered where the occupants had gone. All at once, one of their regular customers, with whom the bank had many dealings, came in to report: "Guiyang's already lost!" It was only two hours by car from Guiyang to Chongqing. Some of the clerks let out a cry in spite of themselves. "Rumours!" she thought to herself.

"What are you going to do?" a male employee in charge of savings deposits asked in alarm.

"You're a local. What are you afraid of? I've decided not to leave. You've had it if you flee, and you've had it if you don't. Might as well stay here and save yourself some trouble," the middle-aged customer said calmly, as if not in the least afraid.

"I'm sending my family away tomorrow," another man in charge of remittances announced.

"But if the Japs are really coming so fast, you'll never get away in time," the savings-deposit clerk declared.

"Rumours!" she protested mentally.

But such rumours were being ceaselessly spread, and the bank was beseiged the whole morning by them. The manager and the departmental heads telephoned everywhere to try to get some information, but although the news they obtained was contradictory and not very reliable, there was not one item that was not worrying. No one had the heart to go on working. Every sudden noise made them think of an air-raid alarm.

She could not bear this atmosphere. Suddenly her family came to her mind. She thought of her husband and her son. She at once wrote a letter to Xiao Xuan, telling him to ask for leave to come home, and gave it to the office-boy to post. As time passed, her disquiet grew. Unable to sit there any longer, she left work early without asking permission, and no one tried to stop her.

As she walked along the street, everything seemed different from usual. She felt as if she were in a dream, unable to distinguish her past from her present. "What am I doing? Why am I going home? Where indeed is my home? Why on earth am I hurrying like this?" she asked herself. "Have I decided? Why can't I decide? What shall I do?"

She could not find an answer in such a short time: she was already home.

A crowd had gathered at the entrance of the building discussing the situation. Porters with large suitcases suspended from carrying-poles were hurrying from the passageways. People were either moving house or leaving the city. She was a little worried, and dashed promptly up the stairs.

The second floor was exceedingly quiet. Mrs. Zhang, who had claimed not to know what to do, had moved with the whole family early that morning. No one knew where to, but the door of her flat was locked. The Wang family's door, which was usually only closed, today was firmly bolted. Unable to push it open, she knocked several times.

Naturally, it was his mother who came to open the door. After she entered the room, she noticed at one glance that he was not there. His bed was empty.

"Mother, where's he gone?" she asked in alarm.

"He went to work," his mother replied matter-of-factly.

"But he's not fully recovered yet. How can he go to work today?" she objected.

"He insisted on going. What could I do?" his mother retorted, her face set.

She seemed to have been struck a staggering blow, and it was a moment before she muttered, as if to herself: "You shouldn't have let him go. He could get worse at any time." She had come home with such a warmth of feeling. The complete disappointment on her face and in her voice aroused her mother's hostility.

It was precisely because she had been unable to keep her son back that she was cross. To hear her daughter-in-law criticize her now in this way incensed her even more: even if I have done something wrong, it's not for you to teach me what's right! Besides, you've never shown any concern for him before. All you think about is meeting your boy-friends outside. A bitch who doesn't even want her own family, who's planning to elope with her fancy man, and you have the nerve to tell me what's what!

"Then why didn't you come back earlier and keep him home then? It's all very well to make fine speeches now! This morning you left so early. What was all that for. I ask you!" Her face was purple with rage as she pointed two fingers of her right hand at Shusheng's nose.

"I went to see my boy-friend. Is that clear enough? What business is it of yours?" her daughter-in-law shouted in reply, her face also red with fury.

"It is my business. You're my daughter-in-law! It is my business, and I'll do something about it!   I absolutely will!" his mother screamed.

And so the two women began to quarrel.

17

All this time, Wang Wenxuan was working in the office, oblivious of what was going on at home.

It was not until his wife had already left the flat early that morning when he had got up. After he had finished breakfast, he suddenly announced that he was going to the office. His mother was unable to stop him.

"Don't worry. I'm better already."

"I can't ask for leave too often. If I don't start work again, even my job is going to be in jeopardy."

"We can't have the whole family depending only on Shusheng for its living. The money for the medicine and the doctor these last few days all came from her."

This had been the reasoning he had used against his mother.

She had found no arguments with which to counter him. In fact, she herself was thinking: I'd rather starve, I'd rather suffer any hardship than live off Shusheng.

"Then let me go out and find work. I'll be a servant, or even an amah," she finally cried, looking compassionately at her only son, her eyes brimming with tears.

"Mother, how can you talk like that! You're an educated woman. How can you do work like that!" he said wretchedly, averting his gaze, not daring to look at her.

"My only regret is that I ever studied in the first place. And I shouldn't have let you study either. I've ruined your life as well as my own. Frankly, I don't even know enough to be an amah!" she exclaimed bitterly.

"These days, everyone manages except for useless people like us. I'm not equal to an office-boy in a bank, and you're not

It was precisely because she had been unable to keep her son back that she was cross.

as good as an amah," he said with rancour. At last, he looked
up and, giving a long sigh, left the flat. His mother ran after
him trying to call him back, but he went down the stairs without even turning his head.

When he reached his firm, the office downstairs seemed
quieter than usual. The sign-in register had already been removed. Old Mr. Zhong nodded to him and smiled. He went
upstairs. There were some empty places in the first-floor office. Mr. Wu, who'd just finished a telephone call, glanced at
him, looking displeased, and asked without any real interest:
"Are you better now?"

"Yes, thanks," he answered in a low voice.

"It seems to me that your health is pretty bad. You ought
to take a long period of rest," Mr. Wu said coldly. He was
still wondering what Mr. Wu really meant, when he heard Mr.
Zhou give a cough of displeasure in the small office.

He answered with a vague "yes" and went quickly over to
his desk and sat down.

He had just done so when the office-boy brought a new pile
of proofs and placed them before him: "Mr. Wu says that they
are urgent. He needs them today," the office-boy said brusquely.

He just nodded quietly without a word of complaint, but he
thought to himself: The situation's so tense today, and some of
the others haven't even come to work. Everyone is on such
tenterhooks. Why am I the only one that has to do extra work?
What if I hadn't come to work today? You're all just shoving
me around. It's completely unfair.

The office-boy stood staring at him. "Mr. Wu says they're
needed today," he repeated, as if to torment him.

He looked up, but showed not the slightest indignation, answering gently: "All right." The office-boy left.

As he leafed through the proofs and manuscript in silence,
he began to frown without realizing it. It was a book on Party
precepts, printed in No. 4 type, preceded by prefaces by important people in the Party and the Government. He bent over
his work reading under his breath, first the prefaces and then

the text itself. His mind wandered off to he knew not where. His head was swimming and his limbs were weak. But he forced himself to go on reading and correcting.

During this time, the head of department, Mr. Zhou, left, and so did his section head, Mr. Wu. His colleagues at once broke into noisy conversation, exchanging news of the war. They were all worried and concerned, and no one worked with enthusiasm. Only he continued as before to bury his head in his proofs. "They're needed today," a rude voice kept sounding in his ear. At last, unable to stand it, he answered it mentally: "Stop pushing me! The most I can give you in exchange is my life!"

When twelve o'clock came, the lunch-bell rang. He left the office as if he had been saved. His appetite was still bad, and he had to force himself to eat one bowl of rice. He could feel the mixture of contempt and pity in his colleagues' eyes, as they purposely dropped alarming remarks about the war to frighten him. "I say, Lao Wang, you'll be getting a rise before long. You can still bury yourself in your work at a time like this. You'll really deserve a bonus at the end of the year!" one of his colleagues mocked. Without replying, he returned to take refuge behind his desk. He did not smoke, and did not have the energy to read. He just sat there in boredom, facing the glass windows, and dozed off.

After he did not know how long, someone suddenly called "Mr. Wang." He opened his eyes with a start and straightened up. The office-boy was standing before him again, and announced, with his eyes fixed on him: "There's a message for you. You're to go at once."

The note was on his desk, in Shusheng's handwriting. It read:

"Xuan:
There's something I have to discuss with you. Please come to the International at once.

Shusheng,
Today."

He gave a start. "What can it be about?" he wondered, getting up instantly and hurrying down the stairs.

"Where are you going, Wang, old man?" old Mr. Zhong asked.

He muttered vaguely in reply, and walked out onto the footpath.

He entered the lounge at the International Coffee Shop. There were very few customers. Most of the tables were empty. Shusheng was sitting at a round table inside, her eyes fixed on the entrance, an angry expression on her powdered face. As soon as she saw him, she leapt up, but sat down again immediately. Her eyes never left him as she waited for him to come over.

"I came as soon as I got your note," he said, smiling as he sat down opposite her. "What's it about?"

"I want a divorce," she said, her eyes wide open, her lips in a sullen pout, the words coming out in spite of her.

He could scarcely believe his ears, but there was no mistaking the expression on her face. He knew something must have happened, but he did not dare ask. He looked down without a word.

"I can't stand your mother's temper. Today, I've made up my mind. It's either she or I! You'll have to choose! I've put up with everything this week, but if it goes on, I'll be stifled to death!"

He let out his breath and looked up. It was not as bad as he had thought. Just the same old problem. He could explain to her, he could even apologize to her on behalf of his mother, and her anger would subside.

"What's it about? You'd better tell me all about it," he said, plucking up courage and smiling at her. "You know what Mother's temper's like. She's old-fashioned, she can't get things straight, and grumbles a bit, but she's basically a fine person."

"What's it about? It's about you, of course! I left work early to go home to see you, and when I found you'd gone, I felt she shouldn't have let you go. But when I said something about it, she started a quarrel! . . ." she cried, her face red with excitement.

He interrupted, without waiting for her to finish: "It's all my fault. Mother wouldn't let me go at first, but I insisted, because I was afraid the firm wouldn't be pleased if I took too much time off. And you know how mean our Mr. Zhou and Mr. Wu are. Since I depend on them for a living, I have no choice."

"But you've been coughing up blood! Surely you can ask for leave if you're ill! They haven't bought you life, have they?" she replied.

"A business firm's not a welfare organization. How can they take that into account?" he said with a wry smile. "From what Mr. Wu said this morning, they're mad at me for being ill and even hope I'll resign."

"All right, resign then, resign! Even if you don't work, I can earn enough to support you!" she cried rashly.

For a moment, his face reddened. He looked down and stammered: "But. . . ."

"Yes, I know. It's your mother again. She's not willing," she said, still fuming. "She looks down on me! She hates me!"

"No, you're wrong. She doesn't hate you. And this has got nothing to do with her," he interrupted quickly.

"She hates me, and she despises me. Just now, she said I wasn't properly married to you, that I'm not your wife, that I'm only your mistress. She accused me of not caring about my reputation, of being worse than a prostitute. How I pity her ignorance, but it's beneath me to quarrel with her. I'm not joking with you. I'm telling you straight. If you don't find somewhere else for her to live, I'm divorcing you! With the three of us living together, we'll never be happy. Deep down, she doesn't want you to get on with your wife. With a mother like that, you should never have married!" The more she went on, the more voluble and the more irate she became, until her face grew crimson, her eyes flaming with anger.

"Shusheng, you must be a little more patient," he said timidly. "Wait till the war's won, then she wants to go to Kunming — "

"Wait till the war's won!" she snorted. "You really are dreaming! The Japanese have already reached Guiyang, and you still talk about when the war's won!"

"Then what's the point of going on quarrelling? Wouldn't it be better if we each exercised a little patience?" A forced smile appeared on his face, but his heart was torn apart.

"Patience! Patience! You're always talking about patience! How long do you expect me to be patient, I ask you?" she demanded in exasperation.

"Once our circumstances improve, we'll all get on better," he answered hopefully.

"Once our circumstances improve! You've been saying that for years now, but they're getting worse day by day. I'm not afraid of living with you in hardship. After all, I myself chose to marry you. But I have to put up with your mother's sarcasm day after day. I won't stand for it." She reddened with anger once more.

"Do it for my sake. Forgive her. She's had such a hard life these last few years," he pleaded, his face deathly pale.

"It serves her right, giving birth to a precious son like you!" she said, her face changing colour. Taking 300 *yuan* from her purse, she flung it on the table and, without a word, got up and left, beside herself with rage.

He sat glued to the chair in a daze. It was a few minutes before he leapt up and ran after her.

There were people everywhere. Where was he to go to find her? He looked all about, but her figure was nowhere to be seen. "She must have gone to the bank," he thought, and headed off with long strides in that direction, his body hot and running with sweat.

He was half-way down the street before he finally caught sight of her back. "Shusheng," he called anxiously. She seemed not to hear him. Summoning up all his courage, he ran forward, coming closer and closer. He called her name a second time. She stopped, and turned to look at him. He ran up at once and seized her arm, staring at her with wide-open eyes. It was a moment before he could find his breath to gasp:

"Shusheng, everything I do is for you." His face was flushed by his illness, his forehead dripping with sweat, his mouth hung loosely open, gasping for breath, and the expression on his countenance was a plea for forgiveness.

"Why do you bother to come!" Then she looked at him with compassion and said: "Why don't you go home and lie down? You're not well yet. How can you go on working like that?"

"I should tell you the truth," he said, still as agitated as before. "I went to work because I wanted to ask for an advance."

"But I've already told you that if you need money, I can get it for you. There's no need to go to work," she interrupted.

"I wanted to buy something.... It's your birthday the day after tomorrow.... I wanted to give you a present ... at the very least, I wanted to buy you a cake...." he said disjointedly, looking at the ground in embarrassment.

She was astounded. His words were completely unexpected. Her expression gradually changed: from compassion to gratitude and love. "Is that what you were going to do?" she asked softly, now quite moved.

He nodded, adding: "But I still haven't got the money yet."

"Why didn't you say so earlier?" she said, looking at him with a tender smile.

"If I had, you wouldn't have let me," he replied, his tenseness gone, his face now beaming.

"You still remember my birthday, and I'd forgotten it myself. I really must thank you," she said with a smile of gratitude.

"Then you're not angry with me anymore," he asked, feeling thankful too.

"I've never been angry with you," she confessed in reply.

"Then you won't leave us," he went on to ask, his voice still quivering slightly.

"There was never any thought of leaving you," she replied. Seeing him look more cheerful, she urged him tenderly: "Don't worry. I have no second thoughts. But your mother — " She stopped abruptly, and changing her mind, said: "You'd better go home early and rest. Don't go back to the office."

"I'll go back for a while to tidy things up, and then go home," he said. His wife nodded. They said goodbye to each other at the intersection.

When he arrived back at the office, it was already time for work to begin. His mind was relatively refreshed, but his body was as tired as ever. He sat down and began work immediately. He felt exhausted and could scarcely breathe. He thought of going home to rest, but when the words "they're needed today" recurred to him, he did not dare make a move.

He went through the proofs page after page, unable to make out exactly what he was reading. His heart pounded furiously, while his brain seemed to congeal into a solid mass. His eyes misted over, blurring the black words on the paper. But he could still dimly perceive Mr. Zhou's evil eyes (Mr. Zhou had just come back in). "Even now, you're still pressing me. Only your wealth and power make you better than I!" he thought indignantly.

How it started, he did not know, but he began suddenly to cough, first once, then twice more. Twice in ten minutes, he went over to the spittoon in the corner to spit out the sputum. Mr. Wu gave a cough of displeasure. No, he had simply grunted. But he did not dare go a third time. The sputum worked its way up again, and he had no choice but to swallow it. In the end, he managed to hold on until he had finished the remaining dozen pages of the proof.

After three or four minutes, his throat began to itch again. He tried his best not to cough, but in his mental disarray, a cough finally exploded without his being able to stop it. A mouthful of sputum spattered all over the proof sheets. It was red, the redness of fresh blood. He seemed to smell the stench. He looked at it stupidly. All his effort at self-control, all his struggle and patience had been lost in a single moment.

"Well, I've reached the point of no return," he thought bitterly. The sudden sound of Mr. Zhou's cough brought to his mind the image of his eyes as well. In alarm, he bent quickly over and picked a scrap of paper from the waste-paper basket to wipe away the sputum. Just as he had wiped the sheet clean, he felt another cough coming. He went over to the spittoon and spat into it several times. His mouth was terribly dry. He wanted a cup of tea, but no one paid him any attention. He pressed his hands to his chest, gasping for breath.

Mr. Zhou sent the office-boy to call him to his office.

"Mr. Wang, you'd better not go on working today. Go home and rest. It seems to me that you're not at all well. . . ." Mr. Zhou said, slowly and hesitantly, smiling at him as he leaned back in his revolving chair.

He made a great effort to keep his voice calm: "It's nothing. I can still go on." But his body refused to go on. His head swam, his eyes blurred, his limbs began to give way, and all at once, he began to totter.

"Mr. Wang, you're not well. You'd better go home while there's still time; otherwise, you'll collapse. Medicine costs a lot of money, you know," Mr. Zhou continued.

"Then if I must, I must. If I don't eat your rice, does that mean I must starve?" he thought angrily, but from his lips came a gentle voice: "Then I'd better ask for half-a-day's leave." He quickly covered his mouth with his handkerchief as he began to cough.

"I'm afraid half a day won't be. . . . Well, all right. You go home first and we'll talk about it later," Mr. Zhou said, with an ironic expression on his face, then turned back to his beautiful desk and continued work.

He did not wish to say any more, for he wanted desperately to leave this terrible place at once, but he had no choice but to beg that man against his will: "I wonder if it would be possible to have a month's salary in advance, Mr. Zhou — "

Without waiting for him to give a reason, Mr. Zhou cut him short and, with an irritable wave of the hand, said: "Half a month. Get it from the accounts section."

There was nothing more he could say. Hiding his mortification, he went to the accounts section and collected 3,500 *yuan*. "What can I do with such a small sum?" he thought and with a bitter smile, stuffed the notes into the breast pocket of his inside jacket.

He handed over the proofs he'd finished and went down the stairs. Apart from some pitying eyes that followed him, no one took any notice of him. "Why bother!" was all Mr. Zhou murmured as he shook his head.

He had hoped to see old Mr. Zhong downstairs, to hear from him some words of comfort. He felt so alone. He needed some human warmth. But there was no trace downstairs of old Mr. Zhong.

The sky was still grey, as if it would rain at any moment. The familiar road to his home suddenly seemed so long, so steep and difficult to climb. All around him was a strange world in which everyone seemed so full of exuberant vitality. There seemed to be no connection between them and himself. He leaned forward and, dragging his feet, made his way slowly towards death.

18

He arrived home. He pushed open the half-closed door and went in. His mother was standing at the square table washing clothes. He saw at a glance that it was his gown that was soaking in the old enamel hand-basin.

"Xuan! You're back!" his mother cried, surprised and pleased.

"I'm terribly tired," he gasped in reply. Then smiling with an effort, he exclaimed: "Mother, you're washing my clothes again! Haven't I told you to take it to the washerwoman outside?" He turned the cane chair around and sat down.

"It costs eight hundred *yuan* a month to hire someone to do the washing. It's too expensive! In any case, I've nothing to do at home. I'm not like Shusheng. She can go out and earn a living," his mother grumbled.

"Has she come home?" he could not help asking.

His mother's expression changed at once. She said discontentedly: "She flew into a rage for no reason at all, and stalked out. She gets more impossible every day. You ought to do something about her. With a temper like that, she's absolutely impossible to please! When you're a bit better, I want to go back to Kunming to live for a while. Oh...." Changing her tone, she sighed: "It's over twenty years since I left. I wonder what's become of my second brother and his family in their old age...." Her eyes began to glisten with tears.

The sight of his mother's tears upset him so much that he himself wanted to weep. He quickly comforted her, saying: "Mother, you mustn't upset yourself. I'm your son — "

Without waiting for him to finish, she interrupted: "Yes, and she's only your mistress. She talks of leaving at every turn. It would be better if she did go. When she's gone, I'll find you someone better."

He found his mother's words offensive, but not daring to argue, he said uneasily instead: "Where would a family like ours get the money to marry? We don't even have enough to live on, so who would want to marry me?" He pulled a face.

"Not enough to live on! Who cares! These last few years, who is there with a conscience that lives well? If we hang on and endure, we'll manage to survive. Just because we're poor doesn't mean we have to give up any thought of having a wife and children!" she cried indignantly.

"But I really can't leave Shusheng. We've been married four-

teen years. We understand each other. . . ." he said wretchedly.
But before he had finished speaking, he felt a moment of dizziness and, turning the cane chair round again, laid his head
on the table. He seemed to be sleeping, and for a long time,
said nothing.

His mother went over to him, looking at him with eyes full
of maternal love and compassion. "You really do refuse to give
up until all hope is gone," she murmured, shaking her head
helplessly. "Xuan," she then called. He acknowledged her
without raising his head.

"Go and lie down on the bed," she said tenderly. "She'll
come back. What's the point of getting so upset."

"It's not because of her," he said weakly, shaking his head.
"I know she'll come back. I saw her just a while ago."

"You saw her? She went to the office to find you? She really has no shame! It doesn't embarrass her to complain to you!"
his mother shouted, taking a step back from him, her face
flushing with anger. To herself, she thought angrily: What
game is the bitch playing now?

He glanced at her miserably, and said with a frown: "She
didn't say anything. She . . . she just said that the war situation
wasn't . . . too good."

"What's it to do with her, whether the war situation is good
or bad?" his mother cried heatedly. "If she wants to run off,
let her go by herself and be done with it. Why does she have
to hurt other people!"

"Mother!" he called out, unable to bear it. It was too much!
Why did she hate Shusheng so? Why could a woman never
forgive another woman? "She's not running off. She's already
said so. She's not leaving. She'll be back soon."

"Back? She still has the nerve to face me?" his mother exclaimed in astonished indignation.

"I asked her to come back," he said timidly.

"You still want her back? You don't know what you're
doing! You don't understand anything!" She took several
paces about the room, then suddenly went over to the bed,

sat down on the edge, and covered her face with both hands as if she were crying. Then taking her hands away again, she stood up and muttered to herself: "I can endure any hardship, but I can't stand her temper! I would rather die, I would rather everyone died, than see her again!" She spoke with her teeth clenched, as if she were biting into "that woman's" flesh. And so saying, she paid him no further attention, but retired quickly to her own little room.

His brain reverberated with a confusion of noises of every kind. He gazed after her blankly as if in a dream. The noises gradually quietened. All at once, he understood, and promptly stood up and went into his mother's room.

She was lying in bed on her side, her face turned to the wall, weeping softly.

"Mother," he called. She answered, then turned round and sat up. The teardrops which had formed in the wrinkled corners of her eyes began to fall.

"What else do you have to say?" she asked huskily.

"Mother, you mustn't be upset. I won't let her come back. and that's that," he said gently, as he stood by her bed.

As she wiped the tears away with her handkerchief, a pleased smile appeared on her face. "Is that true?" she asked.

"Mother, it's true," he said, giving it no further thought.

"Then you promise me?" she asked again, still worried.

"I promise you. Don't worry," he answered, his voice full of emotion as he gazed at his mother's care-worn face. He forgot about himself, forgot his illness, forgot even his past and his future.

"As long as you're willing to promise me, as long as I never see that woman again, I'm willing to bear any poverty, I'm ready to endure any hardship!" she said in a voice filled with relief. She stood up. "In fact, how can she be coming back? It seems to me, she's sure to fly off to Lanzhou with that boss of hers," she said with an air of content, feeling that she'd won a victory. Her anger abated, and her misery dissolved away. She came out of her little room in good humour and returned to her enamel basin, soaking her roughened hands once more in the ice-cold water.

He followed her with a sad smile, and silently watched her scrubbing the clothes. All of a sudden, his head felt dizzy, his eyes saw black. Unable to bear the pain in his heart, he almost fell. He leaned quickly against the wall, closing his eyes to regain his composure.

His mother, her head down, saw nothing. She continued to talk to him, saying: "With one woman less in the house, everything will be so much simpler. . . . Xiao Xuan's sure to come back this week. The poor child! His mother's never bothered about him. . . . There are even more rumours about today. Everyone's on edge, as if a great disaster's about to take place. . . . But I don't care. These last few years, what hardship haven't I suffered! Nothing worse can ever happen. . . . Has there been any news at your office?"

"Ah," he answered, as if waking from a dream. "None." He shook his head.

"Then you won't be moving to Lanzhou. . . ." she continued.

"Sometimes we are, sometimes we aren't. I'm not too sure," he answered, and immediately afterwards, coughed several times in succession.

"How is it you're still coughing? You'd better lie down and rest," she said with concern, looking up at him. "You'd better go to bed. Your face is terrible! You've only just got better, and now you might be having a relapse," she cried in alarm.

He bit his lip firmly, trying to keep control. But at his mother's words, his spirit collapsed. Instead of answering her, he staggered over to his bed, and fell onto it, groaning with pain.

"What's wrong? What's the matter?" she asked in panic, hurrying over to the bed.

"I'm going to have a sleep, to have a sleep," he mumbled.

"Xuan, you must be careful. The situation is so bad, what will we do if you're laid up ill?" she asked tearfully in a helpless fluster.

"I'm not ill, I'm not ill," he protested feebly, and then coughed several times. His coughing was weak, but so frightening.

"You keep saying you're not ill! You refuse to rest! If you really collapse again, how will you survive?" his mother reproached him in her anxiety, tears streaming down her cheeks.

"Mother, don't worry. I won't die. Worthless people like me don't die so easily," he said sadly and with effort. But in fact, "death" was precisely the word he was thinking of. "Death" made him pessimistic. "Death" troubled his mind.

"You mustn't talk. You must have a sleep first," she said, holding back her grief and covering him with a cotton quilt.

"Actually, we might just as well be dead. There's no place for us in this world," he said, as if to himself.

"You mustn't think like that. We've never been thieves, robbers or murderers. We've never harmed anyone. Why shouldn't we live?" his mother asked, troubled and resentful.

Just then, the door of the flat suddenly burst open. Shusheng had come back.

"What, Xuan? Why are you in bed again?" she asked without thinking, her voice still just as bright, her face smiling.

"I got tired walking, so now I'm lying down for a while," he replied, pushing himself up quickly into a sitting position.

His mother, startled by Shusheng's return, went crimson, and for a moment was speechless, overcome by shame and irritation.

"Go back to sleep. There's no need to get up. I've brought you some good news: We've taken back Dushan," Shusheng cried happily as she gazed at him. "Here's the evening paper." She passed him the newspaper she was holding in her hand.

"Then we don't have to flee," he said with relief, after he had finished reading the news. He wanted to get out of bed, but as soon as he moved his legs, his body fell backwards. He gave a heavy sigh.

His mother said nothing. She simply put on a stern face and

retired to her room. "Mother," he called from his bed, but she did not even turn her head.

"Let her go, let her go," Shusheng whispered, gesturing with her hand.

Shaking his head, he said earnestly: "You should try to be polite to her for my sake. The two of you should make up."

"She's always hated me. Why should she want to make up with me!" Shusheng replied, still in a happy mood.

"But I can't do without either one of you. When you and Mother go on quarrelling like this, I'm caught in the middle. How can I bear it?" he began to complain.

"Then all that's needed is for one of us to go. Whoever wants to, let her go. Isn't that fair?" Shusheng asked, half-angry, half-joking.

"For you, of course, it's fair. But what about me?" he asked in agitation.

"There's nothing unfair about it even for you. The truth is, that by holding on to both of us, you're just making it hard on yourself," Shusheng replied bluntly.

"But I'd rather be hard on myself," he said miserably. Finally, unable to control himself, he burst into a violent fit of coughing which drowned out their conversation.

His wife went over to his bed at once, while his mother hurried from her little room. The two women stood beside his bed, asking in unison: "Why are you coughing again?"

He turned away, coughing and gasping for breath, his throat itching, his mind in a turmoil. He looked at them, his eyes brimming with tears.

"What about some tea?" his wife suggested. He nodded, but it was his mother who hurried off to fetch it, while his wife stared after her, saying nothing.

He coughed up sputum two or three times, got back his breath and accepted the cup of tea. Still breathing unevenly, he said: "I'm going to die."

"What nonsense! Don't worry. It'll be better in a couple of days," his wife said in tender encouragement.

"I'm not worried," he said, shaking his head. "But I know I won't get better. My whole mouth stinks. I've coughed blood again."

His wife glanced involuntarily at the spittoon by the bed and shuddered. But she continued to comfort him, saying: "Coughing blood's not a lot to worry about. Last time you coughed blood, it was better after a few doses of medicine, wasn't it?"

He looked at his wife, sensible of her concern, and said: "But you don't believe in Chinese medicine yourself. How can this illness of mine be cured by a few doses of medicine?"

His mother said nothing, but with head down, wiped away her tears. His wife seemed to remain just as calm, and continued gently to encourage him: "Even if it is the lungs, it can still be cured if you rest."

He gave a sad smile, his eyes still filled with tears. "Rest? Where would I get the money for a rest-cure? It's always the poor like us who catch these expensive diseases. Even if I took a rest-cure, it would still take three to five years. Where would the money come from? It's a hard enough life for you all even now. How can I just throw money away?"

"As long as you agree to stop worrying and take the cure, I can find a way. The money can always be found," his wife murmured meditatively, though sincerely. She was clearly pondering as she spoke. Her large eyes suddenly brightened, as she remembered what Mr. Chen had said to her just recently: "The business we went into together has already made quite a bit." She had a way! She added with a smile: "Just concentrate on not worrying and getting better. The money's absolutely no problem."

"But I can't add to your burden," he said, shaking his head. "I know your salary's not that big, and you've got quite heavy expenses. Even if you can find the money, how will I repay you later? I can't leave you all with a huge debt."

"Your health is more important than money. You can't neglect an illness just to save a bit of money!" she ventured. "As long as you can be cured, I can get hold of the money."

"But if, after using up so much of your money, I still die, then the money would be wasted! What on earth would the good of that?" he persisted stubbornly.

"But when all's said and done, life is more important than money! Some households provide medical treatment for their cats and their dogs. Why not you then? You're a human being!" his wife said bitterly.

"You should see things straight. These last few years, human beings' lives are the cheapest, especially people with schooling like us, who aren't yet totally devoid of conscience. And of course, I'm the most useless of the lot. Sometimes, I think I'd be better off dead." As he spoke, he began to cough again, not very hard, but it was painful.

"Don't keep talking to him. Doesn't it disturb you to see him coughing so badly?" his mother suddenly scolded, scowling as she looked up.

Livid with anger, his wife stood speechless for a long moment before replying: "I'm doing it with good intentions. All he needs is to agree to undergo treatment, and he's sure to get better." Then she added: "And whether I'm disturbed or not is none of your business!" Turning away, she went over to the window on the right.

"He's coughing so badly, yet you stop him from resting. What kind of good intention is that?" His mother stared at his wife in detestation. She had not spoken loudly, but his wife heard it just the same.

She turned from the window and said with contempt: "I could marry someone else — that would make you happy!"

"I knew long ago that you wouldn't be able to last out — a woman like you!" his mother said scathingly. You've shown your true colours at last, she thought.

"A woman like me is no worse than you," his wife continued, still contemptuous.

"Huh! You dare to compare yourself with me! You're just

my son's whore! I came here in a wedding sedan," his mother sniffed, pleased with herself, for she felt that by using these terrible words, she had wounded her rival.

His wife paled, and almost lost control of herself. She was considering what weapon to use to counter-attack, when he intervened, as husband and son, to have his say.

Why on earth did they never stop quarrelling? Why in this simple household, in these pure relationships could there never be harmony or cooperation? Why must these two women, whom he loved and who loved him, be perpetually fighting like sworn enemies?. . . These long unsolved problems came back to torment him. Their quarrelling voices reverberated in his brain. No, their shrill voices hammered away in his head. His head began to hurt, to swell. He became more and more miserable. Where had the words of love and concern fled to? Now, two pairs of eyes, filled with hatred and contempt, glared at each other, oblivious of his existence. How long would it be before he could find rest?

"Mother, Shusheng, please don't go on. We're one family. If each of you would only give way a bit, there'd be no problem," he implored wretchedly, while to himself he thought: "Have pity on me. Give me some peace!"

"It was your mother who started it. You saw for yourself. I've done nothing today to offend her. What right has she to insult me by calling me your whore? Let her tell me!" His wife's face was crimson with fury, for the blow had struck home, and she wanted amends to be made.

"You are his whore. Who doesn't know! I ask you: When did you marry him? Who was the marriage broker?"

In despair, he covered his head with the cotton quilt.

"It has nothing to do with you. That's our own affair," his wife answered haughtily.

"If you're my daughter-in-law, I have a right to be concerned! It has everything to do with me!" his mother shouted harshly.

"Let me tell you something: It's thirty-three years since the

Empire was overthrown. We're not living in the reign of the Guangxu or even the Xuantong Emperor! It's 1944 today," his wife sneered. "I've never had my feet bound — I can find my own husband, without going through any marriage broker."

"Are you making fun of me because my feet were bound? What if they were? It doesn't alter the fact that I'm still Xuan's mother, I'm still older than you are. I can't stand the sight of women like you. Why don't you just get the hell out of here?" his mother cried, clenching her teeth.

He could not stand it. He felt his head about to explode, his heart rent asunder. The shout "get the hell out of here" was like a violent punch delivered to his chest by a tightly clenched fist. He cried out in pain, threw aside the quilt, and beating his forehead with both fists, cried out over and over again: "I'm better off dead!"

"What is it? What's the matter?" his wife cried in fright, running to his bedside and bending over him.

"Xuan, what's wrong?" his mother asked in terror.

"Stop quarrelling. . . ." he began, sobbing. But it was all he could say before, covering his face with his hands, he began to whimper softly.

"Don't be upset . . . we won't . . . quarrel anymore," his mother said after a while, her eyes filled with grief.

"But you will, you will. . . ." he sobbed in affliction.

His wife looked at him for a moment in silence, biting her lower lip in thought. Then she said compassionately: "Truly, Xuan, we won't quarrel again."

He took his hands from his face, looking tearfully first at his mother, then at his wife. "I'm afraid I haven't long to live," he said. "At least, let me live a few days in peace."

"Xuan, you won't die. Stop worrying and think of getting better," his mother said.

"Just try not to worry," his wife said.

"As long as you two don't quarrel, I might get better faster," he said, solaced, trying to smile through his tears.

But when he had fallen sound asleep and his mother had

gone to fetch the doctor, his wife stood alone at the window on the right, looking out onto the street scene. This 34-year-old woman suddenly felt uneasy, as restless thoughts began to stir in her mind. A doubt echoed in her brain:

"What does a life like this hold for me after all? What satisfaction have I got from it?"

She wanted a clear and definite answer. But her thoughts seemed entangled in a thorny thicket, struggling for a very long time before finding a way out.

"None at all! I've had no satisfaction whatsoever, whether spiritually or materially.

"Then what have I gained in return for sacrificing my ideals?

"And later? Is there going to be any hope later?" she asked herself.

She shook her head involuntarily. Her brain was filled with all the hardships and discords of the last few years. In her ears still faintly echoed his tired, grief-stricken voice, and the scorn and insults of his mother's hatred. In this way, her thoughts gradually ran into a very narrow lane in which she heard a voice cry: "Get the hell out of here!" Just this single phrase.

She coughed slightly. She turned to glance at the bed. His face was a dirty, pale yellow, his cheeks deep-sunken, his breathing loud and urgent. She could see no trace of strength or vitality in his body. "A man about to die," she thought in terror, then quickly turned her eyes once more to the scene outside the window.

"Why should I still look after him? Why should I continue to vie with that woman to have him? 'Get the hell out of here!' Fine! Take him! I don't want him anymore! Mr. Chen was right. I should have made up my mind earlier.... There's still time. It's not yet too late!" she thought. Her heart began to beat wildly and the blood rushed to her face.

"What shall I do?... 'Get the hell out of here!' You're right! I'll go my own way! You can't stop me! Why do I still hesitate? I mustn't be so weak. I mustn't hesitate any longer. I must harden my heart, for my own sake, for the sake of my happiness.

"Can I still achieve happiness? Why not? Besides, I need happiness, I ought to have happiness. . . ."

All at once, the face of a child flashed before her eyes, a child's face with an adult's expression. "Xiao Xuan!" she almost cried out.

"For the sake of Xiao Xuan — " she thought.

"He can do very well even without me. He doesn't seem to have much feeling for me, but I can still go on helping him afterwards. He can't stop me from going my own way. Not even Xuan can."

She turned once more to look at the man on the bed, sleeping fitfully as before. He could not know what she was thinking, poor man!

"Must I really leave him? — or must I sacrifice my own happiness to keep him company? — If he refuses to undergo treatment, he's finished. Can I save him? Can I make his mother not hate me? Can I live together in harmony with his mother?"

She thought for a while, then said softly under her breath: "Impossible." It's no use, she thought. I must save myself. . . .

The deafening roar of a Chinese fighter plane flying low overhead interrupted her thoughts.

She came to a conclusion: find Mr. Chen. He could help her escape this terrible place.

She lifted her head in excitement, her whole body growing hot, her heart beating rapidly. But she was full of courage. She hesitated no longer. Taking her purse from the drawer, she left the flat. She had already reached the corridor outside when she suddenly remembered that, with his mother out, he would be in bed at home alone. Worried, she pushed open the door once more, going back into the flat to see whether he was sound asleep or not.

Just as she reached his bed, he suddenly sobbed in his sleep, calling out her name. Startled, she asked at once: "What is it? What's the matter?" and bent over him.

He turned from the wall, putting out a hand to grasp hers. She gave him her right hand, which he seized and held tightly. He moaned softly. After three or four minutes, he opened his eyes. They found her face, and remained there motionless. "You're here," he said, surprised and pleased, his voice low and weak. "You haven't gone?"

"Gone where?" she asked.

"To Lanzhou. I dreamt you'd left me to go to Lanzhou," he answered. "Left me by myself in a hospital. It was so lonely, so terrifying."

She shuddered, unable to say a word.

"Luckily, it was a dream," he said, sighing weakly. "You won't abandon me and leave me, will you?" His voice was shaking badly. He pleaded not only with his voice, but with his eyes. "In fact, our days together are numbered. I don't think I'm going to recover."

"I won't leave you. Don't worry," she said with emotion, her heart in despair. The decision she had made just a moment before had collapsed in an instant.

"I know that you won't go," he said gratefully. "Mother keeps saying that you'll leave. Please forgive her. Old people always behave a bit strangely."

The word "Mother" struck her like a box on the ears. She was stunned. The flesh on her cheeks quivered slightly, as if she were resisting a force that was compelling her to take back her promise.

"Thank you, oh, thank you," he cried excitedly. "I won't be dragging you down for long. And there's Xiao Xuan. It embarrasses me to mention him. I've never done my duty to him as a father."

"Don't talk anymore." She withdrew her hand, cutting him short rather brusquely. He seemed to be saying these things deliberately to torture her, and she could not bear it any longer. She wanted to find a quiet place where she could weep her heart out for the many wrongs she had suffered. In the end, she remained seated on the edge of the bed.

For a long time, he said nothing. Then sighing suddenly, he called to her tenderly: "Shusheng." She turned to look at him. "Actually, it would be better if you left. I've thought very carefully about what a hard life you have in our family. I'm so sorry. Mother can't change her temperament . . . she's narrow-minded . . . in the future . . . I don't dare think . . . why should I hinder you . . . I've no way out . . . with my health . . . you can still get away. . . ." The hoarse words stuck in his throat.

She stood up, sighed briefly, and said: You'd better sleep for a while. What's the use of continuing to think of these things now? You must concentrate on getting better."

He was suddenly seized by another fit of coughing. He coughed and he coughed. In his efforts to dislodge the sputum which seemed to have stuck in his throat, his face turned bright red. But he failed to cough it up.

She rubbed his back gently, and brought him a cup of boiled water, but after a couple of mouthfuls, he began coughing again. This time, the sputum came up. It was streaked with blood, but she did not notice (in fact, he gave her no chance to see it clearly).

"The doctor will be here soon." She said just what came into her head to console him.

"Actually, what's the use of seeing a doctor again? It's trouble for nothing, and a waste of money," he signed. "I agree to it only because of Mother."

"At a time like this, you still think only of others. You're too good to be true," she said solicitously, but her concern was mingled with a little resentment. "You shouldn't refuse to go into hospital, and refuse to use my money for treatment just because Mother's against it. It's your health that's at stake!" She sighed briefly. "The world wasn't created for the likes of you. You're not only harming yourself, but harming others. . . ."

The sound of footsteps interrupted her. She knew that it must be his mother back with the doctor. She went and sat on a stool by the square table.

The door was pushed open, and his mother came in with the doctor, Zhang Boqing. The doctor greeted them both. It was the same kind, worldly-wise face, the same almost superfluous diagnosis.

"He's just dragging out his suffering. How can *he* cure his illness?" she thought, frowning slightly.

"It's nothing serious, not serious at all. Just take another couple of doses of medicine and it'll be all right," the doctor said confidently.

"I think it's my lungs," he said timidly.

"No, not at all," the doctor replied, shaking his head. "It can't possibly be the lungs. It's inflammation of the liver. If you take two doses of medicine, and don't move about, I guarantee you'll be better." The old doctor smiled affably at him.

"Thank you," his mother kept repeating over and over as she saw the doctor out, but his wife said nothing.

"Mother, there's no point in going for the medicine," he suddenly said.

On hearing him say this, his mother, who'd been reading the prescription in her hand, asked in surprise: "Why not?"

"I don't think it'll make any difference whether I take it or not. This illness of mine can't be cured by drugs," he said decisively.

"There's no illness that drugs can't cure," his mother said, refusing to agree, and folding the prescription. "I'm going to get the medicine." She took her purse, and was about to leave the flat, when he asked:

"You don't have enough money on you, do you?"

"I've got some here," his wife responded at once.

"I've got some," his mother said, gazing at him, refusing to look at his wife, as if she had not heard her speak. His wife reddened and raised her eyebrows, but said not a word. She simply went over to the window.

"Mother, you'd better take this, one thousand *yuan*. I got an advance on my salary today," he said, putting his hand into his pocket to take out the money. "You've taken the money from the food kitty, and you'll have to make it up. You spent all the money calling the doctor just now."

"Don't worry. I've got money. I got some from elsewhere," his mother said.

"Where did you get it? . . . I see. You must have sold your gold ring!" he cried.

"I'm an old woman. I don't need a ring, so it's no use keeping it," his mother explained.

"But it was a keepsake from Dad. You can't get rid of it because of me," he said miserably.

"It won't be long before I see your father again, so it doesn't matter whether I have it or not," his mother answered, pretending to smile.

"But that's the only thing of value you have, and now you've sold even that. All because I'm such a good-for-nothing," he continued remorsefully.

"Since it's done already, what's the use of talking about it? You just get yourself well. As long as you're in good health, I'll be happy," his mother said and, without waiting for him to reply, hurried out.

His wife continued to stand by the window, sunk deep in her own thoughts. In the room, only the sound of the rats gnawing at the timber could be heard.

He thought things over and over, for his brain refused to rest. Unable to sleep, he said with emotion: "Mother has such a hard life. For my sake, she's sold the last precious thing she has." He was speaking to his wife. But she stood quietly by the window without even turning her head.

19

Towards evening the next day, a messenger from Mr. Chen brought a letter with the following words:

> ". . . there have been problems with my air ticket. There will be a delay of one week, but I can definitely go next Wednesday. . . . The matter of your job has already been settled.
>
> "The transfer documents should be ready this week . . . I'll see you tomorrow morning at eight in the Guansheng Garden Restaurant. . . ."

When Shusheng looked up from reading the letter, she met by chance his mother's eyes, filled with hatred and mockery. "I know everything. I know what devilish game you're playing!" they seemed to say.

"You can't stop me!" she thought to herself, giving a slight cough. At the time, she and his mother were eating dinner together, and his mother had put down her bowl first.

He lay in bed coughing all the time, with a dry cough to which they had gradually grown accustomed. Sometimes he would rub his chest gently with his hands. There must be something wrong inside him to cause him such a pain and make breathing so difficult, and rubbing it in this way gave him a little relief. The never-ending itching in his throat kept him coughing, but no sputum would come up. Sometimes it took him all his strength to cough, but the effort would make his chest ache. He endured the pain, doing his utmost not to groan aloud in case it could be heard by the others. He did everything he could to stop them from finding out how things really stood. At the same time, he kept a careful eye on all their actions and listened to all their conversations.

"A letter from the bank. Is it anything important?" he asked weakly. In his concern, he had stopped coughing for a moment.

His wife did not hear. His mother turned to look at him.

She had obviously not heard him clearly either, for she asked: "Xuan, do you want something?"

"Nothing," he replied, shaking his head. But after two or three minutes, he spoke again: "I was asking Shusheng if there was anything important in the letter." This time his wife heard, for he had spoken more loudly.

"It's from someone at the office. It's nothing important," she answered off-handedly. His mother turned quickly to glance at her, her expression seeming to say: "You're lying to him. I know."

"I heard him say it was from Mr. Chen," he said, after some thought.

"Yes," she answered casually.

"Isn't he flying to Lanzhou? Why hasn't he gone yet?" he then asked, after more thought.

"At first he said he was flying tomorrow. But now he says there's trouble with the plane ticket, and he has to delay a week," she said, still in the same cool, indifferent tone.

After a few minutes, she stood up and cleared the dishes from the table, while his mother went outside to fetch a kettle of hot water. Suddenly, he asked:

"I remember you said that the bank was thinking of transferring you to Lanzhou. Why haven't they said anything these last few days?"

His wife turned and looked at him in surprise. Trying to keep her voice steady, she replied:

"That was just talk. It's not likely to eventuate."

His mother came back in with the kettle just at that moment, and caught Shusheng's answer. She grunted, looking at her as if to say: "Liar!"

Shusheng blushed slightly. Her lips parted for a moment, but she said nothing. She turned her eyes away.

"If by chance the bank really does transfer you, will you go?" he pursued. She wondered what was in his mind.

"Not definitely," she replied briefly, for his interrogation was beginning to get on her nerves.

"If they transfer you and you don't go, they mightn't like it." He did not know what she was feeling, and simply wanted to talk for the sake of talking.

"If they don't like it, I'll resign," she answered crisply, but in fact, she had never thought about this problem.

"Resign! How can you! With me ill in bed and Xiao Xuan at school, what would we live on?" he said, as if to himself.

"Then we'll sell something or borrow. We won't starve to death, whatever happens." She said this purposely for his mother's ears, for she felt she had had too much of that woman's temper and was looking for a chance to have a go at her.

He gave a wry smile. "Look, do we have anything of value left? In the last two years, we've consumed everything. And whom would we borrow from? You're the only one who still has a few rich friends. . . ."

"Don't go on, don't talk about it," she interrupted irritably. "You're too ill to talk so much. You'd better have a good sleep." She turned away, refusing to look at him.

"I can't sleep. The moment I close my eyes, it's like watching a film. My brain simply won't rest," he said complainingly.

"You think too much. You shouldn't. You should have a good sleep instead," she said gently to console him, looking at him with sympathy.

"How can I not think? To catch a disease like this when I'm only thirty-four, and not know whether I'll get better or not!" he exclaimed miserably.

"Xuan, you mustn't worry. Of course you'll get better. Zhang Boqing is sure that with this medicine, you'll be better in a fortnight," his mother interrupted.

"I think you should go to the hospital for a checkup. It would be best to have an X-ray. It's more reliable that way. I don't. . . ." His wife mumbled for a while before finally speaking out. But before she had finished, he interrupted.

"What if they discover it's third-stage consumption? What do we do then?" he asked.

"Then we cure it by the methods used for treating consumption," his wife replied without the slightest hesitation.

"It's a very expensive illness. We'd need a stack of money just for the convalescence, let alone the treatment," he said, smiling bitterly.

"Does that mean that poor people must just die?" she asked indignantly, looking at him with concern. "Don't worry. I'll think of something. The medical expenses aren't a problem."

"But I can't waste all your money for nothing!" he persisted, shaking his head. Actually, her words were already beginning to undermine his determination. He still wanted to talk, but something seemed to be pressing on his chest. Breathing became so difficult, that he felt as if he would suffocate. He began to breathe in loud, rasping gasps.

"Let him rest for a while, if you please," his mother cried, glaring at his wife. At the same time, she went up to his bed, looked at him with her eyes full of pity and tenderness, and said gently: "Don't talk so much. It's bad for you mentally, and may even make you worse. Close your eyes and try to sleep."

He answered with a "yes", sighed softly, and did indeed close his eyes.

His wife had been rebuked. She went a bright red, and in her annoyance she wanted to retaliate immediately. But then she thought: What's the use of this everlasting quarrelling? No matter how often we repeat the same meaningless words, no matter how often we look at each other with hatred in our eyes, it will never lead to anything. There will be no reconciliation and no rupture. He had no means of pulling his mother and her together, and no courage to choose between the two of them. There would always be the same pointless compromises. There seemed to be nothing else he could do. Now that he was ill in bed, what more could he give her?

Comfort? Support? . . . He was over there sighing. Now it was her turn to sigh. She had sacrificed her youth for this dark, cold room, exchanged it for hostility and perfunctoriness. She felt her patience fast approaching its limit.

"You know how to toady up to him. All right, I'll let you. He's not the only pebble on the beach," she railed inwardly. She scoffed audibly, then slowly went over to the window on the right to look through the glass at the street below.

The night was bitterly cold. The chill air brushed against her face. Down below was darkness, broken only by a few scattered lamps. This building she lived in was on a boundary, beyond which another district began, and this evening, it was their turn for a power cut. She shuddered, and then shrugged her shoulders. "Why are there always power cuts?" she murmured irritably to herself. No one paid any attention. In this room, no one considered her important! Her loneliness terrified her. She turned around to face the electric light, which stared back at her like the eye of a sick man. It could not add one drop of warmth to her heart. Her eyes strayed to the bed. He was breathing heavily, with his eyes closed and his mouth open. He seemed to get thinner by the hour. "He's really to be pitied," she thought. His mother had gone out. She went to the sick-bed and pulled the cotton quilt up slightly. He opened his eyes at once and looked at her, staring at her fixedly as if he hadn't recognized her. Her heart gave a leap. But then she explained gently: "Your quilt had nearly slipped to the ground. I was pulling it up for you."

"Had it?" he said, and then asked: "Has Mother gone to bed? Aren't you going to rest?"

"It's still early," she replied. "You go back to sleep."

"I just said I couldn't sleep, and then I fell asleep!" he said with a smile. "I've something to talk to you about. Tomorrow's your birthday. . . ."

"I'd forgotten about it myself. What do you want to bring that up for!" she interrupted gently.

"Here's sixteen hundred *yuan*. Please, I want you to order a four-pound cake for tomorrow. I don't dare trouble Mother, so I have to ask you to go and order it yourself. . . ." He held out towards her a trembling hand in which was a roll of banknotes.

"How can I be in a mood to celebrate my birthday? Let's forget about it," she said, deeply touched, almost bursting into tears.

"Go and order it . . . you must order it for me . . . I don't dare go out myself . . . I have to trouble you . . . take the money . . ." he said disjointedly.

There was a knock at the door. "Surely he can't be sending another messenger," she thought, meaning Mr. Chen. She called out casually: "Come in!"

To her surprise, a bald-headed old man entered. It was old Mr. Zhong from his firm. "All right, I'm really grateful to you," she whispered, and took the money.

"Wang, old man, how are you? Have you gone to bed already?" Mr. Zhong called as soon as he walked in. To her, he said: "How are you, Mrs. Wang?"

"Please sit down, Mr. Zhong," she said quickly in greeting.

"Hello, Zhong Lao! What's brought you here? I'm not very ill. I'll be better soon. I'm sorry you've had to come so far. This morning, just after I got up, I was about to leave for work when I suddenly felt dizzy, so I went to bed and have been sleeping till now," he said apologetically, sitting up with difficulty.

"Go on sleeping. Don't get up. I'll just sit for a while and then leave," Mr. Zhong said, coming up to the bed and gesturing for him to lie down again.

"It doesn't matter. I'll just sit up in bed. I'm not sleepy. You see, I haven't even undressed," he said, still sitting up in bed.

"Be careful you don't catch cold. You'd better lie down. We can talk just as well if you lie down," Mr. Zhong said amiably.

"Mr. Zhong, please sit down and have some tea," she said, as she poured out a cup of tea and placed it on the table.

"Thank you, Mrs. Wang," Mr. Zhong said, smiling politely as he sat down on a stool.

"I've just seen in the evening paper that Liuzhai's been re-taken. That's a good piece of news," Mr. Zhong said, lifting his cup and taking a sip.

"Yes," he said, coughing four or five times. "Then the firm won't be moving," he continued, feeling rather relieved.

"Of course not. Moving to Lanzhou was just a lot of talk anyway, and now there's no need to flee," Mr. Zhong said.

"Then can you ask for a day's leave for me tomorrow? I want to go back to work after another day's rest. I don't want too much of my salary docked," he said.

"There's no need for you to go back to work the day after tomorrow. You can stay home and rest a few days. The proof-reading work at the office isn't good for your health, and your health is what's most important," Mr. Zhong said, speaking slowly and hesitantly.

"But you know what Mr. Zhou and Mr. Wu are like. Since we depend on them for our living, it's best to put up with things." He frowned as he spoke. Mr. Zhong was just about to say something, when he asked: "Did they say anything about me after I left yesterday?"

"I'm working downstairs. How would I know?" Mr. Zhong replied. "Only — " Taking a roll of banknotes from the breast pocket of his inside jacket, he got up and went over to the bed, putting the money beside the sick man's pillow "Here's ten thousand five hundred *yuan*. It's your salary for one and a half months. Mr. Zhou asked me to bring it to you."

"One and a half month's salary? He asked you to bring it Why?" he asked in astonishment. After a pause, he suddenly shouted: "He's sacking me, isn't he?"

"He said . . . he said," old Mr. Zhong stammered going red in the face, and unable to continue.

"What have I done wrong? He can't dismiss me for no reason at all," he cried with passion. He felt blood rushing up inside him, his head burning, and a fit of pain in the left side of his chest. He began gasping. "Every day, I've work-ed in that firm, I've been obedient and well-behaved, I've never dared utter a word, I've borne the unbearable, I've put up with every kind of insult, I simply —"

"Wang, old man, you mustn't be angry. He's not sacking you. He says . . . that you're not well . . . that it's def-initely TB. He wants me to urge you to take six months' rest first," Mr. Zhong said after screwing up his courage. "Of course, that's just his subjective opinion. It doesn't look like consumption to me. You're just a little under-nourished, and you're usually overtired. You'll be all right after a month's rest. But that's not what Mr. Zhou thinks. He wants you to rest longer. He said to give you two months' salary, and since you've already drawn half a month's in advance, there's only the pay for a month and a half here. It's just as well. You can have a really good rest for a few days. When you're bet-ter, you can find some other work to do, and you'll be much happier."

He looked down at the ground and said no more.

"It's outrageous!" Shusheng interrupted indignantly. "To work him like a donkey for two years and then kick him out as soon as he's ill. Xuan, Mr. Zhong's right. As soon as you're better, you can find a job that's more agreeable."

"Jobs aren't that easy to find now," he said, looking up.

"I can get people to help. I don't believe that you can't even find something like what you've got now," his wife said. He said no more.

"You're right, Mrs. Wang. In fact, because our firm is neither government nor private, it's not well run. If Mr. Wang loses the job there, it's no great loss," Mr. Zhong put in.

"He's too good-natured. It's easy for others to trample all over him. If you hadn't kept an eye on him these last two years, Mr. Zhong, I'm afraid he'd have come a cropper long ago," his wife said.

"You're being much too kind, Mrs. Wang. How can you say I've kept an eye on him when I haven't helped him even once? I really don't deserve any thanks," Mr. Zhong said, smiling apologetically. "But I get on well with Mr. Wang, and have a great respect for him as a person. The firm knows that he and I are good friends. That's why Mr. Zhou sent me on this commission," Mr. Zhong went on to explain.

"I know, we know what you mean, Mr. Zhong. Since that's how Mr. Zhou feels, Wenxuan had better do as expected and resign," she said with a smile. (It was easy to see that her smile was forced.) She turned to her husband quickly and asked: "Don't you agree, Xuan?"

"Yes, yes," he muttered vaguely in answer.

"You're absolutely right, Mrs. Wang," Mr. Zhong said in approval. "Since there's no future in the firm, it's no use hanging on. You should do your best to get better, Wang, old man. Once your health's better, it won't be so difficult to find another job. . . ." After a few more innocuous remarks, he suddenly got up and said politely: "I won't disturb you any longer. I'll come again another day. Wang, old man, look after yourself. At a time like this, your health is your most valuable asset."

"Zhong Lao, stay for a while. We're not doing anything," he said, trying to detain him. His wife felt that he had spoken for her as well. A guest added to the room some variety, some warmth and some life.

"I won't stay. I'll come and we'll have a proper chat another day," Mr. Zhong said, smiling as he took his leave. "I've still some things to do," he added in explanation.

"Then I won't see you off. Take care," Wenxuan said, disappointed.

"There's no need to see me off. I'll come often in future," Mr. Zhong said politely, as he moved towards the door.

"I'll see Mr. Zhong off," she said.

"Please don't bother, Mrs. Wang. Please don't come out," Mr. Zhong said, already standing in the doorway of the flat.

"But it's terribly dark outside. I'll see you out, Mr. Zhong," she said. She saw their guest to the stairwell, lighting the way with a torch, and then stood at the top, shining the torch for him as he went down the stairs, calling all the time: "Take care, take care!"

"I can see, Mrs. Wang. Please go back inside," old Mr. Zhong called politely from below. She turned around listlessly, intending to go back into the room. Suddenly, she heard the voice of Mr. Zhong talking to someone else.

"She's back," she thought, meaning his mother of course. She felt a surge of displeasure rise up in her and hurried quickly inside.

"Has he gone?" he asked. It was a question that needed no asking and no reply. He had clearly asked it simply to dispel his loneliness. He was already lying down again.

"He's gone," she replied mechanically. The room had lost all its warmth. Only the eternal, sickly, yellow light of the electric lamp and the old dilapidated pieces of furniture remained. And her husband with his everlasting expression that was neither dead nor alive. She had had enough! She at least was alive! She longed to see someone equally alive.

"Can you put this money away for me?" he asked with an ironic smile. "It's money I've sold my life for."

She assented. The last sentence had been spoken so softly, that she did not hear it. She seemed to want to go over to his bed, but suddenly she drew back and said gently: "Give it to your mother in case she's not pleased."

He gave a sigh, but said nothing. His mother's footsteps could already be heard in the corridor, and a moment later, the old woman entered.

"Mother, where have you been?" he asked affectionately, his voice trembling with loneliness in this dark, chilly room.

"I went to Zhang Boqing's for a while. I was worried, so

I asked him to tell me the truth about your illness. He says it's not serious, that it definitely isn't consumption, and that after a few doses of medicine, it'll be better," his mother said gently. But her voice was tinged with anxiety.

"No, it's not serious. I know myself that it's not serious," he replied, touched by her concern. "What did you have to go there again for? It must be very cold outside, and you're tired enough for one day. You're simply our family amah. I'm so sorry." And tears streamed from his eyes.

"You just see to getting better, instead of worrying over such trifles. I've got used to being an amah these last few years. My life hasn't been as lucky as hers," his mother answered as she glanced unconsciously at Shusheng, taking a malicious pleasure in these last words.

At that moment, Shusheng was standing at the table listening to the conversation between mother and son. It was like an unexpected slap in the face, and she cried out mentally. She turned to look at the mother, but she had already reached the sick man's bed, and was still talking: "But Zhang Boqing says that the winter fog is no good for your health, and advises us to move elsewhere."

"Move elsewhere? . . . Where would we move to? And where would we find the money to move?" he replied.

Always these same words that grated on the ear. And so, drop by drop, her life was draining quietly away. Shusheng's endurance had reached its limit. She had committed no crime; why should she be punished? Was not this just a prison in which her life would wither away? She should fly away, she must fly away, while she still had wings. Why should she not leave? She had nothing in common with them. She could not join them in sacrificing themselves. She must save herself.

As his mother continued to talk, her words struck her in the heart like arrows. "Shoot! I'm not afraid! I can't be bothered fighting with you," she thought proudly, and her heart blazed with new hope.

20

On Saturday afternoon, Shusheng came home with her notice of transfer. As she went up the stairs, her heart was filled with contradictory feelings of excitement and pain. She pushed open the door of the flat and found Xiao Xuan at the table reading, while his grandmother sat beside him on a stool. Her husband was still lying ill in bed. They were talking about something, but the moment Xiao Xuan saw his mother, he stood up at once and greeted her. "Mother," he said, a reluctant smile flitting across his pale face.

"Did you get my letter?" she asked, after answering his greeting.

"Yes. The workload at school is too heavy, and a lot of the boys can't keep up," Xiao Xuan replied, his face unsmiling. It was his pretext for not coming home for so long.

She mumbled something in reply, examining her son closely. Anaemic, old for his age, cool-headed, he appeared never to have known youth. He was only a child of thirteen, yet already he was so old and feeble! Her brows came together in a frown as she turned her eyes away to avoid him. She went over to the bed and asked the invalid: "You're better today, aren't you?"

"A little better," he replied with a nod.

The question and answer had become a mere routine. Each day she asked the same question, and each day he answered in the same way, although there was no sign of any improvement whatsoever.

She heard him cough, saw him take the tooth-mug (it now served as a temporary spittoon) from beside his pillow, spit into it and slowly put it down. His cheeks were even more sunken and his eyes stared at her in a kind of terror.

"Have you taken your medicine?" she asked in compassion.

He nodded, looking utterly miserable.

"I still think you should go to the hospital for a checkup," she said. She felt she had to bring up the subject again, even though they had discussed it countless times before.

"Let's see in another few days," he said, shaking his head wearily.

"Why not now? Please! Don't let it drag on," she beseeched him, gazing at him earnestly. A few teardrops suddenly trickled from her eyes, and she turned her face slowly away.

"I'm still all right at the moment. There's nothing much wrong apart from the coughing," he said slowly and hesitantly.

"But the coughing is what's wrong! And besides, you have a temperature every day," she said, turning towards him again. "I'm worried that . . ." She choked back her last words.

"Do you think it's my lungs?" he asked.

She did not dare answer. She seemed embarrassed, regretting having said more than she ought.

"Actually, there's no need for a checkup," he said. "It's my lungs, I know that too. But what's the good of knowing? To go for a checkup would be like a criminal going to hear his own death sentence." And having spoken his thought aloud, he felt upset, and did not want to go on talking.

She looked at him without a word. He knows everything, she thought, even that brutal truth. What was the use of urging him? He lay on the bed simply to get through the days. Whether they passed quickly or slowly, he was after all on the road towards death. What other way did she have of saving him?. . . None. He would not listen to her, would not make a serious effort to get better. She could only wait for a miracle. Perhaps . . . perhaps she should save herself first. Contradictory thoughts surfaced in her mind. That was why she wept secretly, and at the same time nursed a secret hope.

"That's not true at all. TB can be cured. You don't have to worry about the expense. I've told you. I'm willing to work something out for you," she urged with all her energy one last time, holding back her tears.

"Undergoing treatment isn't just a question of money. You

also have to be in a good frame of mind. You know that. With
the kind of life we lead, how can I ever be in the right frame
of mind?" he then said.

"Xuan, you're talking too much. Go to sleep for a while.
Besides, it's almost time for your medicine," his mother interrupted impatiently.

His wife stared at her in silence. She went and sat down
at the table, but once there, she did not know what to do, for
no one paid her any attention. Not even Xiao Xuan came over
to speak to her. She felt weary, but there seemed to be no
place for her eyes to rest.

She sat there for a while, numb with boredom. Surely she
did not have to sit there and wait for his mother to bring the
meal she was cooking, she thought. Even when they began
eating, the atmosphere would be cold and lifeless, and after the
meal, there would be even less warmth. Only the everlasting
dim yellow light of the lamp (or darkness, if there was a power
cut, which was quite often), the tedious, lifeless, idle gossip,
the sickly face. She could not let the last days of her youth
waste away like this for nothing. She could not save others,
but at least she could save herself. Otherwise, she would die
here, die in this room.

Suddenly, she stood up. Once more, she had made up her
mind. It was no use hesitating any longer. The notice of
transfer was still in her handbag. Why should she give up
this opportunity?

She went up to Xiao Xuan. "Xiao Xuan, come with me for
a walk," she suggested.

Xiao Xuan looked up at her. "Without waiting for dinner?"
he asked, without enthusiasm. He spoke just like a grownup,
exactly like his father in fact.

"We can eat out," she answered briefly.

"Without inviting grandmother then?" Xiao Xuan asked,
raising his voice a little.

"We might as well stay, I suppose." She suddenly changed

her mind, exasperated. For some reason, the child's words had irritated her.

Xiao Xuan looked at her in surprise and asked: "Mother, aren't you going even by yourself?"

"No," she said, shaking her head, thinking to herself what a meddlesome child he was.

Xiao Xuan looked up, and turned back to his book, without saying anything more.

"He doesn't seem to be my son," she thought. She remained standing behind him, examining him carefully over and over again. Xiao Xuan noticed nothing. He was reading a play. The sun's rays had gradually weakened, but the electric light they had just turned on was not very bright, and so his head was buried deep in his book. "He'll ruin his eyes," she thought. Her compassion for him made her say: "Xiao Xuan, you should rest for a while. You mustn't work so hard."

Xiao Xuan looked up again in surprise. "All right," he answered. He kept blinking his eyes as if there were something wrong with them. He closed his book, stretched himself, and stood up.

"Why, he never laughs, and he moves so lethargically. He's not a child at all. He's just like his father," she thought.

Xiao Xuan went quietly over to the bed to see his father. "He doesn't show me the slightest affection, as if I were his stepmother," she thought miserably, and sat down in the chair that her son had just vacated.

Xuan's mother sat on the edge of the bed, talking to him, while Xiao Xuan stood by the bed quietly listening. They seemed to be talking intimately about something.

"She wouldn't let me talk to him. Why doesn't *she* let him rest then? The selfish old bag," she thought indignantly. Unconscious of her action, she stretched her hand out and picked up the book Xiao Xuan had just been reading. "She hates me! I'm her enemy! It must be because of her instructions that Xiao Xuan is so cold towards me. Xuan also plays up to her. No, he really does love her more." Her thoughts

ran on, making her more and more irritable. She could not
bear this isolation, this coldness. She had to find something
to distract her. Her eyes fell upon the book in her hand. She
saw first the two characters printed in red, *The Plain*. It was
a play by Cao Yu. She had seen it performed, but had heard
that it had since been banned, why, she did not know. It was
this very play. What a coincidence! The play was about a
mother who hated her own daughter-in-law, and a husband
caught perennially between the two, suffering between two
kinds of love. And how did it end? It was too tragic! *She*
could not bring about such an ending, for *she* was not that
kind of woman! She was superfluous here. She had a chance
to leave. The notice of transfer was still in her handbag. Why
should she let this opportunity slip by? No, it was already decided. The bank would not send anyone else unless she re-
signed. But of course she could not resign, for if she left the
bank, it would be a while before she could find another job.
Besides, she had borrowed part of her salary in advance, and
for the last two months, she had been in partnership with Mr.
Chen in a little bit of speculation.

"Fly! Fly!" a soft, encouraging voice echoed repeatedly in
her ears. The transfer notice gradually expanded before her
eyes. Lanzhou! The words took the form of a plane flying
through her mind. She gradually cheered up. Her courage
returned once more, so that she could look at his mother with
contempt, thinking to herself: "Even if you all unite against
me, I'm not afraid. I have a way out! I will fly!"

2 1

He had a terrifying nightmare: She had thrown him aside
and gone off with another man. His mother also seemed to
have died somewhere or other. He woke from the nightmare,
his eyes wet with tears, listening attentively to the wild beating

of his heart. He stared, open-mouthed, into the darkness, searching for something. But the room was black, totally enveloping his head and body with a curtain of darkness. The air was oppressive, and his breathing came with difficulty. The dull ache in his chest was still there. He closed his eyes wearily, but then opened them again immediately, for the terrible scenes of the nightmare appeared to him again.

"Where on earth am I?" he wondered doubtfully. "Am I dead or alive?" There were no human voices around, but it was not completely silent, for the room was filled with tiny sounds. "I'm alone," he said desolately. Suddenly, a wave of sadness swept over him, and his tears began once more to fall.

"Has she really left, and is Mother really dead?" he asked himself in misery. There was no answer. He tossed and turned over and over again. "Why does nothing stir?" he wondered. "Am I dreaming?" He felt the tears on his cheeks. His throat began to itch, and he coughed.

Suddenly, he tore off the quilt, leapt out of bed and turned on the light. The room was flooded with light, so dazzlingly white that, blinded for a moment, he could scarcely open his eyes. He threw on some clothing and stood by the square table. Thank heavens! The first thing he saw was his wife asleep in bed. She was sleeping soundly, the cotton quilt covering half her face, her long, black eyelashes giving her the look of someone asleep with her eyes open. There was not a wrinkle on her forehead, and she looked as young as she had ten years ago. He looked at himself. His silk gown, padded with silk wadding, was already faded, while his blue top-gown had almost completely lost its colour. His whole body began to ache and hurt, while something resembling sputum began to force its way up his throat. He did not seem to belong to the same generation as she. He had changed! This was not a new discovery, but this time the realization struck him like a fist punching him in the chest. He staggered, and at once held on to the table to steady himself.

He stood by the table for a while. Suddenly, he shivered and, without thinking, pulled his head into his shoulders. The room was still very bright. The rats were once more gnawing at the floorboards. From the street came the sound of footsteps. Someone was walking slowly, calling out in a feeble and dreary voice: "Puffed rice and sweetened water." Helplessly, he sighed.

He turned his eyes to his mother's room. The door was shut, but from inside came the sound of snoring. It was Xiao Xuan. It was not very loud, but he could hear it. They were sleeping soundly. He cocked his ear and listened again, but still heard only Xiao Xuan snoring. "The poor child," he thought, "so unlucky to have been born into our family. Mother too, she's always had a hard life." He sighed once more. "But fortunately, they're all well." The thought comforted him a little.

Then he coughed twice, and felt the sputum stick in his throat. He had to cough it up, but he did not dare cough loudly for fear of waking his wife and his mother. He breathed in slow gasps. His chest began to hurt. He drew out his handkerchief to cover his mouth and, going over to the desk, collapsed into the cane chair.

He cleared his throat noisily many times before he finally managed to cough up the sputum. He tried to spit it onto the floor, but it stuck first to the tip of his tongue, and then to his lips, refusing to fall to the ground. "I don't even have the strength for that," he thought, feeling miserable and discouraged.

After getting rid of the sputum, his throat felt so dry that he wanted to have some tea. And so he stood up. Without meaning to, he knocked something black onto the floor. He bent down quickly to pick it up. It was Shusheng's handbag. As he picked it up, the bag fell open, and a few pieces of paper and a tube of lipstick dropped out. He bent down once more to gather them up, and saw the notice of transfer.

He took it in his hands and sat down once more in the cane chair to read it carefully. Although only a few scrawled lines, he read it untiringly over and over again. He seemed to have stumbled into an icy cellar, and his whole body froze.

"She's been deceiving me," he said to himself in a low voice. Then he wondered: Why has she concealed it from me? I can't stop her. He felt the pain and indignation of a man betrayed. He could not make it out and sat there in silence, biting his lower lip. His chest still ached with a dull pain, and he rubbed it lightly with his left hand. "The germs are eating away my lungs," he thought. "Well, let them eat to their heart's content."

"Does she really intend to go?" he asked himself. He looked down once more at the notice in his hand. It was no use asking again. The piece of paper told him everything. She would leave.

"It's just as well for her to go. She ought to find herself a new place in the world. If I force her to stay, it will only be a complete waste for her," he thought to comfort himself, turning to look at her. She had turned towards the wall, and he could see only her head of black hair. "She's sound asleep," he said quietly. He leaned back in the chair, closed his eyes and rested for a while, still clutching the notice of transfer in his hand.

Suddenly, he opened his eyes again with a start. The room was so bright! So calm! So cold! He turned to look at her again. She was still sleeping, but had turned over again, now facing him, and moreover, her right arm, white and plump, protruded from under the quilt. "She'll catch cold," he thought, getting up and going over to the bed to push her shoulder back under the quilt. He took her hand gently, moving it slowly, but she woke with a start nevertheless.

At first she grunted, and then slowly opened her eyes. "Aren't you asleep yet?" she asked, and then immediately exclaimed in alarm: "What! You're out of bed!"

"I saw your arm outside the quilt, and was afraid you'd

catch cold," he whispered in explanation, the notice of transfer still in his hand.

She gave him a smile of thanks, then slowly her eyes shifted to look elsewhere, and she caught sight of the transfer notice.

"How did you get hold of that?" she asked with a start, sitting up and pulling the collar of her pyjama jacket a little higher. "Where did you find it?"

"I saw it," he answered, looking at the ground and blushing violently, adding at once in explanation: "Your handbag dropped from the desk and fell open."

"I got it only today. I still don't know what I ought to do," she said apologetically. She remembered that she herself had carelessly left the handbag on the desk. She shivered, and at once wrapped the cotton quilt around herself.

"You should go. There's no problem about me," he whispered.

"I know," she nodded, watching him looking at her as if he had so much to say, but was unable to get it out. She was troubled. "At first, I didn't intend to go, but if I don't, what is this family of ours going to live on —"

"I know," he stammered, interrupting her.

"Mr. Chen will help me get a plane ticket. He says we can leave next Wednesday," she continued.

"Yes," he answered mechanically.

"In any case, I don't have much luggage. In the northwest, fur-lined goods are cheap, and so I can have clothes made there," she went on.

"Yes, fur is cheap there," he agreed dispiritedly.

"I can get a travel allowance from the bank, and also borrow some money in advance. I can leave fifty thousand *yuan* behind first for the household expenses."

"Good," he said briefly. His heart hurt terribly, as if it had been battered with a wooden cudgel.

"You look after yourself and get better. Over there, I'll be promoted a grade, so I'll get a rise in salary and be able

to send more money home. You need think only of resting
and getting better." As she spoke, she became more cheerful,
and a smile spread over her face.

Unable to bear it, he said: "I think I'll go back to bed."
He went halfheartedly back to the desk, put the transfer notice
back in the handbag, then returned to his bed and collapsed
dejectedly into it. He covered his head with his cotton quilt
and began to weep softly.

She had just closed her eyes when she heard the sound of his
weeping. Her excitement and happiness vanished in an instant. Countless needles from she knew not where pierced her
heart. "Xuan," she called, but received no answer. She called again, but there was still no reply. But the sound of his
weeping grew louder. Unable to control her own feelings, she
lifted aside her quilt and, pulling his away, fell onto his
body, embracing him in her arms. No matter how he tried to
move to free himself, she continued to pull him towards her.
Tears fell from her eyes as she sobbed: "I don't want to go
either. If it weren't for your mother, if it weren't for everyone's
livelihood . . . I'm so miserable too! . . . I'm a woman,
I. . . ."

22

After that evening, he had even more reason for nightmares.
They tortured him, giving him no peace, even for a single
night. Dream followed dream. In his dreams, he was perpetually saying farewell to her, on her way to Lanzhou
or elsewhere, sometimes, even, she was leaving in resentment
after a quarrel with his mother. On waking, he would almost
always find himself bathed in sweat, and he would give a long
sigh, not knowing what to do. He knew that his illness had
already become very serious.

At night, his wife would sleep beside him, but because of

his illness, he continually avoided turning his face towards her.
Though they slept together, their minds were far apart. His
wife went out during the day and did not return home early
in the evening, because of her social engagements with colleagues inviting her to farewell parties. Whenever she came
home late, she would find his mother in the big room sitting
up with him, but the moment she stepped across the threshold,
his mother would retire to her own little room. Then she
herself would sit on the edge of the bed, or on the stool by the
square table, and chatter on nonstop about the day's happenings. Now that she had become more talkative than usual; he,
in turn, became quieter and more taciturn. He would often
gaze at her unseeingly, wondering whether, after their parting,
he would ever see her again.

When he wasn't dreaming, he liked to count the days and
hours they had left together. As the days and hours diminished, his struggle became more desperate. Should he let her go,
or pull her back? Let her attain happiness, or drag her back
with him into the abyss?

"Will you think of me after you've gone?" he kept wanting
to ask, but in the end, he did not dare to.

The fifty thousand *yuan* was paid: twenty thousand in cash
together with a bank deposit slip. His wife told him it was
for a fixed deposit at seven percent, payable every half month,
after the completion of certain formalities. She knew so much
more about these things than he did! Her luggage was all
ready too, when all of a sudden, she came home with a piece
of good news: The plane tickets might be delayed another
fortnight. The news delighted her, and she also told him that
she would be able to spend the New Year happily with him.
From his point of view, nothing could have given him greater
comfort. Since there was no way he could keep her back, all he
could hope for was to see her more often, to see more often
her beautiful face, which was so full of vitality.

But seeing her like this also made him miserable sometimes.
Even he could see that, day after day, her mind was moving

farther and farther away. Separation from him did not seem wholly painful to her. She would often say laughingly: "In three or four months, I'll be back to see you. Mr. Chen knows the people in the air company, so it'll be easy to get tickets, and coming back and forth will be very convenient." He would mumble something in agreement, thinking to himself: "I wonder if I'll still be here when you come back." And he felt that only a long cry could cheer him up. But when the sputum stuck in his throat and he had to cough with all his might to dislodge it, the left side of his chest would ache so he began to breathe in deep, slow gasps. Though she was accustomed to the sound of his gasps, it would still draw from her a compassionate glance or a look of inquiring solicitude.

He was already sitting up, and even walking freely about the room. Apart from the pallor of his face, his coughing and some of his movements, no one could have guessed that he was ill. He was still taking herbal medicine, but not always when he should. His mother now also proposed that he go to the hospital for a checkup, to have an X-ray. But he always refused. He preferred Chinese herbal medicine because it cost less, and so, regardless of its efficacy, he kept on with it, since it at least gave him a little comfort and hope.

Sometimes he would read, for he was lonely, and moreover, the winter nights were so long that if he slept all night, he could not close his eyes during the day. Besides, he liked to read, to walk about and talk, for it made him feel that his illness was not serious, even forgetting that he was a sick man. But his mother would not let him talk too much, read too much or walk about too much. She kept reminding him that he was ill, that he could not live like an ordinary person.

But why could he not live like everyone else? Lying on his back in broad daylight doing nothing could only make him reflect more deeply on things, and increase his worries and misgivings. It could only exasperate him. Almost every day, he would calculate how much money he had spent and how much was left. There was basically only a limited amount of money, and prices kept rising all the time. How long could his severance pay, the money left by his wife for household expenses and the monthly interest last even when all added together? Day after day, he seemed to see the money flow unceasingly out while his hands were tied, and there was no way of damming the flood. He himself had no income whatsoever, only unending, inexhaustible expenses. . . . It was too frightening. The thought of it threw him into a daze.

Once his mother came home with a chicken she had bought him and happily made him chicken soup, which she served to him in a large vegetable bowl. It was shortly after lunch. For the last two days, his appetite had worsened.

"If you like it, I can make it for you often," his mother said encouragingly.

"It's too expensive, Mother. How can we afford it?" he said, a sad expression on his face. But he accepted the bowl nevertheless.

"I bought it very cheap, only just over a thousand *yuan*. Besides, it will build up your strength," she insisted gently, although she felt as though he had poured cold water over her.

"But we don't have much money," he said obstinately. "My health is so bad, and I've lost my job into the bargain. How can I just sit here idly eating up what money we do have?"

"Don't worry. You mustn't worry," his mother urged, with a halfhearted smile. "In any case, we can manage for the present. We'll talk about it again when you're better."

"Every day, things get dearer and the money gets less. We may have to start using Shusheng's money before she's even gone," he said, frowning at the steam that rose from the chicken soup in his hands.

His mother at once stopped smiling. She turned away, looking for something to fix her gaze on, but finding nothing, turned to face him again and said sulkily and irritably: "Drink up quickly."

Flustered and uneasy, he lifted the bowl with both hands and drank without the help of a spoon or of chopsticks. As

she stood beside him, his mother gave a low sigh. She seemed to see that woman's contented smile before her, and felt her
own face burning. She dropped her head, but the noise of his
drinking drew her attention. "It's very nice, very nice,"
he kept saying in praise, his look of sadness gone. He
kept his eyes glued greedily on the soup, picked up a chicken
leg with his fingers, put it into the side of his mouth and began
to chew.

"Mother, you have some too," he said, smiling, looking up
at her suddenly.

"I'm not hungry," she answered softly, gazing at him with
compassion in her eyes, but still unhappy.

"I'm not ill. It's just that I haven't had enough nourishing
food. From now on, I'll gradually get better," he asserted, as
if in explanation.

"Yes, you'll gradually get better," she repeated mechanically.

He concentrated once more on the chicken meat in the soup.
He seemed never to have drunk or eaten so well before. All
at once, he murmured to himself: "If I'd eaten better in the
past, I mightn't have caught this illness." He continued to eat
as he spoke, while his mother remained standing beside him,
watching him, smiling one moment, rubbing her eyes with her
hands the next.

"He'll almost certainly get better gradually," she thought.
"He can eat. That's a good sign."

"Mother, you have some too. It's delicious, absolutely delicious! People need nourishment," he said to his mother
with a smile of satisfaction after he had finished the meat off
the chicken, still holding the bowl in his greasy hands.

"All right, I'll have some later," his mother answered
vaguely, not wanting him to talk too much. But to herself she
thought: "A skinny chicken like that isn't even enough for
you." She took the empty bowl from him and carried it outside. When she came back, he was leaning back in the cane
chair, dozing. His mother tiptoed about, intending to get some-

thing to cover him, but when she came up to him, he suddenly opened his eyes and grasping his mother by the hand, cried: "Shusheng!"

"What is it?" his mother asked in fright.

His eyes searched all over the room for a moment. Then he asked rather doubtfully:

"Is Shusheng back yet?"

"No, there's been no sign of her at all," she replied, disappointed. He should not be thinking of Shusheng all the time. What good was Shusheng to him? She was simply tormenting him, deceiving him.

He remained for a moment in deep silence before breaking into a sad smile. "I was dreaming again," he said, feeling quite alone.

"You'd better go to bed and sleep," his mother said.

"I sleep too much. My body's sore from sleeping. I don't feel like sleeping anymore," he said, and got slowly up.

"Shusheng's really too busy. She's going soon, and yet she can't get home to spend two days together with us," he said to himself, holding onto the desk for support. He turned around, pushed back the cane chair, and going slowly to the window on the right, pushed it open.

"Be careful, you mustn't catch cold," his mother said with concern. At first when she had heard him pronounce that woman's name, she had repressed her feeling of unhappiness and said nothing, but now, she could not remain silent, for after all, she bore him no resentment!

"It's too stuffy. I need a bit of fresh air," he said, but the cold air that he breathed in reeked of coal. At the same time, something abrasive seemed to scrape against his face, and he felt only pain and discomfort.

The sky wore its everlastingly sorrowful face, and the air was as stifling as always. Pedestrians hurried back and forth along the stretch of dismal greyness that was the road, their eyes fixed to the ground, their heads shrunk in their collars.

"You'd better go to sleep for a while. I can see you're bored with doing nothing," his mother urged again.

He closed the window, turned round, and nodding to his mother, answered: "All right." He looked at his bed. He wanted to go to it, and yet was afraid to. He could not help sighing. "The days pass so slowly," he murmured to himself.

Eventually, he managed to reach his bed, and fell onto it without undressing. But his eyes remained open.

His mother rested in the cane chair, her eyes shut. Hearing him toss backwards and forwards on his bed, she knew that something was troubling him. She felt something like grief and indignation. In the end, unable to endure it, she turned to look at him, saying to console him: "Xuan, you mustn't think so much about these things. Stop worrying and go to sleep."

"I'm not thinking about anything," he answered in a low voice.

"You can't deceive me. You're still thinking about Shusheng," his mother said.

"It was I who urged her to go. She hadn't definitely decided to leave. She hates living here so much. By going to Lanzhou, she gets a rise and goes up a grade."

"I know, I know," his mother said with emphasis. "But you think only of her. Why don't you think of yourself? Why do you worry only about other people?"

"Of myself?" he exclaimed in surprise. "I'm fine, am I not?" But when he uttered the word "fine", even he realized what an exaggeration it was, and so he added: "I'm almost completely cured now, and she's of more help to me in Lanzhou."

"She! You believe her!" his mother scoffed. "She's just a wild bird. Once you've let her go, don't expect to get her back," she said contemptuously.

"Mother, you're so kind to everyone. It's only Shusheng you're so harsh to. She's not that kind of woman at all. And besides, it's only for the family's sake that she's agreed to go to Lanzhou," he said in agitation, sitting up in bed.

His mother looked at him uncomprehendingly. Her expression suddenly changed, and she nodded in submission: "Then have it your way, I believe you. . . . Now stop worrying and go to sleep. If you talk too much, you'll overtax your mind, and you might get worse."

He said nothing. He dropped his head as if meditating. His mother looked at him compassionately, thinking resentfully to herself: Why do you refuse to come to your senses! But she said to him in a voice still tender with love: "Xuan, you'd better lie down and sleep. You'll catch cold, sitting up like that."

He looked up at his mother with something close to gratitude in his eyes. A moment later, he suddenly got out of bed. "Mother, I'm going out for a while," he said in a rush, bending down to tie his shoelaces.

"Going out? Whatever for?" she asked in surprise.

"I've something to do," he answered.

"What?" she asked anxiously. "The firm's already sacked you. It's bitterly cold outside, and you're not well."

He stood up, his face flushed with excitement. "Don't worry, Mother. Let me go," he said stubbornly, and taking his blue top-gown from the nail on the wall, he put it on.

"Wait, I'll help you," his mother said, anxious and worried, and went over to help him with the gown. "You shouldn't go. You can't walk properly!" she said, at the same time taking down his old black-and-white striped scarf and wrapping it round his neck. "You shouldn't go. If you've something to do, write a note. I'll deliver it for you," she added.

"Don't worry. I'll be back soon. It's quite close," he said, and went out. She gazed after him, feeling suddenly as if she were in a dream.

"What's he up to? I simply don't understand!" she said, feeling herself abandoned. After standing where she was and pondering for a moment, she went to his bed, bent over and tidied it up.

Having made the bed, she looked round the room. The floor was covered with dust, with spots of half-dried sputum in several places. She frowned, then went out into the corridor to fetch a broom to sweep the floor clean. The desk was covered with a layer of dust already, for one side of the flat faced the road, and each time a lorry passed, a huge cloud of dust would blow into the room. At this moment, she seemed particularly unable to stand the dirt. And so, taking a cloth, she wiped the table, the desk and the stool.

Having finished, she sat down in the cane chair to rest. Her waist felt sore, and so she rubbed it for a moment with her hands. "How nice it would be if there were someone to massage it for me," she suddenly thought. But realizing at once what kind of life she was living, she rebuked herself: "You've become an amah yourself, and yet you still have such idle thoughts!" she sighed in disappointment, leaning her head against the back of the chair. Before her eyes appeared a figure, at first dimly, then with complete clarity. "I'm thinking of him again." She laughed at herself, but then she whispered: "I don't care about myself. I know that my stars are unlucky. But why don't you protect Xuan? You can't let him pass his days like this!" Overcome by grief, she dropped her head and let fall a few tears.

Soon after, he pushed open the door and saw his mother sitting in the cane chair, wiping her eyes.

"Mother, what's the matter? Why are you crying?" he asked in surprise.

"I was sweeping. Some dust got in my eyes. I've just managed to get it out," she lied.

"Mother, you've made my bed," he said, touched, going over to his mother's side.

"I had nothing to do, and so I got depressed," she replied. Then she added: "Where did you go just now?"

He gasped for breath, coughed a few times, then turned away and said: "I went to see Zhong Lao."

"What did you see him for? Did you go to the office?" she asked in surprise, standing up.

"I asked him to find me a job," he said in a low voice.

"Find you a job? You're still not fully recovered. Why are you in such a hurry? Your health is more important than anything else," his mother cried in disapproval.

"We Chinese are nearly all like this. We say we're ill, but we go on for decades without anything happening. I'm a lot better now, and Zhong Lao says I'm looking much better than a few days ago. He's promised to try to find me something." His face still looked ill and fatigued, and it seemed a great effort for him to speak. He went over to the bed and sat down on the edge.

"Ah, why are you in such a hurry?" his mother exclaimed. "We won't go hungry for a while yet."

"But I can't sleep all day, while you do all the work by yourself. I'm a man. I can't just put my hands in my pockets and wait to be fed," he argued miserably.

"You're my son. You're the only son I have. If you refuse to look after yourself, who's going to look after me in the future? . . ." She could not go on, choked by grief and pain.

He held his left hand to his mouth, biting hard on the thumb. He could not feel the pain, for the left side of his chest was hurting so. After a while, he released his hand without looking at the deep toothmarks. As he watched his mother sitting there silently, his eyes filled with compassion. "Your dreams and your hopes have all come to nothing," he thought. He knew what lay in the "future". The "future" resembled the evil face of a monster, with two rows of frightening white teeth.

The two said nothing more, did nothing more. The terrifying silence was a torture. There was not a breath of life in the room, and not even the noise of the traffic and the people in the street could break the stillness. But, mother and son, each sunk deep in thought, though travelling different roads, converged and met head on at the same point which they both understood, the one gigantic word: Death.

He went and stood behind his mother. "Mother, don't be upset," he said gently. "Xiao Xuan will look after you. He's sure to do better than I in the future."

Understanding his meaning, his mother became even more troubled. "Xiao Xuan's exactly as you were when you were young. He's too like you," she said, seeming to sigh. She had no wish to reveal her misery to him, but these few words enabled him to see more deeply into the loneliness of her life and to see it even more clearly. She was right. Xiao Xuan resembled him too closely. In other words, like him, Xiao Xuan had no future. Who then was going to look after her? He himself had sometimes placed his hopes on Xiao Xuan. Now he realized how uncertain these hopes were.

"He's still young. He'll improve as he grows older. To tell the truth, I really should ask his forgiveness for never having seen to his upbringing properly," he said, still thinking to console his mother.

"Actually, you're not to blame. You've never in your life had a moment to spare, and you've had to suffer every kind of hardship. . . ." At this point, she was so overcome by her emotions that she could say no more. She stood up abruptly and fled from the room.

He walked in silence over to the window on the right, and threw open one side. The sorrowful face of the sky, the dark grey clouds frowning in menace, stared back at him. He shivered. Something cold beat against his cheeks. "It's raining," he said dejectedly to himself.

Behind him, he heard the sound of footsteps. His wife came into the flat, and without waiting for him to turn, she cried excitedly: "Xuan, I'm leaving tomorrow."

"Tomorrow? Why so fast? Didn't you say next week?" he asked, taken aback.

"There's an extra flight tomorrow, and they've already delivered the tickets. I can't spend the New Year with you after all. And it's really a shame, but I'm invited out to dinner this evening as well." At this point, her brows contracted in a frown without her being aware of it, and her tone of voice changed.

"Then you're really going tomorrow?" he asked, feeling let down.

"I have to be at the airport tomorrow morning before six. I'll have to get up before it's light," she replied.

"Then you'd better order the taxi tonight; otherwise, you mightn't make it," he suggested.

"There's no need. Mr. Chen's borrowing a car and is coming to fetch me. But I still have to pack. My suitcases aren't ready yet," she said in some agitation. She bent down to get the suitcases from under the bed.

"I'll come and help you," he offered, going up to the bed.

She had already dragged a suitcase out and, kneeling down, opened the lid and began sorting through her clothes. Every now and then, she would get up to get something to put into it: clothes, make-up and other things.

"Do you want to take this? Do you need this?" he would ask from time to time, each time bringing one or two of her things over to her.

"Thanks," she would reply each time. "Don't do anything. I'll manage."

His mother came in from outside and stood at the door, watching them coldly. She did not utter a sound, but her heart was full of resentment. Noticing her all of a sudden, he announced: "Mother, Shusheng is flying early tomorrow morning."

"If she's flying, she's flying. What's it to do with me?" his mother declared icily.

Shusheng had risen to greet his mother with a few friendly words, but at his mother's icy remark, she knelt down again with a barely audible grunt, her face turning red.

His mother stalked in a huff to her own little room. Shusheng closed the lid of the suitcase and stood up, her anger
already abating.   He gazed at her with beseeching eyes, not
daring to say a word.

"You see. It's she who can't stand me. She really hates me,"
Shusheng muttered in a low voice.

"It's all a misunderstanding. She'll come to understand eventually. But you mustn't blame her," he answered softly.

"I won't hate her, if only for your sake," she promised with
a gentle smile.

"Thank you," he said, smiling too. "Tomorrow, I'll see you
off at the airport." he said even more softly.

"You mustn't. Your health's not up to it," she said quickly.
"In any case, there's Mr. Chen to look after me."

The last sentence stabbed him to the heart. "Then we're
going to say good-bye in this room?" he asked miserably, his
eyes brimming with tears.

"Don't be upset. I haven't gone yet. I'll come back early
this evening and we can have a long chat together," she said
sympathetically, her heart softening as she tried to console him.

He nodded, wanting to say: "I'll wait up for you." But
the words would not come, and all he could manage was
a vague grunt.

"You should lie down. It's too tiring for you to stand. You
still haven't completely recovered," she then said. "I can sit
on the bed for a while."

He did as she urged and lay down, while she half covered
him with the cotton quilt before sitting down on the edge of
the bed. "I wonder what things will be like at this time tomorrow," she said to herself. "In fact, I'm not sure that I want
to go. I still haven't got used to the idea. If you'd tried to
stop me, perhaps I might not have gone." It was the truth
she was speaking.

"Stop worrying and go. Since you've made up your mind,
it can't be wrong," he replied gently, forgetting his own
misery.

"In fact, I don't know myself whether going to Lanzhou will bring me joy or disaster. There's not a single person I can talk things over with. You're always ill, and your mother is only anxious for me to leave you as soon as possible," she said, gazing at him with a mixture of sadness and vexation.

The word "ill" reverberated in his head. They would never let him forget that he was ill! They would always look on him as an invalid! He sighed. They had once been equals, and it was as if he had fallen away from her and his last gossamer of hope had snapped.

"Yes, yes," he kept repeating helplessly, gazing at her with eyes filled with deep concern and love.

"You still don't look well. You must rest more," she advised. changing to a tone of solicitude. "The money problem's easy to solve. You should just stop worrying and concentrate on getting better. I'll send you money every month."

"Yes, I know," he said, averting his gaze.

"I sent a letter to Xiao Xuan's place today," she continued, but before she had finished speaking, a car horn sounded in the street below the building. A little surprised, she turned to look in that direction before going on. "I've asked him to come home on Sunday." The horn sounded repeatedly as if impatient. She stood up. "I have to go," she said, a little flustered. "They've come to pick me up by car." She straightened her clothes, picked up her handbag and opened it to take out a small mirror, a powder compact and her lipstick.

He sat up. "Don't get up, go to sleep," she said, while carefully re-touching her face and lips in the mirror. But he got out of bed nevertheless.

"I'm off then. I'll be back a bit earlier this evening," she said, turning towards him, and with a nod and a smile, she hurried out the door.

The perfume of her powder lingered in the chilly air of the room, but her clear laughter and her voice departed with her. He stood at the table with an air of having been abandoned, lost in thought, staring at the doorway through which her figure had disappeared and from which the whitewash was peeling. "Stay! Stay!" he seemed to hear a voice within him cry. But the light tread of her footsteps had vanished long ago.

His mother came out of her room, eyeing him with compassion. "Xuan, forget your illusions! You'll have to separate sooner or later. How can a penniless bookworm like you keep her!" she cried, feeling the need to release the love and the hate that filled her heart to overflowing.

He looked down at his own body, and then lifted his right hand to his eyes. So thin! So yellow! Just like the claws of a chicken! It was shaking, quivering feebly. He pushed his sleeve up slightly. What a thin, withered wrist! Where had the flesh gone? He felt cold all over. He stood there stupefied, staring at this terrible hand. He was like a condemned man who has just heard the proclamation of his own death sentence. His mother's words echoed over and over in his ears: "Forget your illusions, forget, forget!" Truly, his heart had been sentenced to death.

What right, what reason did he still have for begging her to stay? The problem was in him, not her. This time, he understood thoroughly.

His mother turned on the light, adding a little brightness to the room.

He went silently over to the desk, looked at the objects there as if to bid them farewell, and then collapsed exhausted into the cane chair. He covered his face with both hands, but there were no tears. It was just that he didn't want to see the things that surrounded him anymore. He renounced everything, himself included.

"Xuan, you mustn't upset yourself. There are plenty of women. When you've recovered, you can find a better one." His mother went over to solace him, speaking in a voice tender with love.

He uttered a groan of misery. He let fall his hands and stared vaguely at his mother. He wanted to cry. Why did she have to drag him back? Why did she force him, a prisoner condemned to death, to glimpse once more this busy, bustling world? He had already prepared to accept his fate with calm. Why did she tempt him with this hopeless dream?   At this time, he was incapable of thinking calmly or deciding unhurriedly, for he was experiencing a personal misery that wrung his very heart.   Shusheng had taken with her his love, taken with her his whole being.   The beautiful dreams when they were at university, the sweetness of their life after marriage, their plans before the war for promoting education . . . all had gone, all had ended!

"You'd better go quickly and lie down.   You don't look at all well.   Shall I go and call a doctor, even a doctor practising Western medicine?"   His mother still could not understand him, but his face terrified her.   She became anxious, her voice trembling as she spoke.

"No, there's no need to call a doctor.   It won't be long now, Mother," he said in despair, his voice weak, gasping for breath from time to time.   He stood up unsteadily.

"What did you say?   Wait, I'll help you," his mother cried in alarm, promptly supporting him by the right elbow.

"Don't be afraid, Mother.   It's nothing.   I can manage by myself," he said, as if waking from a dream.   He pulled himself away from his mother's grasp, moved away from the cane chair over to the square table, and with one hand pressed on the table, gazed vaguely around him.   A feeling of coldness emanated from the dim yellow light, from the plain, old furniture, from every object in the room.   Suddenly, without warning, the light went out.   For a moment, the room was pitch-black, then from the darkness slowly emerged an elusive greyness.

"There was a power cut yesterday!   Why is there another one today?" his mother complained in a low voice.

He sighed.   "In any case, we're not doing anything, so it might as well stay dark."

"It's better if I light a candle.   It's so desolate otherwise," his mother said.   She went to fetch the half candle left from the previous day and lit it. The light flickered wildly. Black shadows leapt about the room. A draught from somewhere or other shook the candle flame violently. The wick fell to one side and the wax flowed down like water, welding the upside-down cup which served as a candle-holder to the table.

"Quick, fetch the scissors, the scissors!" It was not at all what he wanted to say, but the words, filled with anxiety, escaped from his lips of their own accord. Incidents such as this were happening all the time. He had had plenty of practice from past experience, and so he acted without thinking and spoke without thinking.

His mother brought the scissors and cut away the drooping wick. The candle flame gradually steadied. "What about eating now? I'll go and warm up the chicken soup," she suggested.

"All right," he answered halfheartedly. The happiness and appetite he had had a few hours ago had completely vanished. His acquiescence was simply to satisfy his mother. "Why does she still want me to eat? Am I not full already?" he wondered doubtfully, looking at his mother vacantly. His mother had just picked up a piece of candle no longer than her thumb and had lit it in preparation to go out.

"Mother, take this longer piece. It's easier," he said. "I don't need the light," he added. Whether I have light or not makes no difference to me, he thought.

"It's all right. This is enough for me," his mother said, and continued on her way out of the room, holding the smaller piece of candle.

He was left in the room with the leftover piece of candle to keep him company.

"Another day gone. I wonder how many more days I have left," he said to himself, sighing in spite of himself.

No one answered. He saw his own shadow flickering on the wall. He did not know whether he should sit or remain standing, whether he should sleep or stay awake. He did not

even know what it was he wanted to do. He remained standing by the table. The bitter cold of the night air gradually
seeped through both his top-gown and his gown. He shivered
slightly. He moved away from the table, a few steps only,
simply to warm himself a little.

"I'm only thirty-four, and as yet I've accomplished nothing,"
he thought uneasily, feeling wretched. "Now, everything's
over," he sighed with regret. The aspirations of his university
days flashed before his eyes like floodlight. The garden-like
background, the young faces, the high-sounding language . . .
all surfaced once more in his mind. "Who would have
thought then that today would be like this?" he said ruefully.

"How naive I was then! I even imagined running my own
ideal high school," he thought with a bitter smile. Before his
mind's eye appeared the faces of young people, lively, brave,
full of hope . . . smiling at him in gratitude. His eyes opened
wide in alarm. The candlewick had grown longer again, and
the light grew gradually dimmer. An infinite feeling of desolation filled the room. "I'm dreaming again," he said hopelessly to himself, doing nothing to trim the wick. Suddenly, he
heard his mother's footsteps in the corridor.

"Food again! What's the point of living like this, neither
dead nor alive!" he thought wretchedly.

His mother came in carrying in both hands a steaming bowl
of chicken soup and rice, and announced with a satisfied
smile: "I've made you some rice with chicken soup. Eat it
while it's hot. Make the most of it."

"All right. I'll eat as much as I can," he replied obediently.
His mother placed the bowl on the table. He went over and
sat on a stool. The hot steam rose and blew against his face.
He watched his mother bend down to trim the candlewick.
She had become even older these last few days. She was so
wrinkled. Her cheekbones had become more prominent, her
cheeks more sunken.

"Even Mother is tired because of me," he could not help
thinking. He stared at the bowl, lost in thought.

"Hurry up and eat! It'll get cold!" his mother urged from beside him.

23

After finishing his dinner, he waited expectantly for his wife, but she came home very late.

Time passed very, very slowly. He either sat in the cane chair, or lay on the bed in his clothes. His old watch had broken down many days ago, but, unwilling to spend the large sum needed for its repair, he left it lying quietly beside his pillow, and had to keep asking his mother the time . . . seven o'clock . . . eight o'clock . . . nine o'clock . . . the hours seemed deliberately to thwart him. The waiting was a torture, but he had immense staying power.

Finally, ten o'clock came. His mother put down her needlework, took off her glasses and rubbed her eyes. "Xuan, you'd better undress and go to bed. Don't wait up anymore," she enjoined.

"I can't sleep. Mother, you go to bed," he said, disappointed.

"It's so late, yet she still isn't back. How can she be thinking of us? If she has to go first thing in the morning, it's only right that she should come home early to spend time with her family," his mother grumbled.

"She has a busy social life, and lots to do. You can't blame her," he explained, still speaking in her defence.

"Social life! What social engagements can she still have! More likely she's gone dancing with that Mr. Chen of hers," his mother sneered.

"No, no. That's impossible," he said, shaking his head.

"You're always defending her, covering up for her! I don't want to purposely pour cold water on you, but I'll tell you something, and you just see! There's something shady going on between her and that Mr. Chen —" She suddenly swallowed her words and, changing her tone of voice, sighed: "You're too honest and trusting. You still believe her, even now. You can't see what's in front of your own nose!"

"Mother, you don't understand her very well. She has her difficulties too. You can't avoid social contacts if you're part of the working world, and she likes people to think well of her. I don't think she likes Mr. Chen all that much. I trust her."

"In other words, I'm slandering her!" his mother cried in agitation, turning pale.

He was astounded. He stole a glance at his mother, not daring to say a word. After a few moments, her anger subsided, and the tension in her face relaxed. In her deep regret at having spoken in this way, she looked at him with compassion, and said kindly: "Don't be upset. I'm old and I'm getting more and more crotchety. In fact, what's the good of all these continual quarrels! — But I don't understand why she despises me. I'm your mother, after all!"

Encouraged once more, he plucked up courage and said: "Mother, you mustn't misunderstand her. She's never said anything against you. She actually has a high opinion of you." He hoped there was a chance of removing the misunderstanding between them.

His mother sighed and, pointing at his face, said: "You're too good a sort! How can she tell you the truth! I can see! I understand her better than you do. She thinks because she earns her own keep and I depend on the two of you to live, she can look down on me."

"Mother, you really do misunderstand her. She doesn't think like that at all," he said, full of confidence in his own words.

"How do you know?" his mother asked, refusing to give in. Just at that moment, the power came on again. The whole room was lit up. The huge black wick of the inch-long candle stub left standing on the upside-down cup looked as if it would go out at any moment. His mother promptly blew it out, and changing the subject, she exclaimed: "It's half past ten already and she's not back! Do you think she's thinking of us!"

He said nothing, but slowly sighed. The left side of his chest ached terribly. He stole a look at his mother, imploring her pity. He even wanted to cry: "Forgive her!" but he said nothing. He suppressed an explosion of feeling (he wanted so much to weep his heart out), saying calmly to his mother: "You don't have to wait up, Mother. You go to bed."

"What about you?" his mother inquired with concern.

"I'll go to bed too. I'm terribly sleepy." He yawned, purposely pretending he could not keep his eyes open.

"Then why don't you get undressed?" his mother asked.

"I'll undress in a moment. I'll just lie down first. Mother, will you turn the light off for me?" he said, speaking hesitantly on purpose. Then he yawned again.

"All right. It's just as well for you to lie down first. But don't forget to undress," she instructed. She turned off the light as he had requested, tiptoed to fetch a stool and placed it behind the closed door. Then she went into her own room, where the light was still burning.

But he had no intention of sleeping. His thoughts seethed and churned. He looked at the door with wide-open eyes, looked at the square table, looked at the cane chair, looked at everything she had sat on, moved or used. When tomorrow comes, he thought, everything will have changed. This room would never see her presence again.

"Shusheng!" he called softly and tearfully, abruptly pulling the cotton quilt over his head, hoping that a hand would lift back the quilt, that a gentle voice would whisper softly: "Xuan, I'm here."

But nothing whatsoever happened. His mother coughed once or twice in her room, then all was still.

"Shusheng, are you really going to leave me like this?" he cried again, hoping to hear a voice reply: "Xuan, I will never leave you." But there was no sound. Yes, there was. From the street came the desolate cry: "Puffed rice and sweetened water!" A sound so weak, so empty, so solitary. The sales cry of an old man, alone in the world! He seemed to see himself, head down, back hunched, hands stuck in his sleeves, in his old, dirty cotton gown, too thin to keep out the bitter cold wind, a man with schooling, yet so lowly, so ill and so frail. Now . . . and the future? At this thought, he began to sob under his quilt.

Fortunately, his mother did not hear his weeping. There was no one to console him. Gradually, his tears ceased. He heard the sound of footsteps in the corridor, her footsteps! Excitedly, he turned back the quilt and uncovered his face, forgetting that his tears had still not dried until she pushed open the door. He at once wiped his eyes with his hand and turned anxiously onto his side so that she would not see his face when she turned on the light.

She came into the room and switched on the light. Looking over at the bed, she thought at first that he was sound asleep. She picked up her slippers, tiptoed to the desk, then sat down in the chair and changed her shoes. From the drawer, she took out a mirror and briefly arranged her hair. Then she stood up, went to open a suitcase, and put the contents of the drawer into it. She did this with great care not to make a noise, for she did not want to startle him from his dreams. But just as she was arranging the things in her suitcase, she suddenly thought of something and, stopping what she was doing for a moment, went over to the bed and stood there quietly, looking at him.

He had not been asleep. He seemed to have been watching her every movement through the tiny sounds she made. He thought she would move away, but who would have thought she would stand there for so long. He wondered what she was doing. He could not bear it. He coughed. He heard her call his name in a whisper, and pretending to wake up as he turned over, he stretched himself, and opened his eyes.

"Xuan," she called again, bending over to look at him. "I came back late. Have you been asleep long?"

"I didn't intend to fall asleep. I don't know how it happen-ed," he lied, smiling at her at the same time.

"I wanted to come home long ago. Who could have guessed that the dinner would go on for so long! Afterwards, they dragged us to a coffee shop. I said I wanted to go home, but they wouldn't let me go . . ." she explained.

"I know," he interrupted. "Your colleagues definitely wouldn't want you to leave." It was just a casual remark, but once out, he felt he had spoken out of turn. He had absolutely no intention of being sarcastic.

"Are you mad at me for not coming home early?" she asked under her breath. "I'm not deceiving you. Even though I was eating out, I was thinking of you all the time. Since we're parting, I wanted to be with you longer. To tell you the truth, I was afraid —" At this point, she turned to look towards his mother's tiny room.

"I know. I'm not mad at you," he said. "Is your luggage all ready?" he asked, changing the subject.

"Almost," she replied.

"Then you'd better hurry and finish packing," he urged. "It must be nearly eleven by now. You'll have to go to sleep early if you're going to get up before it's light tomorrow."

"Don't worry. Mr. Chen's coming for me with a car. It's borrowed already," she answered casually.

"But you still have to get up early or you mightn't make it." He forced himself to smile as he spoke.

"Then, you'd —" She began to feel reluctant to leave, and became rather upset, so the words stuck in her throat, and she could not continue.

"I feel drowsy," he remarked, purposely yawning.

She seemed to reflect for a moment before looking up to say: "All right. You go to sleep. There's no need for you to get up when I go. It's too early, and you might catch cold. You've only just got a little better, and so you must be very careful."

"Yes, I know. Don't worry," he said. It needed all his

effort to force himself to smile pleasantly, but even then, he did not succeed very well. When she turned to go on with her packing, he covered his head with his quilt and wept.

She was busy for about an hour. She thought he was sound asleep, but in fact he was awake throughout. His thoughts were so active, ranging over many places, and even over many months and years, leaping over the bounds of time and space, but revolving all the time around one face: hers. She was still near him now, but he did not dare utter a sound or even cough audibly for fear of alarming her. Their happy memories, the days of their youth, were all in the distant past . . . even the wretched quarrels and mutual torture were in the distant past. Now all that was left to him was this separation (to take place almost at once) and the loneliness to follow. And there was his illness. The left side of his chest began to ache dully once again. Would she come back? Or if she did, would he be able to last until that day? . . . He did not dare go on thinking. Turning his face to the wall, he silently shed tears. Later he slept fitfully for a while, but that was only after she herself had already been asleep for a few minutes.

He awoke in terror around midnight, bathed in sweat, his singlet soaking wet. The room was utterly dark, and as he turned to look out from the bed, he felt dizzy, and was unable to see anything clearly. There was no sound from his mother's room. He cocked his ear to listen. His wife was breathing evenly beside him, sleeping peacefully. "What time is it?" he asked himself, but he could not answer. "She won't over-sleep, will she?" he wondered. He gave the answer himself: "It must still be early, it's so dark. She'll get there all right, since Mr. Chen is picking her up." At the thought of "Mr. Chen", he felt as if his head had been struck by a heavy blow. He was stunned for a few minutes. His mind was in torment, his face and forehead burning hot. "He's better than I in everything," he thought in a fit of jealousy. . . .

Slowly, little by little, he began to sleep once more. She, however, suddenly woke. She leapt from the bed, put on her clothes, turned on the light and looked at her watch. "Heavens!" she cried softly in alarm, and began at once to put on her make-up.

From outside the window, the horn of a car suddenly sounded. "He's come. I must hurry," she whispered, urging herself on. Her hasty make-up completed, she looked towards the bed. He lay there motionless. "I mustn't wake him. Let him have a good sleep," she thought. Then looking towards the tightly shut door of his mother's small room, she said to it: "Good-bye." She tried picking up her two suitcases, but no sooner had she lifted them than she put them down again. She went anxiously over to the bed to look at him. He was snoring, the back of his head towards her. She stood there for a long moment, not knowing what to do. The car under the window blew its horn again. "Xuan," she whispered softly and tenderly, "we'll see each other again. I hope you won't dream that I've forsaken you." She felt a moment of unease, bit her lip hard, and then, turning round, moved away from the bed. But she at once turned to look at him again. She hesitated, went decisively to the desk, took a piece of paper, and hurriedly wrote a few lines with her fountain pen, putting the ink bottle on top of the note to keep it down. Then taking up one of her suitcases, she went towards the door.

She was already in the corridor, turning to go down the staircase, when he suddenly cried out in terror in his dream, and woke up. He had called her name, not very loudly, but in such despair. He had dreamt she was abandoning him and he was calling her back.

His eyes began at once to search for her. The door was open. The light was terribly bright. There was no trace of her. But in the middle of the room stood a single suitcase. He quickly realized what was happening. He turned over, sat up, hastily put on his cotton gown without even buttoning it up, took the suitcase and strode out of the room with it.

He had not reached the stairwell when his shoulder felt sore, his feet heavy, but he held on with all his strength as he descended the stairs. There was no light on the stairs, and the back flap of his gown which he had not buttoned got in the way of his feet, preventing him from moving quickly. He had just reached the landing on the first floor, when two people came hurriedly towards him. He saw the beam of a torch, and closed his eyes slightly to avoid the glare.

"Xuan, you're up!" the person coming up the stairs cried in happy surprise, in a woman's voice familiar to him. The torch shone on his body. "Heavens! You've brought my suitcase down!" She came up to him at once, putting her hand out for the suitcase. "Give it to me," she said gratefully.

He would not let go, wanting to continue down the stairs with it. "It's all right," he insisted, "I can manage it."

"Give it to me," another voice said, a man's voice, young and full of vigour. He was startled. He looked up at the speaker, and in the dim light, perceived a man of imposing presence, sturdy and stalwart, in comparison with whom, he himself was so wretched in appearance. He obediently hand-ed the suitcase over to the outstretched hand, and heard her say: "Mr. Chen, please go first. I'll be down right away."

"Don't be long," the youthful voice directed, and the strong, sturdy figure disappeared. The tap-tap of his footsteps echoed for a moment, and then all was quiet. He stood on the staircase in silence, and so did she. The torch in her hand shone for a moment, and then went out.

The two of them stood in the dark and the bitter cold, listening to each other's breathing.

The car horn sounded, twice. She made a movement, as if awakening from a dream. "Xuan," she said, "you'd better go back and sleep. You really must look after your health. . . . We'll say good-bye here. There's no need for you to see me off. I've left you a note in the room," she said tenderly, put-ting out her hand and pressing his. She thought how thin and hard his hand was (although it wasn't that cold)! She sup-pressed her feelings, and in a trembling voice said: "Good-bye!"

Suddenly, he seized her by the arm and cried in anguish and grief: "When shall I see you again? When will you be back?"

"I'm still not sure, but I definitely will be back. I think, in a year at the most," she answered with emotion.

"A year? So long! Can't you make it earlier?" he whispered in despair, afraid that he would not hold out till then.

"I can't be sure, but I'm sure to be able to find some way to make it earlier," she replied. The hateful car horn sounded again. "You mustn't worry," she comforted him. "I'll write when I get there."

"Yes, I'll wait for your letter," he said, wiping his eyes.

"I'll —" Just as she spoke, she was seized by a sudden anguish, and threw herself lightly against him.

He fell back a step, crying out in alarm: "You mustn't come close to me. I've got TB. It's infectious."

But she would not let go. Instead, she opened out her arms and embraced him, pressing her red lips firmly to his withered mouth, kissing him passionately. Only when she heard once more the detestable car horn did she release him and say with tears streaming down her face: "I truly want to be infected by your illness, for then I would never leave you." Wiping her face with her handkerchief, she sighed softly and added: "Say something to your mother for me. I didn't dare disturb her." Finally, moving decisively away from him, she switched on the torch and ran hastily down the remaining flight of stairs.

He stood there for a few minutes in a daze, and then all at once, ran down the stairs after her. In spite of the darkness, nothing caused him to stumble, but when he reached the main entrance, the car had just started. "Shusheng," he called, his voice hoarse and rasping. He thought he saw her face appear at the window, but the car was already moving forward. He ran after it, calling to her, but the car sped like an arrow into the fog. Unable to catch it, he stood there gasping for breath, then started back home in despair. A solitary lamp, resembling the full moon, lit up the part of the footpath outside the

The two of them stood in dark and the bitter cold, listening to each other's breathing.

main entrance. There, at the foot of the wall, lay a pile of human forms. Examining it carefully, he saw two children of about ten hugging each other so tightly that they were rolled in a single ball. He saw the dark, greasy faces, the dirty, greasy, tattered cotton jackets, the cotton-wool patches over the sores that covered their bodies. Even the cotton had turned a dirty grey. The lamplight gently stroked their sleeping faces.

As he looked at them, he began to shiver all over. In this all-embracing terrible bitter cold night, there were only these two sleeping children and himself. He wanted to waken them, to ask them into his flat. He wanted to take off his cotton clothes to cover their bodies. But he did nothing at all. "Tang Baiqing slept like that," he suddenly thought to himself. At the memory of the words spoken by his old school-friend, he covered his face and ran inside as if fleeing from the plague.

When he reached his room, seeing on the desk the note she had left him, he picked it up and read it aloud:

"Xuan:
I'm leaving. You are sleeping so soundly that I can't bear to wake you. You mustn't be upset. I'll write to you when I get there. Mr. Chen is looking after everything. You needn't worry. I have only one thing to ask you: look after yourself and make sure you get proper treatment.
Please say something nice about me to your mother for me.

Your wife"

As he read, his tears fell. The last words especially, "your wife", aroused in him a feeling of gratitude.

He stood before the desk for several minutes, holding on to the note. He felt his whole body go cold. His legs stiffened like ice. Unable to endure it, he took the note to his bed, placed it beside his pillow and then, taking off his cotton gown, crept in under the quilt.

He was unable to fall asleep, tossing about continually. Sometimes he would wake with a start as soon as he closed his eyes. Terrifying demons lay in wait for him in his dreams, until he dared not sleep. He was feverish, his head was dizzy and his ears rang. Just as daylight came, he heard the sound of a plane. "She's gone," he thought, "gone far away. I'll never see her again." He took the note by his pillow and, pressing it in his hand, began to weep softly.

"An honest, inoffensive good sort like you! All you can do is weep!" He thought of the rebuke his wife had once made, but it only made him weep even more brokenheartedly

24

The second day after his wife left, he was confined to bed once more. While he was ill, he received three letters from her, the first of which read:

"Xuan:
I have arrived in Lanzhou. Everything is strange. Only the air is good. The weather is cold, but an uplifting cold.
"The building for the bank is still being renovated, and so we're all staying at a hotel. Mr. Chen is very nice to me, so there's no need for you to worry. It's not easy to settle down when you first reach a strange place. I'll write you a long letter in a couple of days.
"Does your mother still get into a temper? When I was home, I couldn't do anything right. Now that I'm gone, perhaps she won't hate me so much.
"You must look after yourself. Eat more food that is nourishing and builds you up. You mustn't under any circumstances try to save money. I'll send you money every month. Best wishes.

Your wife,
dated. . . ."

Although she gave no return address, this short note cheered him up except for the reference to Mr. Chen. He waited for the next letter. It was not long in coming. He received it three days later. Not only was it quite long, but it was written with sincerity, with many appeals to him to rest quietly and get better, together with a letter of introduction to the chief physician, Dr. Ding, of the Kuanren Hospital. It was

signed Chen Fengguang. Realizing that this was the full name
of the manager, Mr. Chen, he flushed momentarily. He
brought the matter up casually with his mother: "Shusheng
wants me to go to the Kuanren Hospital for a checkup. She's
even asked Mr. Chen to write a letter of introduction." "Huh!"
his mother snorted. "Who cares for his introduction?" He
did not dare explain any further, nor did he dare bring the subject up again. Then he waited for her third letter, which he
believed would be even longer. After a week, the third letter
arrived, very brief, saying only that she was preparing for the
opening of the bank and for a while would not have time to
write at length, but that he should write more and tell her
how his health was. At the end of the letter, she gave a return
address, but had changed to signing simply her name
"Shusheng".

After reading the letter, he sighed, but said nothing. When
his mother put out her hand for the letter, he handed it to her
without a word.

"She's got a nerve! Only ten days gone, and she puts on
the airs of a VIP," his mother said in displeasure after finishing the letter. She had not read Shusheng's first letter.

"She's probably very busy. It's not her fault. The bank's
just opening, and they must be short of hands. If Mr. Chen's
nice to her, she has to make more of an effort," he said, sticking up for his wife and trying his best to hide his disappointment and his doubts (for he did have some small doubts).

"You still think Mr. Chen is only being nice to her! You
just wait. One of these days, they'll show their true colours!"
his mother exclaimed scornfully.

"Mother, it's time for my medicine," he interrupted, not
wanting her to go on (it upset him too much).

"All right, I'll go and brew it for you," his mother said, the
thought of his illness driving "that woman" from her mind.
She looked at him with eyes filled with love and affection.
He was still just as pallid, but the expression in his eyes seemed

a little brighter, his lips a little redder. She hurried from the room.

He sighed again, turning his eyes to the wall. After two or three minutes, he looked away from the bed again, finally resting his eyes on the ceiling. No matter where he looked, he saw her smiling, happy face, made-up like that of a beautiful stage actress. His whole face burned, in his ears echoed a monotonous ringing sound, his eyes were so dry that they seemed about to catch fire. Finally, he fell into an uneasy, fitful sleep.

He had a short, but bizarre dream, moaning from time to time, waking only when his mother came in with the medicine and called him. He was startled, and was sweating profusely. He stared at his mother beseechingly.

"Xuan, what's the matter?" she cried in alarm, almost spilling the medicine from the bowl.

He did not seem to understand what she said. It was a moment before he breathed out very slowly and, his expression changing, said with an effort: "I had so many frightening dreams. I'm better now."

His mother looked at him, not really comprehending. "The medicine's ready. It won't scald you. It's just right to drink now. Will you sit up to take it?" she asked solicitously.

"All right, give it to me," he said, pushing back the cotton quilt and sitting up.

"Quick, put on your jacket, in case you catch cold," his mother enjoined anxiously. After giving him the bowl, she took his cotton gown and placed it over his shoulders. "It's freezing today. It's snowing outside," she observed.

"Is it heavy?" he asked, looking up after taking two large mouthfuls.

"No. It's not sticking to the ground. But it's cold, so if you get up, you must put on plenty of clothes," she told him.

He finished his medicine and gave the bowl back to her. Suddenly, he seized her red, swollen hand and cried in alarm: "Mother, you've got chilblains this year!"

She drew back her hand. "I had them last year too," she said indifferently.

"They weren't as bad as this last year! I don't think you should wash the clothes yourself when it's so cold. It's better to send them out to the washerwoman."

"The washerwoman! Do you know how much it costs for a month?" And without waiting for him to reply, she added: "Fourteen thousand *yuan*. It's almost doubled."

"If it's doubled, it's doubled. But you can't let your hands suffer just to save fourteen thousand *yuan*," he said in distress. "I've really let you down," he added.

"But money's still money. I'd rather save fourteen thousand for your medicine than give it to those washerwomen," his mother said.

"But didn't Shusheng say she'd send money every month? There's no need to save a little sum like that at present," he objected. He stretched himself, took off the cotton gown and lay down again.

His mother said nothing, but her displeasure showed in her face. She turned away abruptly so as not to let him see.

"Mother," he called tenderly. Slowly, she turned back. "You should look after your health too. Why must you bring so much suffering on yourself?"

"I don't suffer," she said, forcing a smile, unconsciously rubbing her itching, swollen hands.

"Don't try to fool me. I know you don't want to spend Shusheng's money," he answered.

"That's not true! I've already been using her money, haven't I?" she said, her voice sharp, her face changing colour and her eyes brimming with tears. She turned away from him, biting her lip.

"Mother, I've really let you down. You've raised me to adulthood, but up to now I still haven't been able to support you," he replied. How she wanted to run to her tiny room and weep her heart out!

"Do you still hate Shusheng?" he asked after a while.

"I don't hate her. I've never hated her," she contended. She was anxious to leave the room at once, for she was afraid he would bring up Shusheng's name again.

"She says she has no hard feelings towards you either," he said.

"Thank her very much," she interrupted coldly.

"Then if she writes to you, will you reply?" he asked timidly.

She considered a moment before answering: "Yes." But she still kept her face from him.

"That's good then," he said with relief, letting escape a sigh.

"You think she'll write to me?" she suddenly asked, turning towards him.

"I think she will," he replied, not altogether confident.

She shook her head, wanting to say: "You're dreaming!" But she got no further than "you" before closing her mouth again. She did not want to shatter his dream, and at the same time, she even hoped that his dream might be realized.

This was all they discussed of Shusheng's doings. In the evening, after his mother had fallen asleep in her little room, he climbed out of bed, put on his clothes, and bent over the desk to reply to Shusheng's letter. He told her about his present situation and his conversation with his mother, asking her to write at once a long letter to his mother expressing her apology and her good feelings towards her. After sealing the letter, he climbed back into bed in utter weariness, and fell into a fitful sleep.

Early next morning, in spite of a fever, he handed the letter to his mother, giving her strict instructions to take it to the post office early and to send it by registered airmail. His mother took the letter without a word, waiting till she had left the flat before shaking her head silently. He had no time to try to guess her thoughts. His cheeks were flushed (from the fever), but his eyes were bright with hope, as if in expectation of a miracle.

Because of writing the letter, he had to spend the next four days in bed. But a week passed without the postman's knocking at the door. The next week, her letter came, registered airmail as before. He tore it open, his heart beating fast. But as he finished reading, his face clouded. Enclosed with a postal remittance was a one-page letter consisting of a few scrawled lines: The opening of the bank was imminent; she was too busy to write his mother a long letter, please excuse her; she was sending a postal remittance by air for the household expenses; she hoped he would be sure to go to the hospital for a checkup.

"What does she say?" his mother asked, when she saw the expression on his face.

"She's well, but busy," he answered briefly. He handed the money order and the envelope to his mother: "Here, you'd better take this."

His mother took it, frowned, but said nothing.

"Mother, you'd better give the clothes to the washerwoman in future. It's decided today," he said. "You don't have to economize so hard, since Shusheng will be sending money every month."

"But this ten thousand *yuan* won't go far," his mother protested.

"Mother, you forget the money for household expenses she left behind," he reminded her.

"But we've already spent part of it, haven't we? What's left may not be enough for Xiao Xuan's tuition and boarding fees. Last time it was already over twenty thousand. This term, who knows? It might even come to fifty thousand." When she saw that he did not answer, she waited for a moment before adding: "In fact, I've been thinking of getting him to change schools. How can children of poor families like us attend such a posh school? If he goes to a state school, it'll save a lot of money."

"It's his mother's idea. I think it's better to leave him there. Last time he sat the entrance exams, she had to talk to all sorts of people for ages before he was finally accepted," he said, disagreeing with her. I can't go against her wishes, he thought.

"Then you should write and remind her that there's still not enough for his tuition and ask her to do something about it soon," she declared.

"All right," he answered curtly, though he had not decided whether he would write any such thing.

"I still think we should get Xiao Xuan to live at home, and then there'd be one more person to keep you company," his mother said, changing the subject.

He thought for a moment before saying: "Since he wrote to say that he wants to stay at a friend's place for the holidays, because it makes revising easier, we might as well let him go. Why make him come home?"

"It seems to me that you're too lonely. If he comes back, there'll be a warmer atmosphere at home," his mother observed.

"But he might catch what I've got. It's best that he stay away from me. He's too young, and it's easy for him to catch something," he murmured in a low voice.

"All right, as you wish," his mother answered simply. Although upset, she put on an air of perfect calm. She moved away. But just as she reached the window on the right, she turned towards him again, and looked at him with love and affection: "You should relax a bit and not think so much about your illness. You're still young after all, so you shouldn't keep tormenting yourself all the time."

Lifting his head slightly to look at her, he nodded and replied: "I know. Don't worry."

"I can survive this kind of life. I'm a useless old woman, but it's really too hard on you. You shouldn't have to live like this," she suddenly remarked after a while, for she was unable to restrain the feelings surging inside her.

"Mother, don't worry. I'm sure we'll manage to survive. If we last out till the war's over, then you'll be all right." The words were spoken to comfort his mother. He said "you" and not "we" because he was afraid, no, he was sure that he himself would not survive till then.

"I'm afraid I won't last till then. By the look of things, that will be in the dim and distant future," his mother said, sighing with emotion. "I met a man on the first floor today who said the war would be over this year. In fact, the year's just begun, there are twelve months to go. And what are we going to win with, I'd really like to know!"

"You worry about it too much, Mother. In any case, the Japanese can't reach here at present. Everyone will be pleased if we can only hold on." He smiled sorrowfully as he spoke.

"Yes, that's right. When the Japanese were approaching Guiyang these last few days, everyone was scared out of his wits. Now they've withdrawn, it's as if nothing happened. The rich can eat and dress well again, and the officials and big businessmen are as overweening as ever. To speak no one else, look at that manager, that Mr. Chen of hers ..." his mother said.

"They're holding on too," he replied, with a sad smile.

"Well, if we hold on till the war's won, they'll still be the lucky ones," his mother said resentfully.

"Of course, that goes without saying," he answered with a bitter smile.

His mother said nothing more, but watched him in silence. He too would cast his eyes in her direction from time to time. The two of them had the feeling of having said all there was to say. The room seemed especially big (though it was not in fact large), especially cold (though the sun was shining in, but rather weakly). Time seemed to have stopped. The two of them sat there listlessly: he in the cane chair, his back to the desk, his hands in his sleeves, his head becoming heavier and heavier, his body hunched more and more; his mother with her hand on her cheek, her elbow resting on the square table, feeling herself blink continuously from boredom. A big rat ran back and forth in front of them, carefree and leisurely, but they did nothing to chase it away.

As the room grew gradually darker, their mood also seemed to grow more dismal. They felt the chill night air creep slowly through the soles of their shoes up their legs.

"I'll go and cook," his mother said, getting up lazily.

"It's early yet. Wait for a while," he said, as if pleading with her.

She sat down again in silence, unable to think of what to say. A moment later, the room became almost totally dark. She stood up again. "It's not early now. I'll go and cook."

He stood up too. "I'll come and help you," he said.

"You stay where you are. I can do it on my own," she answered, stopping him.

"It's better if I do something. Sitting by myself is so depressing," he said, following her out.

They prepared a simple meal and ate mechanically. Neither of them ate much. After eating and washing the bowls and chopsticks, the two sat down again where they had been before, and after a few desultory remarks, felt once more that they had exhausted all there was to say. When he looked at the time (on his mother's watch) and found it was seven o'clock, it still seemed early. They suffered time to pass, holding on until finally at half past eight, his mother retired to her small room, and he climbed into bed to sleep.

This was not just one day in their lives. Every day of the winter passed in this way. The only differences were that sometimes there was a power cut and they went to bed earlier; sometimes she would relate to him some old story she had told him dozens of times before; sometimes Xiao Xuan would come home for a night, adding a little warmth to the room (though how much warmth could that little bookworm add, who disliked talking and never laughed); sometimes his health would be better; sometimes his spirits would be at a low ebb.

"Apart from eating, sleeping, being ill, what else can I do?" he frequently asked himself. But there was never any answer, and he would brush aside the question with a despairing smile. Once he almost obtained a reply. At the terrible word (Death), a shiver ran up his spine, and his whole body shuddered. He could almost see his own body rotting, the maggots crawling all over it. For many days afterwards, he dared not let his mind stray at random.

His mother could not comfort him, for it was his secret. Even less could his wife of any consolation, although she wrote him frequent short letters (at least once a week). She was always busy, but never failed to show her concern for his health, and in each letter, she would ask after his mother, though she never wrote a single letter to her directly as he had asked. From this, from her "busyness", from the "brevity" of her letters, he felt that she was becoming separated from him even further. He never said a word to his mother about his wife, but frequently he would secretly calculate the physical distance that separated him from her.

25

The bitter cold of the winter days finally passed like a nightmare. Spring brought with it hope, dispersing the thick fog with its breeze. People discussed the news of the war with smiles and laughter.

But Wang Wenxuan's life did not change at all. As before, his health improved on some days, deteriorated on others. When he felt better, he would go for a walk; when worse, he would lie all day in bed. His mother cooked the meals as usual, swept and tidied the flat, and when he was ill, prepared the medicine as well. Xiao Xuan came home once a fortnight, stayed the night and would talk briefly about one or two events at school, but it was even more difficult to get a smile out of the child. When he was home, no sound of laughter echoed in the room, but once he was gone, the flat became even more desolate. His wife continued to write, a letter every week, a postal remittance every month. The letters were never more than three pages, though the words and phrases were filled with boundless, deep feeling. She was forever busy. But he remained always patient, posting a letter every week, frequently fabricating lies to hide from her his true condition. Writing letters became his only distraction, his only work even.

As the spring days grew longer, how to get through the day became a painful problem. He felt that he would soon lose the power of speech. Once, having caught a cold, he almost lost his voice and could speak only in a hoarse whisper. His mother looked much older, talking less and less. Often, mother and son would sit in the room, facing each other without a sound. Sometimes, he spoke fewer than thirty sentences in a day.

Time passed as if being dragged slowly along by an aged, sick rickshaw puller, so slowly that at times it even seemed to him that the rickshaw had come to a halt.

But he continued to live, continued to feel, continued to think. Frequently, the left side of his chest ached. At night, he often perspired, often had a dry cough. From time to time he would cough blood — or rather, sputum streaked with blood. His misery continued, and became worse and worse. The sound of happy laughter had already become a vague memory in a distant past.

He neither groaned nor showed resentment. Silently, he saw one grey day out, to welcome in one even greyer. His speech became less frequent, for he was afraid of hearing the rasping of his own voice. Sometimes, he was so depressed that he did not know what to do. He could only sigh at length, but not wanting his mother to hear, he would sigh only when no one was present.

The days grew longer and longer, and more and more difficult to endure. One thought tortured him: His spiritual strength was fast becoming exhausted, and he would not be able to hold out.

But no one would allow him not to go on. His wife kept urging him to rest and get better, to wait for her return. Old

Mr. Zhong promised to do something about finding him a suitable job. His mother continually bought medicine for him to take, bringing home both traditional Chinese prescriptions and famous Western medicines. He did not know whether they were beneficial to his health or not. He simply kept taking them, obediently and continually, largely as a duty to his mother. Once his mother even dragged him to the Kuanren Hospital for a checkup. He thought of the letter of introduction sent by his wife, but could find it nowhere. In fact, his mother had long since torn it up. Not wishing to spend too much money registering as a special patient, he signed in as an ordinary one, and had to wait altogether three hours. Since his mother had already given in so far as to drag him to the hospital, he just had to put up with it and wait his turn, regardless of how crowded the outpatients' department was. And the courtyard was so cold (it was before the coming of spring). A doctor with a thin moustache gave him an icy stare, ordered him to unbutton his clothes, listened for a moment with his stethoscope, tapped him here, there, and everywhere, then frowned and shook his head. Telling him to button up again, he then wrote out a prescription and instructed him to go to the pharmacy section to buy a bottle of medicine. The doctor did not seem very communicative, simply telling him to come back the next week for a screening by fluoroscope. An X-ray would be better, he said, but a screening was cheaper. When he came out, he asked the cost of a screening at the inquiries' desk, and silently left the hospital, his tongue curled between his teeth. Afterwards, he went to the hospital again, when the doctor told him once more to come for a screening the following week, but after calculating quickly how much he had already spent in a month, and guessing at the likely result of a screening, he dared not go to the hospital again.

"What will be, will be. Let it happen," he said to himself, deciding to "listen to the will of Heaven". In reality, there was no other way he could set his mind at ease.

One day after lunch, he went for a walk. The weather was fine, but the road was still covered in dust, with cars and carts absolutely chock-a-block and in complete chaos. Heaped on a street corner was a huge pile of rotting rubbish, giving off a stench which made him hold his nose as he crossed the road. Turning his head casually to one side to have a look, he found himself staring at the glass windows of the International Coffee Shop, in which were displayed several large birthday cakes and several different kinds of American sweets. It was exactly as it had been some months before. The sole difference was that there was one person whose voice he failed to hear, and whose alluring figure he failed to see.

He went in. There were quite a large number of customers in the lounge, but so happened that the small round table at which he had previously sat was empty, and so he pushed his way in and sat down. Two waiters were running hurriedly about with trays, while the customers competed for their attention in a hubbub of voices. He sat down timidly in the corner and waited in silence.

A waiter in a white uniform eventually came over. "Two cups of coffee," he ordered in a low voice.

"Huh?" the waiter grunted rudely.

"Two cups of coffee," he repeated, raising his voice.

Without replying, the waiter turned abruptly and went off, returning a moment later with two cups of coffee, one of which he placed in front of Wang Wenxuan, and the other opposite him. "Milk?" the waiter asked, holding up a tin of milk. He shook his head. "No," he replied, but pointing to the cup opposite, said: "Milk for this one." The waiter poured the milk into the cup and went off still holding the tin. Picking up the teaspoon, he scooped up some sugar, putting some first in the cup opposite and giving it a stir with the spoon, before adding sugar to his own cup.

"Go on, drink!" he said softly, raising his cup to the empty seat opposite. In his imagination, Shusheng was sitting there

facing him. She liked white coffee. He seemed to see her
smile at him, and feeling very happy, he took a large mouthful.
He smiled. He stared with wide-open eyes at the seat opposite
him. It was empty, and the cup, full of coffee, remained untouched. He drank another mouthful. On his lips was the
same smile as before, but gradually the smile changed into a
smile of desolation. "Do you still remember me?" he whispered,
his heart throbbing uncontrollably. He felt his nose tingle.
He turned to look at the other customers. The room was
crowded with people talking animatedly in a thick haze of
cigarette and tobacco smoke. No one paid him any attention.

"I'm willing to guarantee that in two months Germany will
surrender. The Japanese can't last a year. We might even be
celebrating the next New Year in Nanjing!" a big man at the
neighbouring table, wearing a Sun Yat-sen jacket, shouted exul-
tantly, his eyebrows dancing and his face radiant.

Startled, he looked at the speaker. The prediction gave him
a strange feeling, not of happiness, but rather of admiration
and jealousy. He gazed once more at the empty seat and the
cup full of coffee. A distracted sigh escaped him. He stood
up, paid his bill, and left.

Just as he reached home, he ran into his mother carrying a
pile of wet clothes from the flat.

"Mother, why are you washing the clothes yourself again?"
he asked in surprise.

"It's nothing. I can wash them," she replied, smiling.

"But you shouldn't try to save such a little bit of money, and
you shouldn't tire yourself so much," he said.

"But the washerwomen have raised their prices again, and
Shusheng sends so little that if we don't economize, there
won't be enough!" his mother said in some agitation. "I don't
know how much prices have gone up since the New Year, but
our income doesn't go up. What else can I do!"

"She still sends more than I get when I'm earning,"
he thought, but he did not dare contradict his mother. Instead,

he went silently into the flat, leaving her to hang out the clothes to dry on the sunporch.

He was alone in the flat. He had no desire to sit, to lie down or to read. He just paced backwards and forwards about the room.

"Why is she always so busy? Why does she always write such short letters? Since she's concerned about me, why doesn't she let me know what her life's like?" he thought in agitation, his mind full of doubts.

There was no answer. He would never find the answer.

But then came an interruption. He heard the sound of heavy footsteps. Then a postman pushed open the door and shouted: "Letter for Wang Wenxuan! Stamp the receipt!"

He took the letter, a thick letter in an envelope covered all over with stamps. He recognized Shusheng's handwriting at a glance.

In a wave of happiness, he stamped his seal on the receipt, which he gave back to the postman. "Thank you so much," he said gratefully.

A long letter had finally arrived. This was just the answer he needed. He kissed the letter over and over in gratitude, laughing softly to himself as he read the address on the envelope over and over again, forgetting his anxieties, forgetting even his illness.

Then he tore open the envelope and took out a thick sheaf of letter-writing paper.

"She's written me a long letter! She's written me a long letter!" he repeated to himself many, many times, chuckling to himself. He spread out the pages, but had read only the word "Xuan", when he quickly folded up the letter again, and waltzed excitedly about the room a few times.

Finally, he sat down in the cane chair, and slowly and unhurriedly unfolded the sheaf of pages, and began to read her letter.

26

The pages were all in her handwriting, the characters very neatly written, but the tone was quite different from usual. She no longer talked of being busy or of the affairs of the bank. Instead, she revealed her innermost thoughts, pouring out her misery. His hands began to tremble as he followed the words, holding his breath as he read on. The words were like iron claws tearing into his heart. But he could not help thinking: "Why does she say all this?" for already, he had a premonition.

She continued to lay bare what was in her mind:

". . . I know that this temper of mine may eventually destroy me, may bring misery to the people who are kind to me. I know too that in the last two or three years, I have given you not just a little pain and grief. I admit too that during these two or three years, I have not been a good wife to you. Yes, I realize that there are many ways in which I have let you down (but I have never done anything scandalous behind your back that is not fit to be revealed). Sometimes, I have been reproved by my conscience, but . . . I don't know how best to say it, I don't know how to make you understand my thoughts.... Especially during the last year or two, I have felt that together we cannot be happy, that there is some vital link missing between us. You don't understand me. Often, when I got angry, you would give in to me. Instead of answering back fiercely, you would just look at me with beseeching eyes. How I came to fear that look, to hate that look! Why are you so weak! At those moments, how I hoped that you would quarrel with me, beat me, curse me. I would have felt happy. But you only implored, you only sighed, you only wept. Afterwards, I was always sorry, and I would often apologize to you. I told myself that in future I must be nicer to you. But I could only pity you, I could not love you anymore. You didn't use to be such a weakling! . . ."

A knock at the door suddenly interrupted him. A man shouted from outside the door: "Wang, old man!"

He was startled, and promptly folded the letter and slipped it into the breast pocket of his inner jacket. Old Mr. Zhong had already entered the room.

"Wang, old man, you're home. Have you been keeping well? You haven't been out?" Mr. Zhong said in a hearty voice, his face beaming.

"Please sit down, do!" he said politely, forcing himself to smile, his mind still on the letter. "I suppose you've been pretty busy lately," he said casually, as he poured a cup of boiled water for his guest. His movements were very slow, for before his eyes he still saw the face of a woman, the face of Shusheng, serious and severe.

"No thanks, no tea, no tea. I had some just before I came," Mr. Zhong said politely, nodding his head the while.

"We've got only boiled water here. Have a cup while you're here," he said, slightly shame-faced, placing the cup in front of old Mr. Zhong.

"I'll have some water then," Mr. Zhong said, smiling. "Boiled water is good for the health." He accepted the cup, took a sip, and then putting down the cup, said: "Isn't your mother at home? Has she been keeping all right?" He looked all around.

"Quite well, thank you." He also smiled, but at once became serious again, for his heart was pounding furiously, his thoughts still on the letter. "She's just gone out," he added hastily, remembering suddenly the other's question. He did not explain that his mother was out on the sunporch hanging up the clothes.

"I've got some good news for you," Mr. Zhong said, a pleased smile spreading slowly over his face. "Mr. Zhou at the office has been promoted and has left. The new head of department, Mr. Fang, is not a manager. He's very kind to me. Yesterday, I talked to him about you. He sympathizes with you, and wants you to come back to your old post. He asked me to come and talk it over with you first. So there's no problem about your job, old man!"

"Yes, I see," he replied, just smiling indifferently, showing no sign of joy at all. His eyes were directed elsewhere, as if he were not listening.

"Then, when will you start work, old man?" Mr. Zhong asked, surprised at his reaction. He had thought that he would be overjoyed at the good news he brought, and had never imagined that he would show not even the slightest excitement.

"What about in a couple of days? Ah! Thank you for the trouble you've taken," he said, as if waking suddenly. He had raised his voice, and was about to smile, when he changed his mind midway, and became serious and unsmiling once more.

"Is your health all right? Is there anything still wrong?" old Mr. Zhong asked, this time with an air of concern.

"No, I'm fine," he answered, looking at his interlocutor with a start and shaking his head. He was still thinking: What was behind what Shusheng had written? Surely she didn't really — he suddenly reddened, and his face began to twitch.

"Then come to work as soon as possible. If you wait too long, they might change their minds. It's not an easy chance to get," Mr. Zhong urged again after a moment's pause.

"Yes, I'll definitely come in two days' time," he answered briefly, and then said nothing more. Mr. Zhong glanced at him in surprise, realizing that there must be something on his mind, yet afraid to ask. To continue talking was not going to arouse his interest. The kindhearted old man then sat a little longer, chatted a little longer and then, feeling that there was no further point, said good-bye and left.

He accompanied old Mr. Zhong to the door, without making any effort to detain him. At the stairwell, Mr. Zhong asked him politely to go back in, but he insisted on seeing his guest to the main entrance.

"Wang, old man, please come and start work as soon as you can," Mr. Zhong urged once more as he said good-bye to him at the front entrance.

"Definitely," he replied, bowing respectfully, and turning, hurried back up the stairs, running into an old servant on the way carrying a pot of boiling water. Drops of water splashed onto the back of his foot, scalding him and causing him to cry out.

The old woman broke into foul language. He apologized at once, and fled up the stairs, supporting the pain as best he could. His mind was still bound to those pages of writing-paper. Nothing else could be of any concern to him. Not even the "good news" brought by Mr. Zhong could give him any joy.

When he came back into the flat, his mother was still absent. She usually came back in after putting out the clothes to dry, but she was not there, giving him just the chance he needed to read the letter in peace. Sitting down in the cane chair, he took out his wife's letter again, but before he had even commenced reading, his heart began to beat wildly and his hands began to tremble as if with cold.

Finding the place where he had been interrupted, he continued to read:

". . . Everything I say is true. Please believe me. I feel that there is no happiness in the life we have led, and there can be no happiness in the future. I cannot say it is your fault, nor can I say that I am faultless. We made each other miserable, we made your mother miserable, and she made you and me miserable. I don't understand why this was so. Moreover, we have no way of getting rid of or of lightening this misery. It is no one person's fault. None of us can blame anyone else. But I don't believe it is due to fate. At the very least, these wrongs can be blamed on our circumstances. I am quite different from you and your mother. Your mother is old, and you are weak and always ill. But I am still young, still full of vitality. I cannot be like you two and live out these unchanging, monotonous days. I cannot dissipate my life in tedious quarrels and lonely suffering. I want movement, I want excitement. I need a life of enthusiasm. I cannot wither away in a home like yours that resembles an ancient temple. I cannot lie to you: I really did try to be a good wife, to be a virtuous wife and a worthy mother. I know that you still love me now, and I don't have any hard feelings towards you. I really did want to do everything possible to make you happy. But I failed to do it, I can't do it. I devoted a great deal of energy to this, and I have refused every kind of temptation. I once vowed never to leave you, to remain always with you, to go through a life of poverty and hardship with you. But each time I tried to keep this vow, I failed.

"And you did not understand the suffering I went through. Moreover, the kinder you were towards me (and you have never done anything to me that you need regret), the more your mother hated me. She seemed to hate me to the very marrow. In fact, I have for her only pity, that in her old age, she has to taste poverty and hardship. No matter how much she boasts of being well-educated, of being moral, now that she is over fifty, she is merely a second-class amah, cooking meals, washing clothes, cleaning the house, and which of these does she do to perfection! But because she looks on me as the mistress who enslaves her, she hates me, to the point where she no longer cares whether she smashes our love and our happiness as a family. I still remember the expression of cruel satisfaction on her face when she cursed me as your 'whore'.

"But all this is idle talk. Please forgive me for commenting on your mother to your face. But I do not hate her. Why should I hate her? The life she has led has been many times harder than mine. She was right when she said that we were never formally married, and that I am only your 'whore'. That is why I am writing to you formally to say that from now on, I am no longer your 'whore', that I am leaving you. I may perhaps marry someone else, in which case, I will be certain to indulge in a little extravagance to let your mother see. . . . On the other hand, I may never marry. What significance would there be in leaving you to marry someone else? In short, I do not wish to come back to your family, to live the life as your 'whore'. You wanted me to write her a long letter expressing my apology. How deeply you wounded me! Even if I had been willing to write, willing to give her a handle against myself, do you think she would really stop hating me? You expect me to flaunt myself as your 'whore', become a slave daughter-in-law, so that she can humiliate me, so that you can live a sweet family life. You really are dreaming!"

He cried out in pain, as if someone had struck a gong in his ear, causing his whole head to reverberate until it was numb. After a long while, he finally let escape a sigh. The pages of the letter were strewn all over the floor. He hastily picked them up and read greedily on, his forehead moist with sweat, his body damp.

"Xuan, please forgive me. I am not taking a pique against you, neither am I joking with you. I'm telling the truth, and moreover, I've thought it over for a long time. If we live together, we can only be a torment to each other, we can only harm each other. Moreover, while your mother is alive, there can never be any peace or happiness for us. We must separate. Apart, we can perhaps still remain close friends, but together, we will one day become strangers. I know that leaving you while you are ill may upset you. But I am thirty-five this year. I cannot continue to waste my life. Time for us women is short. I'm not being selfish. I simply want to live, to live a life to the full. I want to be free. Unfortunately, I have never achieved happiness in all my life. Why shouldn't I live in bliss and comfort for once? Each of us lives only once, and once the opportunity is lost, everything is over. It is for my future that I must leave you. I want to be free. I know you will forgive me, sympathize with me.

"I haven't brought up the word 'divorce', because according to your mother, we were never married. And so our separation does not require any formalities. I don't ask for alimony from you, nor do I need any written document from you. Even less do I demand to take Xiao Xuan with me. I don't want anything. I only beg you to let me help you get better. From today onwards, I am no longer your wife, no longer Mrs. Wang. You will find another woman with a good temper to be your wife, one who will understand you, who will love you more than I do, and who will worship your mother. I am no good for you. I am neither a virtuous wife nor a worthy mother. These last few years, there have definitely been ways in which I have let you down, let Xiao Xuan down. I am not worthy to be your wife or his mother. I am not a good woman, and these last two years, I have changed a good deal. But I have no way out. When I leave you, you may perhaps be miserable for a while, but at most, it will not be for more than one or two years. After that, you will forget me. There are so many women better than I am. I hope the woman who fills my place will make your mother content. You had better let her choose, and moreover, make sure the bride rides in a sedan chair to take part in a grand ceremony in a church. . . ."

He let out a groan, and with one hand madly seized his hair. The left side of his chest had been aching terribly, but now not only the left side, but his whole chest was in pain. Why did she wound him so cruelly? She must know that each word would be like a sharp needle, and that each needle would suck up his life's blood. In what had he ever wronged her? Her hatred for him was so deep after all! She couldn't be thrusting such needles into a man powerless to resist simply to be free! At this thought, he looked up, groaning like a man wrongly accused. He wanted to cry: "Why do the catastrophes all fall on my head? Why am I alone punished? What after all have I done wrong?"

There was no answer. He could not find a fair judge. At that moment, he could not even find one person to share the burden of his misery. He sat there, gazing unseeingly at the ceiling. But at what? He himself did not know.

After some time, suddenly realizing that he had not finished the letter, he bent over to fix his eyes on the pages and continue reading:

"[Two and a quarter lines were crossed out, and he was unable to make out what the words were] I myself do not know why I am writing so much. My first idea was actually this: I don't want to see your mother again, and I want to be free. Xuan, please forgive me. You see, I really have changed a great deal. At this time, in this kind of life, what way is there for a woman alone like me, who has never harmed anyone, who has never done anything evil? Don't speak to me of ideals, for we are no longer qualified to talk about ideals or about education. Xuan, don't be upset. Let me go. Release me quietly. Forget me, and don't think of me anymore. I am not worthy of you, but I am not a wicked woman. I have committed only one wrong: to desire freedom and happiness.

"I don't want to write to Xiao Xuan. Please explain to him for me. I cannot make it clear to him myself, and besides, it is not certain that before long, I will have lost the right to be his mother. But I hope you won't all misunderstand. I am not leaving you because I wish to marry someone else, although someone has already proposed to me. Up till now, I have not yet accepted. Moreover, I do not wish to accept. But you must also understand my situation. There cannot but be times when a woman is weak. I am afraid for myself. I have my weaknesses, and I cannot find a genuine friend who can help me. Xuan, dear Xuan, I know you love me very much. I beg you then to let me go, to give me my freedom, and not to call me any longer by the empty name of 'wife', so that this world of contradictory feelings, this hatred of your mother's, will not force me into this dead end that can lead only to ruin and disgrace. . . .

"Please forgive me. Don't think of me as an evil woman. Please give my regards to your mother. I am no longer her son's 'whore'. She need not waste her energy any more in hating me. Be sure to look after your health, and concentrate on getting better. I shall continue to send every month the household expenses given by the bank, so that Xiao Xuan's schooling will not be interrupted. Also, please allow me to remain your close friend and continue to write to you. I hope you are all well.

"If possible, I hope to hear from you soon. A few words will do.

Shusheng,
Dated. . . ."

The letter ended, and for him too, all had ended. He fell dejectedly against the back of the chair, closed his eyes, remaining a long moment as if dead. He was suddenly wakened by his mother calling. He sat up in alarm and relaxed his grip, letting the pages of the letter fall to the ground.

"Mother, why has it taken you so long to put the clothes out to dry?" he asked.

"I went out. Xuan, why don't you go to bed and rest?" his

mother said. Seeing the pages of the letter on the ground, she asked: "Who's the letter from?" and went to pick up the pages.

"Mother, I'll do it." He bent down at once to gather the pages, explaining as he did so: "It's from Shusheng."

"Such a long one. What did she have to say?" she then asked.

"Nothing much," he replied, flustered, and promptly slipped the letter under his gown, obviously trying to conceal it. My daughter-in-law must have said something against me to her husband, his mother thought. She could not help remarking:

"She must have said something nasty about me. I don't care. Let her say what she likes!"

"Mother, she hasn't said anything about you. She was writing about other things, about . . . her life there, about Mr. Chen's attitude to her . . ." he said, defending the letter-writer aloud, but before he was halfway through, his voice became husky, and he had to stop in mid-stream.

Noticing this, his mother asked no more about the letter. She thought of something else and changed the subject:

"I ran into Mr. Zhong just now. He said he'd already spoken to you, that your job is all fixed, and that you can go back to the firm to work. But I said, if the new head is easy to talk to, it would be best to let you have another couple of months' rest before starting work. As long as he's willing to help by arranging things first, there won't be any difficulty."

"I think I'll go tomorrow," he said, his face showing not the slightest joy.

"Why be in such a hurry? There'll be plenty of time if we wait till Mr. Zhong comes back with his answer," his mother said.

"Zhong Lao wants me to go as soon as possible. He says if we wait too long, things might change," he answered, making an effort to appear indifferent. But he felt as if worms were gnawing at his lungs, eating into his heart.

"But tomorrow's a bit too early. Perhaps you could go the day after tomorrow to see what the situation's like. Don't go tomorrow. Tomorrow, I'll cook you some nice dishes. I want to invite Zhang Boqing as well. He's been to see you so many times, and we haven't much money to give him," his mother said, assuming an air of happiness.

After a moment's thought, he looked at his mother's face, and then cried wretchedly: "Mother, what have you pawned this time? What have you sold? For my sake, you have sold every little thing of value that you have!"

"It's nothing. Don't you worry about it," his mother replied, her smile becoming more and more unnatural.

"But you don't think! What if I were to die? What would you do then? What would you live on?" he cried, pointing at his mother as if he were arguing with her.

"Don't you worry. I'll die before you do. Besides, there's still Xiao Xuan. He'll grow up one day. And there's Shusheng. She's your wife after all, and my daughter-in-law," his mother said, smiling and putting on a nonchalant air, but she felt as if her heart was in the grip of iron claws.

"Mother, how can you rely on them! Xiao Xuan is so young, and Shusheng — " As soon as the last words slipped out, he stopped instantly. But the feeling he had let escape could not be retracted. Tears sprang from his eyes. He stood up abruptly, saying nothing at all, and left the flat.

He heard his mother calling him, but instead of answering, he hurried quickly down the stairs. But when he reached the main entrance, he began to hesitate. He stared at the dust from the street, not knowing which way to turn. He stood on the footpath outside the building as if his feet had taken root, looking first to the east and then to the west. Before him were the figures of strangers with whom he had not the slightest connection. In this vast universe, only he, a tiny weak invalid, was unable to find a place on which to set his feet! He was all alone, and how deep his loneliness was, even he could not tell. The tear stains on his face had still not dried. His mind was a complete void.

The counter of the draper's shop next door was piled with cloth of every kind and colour. Business seemed good. Three fashionably dressed young women (perhaps not so fashionable after all) were laughing and chatting as they selected cotton prints. On the other side, in front of a newly-opened eating-place, stood two billboards, from one of which a young woman smiled enticingly at the passers-by.

"They're all happier than I am," he reflected. But he never thought about who "they" might finally be. He felt his chest begin once more to throb and ache, and unconsciously pressed his hand to it.

"Xuan! Xuan!" He heard his mother's voice calling from behind him. He turned his head vaguely. As soon as she reached his side, his mother, panting, asked: "Where are you going?"

"For a walk," he answered indifferently.

"You look terrible. You'd better go another day," his mother urged. "In any case, there's nothing you have to do."

He said nothing. "You'd better go back inside," his mother urged again.

He thought for a while. Actually, his brain was not functioning. He merely stared for a moment and said: "No, Mother, let me go for a walk," and then added in an undertone: "I'm in low spirits."

His mother gave a long sigh, looked at him doubtfully, and urged softly: "Then come back soon. Don't go too far."

"All right," he replied, and brushing past her, he set off, while she stood at the entrance and watched his back slowly disappear.

He walked aimlessly ahead, neither rapidly, nor yet dawdling. He cherished a vague hope of finding a place where he could forget everything, or where he could simply annihilate himself. The burden of his suffering was too great, his shoulders could not support it. He could not bear the piecemeal oppressions, the endless torment. He would rather end it all in exultation.

People ran into him, rickshaws knocked against his legs. His feet hurt as he stumbled on the stones and bricks in the uneven pavement. His eyes could no longer distinguish the light or colours. All was an endless stretch of grey. His whole world was only an endless stretch of grey.

His feet brought him to a stop in front of a small shop. Why? He did not know himself. He went in and sat down on a stool. The wine-shop was not strange to him. He had sat at this place beside the square table before.

The waiter came over and asked: "A cup of *hongzao*?"

"Yes, quickly," he cried, as if waking up, although in fact, the waiter's words had not registered.

When the waiter brought the wine, he gulped a great mouthful unthinkingly. A wave of warm air rushed up his throat, and unable to bear it, he hiccupped. He put down the wine cup and drew Shusheng's letter from under his gown, placing it on the table. Then he lifted the cup to take another mouthful of wine. He hiccupped again. He was too resentful to drink. He took the letter and casually turned the pages, reading a few sentences under his breath. He was so upset that tears flowed once more. He tried not to read the letter, but as soon as he folded it, he could not stop himself from unfolding it again, reading a few sentences softly. He became even more upset, and tears streamed down. He lifted the wine cup determinedly, drinking in huge gulps. He felt a rush of hot air enter his stomach. His throat itched and his stomach churned. His head was afire, his thoughts stopped and his mind became more and more confused. But the words and sentences in the letter lashed unceasingly like a whip at his benumbed emotions.

The wine shop was very quiet in the daytime. Apart from himself, there were only two customers, drinking together in a tête-à-tête. All the other tables were empty. No one paid him any attention. Seeing his wine cup empty, the waiter came over to ask: "Do you want some more *hongzao*?"

"No, no." He shook his head vaguely, his face crimson, although he had drunk less than two ounces of wine.

The waiter stood to one side, looking at him in wonder, but he did not notice. He kept turning the pages of her letter, without knowing how many times he read it.   He was no longer weeping.   He simply kept shaking his head and sighing.

"Some more *hongzao*?" the waiter came again to ask, seeing that he neither moved nor left.

"Yes, all right," he answered briefly.   As soon as the wine arrived, he drank a big mouthful at once.   He put down the cup.   His body felt hot and his head was dizzy.   He looked down and stared at the letter, but his mind was elsewhere.   All at once, he sensed that someone had sat down opposite him, but he kept his head down, drinking.   When he looked up, he stared with wide-open eyes.   There was no one there.   "I was thinking of Tang Baiqing," he muttered, rubbing his eyes. He looked down again and dimly perceived Tang Baiqing looking at him with a bitter smile.   "How can I have reached the same point as he?" he asked miserably. He leapt up suddenly as if he had heard an alert, paid and went out.

All the way, Tang Baiqing's shadow pursued him.   He had only one idea: to reach home.

It was not until he arrived home that he felt calmer.   As soon as he entered the flat, he sat down and wrote Shusheng a letter.   He gave vague answers to his mother's chatting without hearing a word she said.   In his letter, he wrote:

> "I received your letter and have read it several times.   Apart from apologizing to you, there is nothing I have to say.   To have ruined your youth is a great wrong on my part.   The only way to redress this is to give you back your freedom.   Everything you say is true. We will do everything as you say. I only beg you to forgive me.
> "The firm has agreed to give me back my job.   I start work tomorrow.   Please do not send any more money for household expenses; my mother and I can manage on my salary.   Please don't worry.   I am not writing out of pique, because I shall love you till I die. Wishing you every happiness!
>
> > Wenxuan,
> > Dated. . . ."

He wrote all this without effort, in a single breath.   But as soon as he had finished, he felt drained of all his strength.   It was as if the whole building had collapsed.   He was finished.

His whole world was in ruins.   He fell onto the desk in despair and wept softly.

"Xuan, what is it?   What's the matter?" his mother cried in alarm, running at once to his side.

He lifted his head, letting her see the tear stains covering his face, and weeping like a small child, he said: "Read her letter." But the letter he gave her was the one he had written and not Shusheng's.

His mother read the brief note. There was no need for him to explain. She understood everything. "I told you long ago," she said, "that she wouldn't stay with you forever. Now what! I saw through her ages ago!"

She was indignant, but also happy and content. Her first reaction was to look on it as a blessing. It never occurred to her that she ought to sympathize with her son.

27

Shusheng's letter was like a stone thrown into a pool, raising ripples for a moment and disturbing the entire surface of the water, then the surface became calm once more, and the stone sank to the bottom, to remain there forever, impossible to remove.   Afterwards, she kept writing, at least three letters a month. She wrote briefly, saying nothing of her own life, simply asking after Xiao Xuan's health and his own, and about how they were getting on. She continued to send the monthly money orders. His mother wanted him to send them back, but instead of doing as she asked, he kept the money. He did not use it, but neither did he send it back. He put it all in a fixed-deposit account as she had suggested, and wrote to her, requesting her not to send any more. But she did not seem to read what he said, for the following month, she sent the money as usual. He asked her to tell him how she was, but she never said a word, apart from reporting now and then that she was busy or that she was fine. He bore all this in silence, not wanting to write or to do anything that might wound her.

He had work and an income. Two days after receiving her long letter, he went back to work at the office. The new head, Mr. Fang, a middle-aged man, was not at all severe. Indeed, not only was he polite to him, he even said a few words of comfort to him. His colleagues all greeted him with a nod, although, apart from old Mr. Zhong, their faces expressed no welcome. He was happy, and because of this, neither the bizarre translations nor the formalistic documents annoyed him particularly.

As always, his home lacked the sound of voices. Apart from Saturdays or Sundays (mostly once a fortnight) when Xiao Xuan came home and sat around, eating one or two meals and staying the night, there were only his mother and himself, and sometimes, only one of them would be at home.

The days passed monotonously one by one, neither fast nor slow. He had the feeling only of holding on, of being dragged along. He had no distractions and no hobbies. Not even writing letters or conversing gave him any happiness. Spring, which brought him no pleasure, finally came to an end.

In the summer, he became even more pallid. His health did not improve at all, but grew worse. What force sustained him and kept him on his feet, he could not tell. Every afternoon, he ran a fever; every night, he sweated. If he walked too much, he became breathless, and coughed incessantly, sometimes coughing sputum streaked with blood. The left side of his chest was exceedingly painful, and now even the right side began to ache. At first, he gritted his teeth and bore it, but in the end, then gradually he grew accustomed to it. It was not difficult for him to get through these days, since in any case, his life was just a dark stretch of grey. He took no interest in anything, not daring to nurse any further vain illusions. Even Germany's surrender brought him no comfort or joy. He heard people prophesying that Japan would collapse within a year, but was unable to express any joy or pleasure. Those bright, beautiful dreams seemed to have no connection with him. He was like an old, feeble carter, moving forward one step at a time, devoting all his energy to pushing his heavily loaded cart, having stopped thinking long ago about when he would reach his goal and put down his burden. Nor did he calculate how far he had already gone, concentrating solely on moving forward step by step, pushing until his strength was exhausted.

One evening after dinner, his mother suddenly looked at him and asked: "Xuan, there hasn't been anything wrong with you these last couple of days, has there? You look so terrible!"

"I'm all right. There's nothing wrong," he said, trying to look happy. But his throat refused to keep up the pretence. He coughed several times in succession, covering his mouth at once with his hands, afraid that he might cough up blood as he had that day in the office. Although he had carefully wiped away the traces of blood from the proof-sheets, the red stain on the paper could still be seen dimly.

"But you must be careful. You're coughing again. Your cough doesn't seem to have got any better," his mother said, frowning.

"Oh, yes. It's been better for a while, but I haven't got rid of it completely yet. When I'm tired, it starts again," he explained. He knew this was not true, but he wanted to say it, for he wanted to deceive not only his mother, but himself as well.

His mother was silent for a long time, before she said with a sigh: "In fact, you shouldn't be working. But what other choice do we have?"

He felt very upset, but could not think of a reply. The more he tried not to cough, the more violent the coughing became. Once he started, he could not stop. He went red in the face, tears springing to his eyes. His mother became so anxious that she ran from the room to fetch boiled water, then massaged his back. Finally, he managed to get his breath back, and taking a handkerchief from his mother's hand, wiped his face.

"It's all right," he said with an effort, looking at his mother with gratitude in his eyes.

"You'd better lie down," his mother said tenderly.

"It's nothing. I'll just sit for a while," he answered hoarsely.

"Xuan, I'll go to the office tomorrow and ask for one or two months' leave for you. You must rest. You mustn't worry about earning a living. If there's really no way out, I'll get a job as an amah," she said decisively.

Shaking his head, he said weakly: "Mother, you're old now. How will you stand it? What's the use of this way out? We're not the only ones suffering. Even if we can't hang on, we must!. . ."

"In that case, it would be better not to live," his mother cried indignantly.

"These last few years, you can't even die if you want to." As he said this, he felt the dull pain in his chest. The germs were eating into his lungs. He had no strength left to resist. He would die. Whether he wanted to or not, he would soon die.

His mother stood there, looking at him blankly. He seemed not to notice, thinking of the day in the office when he heard his colleagues idly talking about tuberculosis. It was at lunch time. Xiao Pan, as if to show off, was talking about a relative who had died of TB. "There's nothing more tragic or miserable than someone dying of TB. If I had such an illness, when it reached the second stage, I'd kill myself," Xiao Pan had said, and his eyes had rested on his face. He had said it deliberately for him to hear.

"I hear there's an especially effective medicine which is imported, but outrageously expensive," old Mr. Zhong had put in.

"It's not really effective. Besides, you can't cure this kind of disease just by taking medicine," Xiao Pan had said, pleased with himself.

"Nothing more tragic or miserable," he thought. He could not chase the thought from his mind. From afar, despair and horror pressed close on him. He shuddered without realizing it (although it was summer, he still felt cold, as if his whole body had fallen into an icy cellar).

"Why is there no really effective medicine that everyone can afford to buy? Must I really die so tragically and so miserably?" He asked himself in despair.

His mother, seeing him in poor spirits, his face terribly pale, his eyes motionless and filled with terror, was herself filled with anguish, and dared not talk with him anymore. Instead, she urged: "Xuan, you'd better go to bed a bit earlier. Don't think about things. We'll talk about asking for leave again tomorrow."

He started, as if waking from a terrifying dream. But when he looked all around him, the pale light in the room was just beginning to dim. The hubbub of voices downstairs, the gongs of the opera, the quarrelling in the street — strange sounds of every kind became mixed in a single, confused din. His mouth felt dry, so he went to fetch the teapot to pour himself a cup of slightly warm boiled water. "All right, I'll go to bed," he said, smiling bitterly. "Mother, you go to bed as well. I can see you're lonely too."

"I'm used to it. In any case, I'll soon be in my grave. I'm not afraid of being lonely," his mother said, sighing softly.

She went to her room and closed the door, while he crept into his bed. The left side of his chest was still aching, but not only the left side. His whole body was in pain. His mind was wide awake. He could not fall asleep. The gongs in the street and the strains of the operatic arias had still not ceased. Some family or other had invited a shaman to perform rites for the dead, while at the same time, some female impersonator was singing at the top of her voice. He did not want to hear the words of the opera, but they forced themselves insistently into his ears, troubling his thoughts. He tossed about on his bed, but the more he tried to sleep, the more anxious he became, so much so that he began to sweat profusely. But he did not dare throw aside the thin quilt for fear of catching cold, and he had no wish to damage his own health through neglect, even though he had been thinking at first that the disease would soon eat up his insides completely, and that death was already close.

There was still a light in his mother's room. She was not yet asleep, for he heard her cough from time to time. What was she doing? Why did she never stop working all year? What did she get from it all? Her whole existence seemed to be for him and for Xiao Xuan. But what could he do to repay her? At this thought, he clutched at his hair.

Then Shusheng appeared, her beautiful face smiling at him. Was she laughing at him or did she pity him? Another letter had come for him the day before yesterday, asking in the manner of a familiar friend, about his health and about the rest of the family. She had also enclosed another money order. Naturally, he put it in the bank as before. He wrote in reply without telling her that he had never spent any of the money she had sent. What did she mean by it, in fact? She had said that their relationship as husband and wife had ended, and they had done as she had wished. Then why did she not forget him? Why did she still write and send money every month? The more he thought about it, the less he understood, but these thoughts aroused in him a hope.

Ill and on the verge of death, he nevertheless nourished the hopes of a healthy man, hopes that tormented him cruelly, because he understood that they could not be realized. But he could not suppress or extinguish them. As he struggled with his thoughts, his singlet, wet through, clung like ice to his burning back.

"I want to live, I want to live!" he called out, unable to control himself, but his voice was beginning to become hoarse.

No one heard him call, no one paid him any heed. From outside the window echoed the sound of every kind of noise. Crowds of people were coming and going. At the entrance of the lane noodle-stands had recently been set up and were in their busiest season. A shaman was shouting loudly, and custom-

ers were talking at the tops of their voices. He could hear
the hawker's cry: "Puffed rice and sweetened water!" But it
was the voice of a young man. Several women's voices, shrill
and clear, called out for "boiled water" or "puffed rice and
sweetened water, over here!" Now, even the sellers of puffed
rice and sweetened water had changed and, moreover, were
busy. He alone lay quietly in bed, and although he was already
near death, no one came to care for him.

"I want to live!" he cried again in a voice audible only to
himself. But who was he calling to finally? He could not tell.

28

Little by little, he lost his voice. At the same time, his strength
gradually diminished.

Each day, when he came home from work, he would come
through the door panting for breath and collapse on the cane
chair, remaining there for a long time as if dead before he could
move or talk.

"Xuan, you must ask for a few days' leave. If you go on
like this, you'll have a relapse," his mother urged, pitying him.
She knew that his illness was worsening, but what could she
do to save him? Zhang Boqing was of no use, neither was the
hospital. The two of them, mother and son, were helpless,
completely without resources of any kind.

"It's all right, I can still manage," he replied, assuming an
air of indifference, but his heart felt as if it had been pierced
through by a huge handful of needles. He remembered clearly
how he coughed in the office as he read the proofs, how
breathless he became after a long spell of reading. He remembered too the detestation in the eyes of his colleagues at lunch
time. How much longer could he endure? He did not dare to
think about it, but could not stop himself. And he did not
want anyone else to bring the subject up with him.

As his mother gazed at him in silence, she thought in anguish:

Why are you so obstinate? "But you must take care of your-self," she could not help saying. She saw him shake his head slightly with an expression of helplessness on his face. All at once, she suddenly reflected: It's I who have harmed him; it's I who have tired him. She wanted to cry, but restrained herself with all her might. "No, it's that woman who has harmed him," she thought in revolt, raising her eyebrows.

From the road outside the window came the sound of crying and the noise of firecrackers. A woman was sobbing her heart out.

"Who's crying?" he suddenly asked in a voice tinged with fear.

"Someone has died in the tailor's shop across the road. He caught cholera. He was fine yesterday, but he died in less than a day," his mother explained.

"That can be counted a blessing. Why cry?" he thought for a while, then muttered pensively to himself.

"You'd better be careful when you're out these next couple of days. I know you never eat anything raw or cold, but you're still very weak, so you must always be careful," his mother exhorted him, full of concern.

"I know," he said off-handedly. But his mind was preoccupied with another matter: When a man dies, is there a soul that survives? Does he still recognize those dear to him in life?

Who could give him sure answers to these questions? He knew that they were questions forever unanswerable. Someone had once asked him the same questions, and he had laughed in his face. Now he himself was posing this questions! Must his mother, Shusheng and even Xiao Xuan say good-bye to him forever?

Without realizing it, his eyes fell on his mother's face. Such an affectionate face. "Mother," he called gently.

"Huh?" His mother's eyes turned towards him, but seeing that he said nothing, she asked: "What is it?"

"I was watching you," he said affectionately. He gave a re-luctant smile, and then said: "Xiao Xuan's coming home the

day after tomorrow. I wonder if he's lost weight this last fortnight."

"His constitution's much the same as yours. He doesn't look
too well either. But a tonic is so dear, otherwise, it would be a
good idea to buy him some," his mother said, looking at him
closely. Then suddenly, she turned her face away to hide the
teardrops hovering in the corners of her eyes.

Xiao Xuan's return gave two lonely people a little extra
warmth, providing them with at least one more person to talk
to. The grandmother lovingly asked her grandson about his life
in the last fortnight, his schoolwork, his food and drink, everything in fact. Xiao Xuan replied briefly, for he was a taciturn
child, but his grandmother's questions demanded answers, so
even someone of as few words as he was forced to say something.

"Your father hasn't stopped thinking of you these last two
days. He wants to see you very much. When he comes back in
a moment, he's sure to be delighted," the grandmother assured
her grandson.

"Yes," Xiao Xuan answered tersely, without the trace of a
smile.

"How can the child have changed so and become even
more like a grownup?" his grandmother thought, rather disconcerted. She continued solicitously: "Do you feel unwell
or anything?"

"No," Xiao Xuan answered, as briefly as ever, but after some
thought, he frowned and added: "I can never keep up with my
schoolwork."

"Even so, that's nothing to worry about. It'll come in time.
In any case, you're still very young," she said gently to cheer
him up.

"But the teachers are on our backs all the time. I'm terrified
of failing and being kept back a class, and letting you all down,"
Xiao Xuan said, as if in complaint.

"You're so young, and you worry about being kept back a

class! The most important thing is your health. You mustn't get like your father," his grandmother said plaintively.

Just then, the father pushed open the door and came in. He was panting for breath, his face as grey as the tough dust-covered paper used for windows He went directly over to the desk and collapsed so heavily into the cane chair, one of whose legs was already splayed outwards, that it shook briefly. He said nothing, simply closing his eyes tight and remaining completely motionless.

The grandmother signalled to her grandson with a glance not to disturb his father. She stared at her son in dismay.

A few moments later, he suddenly opened his eyes. "Mother," he called, his voice almost completely inaudible, while his eyes tried to focus as they searched for her.

She went over and asked him gently: "Xuan, what is it?"

He put out a shaking hand, found hers and seized it, grasping it tightly, refusing to let go. "Where's Xiao Xuan?" he asked lethargically, his eyes seeking his son. Xiao Xuan was standing on his right, but a little behind him, so that he failed to find him, for his eyes wandered constantly to and fro, searching only the region space in front of him.

"Come here quickly, quickly! Your father's calling you!" his grandmother called to Xiao Xuan, her voice tragic with grief. She thought that he was already on the verge of death and that he was about to bid farewell to his family. Her voice shook violently and her heart beat even more violently. Xiao Xuan came over instantly and stood before his father.

He seized the child with his other hand and examined him closely. "Are you all right?" he asked. He seemed to want to smile, but failed. He closed his eyes, the hands of his mother and his son still firmly pressed in his own.

His mother wept, while the child stared at him, stupefied. Sure that some tragedy was about to be enacted, they thought. "It's over," his mother thought, darkness beginning to veil her eyes. The only thing that gave her any hope was that his hand never went cold.

"Xuan," his mother called, unable to contain her sorrow. "Dad," his grief-stricken son called in turn.

He opened his eyes and forced a smile. He stirred. "Don't be afraid, I won't die," he said.

His mother breathed a sigh of relief, relaxing slightly. Holding back her tears, she asked in a low voice: "Do you have something on your mind?"

He shook his head, saying: "Nothing."

Xiao Xuan continued to stare at him, his eyes never moving. "Then you'd better lie down. I'll go and get the doctor," his mother said gently.

He let go their hands, changed his position slightly, and said with an effort: "There's no need, Mother. I'm not ill."

"Xuan, you mustn't be stubborn. How can you say you're not ill?" his mother said. "Illness is nothing to be frightened of. It just needs to be treated in time."

He shook his head again and said: "I'm not afraid." He felt about under his gown and drew from his breast a crumpled letter, putting it into his mother's hand without explaining what it was.

She opened it, and in a low voice, read out the following words:

"Dear Mr. Wang,
   We, your colleagues, are all small clerks who depend on a salary to live. We are all undernourished and overworked, weak in health and frequently ill. We therefore express our sympathy to you for your lung trouble, and there is no question of our looking down on you. But your illness has now reached the third stage, and you should by rights ask for and undergo treatment. But because of the need to earn a living, you cannot but come to work. However, in consideration of others, it would be better if you did not eat with them at the same table, or use the same teacups, so to avoid spreading the infection, bringing harm to others. Hence, motivated entirely by our concern for the interests of all, we beg you to leave our lunch group, and take your meals at home. Please put this into effect immediately. Otherwise, we shall be forced to take exceptional measures. Please do not say that you have not been given due warning. [This was followed by six signatures and the date.]"

"They gave this to you personally?" his mother asked, completely bewildered.

"They asked the office-boy to give it to me. Xiao Pan drafted it, and out of seven people at our table, only Zhong Lao didn't sign," he replied. After a moment, he added: "What they say is right, of course, but they shouldn't have expressed it like that. If they had something to say, they could have put it more nicely. I'm a human being after all . . ." His voice gave out, and he was forced to say no more.

"It's outrageous! People who can't even write properly should put on such airs! You've all been working together for nearly two years, yet they don't even have a spark of human feeling!" his mother cried at length, her voice shaking with fury, and her face reddening with anger. In a few moments, she had torn the letter to shreds.

"I think you should ignore them, Dad. See what they can do about it!" Xiao Xuan unexpectedly said, his face pale with indignation.

"You all work together, why can't you eat in the dining room? If TB is so easy to transmit, then why isn't everyone here dead? It's only the cowards who are afraid!" His mother's anger would not subside and she continued to rage.

Shaking his head, he managed with great effort to say hoarsely: "Actually, it's my illness that's to blame. It's incurable." His mother and son looked at him in surprise and bewilderment. After a moment, he continued: "You can't blame them. They're afraid of an illness like this too. If they really did catch it, what would they do?. . ."

His mother spat on the ground in anger. "You really are impossible!" she interrupted. "You're in this situation and you still think about them. If I were you, I'd make sure they all caught it. If there's to be suffering, let them suffer. Don't let a single one of them gloat over others' misfortunes."

"But what good would that do me?" he asked with a bitter. smile. The huskiness of his voice made it seem as if his throat were beginning to fester. He stood up unsteadily, saying to himself: "I'd like a cup of tea."

His mother caught hold of him at once, at the same time telling Xiao Xuan: "Go and pour your father some tea."

Xiao Xuan obeyed, quickly bringing the teacup from which the steam was still rising. He took the cup, glanced into it, and said sadly: "Boiled water." Then lifting it up, he drank it all down in great gulps. He gave the cup back to Xiao Xuan, instructing him carefully: "Xiao Xuan, remember to wash the cup clean with boiling water." He made a great effort to make his meaning clear to Xiao Xuan.

"There's no need to wash it so carefully. I'm not afraid of catching anything. Surely we're not going to start writing letters against you in our family!" his mother exclaimed, miserable with grief.

He looked at her and then at Xiao Xuan before saying: "But Xiao Xuan is very young after all. In this Wang family of ours, we have only one son . . ." Slowly, he went over to his bed. "I'll lie down for a while," he murmured under his breath as he reached it. Then he collapsed onto the bed and stretched himself out.

The next day, he went to work as usual, wearing his long gown of cheap cloth, which had grey soil spots in several places on the back and front. He sweated and panted as he climbed the stairs, went to his desk, sat down, opened the drawer and took out the proofs that he had failed to complete the previous day.

Before he even began work, he already felt too unwell to carry on. He continued to sweat profusely, his mind was a blank, and he had no idea what he was doing. He simply gritted his teeth, took hold of himself, and forced himself to begin.

Spread in front of him were the proofs of a great work singing the praises of great deeds and sterling virtues. He corrected one word at a time. The author bragged unblushingly of the progress and reforms made by China in recent years in transforming herself from a semi-colonial country into one of the four great powers among modern nations; of how the standard of living of the people had risen and human rights had been extended; of how the Nationalist Government's concern for the suffering of the people had brought the grateful thanks of the people and inspired their enthusiastic participation in military service, the payment of taxes, delivery of grain, . . . "Lies! Lies!" he kept thinking, but he had no choice but to keep on reading carefully, changing wrong characters and removing misprints.

He was already not up to the work physically, but he had to grit his teeth and continue, working on slowly. At any moment, he might have keeled over onto the floor, but all along, he supported his cheek in his left hand and went on working. He coughed unceasingly, but there was no longer any need to worry about alarming his colleagues, for by now his coughing had become soundless. Of course, he coughed up sputum, sputum streaked with blood. He would spit it onto a piece of paper, roll it into a ball and throw it into the wastebasket. Once, through lack of care, some blood fell onto the proof-sheet, and he tried to wipe away the mark with a scrap of paper, lightly, taking care not to apply any pressure lest he tear the bad-quality paper of the proof-sheet. When he took away the scrap-paper, the stain of his blood was still visible among the words and phrases glorifying the standard of living of the people. "For the sake of your lies, my blood will soon run dry!" he thought with rancour, seized by a desire to tear the proof to shreds. But he did not dare. He stared at the pale bloodstain, breathed a long sigh, and finally finished reading the sheet and turned over the page.

All of a sudden, there was a commotion downstairs, as if something out of the ordinary had occurred. Some people dashed downstairs. An agitated discussion broke out on his floor, until everyone was talking at the top of his voice. He, however, shrank back into his seat, his eyes glued to his proofs, his head reverberating as if with the cries of crickets. He did not dare move. Suddenly, the words "Zhong Lao" came to his ears, and he heard "Zhong Lao" repeated over and over again. He looked up in alarm. The department head was talking to the section head, his face grave.

"What's happened to Zhong Lao?" he wondered. He wanted to stand up, but unable to summon up the courage, he stayed where he was, as if rooted to his chair.

Then the department head and the section head went downstairs. He watched them go, his mind full of questions. Soon after, the section head came back upstairs alone. The commotion below had already abated.

"He's gone. It must be cholera. Luckily we managed to get a car to take him. It's nearly ten miles!" He heard the section head say to someone.

"Has anyone gone with him?"

"Xiao Pan has. He'll come back in the same car. Later, we'll send one of the office-boys to see how he's getting on," the section head said.

"Xiao Pan!" he thought in astonishment. "Then he's not afraid of catching something anymore! He was just bullying me!" He felt a stab of pain in his chest.

When lunch time came, he did not go down. The department head who was the last to leave, seeing him sitting there motionless, asked him: "Aren't you going to eat?"

"I don't feel like it," he answered, embarrassed.

"Aren't you feeling well?"

"No, it's not that," he said, standing up instantly and shaking his head. "He doesn't know," he thought with relief.

"Have you ever been inoculated?"

"No," he replied, shaking his head.

"Then you'd better be," the department head advised him, showing his concern. "Zhong Lao has already been sent to hospital. It's almost certainly cholera."

"Yes, thank you," he replied.

"Your voice has been hoarse for quite some time now. Haven't you seen the doctor?"

"Yes, I have. I'm taking medicine all the time, only up till now, it doesn't seem to have done any good," he replied, keeping his eyes to the ground.

"You must take care," the department head said with a frown. "If you're not well, it won't matter if you take a few days' leave."

"Yes," he answered, unable to look up.

The department head went downstairs. He remained upstairs alone. A thought suddenly crossed his mind. "Was he hinting that I should resign?" He felt uneasy, as if his body, already weak, had suffered yet another unexpected blow, and he would collapse, never to stand up again. He cupped his face in his hands, and sat there staring at the proof-sheets in perplexity.

"It can't be. He seemed very courteous towards me," he suddenly murmured to himself. The thought assuaged his suffering and his doubt, making him a little easier in his mind.

Xiao Pan had no news at all. About an hour before office was due to end, the young man suddenly came back. He said something to someone downstairs first, then came upstairs and went into the director's office.

"The car broke down on the way and we were held up for almost two hours," Xiao Pan began.

"How's Zhong Lao? It's not serious, I hope," the department head asked with concern.

"The hospital's a temporary setup. Bloody awful! There were altogether only two doctors, four nurses and twenty beds, and they've already taken in over thirty patients. Some were lying in the corridors and on the floor, and there wasn't even time to give them a saline drip. There was piss and shit all over the floor. The stench was absolutely unbearable! And patients were being brought in all the time. It's the only epidemic hospital in the whole city. Cars can't drive as far as the entrance, and the patients have to be carried in on stretchers. When we got Zhong Lao to the hospital, the doctors examined him and confirmed it was cholera, but we had to wait over an hour before anyone came to give him a drip. The doctors and nurses just can't cope and they're terribly exhausted as well. From the look of things, we'll have to send someone from the office to look after him...." Xiao Pan poured all this out excitedly in one breath.

"What did the doctor say? Since it's cholera and he's on a drip, his life can't be in danger then," the department head said.

"The doctor didn't say anything. He just shook his head and sighed. He seemed to be saying that he was just an ordinary doctor, and that to put the lives of a whole city into the hands of two of them, was a responsibility they couldn't handle," Xiao Pan said.

"All right, let's do it this way. Tomorrow, we'll take the day off, give the place a good scrub and also disinfect it thoroughly, so that no one else catches anything," the department head said after some thought.

The people in the office continued to talk about what had happened to old Mr. Zhong. Wang Wenxuan alone remained with his head buried in his proofs, not daring to put in a word. But old Mr. Zhong's kind, humorous face kept surfacing in his mind. He felt as if he were in a dream. He had not seen Mr. Zhong that day, for when he signed the register, old Mr. Zhong had not yet arrived. He had probably not been well when he came to work, that was why he had been late that day, and then he had suddenly been taken ill. Could Mr. Zhong be in danger? It was impossible. He had been so well yesterday, so sturdy and robust, quite different from Wang himself, who was getting thinner day by day. Then why did Xiao Pan speak so fearfully? He began thinking. Old Mr. Zhong was his only friend in the office, and had refused to sign that letter. He could not help thinking of him.

When he got home after work, he told his mother the unhappy news. She sighed once or twice, uttered a few words of sympathy, and then never mentioned Mr. Zhong's name again. But he did not sleep well the whole night. The mosquitoes and flies kept tormenting him, the rats kept racing around the room, while in the street beneath his windows, noisy quarrels, tearful recriminations, laughter and chatter and shouted abuse continued until midnight. He kept seeing before him old Mr. Zhong's smiling face, his shiny bald head and his red nose. He thought of him all the time. Would he die, or wouldn't he die? Could science save this old man? Cholera was not a strange name to him. Since the age of eleven or twelve, he had seen the power of this dreaded disease.

That night, he slept fitfully, tossing restlessly about, moaning softly all the time, as if some terrible weight were pressing down on his chest. He dreamt not only that old Mr. Zhong had died, but that everyone in the firm had died. He wept quietly, his sobs audible only to himself, so that his mother was not awakened.

When he got up the next morning, his head felt dizzy and his limbs were without strength. His mother asked him with concern: "Xuan, why are your eyes so red? How did you sleep last night?"

"Not very well. I don't know how many times I woke up," he answered.

"Then you'd better not go out today. Since you've a day's holiday, you'd better stay in bed and rest for the day," she said.

"I want to see if Zhong Lao's any better," he mumbled.

"You're going to the hospital?" his mother asked in surprise.

"I'm going to the office. They'll have news of him there," he explained.

"They're taking a holiday today. How can you get any news from there?" his mother objected in disagreement.

He looked at her, but said nothing more. That day, he stayed at home all day sleeping, doing exactly as his mother said, but his mind was on old Mr. Zhong all the time. Would he be lucky or unlucky? He almost wanted to pray. Let him live! Use all the resources of science to save him! All day, he repeated this cry; all night he clung to this hope.

He could not stop thinking about it, and could not get any peace whatsoever. It was difficult to endure until the day came, to endure until it was time to go to work. When he arrived at the office, everything was as before, with only old Mr. Zhong's place empty. After going upstairs and sitting down, he opened up the proofs at the place he had reached two days before, and began his proof-reading. Shortly after, an office-boy brought a note from the section head, Mr. Wu, asking him to write an advertising blurb for the "great work" he was correcting.

This was tantamount to an order he could not refuse to obey. He thought for a while, pulled out a sheet of letter-writing paper and picked up his brush, intending to write a short draft of between one and two hundred words. But after one sentence, he could not think how to continue. The words and phrases lay in a great muddled heap in the middle of his brain, and he could not disentangle one from another. His thought processes were blocked. He moistened his brush over and over again in the ink on the inkstone, but for a very long time, could not write a single word. His forehead was beaded with sweat, his whole face burning as if on fire. There was nothing he could do but put the writing paper aside and go on with his proof-reading.

Suddenly, he heard Mr. Wu give a cough. He was alarmed. Mr. Wu had coughed purely by chance, but he thought it was an indication of Mr. Wu's dissatisfaction with him. He promptly set his mind to work, picked up the sheet of writing-paper again and spread it out before him. "It doesn't matter. I'll just write a few stock phrases," he thought, and absent-mindedly put together about a hundred and fifty words. He read it over to himself. "Lies! All lies!" he reprimanded himself. Nevertheless, he took the draft, went to Mr. Wu's desk and respectfully handed it to him.

"It's not very suitable. It's not complimentary enough,"

Mr. Wu commented, shaking his head and frowning. "A work of this importance has to be promoted in a very serious way; otherwise Mr. So-and-so will be highly displeased when he sees it."

Mr. So-and-so, the author of the book, was an alternate member of the Central Committee of the Kuomintang and consequently a busy man in government circles. Did he have time to read the advertising blurbs of publishing houses? He did not quite believe Mr. Wu, and so he said offhand:

"Mr. So-and-so is not likely to see it though, is he?"

"How do you know? People in high places notice everything. Mr. So-and-so is from cultural circles, and pays great attention to culture. His interest in writers and writing is as great as his interest in political activity, and besides, he's a permanent director of our company," Mr. Wu said, assuming an air of severity.

"Yes, I see," he replied, dropping his head.

"You'd better go back and write it again," Mr. Wu ordered, giving him back his draft.

He murmured his agreement, and was just about to turn and leave, when he heard Mr. Wu command:

"And that book you're proof-reading, you must take special care. You can't afford to have a single word wrong, because Mr. So-and-so always takes particular note of printing errors in books."

He muttered something in answer, disgusted, and without turning his head, went back to his own desk. He said resentfully to himself: "All right, I'll boost him up then." Taking up his brush, he made an effort to draw from the recesses of his mind some words of the highest praise, and scattered them liberally throughout the article. "You see, I can lie too," he said sullenly to himself. Luckily, there was no risk of these unspoken words being overheard.

Suddenly, he heard Xiao Pan's footsteps. Xiao Pan ran up the stairs, breathless and pale, and dashing into the department head's office, cried out in loud gasps: "Mr. Fang,

Zhang Haiyun's just telephoned. Zhong Lao died early this morning. He's been telephoning again and again, but has only just got through."

Everything went black before his eyes. He was deafened by the sound of bells ringing in his ears. He had to quickly support his head in both hands.

29

Old Mr. Zhong had been his only friend in the office. After his death, he lost all contact with others in the firm, for it could now be said that the firm meant nothing to him. After finishing work, he tidied up his desk carefully before going downstairs, but just as he was about to go out the main door, he stood for a moment at Mr. Zhong's empty seat. Why, he could not tell. After leaving the building, he looked back at the entrance with a strange light in his eyes, feeling that he too would soon be saying farewell to the place forever.

But in fact, he came back the next day, the third day, the fourth day, right up to the sixth day.

On the afternoon of that day, several people in his office had arranged to visit old Mr. Zhong's grave, and he was going with them. They were to make the journey there and back by long-distance bus. They were packed like sardines, with so little room to stand that he had to keep his left foot suspended in midair. The coach bumped so alarmingly throughout the journey, the heat inside was so stifling, the air so foul, and his mind in such disarray, that he almost vomited.

Mr. Zhong was buried in a small plot on a slope not far from the epidemiology hospital. The earth on the grave was already dry, with no grass as yet. On the grave lay a single wreath of red, green and white paper flowers. On one ribbon was written: "May Mr. You'an rest forever in peace," and on the other, "With sorrow, from the Yizhong Book Company." Apart from this, there was another wreath, tied to a small but tall stand placed before the grave. On one ribbon was again written: "May Mr. You'an rest forever in peace," and on the other, "With respect from younger brother Fang Yong-cheng." This had been sent by the director and was also of paper. There had not been time to place a headstone, and so these two odourless wreaths, one standing and one lying, were the sole companions of the kindly old man.

"So this is the kind of mourning the firm organized. It really is too simple and crude. They can't have spent more than a few pence altogether," one of his colleagues remarked.

"This is already something. If Mr. Zhou were still here, there wouldn't be even this much," another colleague commented.

"Well, when all's said and done, once a man's dead, whatever you do is meaningless. It would be better to have treated him better when he was alive," a third put in.

"Yes, that's what I think. Since they treat us who are living like this, why not the dead?" the second speaker added.

No one spoke to Wang Wenxuan. They seemed to be avoiding him. He stood by himself in a corner, gazing timidly at his friend's grave, as if afraid that they might really chase him away at any moment.

Tears blurred his sight. His lungs ached, his throat ached, and now his eyes began to ache. He rubbed his eyes, rubbing them hard. Why was his name, Wenxuan, on the wreath? He steadied himself. He had seen wrong, for there, clearly written, was the name "You'an". No, he had not seen wrong. He had been thinking of another similar wreath, on the white ribbon of which was indeed written his name. He too would lie under a similar mound of earth, in similar barren surroundings.

His colleagues left for the city. They did not even call him when they were about to go. He stood alone before the grave, looking now and then from left to right, as if, instead of paying his respects to a friend, he was looking at his own simple, crude last resting place.

Black clouds gathered more and more thickly in the sky, until all around, the scene became gradually so dark that even he noticed it. He could not stay any longer. He hurried to the bus stop, without running, yet by the time he reached the stop, he was bathed in sweat and completely out of breath. He waited for half an hour before being pushed aboard by the crowd. He had to stand for nearly an hour and a half before reaching the stop near his home. Normally, it would have taken only forty minutes or so, but this time, it began to rain heavily halfway, forcing the bus to stop in midjourney.

When he reached home again, he fell, exhausted, onto his bed, and from that time on, he never returned to the office.

He would lie in bed all day, slightly feverish, dripping with sweat, breathing in short, noisy gasps. When he spoke, his voice was hoarse and rasping. His chest and his throat were in terrible pain, but he groaned only rarely, suffering all in silence. He did not ask Xiao Xuan to come home, and to his mother he now spoke much less, but when he saw her weeping for him, he would smile sadly at her.

He had given up completely, but his mother still refused to abandon the hopeless battle. She called in a Western-trained doctor to diagnose, but he simply shook his head as a sign that the illness was already too far gone for any medicine to be effective. Zhang Boqing was her only recourse, for he had once given her a ray of hope, but now, even Zhang Boqing felt that there was no way of saving him.

Finally, he lost his voice completely, becoming inaudible even to himself. When he first discovered this, he was so upset that he wept for a long time. Tears streamed from his eyes, but no sound came from his throat. His sobbing nevertheless gave him some relief. Seeing him cry, his mother came over to ask him why. Unable to make himself heard, he could only open his mouth and point to his throat. She understood his suffering, and stood there in silence for a long time before finally saying with tenderness and love:

"Xuan, you mustn't be upset ... You're a good person ... Heaven has eyes ..." and for a time, she too was unable to speak.

"Mother, I'm not upset. When did you start believing in Heaven?" he wanted to say, but could not. He could only make every effort to restrain his sorrow and, shaking his head, pretend to smile.

"Don't be afraid. You won't die," she said.

"I'm not afraid. Everyone has to die, but it grieves me to leave you to suffer hardship alone. And Xiao Xuan is so young ..." he tried to say, with effort, but all his mother heard was his gasping. She did not know what he was saying, but the sight of his struggle terrified her even more. Gazing at him, she interrupted:

"Don't try to talk. You'd better have a good rest." Her face twitched, and her eyes filled with tears.

He gave a long, long sigh, opened wide his tear-brimming eyes and looked at her imploringly.

The room was exceptionally hot and close, so much so that the wooden walls seemed as if they might burst into flames at any instant. He pushed aside even the cheap cotton bed-sheet that covered him, revealing the holes in his old singlet, through which he could see his yellow chest, now mere skin and bones.

After this, his mother bought him a bell. When he wanted something, instead of calling her, he rang. When he wanted someone to do something for him, he wrote it down on paper. This someone was of course his mother, for apart from her, no one much ever came into the room other than the doctor or the postman. But the postman did not come often, for Xiao Xuan seldom wrote, while Shusheng's letters now came less frequently. She still sent the monthly remittances, and now, they made use of the money. Bit by bit, his mother withdrew the money which up till now they had always paid into a fixed deposit account. It was she herself who had asked him for the deposit slip. Now that it was a question of her son's life, she was willing to do anything, except be the first to write to Shusheng. He wrote to Shusheng himself, without asking his mother's help. In each letter, he wrote things like: "I'm fine; I'm gradually getting better; please don't worry." As for the letters to Xiao Xuan, sometimes he wrote, sometimes his mother. He asked his son not to come home (the child was staying at a friend's place for the summer), to study hard and to review his lessons properly. His mother's letters said a little more, but she could not bear to tell him the true situation either, and besides, she secretly clung to a tiny shred of hope.

But instead of her hopes being realized, his condition gradually worsened. He was fully aware that his insides were rotting away day by day, and that his throat and lungs were becoming daily more painful. Even his mother could see that he was moving slowly along the road towards death.

But she could not give up hope easily. She continued to give him medicine, to make him drink fresh milk and chicken soup. She helped him dress, helped him carry out his natural functions, doing everything for him, even things that an old amah would have been unwilling to do. Nevertheless, after great effort, he finally wrote these words on a piece of paper: "Mother, give me some poison. Let me die quickly. I can't bear to watch you suffer. It tortures me too much."

As his mother read this note, he watched her, his eyes brimming with tears.

"I can't. You're my only son," she sobbed.

He then wrote: "I have to die sooner or later."

"If you die, I'll die with you. I won't want to live either!" his mother cried, breaking into loud sobs, unable to hold back her grief and pain.

He put down his pencil, and let his head fall wearily back onto his pillow.

The heat intensified his suffering. The noise around him was like adding oil to a fire. The cholera took many lives in the city, and his own street was continually filled with the heart-rending wailing of the bereaved. He lay on his bed all day, on his back, on his side, on his stomach. His mind would not rest, and he never managed to sleep soundly for even fifteen minutes.

He could not dress himself, or sit up freely by himself. Each time he wrote to Shusheng, he had to summon up a desperate determination and suffer the most excruciating pain before he could write four or five lines. "I'm fine, I'm managing to survive," he was forever telling her.

"Why do you make yourself suffer? I'll write it for you," his mother said, in a voice of supplication. But it was no use. In this, he was unwilling to listen to her. If he did not write himself, she would know that he must be seriously ill.

"Why not let her know?" his mother burst out one day, unable to bear it.

He hesitated a long time before writing in reply: "I want her to be happy."

His mother thought: "She already belongs to someone else. Why not let her suffer a bit, let her conscience prick her a little?" "You're so foolish," she reproached him gently. But as she looked again at the shaky writing on the paper, her heart softened. Then she thought, what happiness had he had in his life in this world? He had lived a life of hardship. Why was she unwilling to help him fulfil even this tiny wish of his? He was after all her own flesh and blood. She looked in silence at his thin, lustreless face, and her heart hurt as if it were being torn apart. She wanted to laugh, she wanted to cry out. She wanted the ground to open up so that she could leap into hell. She wanted a bomb to fall from the heavens and destroy this tiny, tiny world of hers.

That afternoon, a young man in the family next door died of cholera. The heartbreaking sobs of two women penetrated his room. After listening for a moment, he wrote suddenly to his mother: "Mother, when I die, you mustn't weep."

"Why do you say things like that?" his mother asked miserably.

"When I think of you weeping, I can't die in peace. I feel too wretched," he replied.

"You won't die! You won't die!" his mother cried through her streaming tears.

The hottest period passed. The air in the room became a little easier to bear. But his illness continued in its advance, and his suffering went on increasing. He fought the disease by an even greater endurance. Sometimes, when it was more than he could bear, he would groan, but even in his suffering, his groans were noiseless.

One evening, his mother brought him some chicken soup, feeding him with a soup-spoon. After swallowing two mouthfuls, he abruptly pushed her hand away and shook his head in refusal.

"Have a few more mouthfuls. It's no good for you to eat so little every day," his mother urged.

He took his pencil with a shaking hand and wrote: "My throat is sore."

She shuddered. Her hand holding the spoon also shook. Controlling her sorrow, she urged again: "Put up with the pain and drink. How can you not eat?" She lifted the spoon to his lips again. He opened his trembling lips and forced himself to swallow. He turned his eyes to the ceiling, once, twice, grasping the thin bedclothes in his hands.

"Xuan," his mother called softly. He looked at her with tears in his eyes, and slowly let out his breath.

His mother clenched her teeth, and again lifted the spoon to his mouth. As before, he swallowed painfully, and eventually managed to swallow two more mouthfuls, but the next time, the whole spoonful of chicken soup came up again. He coughed soundlessly. His mother at once put down the bowl and began to massage his chest.

Slowly, he closed his eyes. He wanted to sleep, but the pain kept him awake. He could not groan, he could not cry out. He fought against the pain in silence. His mother's hands brought him some relief. He concentrated all his thoughts on his mother, hoping for a time to forget his pain and suffering.

Suddenly, the streets echoed with the explosions of firecrackers. Although such a sound was rarely heard in this mountainous city, they were in no mood to pay it any attention. Unexpectedly, the noise of the crackers continued. From far and near, people began letting off firecrackers, as if some great, joyous event had taken place. There was a confused hubbub of voices, with people running about, people singing at the tops of their voices, people laughing and talking.

"What is it?" he wondered, a thought which his mother expressed aloud.

"Japan has surrendered! Japan has surrendered!" Children's voices in the streets were followed up by the voices of other young people.

He was stunned. His mother, forgetting everything, shouted: "Xuan, did you hear? They're saying that Japan has surrendered!"

He shook his head, still not believing. The explosions of the firecrackers outside became more frequent.

Below the window people seemed to be rushing past the street in waves.

"It must be true, or they wouldn't behave like this!" his mother cried excitedly.

He still shook his head. The news had come too suddenly!

"United Press telegraph: The Japanese Government has surrendered unconditionally to the four powers of China, the United States, Britain and the Soviet Union!" someone in the street was shouting.

"Do you hear? Isn't this true? Japan has surrendered! The war's won! We won't have to suffer anymore!" she shouted hysterically. She was laughing and weeping at the same time. She seemed to have forgotten that she was in a dismal room, lit by a single candle placed on a wooden stool by the bed, its flame flickering wildly, its wick drooping to one side, the wax pouring through the little gap that had formed.

He stared at his mother with wide-open eyes, as if not understanding what she meant. Suddenly, tears sprang from his eyes. He wanted to laugh and he wanted to cry. But he soon calmed down. He gave a long sigh as he thought: You're finished, and I'm finished!

"Extra! Extra! Japanese surrendered!" cried a newspaper seller running past below the window.

His mother seized him by the hand and, smiling, asked him gently: "Xuan, are you happy? We've won! We've won!"

He took his pencil with a shaking hand, and wrote painfully on the paper: "Now I can die with my eyes closed."

When his mother saw these shakily written words, she forgot everything. Laughing and crying at the same time, she shouted: "Xuan, you won't die! You won't die! The war's won! No one will ever die again!"

Tears cascaded from her eyes, and she squeezed his hand tightly, not knowing whether what she felt was joy or grief.

30

His mother's hope was not realized. One evening after she had expressed this wish, she sat by the bed watching over her son. The electric lamp still gave only a dim light, and on the wooden stool by the bedside stood a small rice bowl full to the brim of chicken soup in which a spoon was dipped.

"Xuan, drink a couple of mouthfuls," she said.

His eyes turned to look up at the ceiling. He moved a little, making a weak gesture with his hands, but made no effort to pick up his pencil. He did not answer.

"Xuan, you haven't taken anything for two days. Try to bear the pain and eat a little," she begged insistently.

He moved his head slightly. He opened his mouth, and with

a great effort, lifted his arm to the side of his mouth and grasped his lower lip. Then loosening his grip, he put his fingers
into his mouth, clawing at his tongue.

"Xuan, are you in pain? Try to endure it," she said miserably, grasping his other hand firmly.

He nodded, took his hand from his mouth and pressed it
to his throat. He gazed at his mother, his eyes filled with tears.

"You mustn't be upset. You won't die," she comforted him.

He kept rubbing his throat with all five fingers, but the
movements were slow and awkward, for his fingers were stiff.
Suddenly, he heaved his chest upwards.

"Xuan, what do you want?" his mother asked.

He did not reply. After a long time, he seized himself madly by the throat. His fingers now seemed to have become rigid.
His body and the bed creaked.

"Xuan, try to be patient," his mother said. Letting go his
left hand, she stood up and pulled his right hand from his
throat. But within two or three minutes, he had moved it back
to where it was. He breathed with effort, through his wide-
open mouth. His eyes were turned upwards, their whites
showing. He clawed madly at his throat with his fingers, the
untended nails leaving behind streaks of blood.

"Xuan, you must be patient. It's no good doing that. You
mustn't do that," his mother implored in grief and anguish.
His eyes turned slowly towards her. It was his eyes that spoke:
"I'm in such pain." His body rocked to and fro on the bed,
shaking and quivering.

"Xuan, are you in great pain?" she asked.

He nodded. He took his right hand from his throat, clawing
wildly at the air, but she did not know what he wanted.

"Xuan, what do you want?" she asked.

His eyes moved slowly to the pencil by the pillow.

"Do you want to say something? Do you want the pencil?"
she asked, picking it up at the same time and handing it to him.
He tried to seize the pencil, but his fingers trembled so violently as he took it that he almost dropped it onto the bedclothes.

His mother gave him a book. "Write it on the back," she said.

Holding the pencil in one hand and the book in the other, with great effort, he wrote on the back of the book the single character "pain". In fact, it only partly resembled the character. The number of strokes was correct, but they were arranged shakily and unevenly.

His mother looked at the word and burst into tears: "Xuan, bear it for a little while. Wait till Xiao Xuan comes and fetches Zhang Boqing, then everything will be all right." Although she was trying to comfort him, as soon as she finished speaking, she turned her face away and began to weep softly.

His mind was perfectly clear. He could feel the pain keenly, feel his own weakness. He knew that every organ of his body was gradually dying and was moreover approaching its last extremity. But as this happened, he felt even more strongly his desire for life, his fear of death. He could also see the suffering he was causing his mother. He saw her go to the window weeping, but what could he do? If only he could speak, leave a few words as his testament. "What wrong have I ever done? I've been a law-abiding, harmless good sort! Why must I suffer this punishment? And my mother, when I'm dead, how will she survive on her own? What will she live on ? How will Xiao Xuan live? What wrong have they ever done?" His heart was filled with resentment. He wanted to cry out, to scream. But he had no voice. No one would hear him. He demanded "justice", but where could he find justice? He could not cry out his grief and indignation. He had to die in total silence.

In the street, a husband and wife were quarrelling, the woman was shouting and crying, the man was cursing her and beating her, while a third person tried to make peace between them. Someone passed the window singing an aria from a Sichuan opera.

"Why may they live, and I die? And die in such a painful way?" he thought. "I want to live!" he cried soundlessly.

His mother turned to look at him, her eyes swollen from weeping, her face sallow and wan, as if she would collapse from illness at any moment.

"It's too hard on her too," he reflected miserably. He moved his head. Suddenly, he was seized by an intense pain attacking both his throat and his lungs, so painful that he could not stand it. He clutched wildly at the air with both hands. He opened his mouth to cry out, but no sound came. With all his strength, he opened his mouth still wider, but still failed to produce any sound. His head was bathed in sweat, he felt someone take both his hands, heard his mother's voice say something . . . but the pain was so intense, he fainted.

He was woken by the sound of his mother's weeping. He was lying in bed in a cold sweat, and had wetted his trousers. He grasped his mother's hand tightly, staring blankly at her dear face. The pain had eased slightly. He wanted to smile at her, but instead came tears beyond his control.

"Now that you're awake, everything will be all right," his mother said, sighing affectionately, tears still staining her cheeks and the corners of her eyes.

He shook his head in disagreement.

Xiao Xuan came into the flat from outside, calling as soon as he entered the room: "Grandma, Zhang Boqing has malaria. He can't come."

For a moment, she was stunned. That was the end! Her heart had been struck by a stone. "Why were you so long?" she asked.

"The streets were so full of people everywhere, getting ready for the victory celebrations tomorrow. I took the wrong road and I was held up at Zhang Boqing's place for a while." Xiao Xuan replied. Then he added in explanation: "It's going to be pretty lively tonight. They've put colour lanterns up everywhere!"

"Are you hungry? You've got some money on you still, so you'd better go and buy yourself two bowls of noodles.

I didn't cook this afternoon, and I fried and ate the rice left over from this morning. Hurry up and go and eat," she said.

"All right," Xiao Xuan answered.

He heard the whole conversation. "They're celebrating," he thought, wanting to smile at them, but prevented by the pain. "Will victory bring them salvation?" he then wondered, meaning by "them" his mother and Xiao Xuan. But the pain returned once more and interrupted his thoughts. He was overcome by the pain. The pain invaded his whole being, increasing slowly, increasing continuously, chasing away every other thought. Pain made him forget everything. He could think only of how to endure it, of how to escape it. A hopeless battle was in progress. He lost. But he had to continue the struggle. He cried out in noiseless grief: "Then let me die. I cannot bear such pain!"

But his beloved ones, his mother and his son could not understand this soundless cry. They could not help him find release from his pain.

The pain went on, growing all the time.

The third of September, day of victory, day of joy and laughter, brought no change to the room. In the streets, people paraded in the victory celebrations, wreathed in smiles, while overhead, planes performed their aerobatics, scattering celebration leaflets, but in Wang Wenxuan's flat, there was only suffering and tears.

That day, he lost and regained consciousness three times. He felt he had reached the limit of pain that any man could endure. He wished that "death" might come at once to deliver him, but he continued to live. His mother and Xiao Xuan remained by his bedside throughout, while he gazed at them, his eyes brimming with tears, begging them to help him die sooner.

His life ebbed away minute by minute. And although unable to think much, his brain retained its lucidity to the end. In those last moments, he was unwilling to take his eyes from the faces of his mother and Xiao Xuan. Later, as their faces gradually blurred, he seemed to see another face, that of Shu-sheng. He had not forgotten her. But not even these three faces could reduce his pain. He was in pain until the final moment. He clung to his last breath, and for a long time, refused to die. His mother and Xiao Xuan, each held and pressed one of his hands, watching over his breathing.

Then he breathed his last, his eyes half-closed, the pupils turned upwards, his mouth wide open as if demanding "justice" from someone. It was about eight o'clock in the evening. The streets resounded with the deafening noise of gongs and drums, and people celebrated victory by letting off firecrackers and lighting dragon-lanterns.

Epilogue

One night about two months later, there was a power cut in the mountainous city, on the grounds that they were repairing all the boilers in the town. It had rained in the morning, in the afternoon the weather had suddenly turned bitterly cold, and a chill wind, gusting through the city, had chased the customers from the stalls and spread everywhere the smell from the carbide lamps, the flames of which flickered desolately in the cold.

A rickshaw passed through the dim, cold, desolate streets and stopped at the door of a large building. From it descended a woman dressed in the latest fashion. She walked through the swing doors, her handbag under her arm, shining a torch to light her way as she crossed the dark cavern of the foyer and mounted to the first floor, and then to the second floor.

She stood before the door of one of the flats, her heart beating furiously, and excitedly knocked at the door.

There was no answer. She could see there was a light in the room, and that the door was not locked. There must be someone there, she thought. Perhaps they were asleep. She knocked harder, twice more.

"Who is it?" a woman's voice called from within. The voice seemed familiar to her, but she could not place it.

"Me," she answered casually, in a single word.

The door opened, letting out a faint glimmer of light. She glimpsed a candle burning on a table. It was a woman who came to the door. Her face was hidden by the light, so she could not see clearly who it was.

"Whom are you looking for?" the woman asked in surprise.

"Does the Wang family live here?" the visitor asked, even more surprised.

"There's no one called Wang here," the other replied.

"Didn't there used to be a Wang family here? It's definitely this flat, it's the same furniture," the visitor exclaimed, her amazement becoming even greater.

"Oh, you're Mrs. Wang! Please come in and sit down. There's a power cut tonight and I couldn't see you properly," the woman who answered the door cried, smiling as she stepped aside to let the visitor in.

"Mrs. Fang! Didn't you use to live on the first floor? When did you move up here?" The visitor recognized the woman who opened the door as Mrs. Fang who used to live on the first floor, and now that she had finally met someone she knew, she felt a little more at ease. The furniture in the room had not changed, although the walls were much whiter and a little more pleasing to the eye.

"The middle of this month," Mrs. Fang replied. "Mrs. Wang, ah, I don't know how I should address you now. Aren't you in Lanzhou? When did you come back?"

"I just arrived today, Mrs. Fang. I haven't changed. I'm the same as before." Shusheng blushed as she spoke. Then she added in a trembling voice: "Mrs. Fang, where have they moved to? I mean Wenxuan and the others."

"You mean Mr. Wang? You don't know?" Mrs. Fang asked in surprise.

"I really don't know. I haven't had a letter from them in two months," Shusheng said uneasily.

"Mr. Wang passed away," Mrs. Fang said softly.

"Passed away? When?" Shusheng tottered and paled as she cried out in alarm.

"Last month, on the day of the victory celebrations," Mrs. Fang explained. Shusheng shuddered violently. "The old lady left with her grandson. She let us have this flat, together with the furniture. We paid her some money for it."

Shusheng felt as if someone had poured a bucket of cold

water over her. Her whole body went cold, her face turned deathly pale. It was a long time before she could utter a word. "Where have they moved to?" she then asked, wiping her eyes with her hands and turning her face aside.

"I don't know. I asked the old lady. She said first she'd go and stay a few days with some relatives, and then something about going to Kunming. I think I also heard her ask someone to buy her some boat tickets," Mrs. Fang said, trying to think, her voice without emotion, as if not very sure of what she was saying.

"You don't need boat tickets for Kunming. And they haven't got relatives around here," Shusheng said doubtfully. "I wonder where they've gone."

"Well, that's what the old lady said," Mrs. Fang replied. "But I think they've most likely gone to Kunming. Before they left, they sold almost everything. They set up their things on the ground at the main entrance. Ah, Mrs. Wang, you've been sitting here so long, and I haven't even made you a cup of tea," she said apologetically, standing up and going to a tea-table where stood a thermos flask, a teapot and some teacups.

"Mrs. Fang, please don't bother. I'm not thirsty," Shusheng said at once, half rising to block the way. "Please tell me, do you know how Wenxuan was before he died? Where is he buried?"

"Mrs. Wang, don't be upset. Stay and rest awhile. Have a cup of tea first," Mrs. Fang said gently, placing a cup of tea before her.

"Thank you, but please tell me how he was just before he died. When I was in Lanzhou, I thought he was gradually getting better. He used to say in every letter that his health was all right. Please tell me, I'm not afraid. Tell me the truth."

"Actually, I don't know, I really don't know. When Mr. Wang was ill, I saw old Mrs. Wang only once. I know only that he lost his voice and died after less than two and a half months or so in bed. When I saw him in bed that time, he couldn't speak, and was so pitiably thin — " Mrs. Fang said, in a voice full of sadness.

"Where is he buried? I must go and see him!" Shusheng interrupted, forgetting everything. She felt a moment of intense pain. She was filled with regret, genuinely wanting to go to his grave instantly.

"I don't know. I heard that when Mr. Wang was dying, there was no money, and the body had to be left in the room with no preparations made until, after old Mrs. Wang had spent two whole days running about, they finally scraped together enough to buy a coffin and dress the body for burial. I don't know where Mr. Wang is buried. I asked the old lady, but she wouldn't say. She really suffered so much. During the two months, she became so much thinner, and her hair turned all white," Mrs. Fang said, looking at her sympathetically.

Shusheng bit her lip as she listened. The tip of her nose tingled and her heart jumped wildly, a feeling of bitter remorse tore at her breast. Tears ran down her cheeks. But she did her best to control herself. "Then there must be some neighbours who know where he's buried? He can't have disappeared without a trace. There must be someone from the office who knows. At the very least, Mr. Zhong must know," she said, as if debating with someone, not knowing that old Mr. Zhong was no longer in this world.

"No one here knows. The coffin was taken out very early in the morning. No one went to the funeral. Old Mrs. Wang didn't inform any of us. But there must be someone in Mr. Wang's office who knows," Mrs. Fang said kindheartedly. She wanted very much to help her visitor, but she knew that she herself could do nothing.

"I'll go to the office tomorrow and try to find out," Shusheng said in disappointment. She dropped her head and wiped her eyes with her handkerchief. "When did the old lady move out?" she asked.

"I remember it was the twelfth. She moved out that day,

and the next day, we whitewashed the walls, and the fourth day, we moved in. My husband uses the room downstairs for meeting visitors and as a business office. Ah, Mrs. Wang, I haven't asked you where you're staying?" Mrs. Fang asked solicitously.

"For the time being ... at a friend's place. ... I'll be going back in a few days," Shusheng said hesitantly.

"Then are you going to look for the old lady and her grandson?" Mrs. Fang pressed on with her questions.

The sound of a baby crying suddenly penetrated the room. Without waiting for her visitor to answer, Mrs. Fang at once got up, saying anxiously: "My daughter's awake. Please sit down for a while." She hastened into the small room.

Shusheng escaped having to answer a difficult and painful question. She continued to sit there, alone with the candle. All at once, she had the feeling of being in a dream. This was her own flat. She had used this furniture herself: the square table, the desk, the small bookcase, the crockery cupboard, the bed ... everything was familiar to her, although the broken items had been repaired, the old things cleaned, and the walls whitewashed till they gleamed. But now, sitting on the stool that she had sat on for so many years, she had become a stranger, so much so that she could find no trace of the past in these familiar objects. A candle was burning as it had always done, but it seemed so much brighter than before. In less than a year, everything had changed. He was dead, his mother and her child gone. Where was he buried? Where had they gone? She did not know. Why had they not let her know? How could she find out? Another's child was crying in the room. What a strange sound! Now the young mother was pacing back and forth in the tiny room, cradling the child in her arms, singing a lullaby. She had done this in the past, over ten years ago, for Xiao Xuan. But now, where was Xiao Xuan? That child had never been sorry to part from her, and she had never fully expressed to him a mother's love. She had neglected him, and now she had lost him forever. He was her one and only child. Mrs. Fang still did not come out. The baby continued to cry fitfully, while Mrs. Fang patiently sang the lullaby, walking up and down, patting the child. The woman seemed to have forgotten her existence. In her concern for the child, she had forgotten her visitor, leaving her sitting cold and cheerless in the outside room, surrounded by the torment of her memories. Suddenly, she thought of the scene in the stairwell. They had shaken hands in the dark. She had thrown herself in tears against his body and kissed him. "I wanted you to take care of yourself. Why didn't you tell me, even when you had become so ill?" she thought in misery. When she got off the plane today, she had been thinking: "I've come back just for your good. I've never done anything to you that I need feel sorry for." She could say this to him in all honesty. But now, it was too late. She did not dare think about how he had died. It was too late, too late! For the sake of her own happiness, she had helped destroy another person's. . . . Her thoughts went on and on. All at once, she stood up. Why was she here? She could not stand this room or its furniture. Every piece told his story and hers. Every piece hurt her. She almost could not bear the young mother's lullaby. It reminded her of when she herself had been a mother, calling up memories that she had long since buried. She had to go.

"Mrs. Fang, I'm leaving. Please don't come out," she called, picking up her handbag and moving towards the door.

Mrs. Fang hurried out with the child in her arms and cried earnestly: "Mrs. Wang, stay for a while. It's early yet!"

Shusheng stopped and turned to look at her. "I have to go, but thank you," she said.

"Then take care," Mrs. Fang said gently, adding: "You'll come back again, won't you?"

"Thank you, but I won't be back," Shusheng said, shaking her head. This time, she did not weep, but she felt even more miserable than if she had.

"Then wait. I'll fetch a candle so that you can see. It's so dark outside," Mrs. Fang said solicitously, carrying the child in one arm and picking up a candlestick in her other hand.

"Mrs. Fang, please don't come. I've a torch. I can see. I'm used to the place," Shusheng said politely, and hurried out into the corridor.

"Mrs. Wang, wait! Wait! I'll see you to the stairs," Mrs. Fang shouted, and then added peevishly: "It's terrible. There are still power cuts. It's over two months since the war was over, but nothing's got any better. Instead it's worse."

Shusheng had already reached the staircase. She turned and, waving her torch towards Mrs. Fang, cried: "Mrs. Fang, please go back in. I'm leaving now." Without waiting for a reply, she hurried down the stairs. She really was familiar with the place, and once she began to descend, she did so without difficulty.

Just as she reached the entrance, she was met by a bitterly cold gust that made her shudder. "It's only the end of October, yet it's already so chilly at night!" she thought, feeling her autumn overcoat not warm enough. From the entrance, there was no rickshaw to be seen. She looked back at the entrance and the dim lamp above it and let out a sigh. She did not know where it was best to go now. Her mind was a complete void. She just wanted to find somewhere to lock herself in and weep. But there was nothing she could do, except walk slowly along the footpath.

"Excuse me, miss. We're refugees from Guilin. We've lost everything . . . " A black figure darted suddenly from the darkness and was beside her in a flash. She was startled by a thin, withered hand stretched towards her face. She looked closely. It was an old woman.

Opening her purse, she took out a note, and thrust it into the dark hand.

"Thank you, miss," the old woman said, shrinking back into the darkness.

She shook her head and continued to move ahead. Then she saw a light.

"Bargain . . . for sale . . . 500 *yuan* . . . 300 *yuan* . . . 200 *yuan* . . . "

The bitter cold wind blew the stench from the carbide lamps into her nostrils. From smiling lips came a voice wailing as if in grief. A young woman was sitting on a low stool, cuddling a sleeping baby in her arms, while staring with dead eyes at the heap of goods she had been unable to sell.

She shuddered again. "The night is so cold!" she thought. "She is a mother too," she also thought. She stood for a moment before the goods spread out on the ground, looking with sympathy at the woman and the child in her arms. "I must find Xiao Xuan," she told herself. Then she looked once more at the woman and the child before her. "They also set their things out on the ground like this," she thought. This "they", needless to say, was old Mrs. Wang and Xiao Xuan. She became even more upset.

"When are you going?" someone near her was saying.

"I can't. How can ordinary people like us get boat tickets!" another answered.

"You should think of a way. Stowing away always works."

"Now that the officials are going back to their posts, ordinary people can't get back. I've a relative who couldn't buy a ticket and tried to stow away. He was caught on the ship. He paid out all that money for nothing."

"At least you're all right if you can't go. If you stay in Sichuan a few more months, you won't have to worry about not having enough to eat. But if I can't get away, I'll starve. I'll soon have sold or eaten up everything. At first, I thought, with the war over, I'd be able to go home."

"But they won the war, not us! We never made any money out of the disaster to our country, and so winning is bad luck for us. I knew all along I should never have taken part in the victory celebrations that day."

Again she shuddered. She felt as if she had suddenly step-

The night was so cold. She needed warmth.

ped into an icy cellar, and her whole body froze. She looked around her vaguely, conscious of the falsity of everything she saw. It was as if she were in a dream. At this time yesterday, she was still dining in the noisy restaurant of another city, listening to another man's flattery. Today, however, she was standing in front of these wares laid out on the ground, listening on a bitter cold night to the complaints of these strangers. Why had she come back? And what was she feeling now that she had left the flat? ... What should she do now? ... She was waiting for the morrow.

The dead were dead, the departed had gone. Even when the morrow came, the most she could do would be to find a dead man's grave. But could she find Xiao Xuan again? Could she change anything of the present? What should she do? Should she search the world in what she clearly knew to be a vain search? Or should she go back to Lanzhou and accept the other man's proposal?

She had only a fortnight's leave, and in these two weeks, she must decide her own future. . . . At least she still had twelve to thirteen days, and the matter was not that difficult to decide. Why must she stand in front of these wares enduring the blast of the bitter cold wind?

"I've time to decide," she finally told herself. She moved away, her steps slow but steady. Just as she walked down this dim street, she was suddenly overcome by a strange feeling. She kept turning to glance again and again at the two sides of the street, afraid lest the flickering carbide lamps be blown out by the bitter cold wind. The night was so cold. She needed warmth.

Completed on December 31, 1946

Afterword

In the winter of 1944, when Guilin had fallen to the enemy,
I was living in a room, so small that it could not have been
any smaller, on the ground floor of the Culture and Life
Publishing House in Minguo Road in Chongqing. In the
evening, I often used to prepare a candle to light my desk,
and at midnight I would take my thermos to the old man who
used to call, "Puffed rice and sweetened water!" to buy some
boiled water with which to quench my thirst. I used to go
to bed late, but the rats, gnawing incessantly under the concrete floor all night, would prevent me from going to sleep.
In the daytime, the whole house would reverberate with the
cries of hawkers, the noise of quarrelling, the hubbub of conversation, and the beating of the gongs and drums of the
theatre. Noise seemed to come from every direction, and even
though I locked myself in my room, I could not get any quiet.
At the time, I was correcting a full-length novel by Gorky
translated by a friend of mine, and sometimes, I would do some
small jobs for friends who had taken refuge from Guilin. One
day, a friend, Zhao Jiabi, came unexpectedly to the Culture
and Life Publishing House to look for me. He had come
empty-handed, after the business he had set up in Guilin had
been completely destroyed by enemy gunfire. Although he
had managed to save a part of his stock of books, these had
then been destroyed by the great fire at Jinchengjiang. This
loss caused him great pain, but he was not downhearted. He
decided to establish a new base in Chongqing, and I agreed to
help him.

And so, one cold winter night, I began to write the novel

480

Bitter Cold Nights. I have never been a great writer, and even
in my dreams, I would never dare think of writing an
epic. As a "critic", "who looks at life through a crack . . ."
has said, I "dare not face the cruelty and the bleeding reality"
and so I write only of things I have seen myself; I write only
of a tuberculosis sufferer's blood-stained sputum; I write only
of the life and death of an insignificant intellectual. But I
have told no lies. I saw the blood-stained drops of sputum
with my own eyes. They are still deeply impressed on my
mind, and they forced me to take up my pen to speak out on
behalf of those who have died after coughing up all their blood-
stained sputum, and those who have not yet finished doing so.
I wrote this novel in fits and starts, finishing it after two years,
but the bookshop for which Zhao Jiabi worked was already out
of business (the Chenguang Publishing House has only recently
been founded). Besides, during this period, I lost a good
friend and an elder brother, both of whom died in loneliness
after coughing up their blood and sputum. During this period,
"victory" brought us hope, and then gradually took hope away.
I have not, as suggested by the "critic", added the words "Hail
to the dawn!" to the end of the novel. This is not because I
am afraid of being arrested and hung. The sole reason is that,
when they died, those who were destroyed by the unjust
system, dragged to their death by their conditions of life, did
not have the strength to hail the "dawn"!

But I have had cause to cry out once or twice. For example,
six years ago, in an essay "The Long Night" I wrote in Guilin, I
wrote: "This is a cry for light, which can awaken us to the
dawn, for the long night is drawing to its close." That essay
really was written in the depths of a bitter cold night, and I
wrote down faithfully the feelings and thoughts that I had then.

I wrote these words a year ago. Now that *Bitter Cold Nights*
is about to be republished, I do not wish to write another after-
word, because there would be too many things I wanted to
say. If I wrote them all down, it would be another even
longer *Bitter Cold Nights.* Today the weather really is

terribly cold. The *Dagong Bao*, spread out at my left hand, has a headline reporting: "Temperature Below Zero All Day! Over 100 Corpses Picked Up from the Roads in Two Days!" Outside the window, a bitterly cold wind is howling, and my door, which is not securely locked, creaks from time to time. My feet, seeking refuge in leather shoes, are almost frozen stiff. A year ago, even two years ago, we had not yet suffered such a "bitter cold night." I am still alive. I have not died of tuberculosis, nor have I frozen to death. I was born under a lucky star. This book has sold five thousand copies, but it is not something to rejoice over. I know of many worse written books that have sold even more copies.

Ba Jin, end of January 1948 in Shanghai
Translated by J. Hoe, June 1984

On *Bitter Cold Nights*

I recently saw the Soviet film *The Overcoat*, adapted from Gogol's short story. The film was really not bad, and the audience was greatly moved by it. However, after the film, I was troubled all night, feeling suffocated by something continually pressing of my mind. Before me, a figure kept appearing and disappearing, needless to say, that of the petty clerk Akasi Bashmakin. Only after a day, did his figure begin gradually to fade. But another man's face appeared in my mind, that of my hero Wang Wenxuan, a small clerk who died of tuberculosis.

Wang Wenxuan is not a real person, yet I have always felt that he was a very close friend. In the past, I saw him every day, I saw him everywhere, his face always wan, his eyes lifeless, his cheeks thin, his head bowing before others, his hands, hanging by his sides, coughing slightly, walking on tiptoe like someone afraid of others. He was kindhearted, and would never have thought of harming anyone, hoping only that he himself would suffer no illness or catastrophe, and would just live a plain and simple life. I have in fact seen a great many people like this, and also known quite a few. In the old society, they met with disdain everywhere and accepted without protest every kind of unjust treatment, doing their work laboriously and conscientiously, day in, day out, year in, year out, but without ever succeeding in clothing or feeding their families. Step by step, they travelled along the road to a tragic death, and only when they finally breathed their last did they obtain rest. But because no arrangements or guarantees had been made for the livelihood of their wives and children, they could not close their eyes in peace even in death.

In the old society, how many people caught tuberculosis and died in pain and misery! How many families lived an inhuman life of poverty and distress, in which there was no assurance that the life which began in the morning would not end by the evening! There were countless people like Wang Wenxuan! In the past, most kind and honest people believed that "the good would be rewarded with good". But in the old society, there was absolutely no way in which the good could be rewarded with good. On the contrary, the most commonly seen phenomenon was that of "evil men prospering". I began writing *Bitter Cold Nights* in the early winter of 1944 in a small room, so small that it could not have been smaller, under the staircase of the Culture and Life Publishing House in Minguo Road, just at the time when evil men were prospering. After writing a few pages, I put down my pen, but in the early winter of 1945, I took up my pen again and continued from where I had left off the previous year. In Chongqing and the Kuomintang-controlled areas, that was still a time when evil men were prospering. I wrote my novel to explain that the good could not be rewarded with good. My sole aim was to let people see what the society under the rule of Chiang Kai-shek and the Kuomintang was like. When I started to write, I seemed to hear perpetually in my ears, a voice crying: "I must redress the wrongs of these nobodies." This was of course my own voice, for I had not a few friends and relatives who had died in the same tragic way as Wang Wenxuan. I felt for them. Although I did not approve of the way they kept their place, enduring humiliation to seek momentary ease, nevertheless, I suffered miserably, for I saw with my own eyes how they went towards death while I could do nothing to help them. Even if I could not redress their wrongs, I could at least describe their life and circumstances, and leave behind a work by which I would always remember them, and which would warn bystanders not to take them as a model.

The characters of *Bitter Cold Nights* are fictional, but the background, the events, etc., are completely factual. I am not saying that I used a camera to take photographs all day, nor am I saying that what I wrote was a news report of true people and true events. I am saying that the whole story took place all around me at the place where I was living at that time, upstairs above my room, at the doorway of the big building where I lived, in Minguo Road and the neighbouring streets. People sheltered from air-raids, drank wine, quarrelled, fell ill ... all these things were happening every day. The prices kept shooting up, life was difficult, the war was suffering setbacks, and people were in constant anxiety.... No matter where I went, and even when I was sitting in my small room, I would hear the "nobodies" venting their grievances and pouring out their woes. Even if they are not people to whom I can give a name or a surname, people who are known to every household, even if they are not events which everyone has witnessed and which can be recorded in the history books, they are nevertheless people and events I actually often saw and heard at that time. These people lived, and these events occurred continually. Everything was so natural that I seemed to be living in my own novel, I seemed to be watching the people around me acting out a tragic drama of joy and sorrow, reunion and separation. I was familiar with the wine-shop selling cold snacks, I was familiar with the coffee-shop, I was familiar with the semi-government, semi-private book company, I was familiar with every place in the novel. I lived in that small room in peaceful coexistence with the rats and the bedbugs, continually observing what was going on above me, below me and all around me. From their midst, I selected a part to incorporate into my novel. I often went in and out the main entrance through which Wang Wenxuan and his wife passed several times a day. Early and late, I used to stroll through those streets that appear in the novel. I was an old customer of the old man who sold "puffed rice and sweetened water"; the power cuts that lasted all night also drew from me not a few complaints, and I could not stand the dim, lifeless surroundings. The cold, cheerless scene of the first chapter of *Bitter Cold Nights* in which Wang Wenxuan shelters from the air-raid, was an event I saw just an hour or so before I picked up my pen. From then on, I wrote continually, although it was only after a year that I resumed the writing, and moreover I wrote with many breaks in between, the last two thirds of the manuscript being completed in Huaihai Lane after I returned to Shanghai, the final date of completion being late at night on December 31, 1946. Although I wrote off and on and was interrupted by a major shift from Chongqing to Shanghai, I felt the writing flowing smoothly as if guided by my pen to put down the biography of a close friend, as if recording the memoirs of this husband and wife. I seemed to live together with this family, each day crossing the long, narrow corridor to go up to the second floor to pass a few moments in their flat, sitting quietly in a corner, listening to them converse, air their grievances, quarrel and make up; I seemed every day to have the opportunity to see Wang Wenxuan off to work, to walk with Zeng Shusheng to the bank, to accompany old Mrs. Wang to the market to buy vegetables ... and each and every one of them spoke to me openly of their individual hopes and sufferings.

When I wrote the first chapter, I really had the feeling that although Wang Wenxuan's family had lived in the same building as I for several months, we had only recently begun to converse. As I wrote I gradually came to know them. The more I wrote, the more I understood them, and the deeper the friendship between us became. The three of them were my friends. I heard plenty of their quarrels. I saw the shortcomings of each of them, I understood the reasons for their quarrelling. I knew that each of them was moving inexorably towards an unhappy end, and I had also admonished each one of them. I criticized them, but I sympathized with them, with each and every one of them. My feeling for them grew. When I came to write about Wang Wenxuan's death, I was extremely upset. I really felt like crying out to release the indignation bottled up inside me. When I came to write about Zeng Shusheng walking alone in the dim street, I really wanted to drag her back, to implore her not to go forward, to prevent her one day from falling into the abyss. But since there was no way in which I could change their destiny, what pain and misery I felt for their unhappy fate!

I know that some people will accuse me of wasting my sympathy; they claim that these people are all in the wrong and do not deserve any pity. There have also been readers who have written to me to ask: Of these three people, who is right and who is wrong? Who is the hero? Who is the villain? With whom does the author sympathize? My answer is: None of them is a hero, and none a villain. Each one is in the right, and each is in the wrong. I sympathize with them all. What I want to say is that you cannot blame the three of them. The fault lay with Chiang Kai-shek and the reactionary Kuomintang government. The fault lay with the society in Chongqing and the Nationalist-controlled areas. They were all innocent victims. My purpose here is not to defend myself. In a creative work, an author's self-praise or self-justification is of no use whatsoever. I am merely explaining what I actually thought at the time I picked up my pen to write about this family.

I have already explained that the setting of *Bitter Cold Nights* was Chongqing, the place where Wang Wenxuan's family lived being the three-storey building in Minguo Road where I was living at the time. I lived on the ground floor of the Culture and Life Publishing House, while they lived on the second floor. In July 1942, when I first arrived at Minguo Road, I lived on the second floor. At the end of 1945, when I resumed writing *Bitter Cold Nights*, I had already moved to the first floor, to a room facing the street. The building was old and dilapidated, and not long before, had been rebuilt out of the rubble from the bombing. But in Chongqing in those days, even a building of this kind was not to be sneezed at, and besides, it had been fitted with swinging doors with ornamental engravings. On the ground floor were a shop and an

office. Upstairs were offices and the lodgings of the office-
workers, as well as flats for private individuals. Some flats
were clean and tidy, some were rickety, and through the wood-
en partitions that separated them, voices could be heard nearly
all the time coming from all directions. If the flats were available for renting, the price was not cheap, and moreover, such
flats were not easy to get. But while the building was being
rebuilt, some people forked out a lot of money and were able
to move in for several years without paying anything further in
rent. Needless to say, it was through Zeng Shusheng's social
contacts that Wang Wenxuan's family was able to move in,
and the rent was paid by her. They did not of course move
there because they liked the noise and the confusion, all of
which merely added to their agitation and could not ease their
loneliness in any way. The only reason was that it was close
to the places where they worked. Wang Wenxuan was a proof-
reader in a semi-government, semi-private book publishing
company. I did not reveal the company's name in the book,
and I should like to make it known now — it was the Zhengzhong Book Company, run by the Kuomintang. I did not know
anything of the inner goings-on at the Zhengzhong Book Company. But I was not writing about its vile history. The
true situation could only be more hideous than what Wang
Wenxuan saw or suffered, many times more hideous. I was
writing about Wang Wenxuan, a minor intellectual, honest,
sincere and kindhearted, whose status under the Kuomintang
rule was lower than that of anybody, a petty clerk, humiliated
everywhere like Bashmakin. He worked hard and conscientiously, never sought to be lazy, but he was confined to a low
position, on a low salary, and despised by all. As for his wife,
Zeng Shusheng, she was a clerk in a private bank, the Bank
of Sichuan, also located near Minguo Road. In the bank, she
really was a so-called "flower vase" a kind of ornament; that
is to say, her role was purely decorative. She went to work
every day, but the work was not important. As long as she
was beautifully dressed, could talk and laugh, keep the manager

and the heads of department happy, then she had fulfilled her
duties. Her salary was by no means small, and she also had
the opportunity to take part in a little speculation. She
relied on these sources of income to help with half the household expenses (the other half coming from her husband), pay
for her son's schooling, and also enable herself to live a life of
comparative comfort. Then there was Wang Wenxuan's
mother. She was well-educated, and could have been a woman
of talent in Kunming in Yunnan Province. Before the war,
she had led a happy life of comfort and ease in Shanghai. At
the beginning of the War of Resistance, she returned to Sichuan
with her son (he was Sichuanese), and a few years later she
became, in the words of her daughter-in-law, a "second-class
amah". She could not stand her daughter-in-law's life as a
"flower vase", and did not want to depend on her to live, but
she could not help using her daughter-in-law's money indirectly. She loved her son, and his plight made her resentful.
The more she loved her son, the more dissatisfied she became
with her daughter-in-law, for unlike her, her daughter-in-law
did not devote herself heart and soul to this one person.

In my novel then, this was the kind of family I was writing
about. Two kindhearted middle-class intellectuals, two grad-
uates in education from a university in Shanghai, depend on
proof-reading and on being a "flower vase" to earn a living.
A life of privation and hardship, in a kind of living death, in-
creases the conflict between the incompatible ideas of mother
and daughter-in-law, while the little clerk, as son and husband
caught in the middle, can only silently choke back his tears
and let his lifeblood drain slowly away, drop by drop. This
was the tragedy of a good, kindhearted intellectual's life under
the Kuomintang rule. Although the tragedy did not always take
the same form, the conclusion was inevitable: families broken
up and destroyed. Wang Wenxuan's family of four consists
of three generations, including a grandmother and a grandson.
But the thirteen-year-old junior secondary school pupil is a
boarder at school. Weak physically and always busy at his

lessons, he does not talk much when he comes home, nor does
anyone pay any attention to him at home. And so in this
novel, I concentrate on only the three people mentioned above.
About them, I should also like to state that, although the setting and background are real, the characters themselves are
composites. At first, there was no real Wang Wenxuan in my
mind. It was only after the manuscript was completed that I
saw his face clearly. Four years ago, Mr. Wu Chufan came to
Shanghai and invited me to see the Hong Kong Cantonese film
of *Bitter Cold Nights* that he had brought with him. He acted
as interpreter for me. I felt that the Wang Wenxuan of my
imagination was the very person that he had portrayed. Wang
Wenxuan came alive before my eyes. I praised his outstanding
acting skill, for he seemed to have shrunk his own physical
stature! In general, a tall person often frightens people, or at
the very least, others dare not bully him freely. In fact, in the
old society, where money and position held absolute sway,
physical stature had long since lost any connection with importance. If Wang Wenxuan had suddenly obtained someone's
backing and been promoted to manager or departmental head
in the Zhengzhong Book Company, become the manager of a
bank or the boss of a business firm, etc., even if he had been
as thin as a matchstick or as hunchbacked as a camel, he would
have received the respect of others. Who would have cared
whether he had deep learning or not, whether he had high
ideals or not, and whether he had done well at university or not?
Wang Wenxuan ought to have known that this was how things
stood. But he did not. He naively believed the lies of rascals,
and patiently waited for better days to come. As a result, what
did he gain in the end?

I said above that with regard to the three main characters of
the novel, I sympathize with all of them. But I am also critical
of each of them. They have failings and, of course, they have
good points. They love one another (except for the misunderstanding between mother and daughter-in-law), and they harm
one another. They are all pursuing happiness, but instead, they

are heading inescapably towards annihilation. As for Wang Wenxuan's death, his mother and wife both have a responsibility. They do not want him to die of illness, they want to do everything they can to save him, but what they actually do pushes him, and forces him to an early death. Wang Wenxuan himself is the same. He wants to live, and even after having plumbed the very depths of suffering, he still loves life strongly. But he finally turns his back on what he most desires, listening to the exhortations of neither his mother nor his wife, and consciously or subconsciously ruins his own health, hurrying off in long strides towards destruction. Why do they do this? Can it be that all three of them are crazy?

No, they are not crazy. But not one of them is a free agent. Each of their actions, each of their movements comes not from their will, but is directed from off-stage by the old society, the old system and the old forces that are on the verge of collapse. Because they do not resist, they become their sacrificial victims. The old forces seek to destroy them, but they do not think of protecting themselves. In fact, they do not even know how they can protect themselves. These pitiful people are indeed as described by one critic, people who never at any time "stand up to fight to change their lives". Some among them put up with everything, like Wang Wenxuan and his mother; some, not content to submit, try to find another road, like Zeng Shusheng. But what way out does Zeng Shusheng have, accepting as she does her role as a "flower vase"? She wants to escape the destruction that is to be her fate, but it is impossible to reach the north by heading south.

I think again of the film in which Wu Chufan acted. The female lead in the film is almost as I imagined, differing in only one point from the character I had in mind. In the film, Zeng Shusheng fears her mother-in-law. Because she has not gone through a wedding ceremony before living together with Wang Wenxuan, she is despised by his mother, and she herself feels ashamed. If only her mother-in-law will forgive her, she is willing to be a filial daughter-in-law. But her mother-in-law absolutely will not forgive her, treats her failure to hold a wedding ceremony as a major crime, and because of this, even prefers to destroy the happiness of her son's family. This is the way the Hong Kong film-makers interpreted the story, perhaps because of difficulties which they would rather not discuss. But the character in my story is not like that at all. In my novel, the principal criminal in bringing about the tragedy in Wang Wenxuan's household is the Kuomintang under Chiang Kai-shek; it is the rule of their reactionary regime. When I was writing about these characters, and gradually developing the situation and plot, this is how I understood them, this is how I knew them to be:

Wang Wenxuan's mother really loves her son dearly, and wants to share her son's hardships. But her love is a selfish one. Just as her daughter-in-law says, she is a "selfish, pigheaded, old-fashioned" woman. She does not like her daughter-in-law because, firstly, her daughter-in-law is not like herself when she was young, she is not a filial daughter-in-law who is one hundred percent submissive to her mother-in-law; secondly, she cannot get used to her daughter-in-law's "dressing and making herself up every day in such a bizarre fashion", going to restaurants, attending dances, living the life of an "flower vase"; thirdly, her son's love for his wife is greater than his love for her. Her accusation of "You're only my son's 'whore'! I came here in a wedding sedan!" is just a weapon she uses at the height of anger, an insult for wounding her enemy and that is all. For in 1944 already, no one made much fuss about "wedding ceremonies". Since her son cannot even earn enough to support the family, why should his mother worry so incessantly about an extravagant ritual of this kind? What she really wanted to have restored is the power and the comfortable life of mothers-in-law in the past. Although she knows quite well that the past cannot be restored, and that only dependence on her daughter-in-law's ornamental existence enables the family to barely survive, she nevertheless continues unconsciously to put on airs and to fly into a temper in the presence of her daughter-in-law. Moreover, it is precisely because she is indirectly dependent on her daughter-in-law's money that she becomes even more unhappy with her, and constantly finds pretexts for pouring onto her daughter-in-law her own frustrations and resentment. However, her daughter-in-law is not one to submit easily, and is always answering back. Life is hard, their circumstances are bad, and so it needs only a small incident to release their grievances, and the more often this happens, the more difficult it becomes to control themselves. Because of this, disagreements between mother and daughter-in-law grow deeper and deeper. Neither is willing to give way. When her anger rises, this mother, who normally loves her son so much, will not even listen to what he says. The result is that the happiness of her son's household is shattered. Although she frequently thinks of giving her all to save her son's life, and would willingly do so, her fits of anger can only aggravate his illness and drive him to an early death.

When Wang Wenxuan, this honest, sincere and kindhearted intellectual, studied education at university, his mind was full of ideals, and he nursed high hopes of helping others and remaking the world. But in all the years he worked in the old society, his position sank lower and lower, his life grew harder and harder, his will and spirit became weaker and weaker, until in the end he becomes a petty clerk, timid and afraid of getting into trouble, bowing his head before others, cowardly and obedient, willingly accepting humiliation. For the sake of a job that provides him with neither enough to wear nor enough to eat, for the sake of a life which is neither dead nor alive, he pitifully sacrifices everything that he valued in his youth, even his own aspirations. Nevertheless, the momentary ease of the situation cannot long be maintained, for he finally contracts tuberculosis, is dismissed from his job, coughs up blood, loses his voice, and dies in pain and suffering. He "wants to live" and "demands justice". But the old society does not allow him to live, nor does it grant him justice. He

thinks all the time of his wife, but is unable to hold out until
she returns once more to see him.

Zeng Shusheng is like her husband, for at one time, she too
had ideals. When the couple, husband and wife, left the university, they were determined to give their lives to education.
By the time of *Bitter Cold Nights*, she has abandoned everything. She relies on her beauty, her dress sense, and her social
poise to obtain a comparatively highly-paid post to enable her
to "raise" her own standard of living, send her son to school
and help with the household expenses. She does not wish to
be a flower vase", and because of this she often feels depressed
and full of grievances. But in order to solve the difficulties of
life, in order to avoid a life of hardship, she finally accepts her
role as a "flower vase" willingly. Every time she opens her
mouth, it is to spout about "freedom", but the freedom she
pursues is illusory. This is clear from her own words: "I
want movement, I want excitement. I need a life of enthusiasm." In other words, she is merely seeking after individual
pleasure. She writes to her husband to say: "I want ... to
live life to the full. I want to be free." In reality, apart from
that limited pleasure, what kind of "full life" can she possibly
have? What kind of "freedom" has she had? Sometimes,
she too is aware of her own shortcomings, and sometimes she
also feels depressed and empty. She may think of this as a
melancholy without a name, but she absolutely will not consider
it, and is reluctant to admit it as a depression with no exit, or as
an unresolvable contradiction, because she has never striven to
change her life. What she pursues is simply a kind of escape.
Even after leaving Wang Wenxuan, she is unwilling to give up
her life as a "flower vase". She could very well accept Mr.
Chen's proposal of marriage, even if it meant continuing her
ornamental existence afterwards. In fact, she is not altogether
sure she wants to marry Mr. Chen, who is two years younger
than she, but unless she changes her style of living, it will
be difficult for her to escape entanglement with him. They
are already closely tied together economically. She relies on his

help, and joins in partnership with him in a business of hoarding and speculation which has already earned a tidy sum.   If she breaks with him, she will have to leave the Bank of Sichuan and rearrange her life.   But she lacks the courage and deter- mination to do this.   Once her husband has died, her feelings can range with an ever greater "freedom".   It is very possible that she will now seek comfort and intoxication in Mr. Chen. But he cannot give her any great happiness.   For her, the days of old age and the fading of her beauty are already not far-off.   Mr. Chen cannot long be kept by her side.   This kind of thing was a common sight in those days.   If she cannot change her life, then life will change her.   If she does not stand up to fight, then she can only remain forever in a passive position.   She has a thirteen-year-old son.   She is not con- cerned about him in the way most mothers are concerned about their sons.   Nor is he very affectionate towards her.   The son resembles the father, and likes his grandmother, and so of course cannot win her love.   She spends not a small sum in sending him to study at a "posh school", as if simply to fulfil her duty.   While she is enjoying her so-called "freedom", she gives him no thought whatsoever.   Finally, in the epilogue of the novel, when she comes back from Lanzhou to her old home in Chongqing, all she sees is darkness and desolation. Her husband is dead, her son has followed his grandmother to she knows not where.   In the film, Zeng Shusheng leaves a ring on the grave of Wang Wenxuan to show that she will never be separated from him, even by the grave.   Unexpec- tedly, she meets her son and mother-in-law there.   Her mother- in-law speaks a few kind words to her, and contrary to all expectation, she agrees gratefully to go with the grandmother and grandson to their home village, for she is willing to do anything as long as her mother-in-law is willing to take her in. This is definitely not the Zeng Shusheng that I wrote about. Zeng Shusheng would never have bowed her head to her mother-in-law and admitted she was wrong.   She cannot give up her "pursuit".   Even less can she break the "flower vase" of her own accord. Moreover, if she, her mother-in-law and her son had gone back to the village in the late autumn and early winter of 1945, what would they have lived on? Under the reactionary rule of the Kuomintang, to raise a family of three was not easy. If Zeng Shusheng had been able to put up with hardship, she would have taken a different road long before. She would never be able to go through endless trials and tribulations to seek those two living people. She may have found her husband's grave. At the most, she would have wept bitterly for a time. Then, she would have flown back to Lanzhou, and dressed herself up gorgeously to entertain at grand dinners, in her capacity as wife of a bank manager. She and Wang Wenxuan's mother are women who are equally selfish.

Naturally, I do not approve of these two women. On the contrary, I describe them with a reproving pen. But I recognize myself that there are times when my writing frequently betrays a note of sympathy and forgiveness. At the time, my thoughts were as follows: I wanted through the suffering of these insignificant nobodies to condemn the old society and the old system. I intentionally made the ending gloomy, hopeless and without exit, to make the novel a "deeply-felt bitter denunciation". According to the propaganda of the Kuomintang reactionaries, after the victory in the War of Resistance, everything would be possible. But Wang Wenxuan died just when gongs and drums were resounding to the heavens in the street and people were celebrating victory[1]. My hatred was intense. But I forgot the following fact: What stirs the enthusiasm of people to fight is hope, not despair. Especially at the end of the novel, when Zeng Shusheng disap-

---

[1] In the synopsis for the new edition of *Bitter Cold Nights* published after Liberation in 1949, appear the following words: "This novel is about life in Chongqing, the so-called wartime capital under Kuomintang control, in 1944-45. . . . The hero dies just as gongs and drums are resounding to the heavens in the street and the people are celebrating victory with tirecrackers and dragon-lanterns. This is a deeply-felt bitter denunciation of the reactionary rule of the Kuomintang."

pears alone into the desolate, bitter cold night, the melancholy feeling after the people have gone and the buildings are deserted is a purely petit-bourgeois emotion. And because of this, my "denunciation" also has no exit, has no force, and is simply a letting-off of steam.

A thought has just occurred to me: In the days after victory, especially at night during the power cuts, I would often wander by myself along Minguo Road. What Zeng Shusheng saw was what I saw. I myself wanted to go back to Shanghai, but I could not. I had had enough of listening to strangers pour out their grievances, and I myself was depressed to the point of nervous frustration. I was also conscious of the dejected mood of other people. At the time, I had published a short essay about what I had seen while standing in the cold wind before some goods laid out on the ground. After over a year, when I was writing the epilogue of *Bitter Cold Nights*, I had a look at this short essay again. Moreover, at that time (the last two days of 1946), my morale was at a very low ebb. No wonder I was able to write such a conclusion. At the end of 1959 I was in Shanghai, editing the last three volumes of a collection of my literary works, and at the end of 1960 I was in Chengdu, reading and correcting the proofs of *Bitter Cold Nights*. On both occasions, I toyed with the idea of re-writing the epilogue of *Bitter Cold Nights*, but after thinking it over carefully, I felt that to change only the ending was not enough. If I was to change anything, then I would have to start right from the beginning, and so it would be better to write something quite different. Because of this, I left it as it was. In any case, it was an old work written before Liberation. That was how I thought at the time. Besides, the work had already appeared before readers in that form. There was no way in which I could hide that, and I had no desire to defend its shortcomings either.

I want to say something now about old Mr. Zhong. There is not a great deal that needs to be said. I do not intend to talk about him as such, for kindhearted people like him were by no means rare in the old society. But in the old society, old Mr. Zhong could not play a useful role. The most he could do was to give a little help to people like Wang Wenxuan who suffered even greater hardship than he did and were in even more unfortunate circumstances than he was. No one would have thought that he would die before Wang Wenxuan. I wrote that he died of cholera, because in the summer of 1945 in Chongqing, a cholera epidemic was raging, and the head of the city Bureau of Health shamelessly and unblushingly issued a public denial of the fact. The son of Mrs. Tan, the cook of the Culture and Life Publishing House, suddenly died of cholera. This woman of about fifty years old was a Roman Catholic. She was so worried that in her alarm and desperation she ran to a Chinese Boddhisattva to beg for the ashes from the incense to treat her son's illness. At the time, the child, who was only fifteen or sixteen, lay on a bed near the kitchen, and was already sinking fast. We urged Mrs. Tan to send him to the epidemiology hospital at Xiaolongkan, and she managed to find a stretcher to carry her son there. Two days later, he died at the hospital. When I heard an office-boy of the Culture and Life Publishing House talking about the situation at the epidemiology hospital, I felt an intense hatred for the bureau head. In the introduction to *Ward No. 4*, I "praised" his "virtuous government", and in *Bitter Cold Nights*, I have written again about this hospital, the only one in the wartime capital for epidemics. If it had not been for the "virtuous government" of this bureau head, old Mr. Zhong very likely would have survived. In the novel, he is not of course a character who has to die. I am writing this just to explain that an author does not always create his incidents out of thin air. If there had not been so many people dying of cholera at that time, if no one had spoken to me about the situation at the epidemiology hospital then, how would I have thought of sending old Mr. Zhong there? Even Mr. Zhong's grave did not spring from my imagination. In an isolated grave, "on a slope", was buried my friend Miao

Chongqun. This essayist, whose prose style is so unique, contracted tuberculosis very early. I met him for the first time in January, 1932. His face was pale and he was coughing all the time. Sometimes he would be better, sometimes worse. In January 1945, he died of illness in the Jiangsu Hospital in Beibei. He was like Wang Wenxuan in several respects. He never liked to trouble people, was always afraid of hurting others, and was nowhere looked up to. He had no family and was all on his own. He lived quietly, a little like old Mr. Zhong. I heard that before he went into hospital, he had lain ill in bed, unable to obtain a mouthful of water when he wanted to drink. He would not say anything, and did not want anyone to know that his illness was racking him with pain. When he died, there was no one he knew present. When I got the news, I hurried at once to Beibei, but he was already in his grave. It was just as I described in the novel. Even the two paper wreaths were as I described, except for the name Chongqun which I changed to You'an. It was said that the immediate cause of death was not TB. I have not seen many people who have died in pain and suffering after losing their voices when the disease spread from their lungs to their throat, but the number I have seen is not too small either. My friends Fan Yu (of whom I wrote in *In Memory of Fan Yu*) and Lu Yan (an excellent writer of whom I wrote in remembrance in *Written for Lu Yan*), and also my cousin . . . all ended their lives in this tragic way. I felt resentful about their deaths, I felt indignant, and because I had done nothing to alleviate their suffering, I felt ashamed. I wrote about Wang Wenxuan's illness, its gradual development up to the final moment of his death, on the basis of what I myself had seen and heard, and on the basis of letters written to me by Fan Yu during his illness. In the novel, I also wrote about my own feelings. Wang Wenxuan should not have died early, should not have suffered so greatly, yet he finally died a tragic death. The people I knew so well should not have died so early either or in such terrible suffering, but their graves have been covered with long grass for a long time now. How full of grief my heart was as I cursed the old society and cried out against its injustice towards them. Today I am ten thousand times happier, and my heart is full of joy as I sing in praise of the dawn of our new society. If those "nobodies" who suffered injustice are able to know this in their death, they will certainly be smiling in their place of rest. Continually advancing science and an incomparably superior new social system have already conquered tuberculosis. No more can the mere mention of the word make people turn pale. These last two days, reading *Bitter Cold Nights* again has been a nightmare. But this nightmare has gone and vanished forever!

November 20, 1961

About the Author

Ba Jin, the pen-name of Li Feigan, was born in Chengdu, Sichuan Province in 1904. The son of a county magistrate, he was taught by a private tutor at home. In his youth, he was greatly influenced by the then prevailing ideas of socialism, especially those of social utopianism.

In 1920, he entered a provincial foreign languages school and began studying English. Three years later, he went to Shanghai for further education. There, at the same time, he did editing work for the magazine *Half-Monthly*, engaged in the propagation of new ideas. At the end of 1926, he left for Paris, where he studied French and wrote his first novel, *Destruction*. He returned to Shanghai at the end of 1928 and later wrote the trilogy entitled *Love* consisting of the novels *Fog*, *Rain* and *Lightning*. He also published, among others, *Family*, the first novel of another trilogy entitled *Current*. In the autumn of 1933, he went to Beijing and worked on the editorial board of the *Literary Quarterly*. The following year he was in Japan. In 1935, he was back in Shanghai and served as chief editor of the Cultural Life Press. Three years later, he published *Spring*, the second novel of his trilogy *Current*.

In 1937, after the outbreak of the War of Resistance Against Japan, he edited, with Mao Dun and others, magazines such as *Outcry* and *Flames*. Later, he was in different parts of southwest China, engaged in various literary activities. Works of this period included *Autumn*, the third novel of the trilogy *Current*, the novel *Fire* and the novelettes *Garden of Repose* and *Bitter Cold Nights*. He also translated Turgenev's *Fathers and Son* and *Virgin Soil*. In 1946, he was once again back in

501

Shanghai, where he resumed editorial work for the Cultural Life Press.

After the liberation of Shanghai in 1949, he attended the First National Conference of Literary and Art Circles held in Beijing and was elected member of the Chinese People's Political Consultative Conference. In September of the same year, he attended its first conference. In 1950 he attended the Second World Peace Conference held in Warsaw, Poland. He visited Korea twice, in 1952 and 1953, and wrote feature articles with the war as their main theme. They were collected in two books and he also published a collection of short stories related to the war.

After 1954 he was elected deputy to the First, Second and Third National People's Congress. After the fall of the "gang of four", he was again elected deputy to the Fifth National People's Congress. At present he is vice-president of the Union of Chinese Writers as well as President of the Shanghai branch of the union.

巴　金　选　集

第二卷

*

外文出版社出版

（中国北京百万庄路24号）

外文印刷厂印刷

中国国际图书贸易总公司

（中国国际书店）发行

北京399信箱

1988年（28开）第一版

（英）

ＩＳＢＮ 7-119-00575-8/Ⅰ·68（外）

01350

10—E—1842ＳＢ